*By Jill Mansell and available
from Headline Review*

Take A Chance On Me
Rumour Has It
An Offer You Can't Refuse
Thinking Of You
Making Your Mind Up
The One You Really Want
Falling For You
Nadia Knows Best
Staying At Daisy's
Millie's Fling
Good At Games
Miranda's Big Mistake
Head Over Heels
Mixed Doubles
Perfect Timing
Fast Friends
Solo
Kiss
Sheer Mischief
Open House
Two's Company

Jill Mansell

take a chance on me

**headline
review**

First published in 2010
by HEADLINE REVIEW
An imprint of HEADLINE PUBLISHING GROUP

First published in paperback in 2010
by HEADLINE REVIEW

3

ISBN 978 0 7553 5748 2 (A-format)
ISBN 978 0 7553 2822 2 (B-format)

Typeset in Bembo by Palimpsest Book Production Limited,
Grangemouth, Stirlingshire
Printed and bound in Great Britain by
CPI Mackays, Chatham ME5 8TD

Headline's policy is to use papers that are natural, renewable and recyclable
products and made from wood grown in sustainable products. The logging
and manufacturing processes are expected to conform to the environmental
regulations of the country of origin.

HEADLINE PUBLISHING GROUP
An Hachette UK Company
338 Euston Road
London NW1 3BH

www.headline.co.uk
www.hachette.co.uk

To Tina LaVenture, my wonderful mother-in-law.
And Michael too!
With my love and thanks for everything.
(Next time you do our garden for us, could
we have the Trevi fountain, please?)

Chapter 1

'Come on, come on, late as usual.' Waiting in the porch, Ash Parry-Jones tapped his watch as Cleo and Will hurried up the gravelled path. 'Better get in there and grab a seat. Place is filling up fast.'

Like it was an Elton John concert or something. Cleo paused to straighten Ash's wonky yellow-and-grey striped tie. 'Don't nag. And I can't believe you're wearing this shirt.'

He looked offended. 'Who are you insulting?'

'You.' She gave his collar an affectionate tweak. 'Stripes and swirls don't go.'

They found somewhere to sit in a pew on the left-hand side of the church. As the organ music played and Will studied the order of service, Cleo composed herself. Of course it was a sad occasion – it was the end of a life, after all – but as funerals went, it had to be one of the cheerier ones she'd attended.

Then again, as deaths went, Lawrence LaVenture's had been better than most. It may even count as enviable. As Lawrence himself had been fond of remarking, the family name was derived from the French word for 'lucky' or 'fortunate', and he'd taken enormous pleasure in living up to it. And what rakish 73-year-old widower, given the choice, wouldn't want to go as he had gone, following a sublime meal and a bottle of delicious Saint-Émilion, in bed with an attractive brunette many, *many* years younger than himself?

Mind you, it had given the poor woman he'd hired for the evening a bit of a shock. One minute they'd been having a high old time together, getting up to all sorts of naughtiness. The next, she'd come back into the bedroom carrying the bottle of cognac and two glasses Lawrence had asked her to bring upstairs and there he'd been, collapsed back against the goose-down pillows, stone dead.

Peering around the church, Cleo whispered, 'Do you think she'll turn up?'

'Who?'

'The woman who was with him when he died!' Who had actually, *technically*, killed him, when you thought about it. 'I want to know what she looks like.'

'She'll be the one in the black leather basque,' Will murmured. 'Stockings, suspenders, spike-heeled stilettos . . .'

Cleo dug him in the ribs then slipped her arm through his, grateful to him for having come along. Will had never met Lawrence LaVenture but she'd wanted him with her today and he'd obligingly taken the afternoon off work. He even knew why she'd asked him and hadn't laughed, for which she was grateful. Meeting Will Newman in a nightclub three months ago had definitely been one of the happier accidents in her life. She'd been nudged from behind in a crowded bar in Bath, her drink had splashed over his sleeve, they'd got chatting as a result . . . and what a result it had turned out to be. Will was handsome and charming, hard-working and intelligent . . . basically, he was perfect in every way. Her Mr Right had finally come along and she couldn't have been happier about it.

'Could be her.' Pointing helpfully to a roly-poly woman in her sixties, squeezing into an already full pew across the aisle, Will said, 'There's a high-class hooker if ever I saw one.'

'That's Effie Farnham from Corner Cottage.'

'There's a studded leather whip hanging out of her handbag.'

'She breeds Cairn terriers. It's a dog's lead.'

'Are you sure?'

'Trust me, Effie's not the whippy kind.'

'You never know. Under that coat she could be wearing something completely outrageous.'

OK, this definitely came under the heading of Too Much Information. Thankfully, before Cleo could start picturing Effie in a tasselled thong, distraction was provided by the arrival of Lawrence's family. Well, such as it was. She held her breath and watched as the three of them made their way up the aisle, two ancient, creaking older sisters swathed in politically incorrect fur and supported by silver-topped ebony canes. And between them, matching his pace to theirs, Johnny LaVenture.

He was looking smarter than usual in a dark suit and with his habitually wayward black hair combed back from his forehead. For a split second he glanced to the left and their eyes met, prompting a Pavlovian jolt of resentment in her chest. She couldn't help it; old habits died hard. Then Johnny looked away, carried on past and took his place between his ancient aunts in the front pew.

Cleo bent her head. OK, don't think about him now. Just concentrate on the funeral. Lawrence might have been an off-the-wall character, fond of a drink and, well, various other lusty pastimes, but he'd been entertaining to have around. They were here to celebrate a life well lived.

After the service, everyone huddled up against the icy wind

and made their way across the village green to the Hollybush Inn where food had been laid on and the drinks were free, as stipulated in Lawrence's last will and testament. For so many years a cornerstone of the pub, he knew how to guarantee a good turn-out.

Ash, catching up with Cleo and Will, rubbed his hands together and said cheerfully, 'All went off pretty well, then. I really enjoyed that, didn't you?'

And *still* he was managing to make it sound like an Elton John concert. Cleo said, 'You're not supposed to enjoy funerals. Next you'll be giving it five stars on Amazon.'

'Actually, that's not a bad idea. We could do it on the show, get the listeners to call in with reviews of their favourite—'

'No you couldn't. That's just wrong. Oh God, look at my *heels*.' As they reached the entrance to the pub, Cleo leaned against one of the outdoor tables and used a tissue to clean away the clumps of mud and grass. 'Did you see me sinking into the ground while we were standing around the grave? I thought I was going to tip over and fall flat on my back.'

'That's why I didn't wear mine.' Ash nodded sympathetically. 'You know, you're looking good today. Scrubbed up well. Even if you don't deserve a compliment when you think of all the grief you give me.'

'It's not grief. It's constructive criticism. Which you badly need, by the way.' Having more or less cleaned her heels, Cleo lobbed the muddy tissue into the bin and adjusted her narrow cream skirt. Of course she was looking good; hadn't she put in a whole heap of extra effort making sure of it? But that was pride for you. It was also the reason she'd dragged Will along for the occasion. When you'd spent your teenage years being mercilessly teased and humiliated, you didn't want to turn up to meet your tormentor

4

looking like a . . . a *donkey*. You felt compelled to prove to them that you weren't still a complete loser, not to mention capable these days of bagging yourself the kind of boyfriend any girl would be thrilled to, well, bag.

And here he was, standing just inside the entrance to the pub, greeting everyone as they came in and gravely receiving condolences in return. Oh well, on an occasion like this at least he wouldn't call her—

'Hello, Misa.' Dark eyes glinting with amusement, Johnny gave her hand a cross between a shake and a squeeze. He may even have been about to lean forward and plant a polite kiss on her cheek but she pulled back before that could happen.

I can't believe he just called me that.

'Hello, Johnny. I'm sorry about your dad. We'll all miss him.'

'Thanks. I guess this village is going to be a quieter place from now on.' His gaze flickered over her and the smile broadened. 'You're looking very well.'

Damn right I am. Turning to indicate Will, Cleo said, 'This is my boyfriend, Will Newman.'

'I'm so sorry for your loss,' Will said politely as they shook hands.

'Thank you. So, Misa, gone and got yourself a new man. Excellent.' Evidently pleased with his play on words, Johnny said, 'From what I hear, the old ones haven't been much cop.'

See what a nightmare he was? Cleo quelled the urge to retaliate with something cutting; it would hardly be seemly, after all. Plus, dammit, she couldn't think of anything fast enough. Instead she turned away. When they were safely out of earshot, Will said, 'I see what you mean. Why does he call you Misa?'

All the old emotions were rushing back. Only someone whose teenage years had been similarly blighted could possibly understand how it felt to have been picked on non-stop.

'Oh, it's a hilarious nickname. I used to work hard at school, pay attention in class, ask loads of questions, answer them too. One day I was so excited about knowing the answer to a really difficult question that I stuck my hand up and yelled, "Me, sir!" Well, everyone practically wet themselves laughing. And that was it, I was stuck with it for the next three years of school. I was officially Teacher's Pet. Some of the other kids thought my name actually *was* Misa.'

'And he's still calling you it, all these years later.' Will jerked his head in Johnny's direction.

'He was the one who came up with it in the first place.' Cleo cringed at the memory. It went without saying that she had never once put her hand up in class for the rest of her time at school, had stopped asking questions and paying attention to the answers. OK, maybe she couldn't blame everything on Johnny LaVenture, but he certainly hadn't helped. Her teenage hormones had been all over the place, she had fallen in with a wilder group of girls and her grades had slipped badly as a result. When her GCSEs had been a complete car crash, she'd felt an almost perverse sense of pride at their awfulness. *See, look at me, look at these abysmal grades! Here's the proof that I'm not a teacher's pet any more!*

'Poor baby.' Rubbing her shoulder in jokey consolation, Will said, 'Want me to beat him up for you?'

'Yes please. Except you'd better not. It's his dad's funeral, after all.' Plus, although Cleo didn't say this bit out loud, Johnny was bigger than him and had always been pretty athletic. It would be frankly embarrassing if he were to reduce Will to a slushy pulp. Still, it was generous of Will to have offered.

An hour and a couple of drinks later, the party had begun to warm up; everyone had begun to relax and Cleo's skin had stopped prickling every time she glanced over at her nemesis. Was it stupid to still feel like this? Maybe, but she couldn't help herself. It was thirteen years since they'd been at school together. She had left at sixteen and plunged into the first of many jobs. Johnny had stayed on to take his A-levels – ha! *Now* who was the swotty teacher's pet? – before heading off to art school. After that he'd moved to New York, returning only occasionally to Channings Hill to visit his father, although Lawrence had evidently kept him updated on the subject of her less-than-dazzling successes on the boyfriend front. You'd have been more likely to spot Elvis around the village than Johnny in those days. Meanwhile, through a combination of hard work and socialising in all the right places, he had begun to make a real name for himself with his wire-constructed sculptures. When it came to the luck of the LaVentures, he'd inherited his share too. As time went by, the sculptures grew and so did Johnny's reputation, culminating in an exhibition during which every last one of the larger-than-life-size pieces had been snapped up by the billionaire owner of a chain of casinos. Overnight, Johnny became a recognised name, a celebrity in his own right with a stunning supermodel girlfriend to match. And Cleo, reading about his star-studded lifestyle in magazines, discovered a level of resentment she'd had no idea she was capable of experiencing, because it was all just so completely and utterly unfair. If a nice person experienced something wonderful, you were delighted for them and rejoiced in their success. But for all this to have happened to someone who so profoundly *didn't* deserve it . . . well, where was the fairness in that?

Will checked his watch and said apologetically, 'I have to go.'

'Of course you do. Thanks for coming.' He had a work meeting in Bristol to get back to, followed by a squash tournament this evening. Cleo hugged him, kissed him quickly on the mouth and said, 'I'll see you on Friday.'

'Can't wait. Will you be all right here?'

'I'll be fine. I've got my big sister to look after me.' Abbie, fifteen years older and light years more sensible, was over by the bar chatting to some neighbours.

'Well, make sure she does. No pole dancing,' said Will. 'No chatting up handsome men.' He indicated a couple of whiskery ancient farmers huddled over their pints in the corner.

'Good luck with the squash competition.' Cleo gave him another kiss.

'Thanks. I'll be over after work on Friday.' Wiggling his fingers at her as he moved towards the door, Will said, 'Bye.'

'Or I could come to you,' Cleo offered, 'if it's easier.'

'Hmm, you know what? I think I'd rather stay at your place.' He smiled and pulled a you-know-why face; the two friends with whom he shared an untidy flat in Redland were the boisterous, heavy drinking, perpetually-up-for-a-laugh types whose presence wasn't exactly conducive to a romantic atmosphere. Will, reluctant to subject her to their ribald remarks, had explained that it wouldn't matter so much if she were just a casual one-off fling, but she wasn't, she was way more important than that.

Hearing this had caused Cleo's heart to expand with hope. Crikey, just imagine where she and Will might be in a year's time. She watched him leave and exhaled happily. Will Newman. Cleo Newman. He really could be The One.

Then her skin started prickling again and a voice behind her said, 'So that's the boyfriend, is it, Misa?'

Chapter 2

Was her blood actually *physically* heating up or did it just feel that way? Cleo kept herself under control and nodded. No need to react and give Johnny the kick of knowing the effect he had on her; she was *so* much better than that.

'And now he's run off and left you?'

'He had to get back to work for an important meeting. He has a very responsible job.'

'He does? Good for him.' Johnny sounded amused.

How did he manage to make even those few words sound as if he was taking the mickey? Cleo marvelled at his talent. Logically she might know her own lack of further education wasn't his fault, but deep down inside, it still kind of felt that way. She loved her job at Henleaze Limos, but who knew, if her schooldays hadn't been blighted, she might have gone on to do anything. The sky could have been the limit . . . she could have become, God, an astrophysicist!

Well, she *might* have wanted to be an astrophysicist. Whatever that involved. Physics, presumably, mixed with . . . possibly . . . Astroturf.

'So is this Will New-Man the love of your life?'

See? Even now he was making fun of Will's surname. How would he like it if she called him Lahhh-Venture?

Instead, taking the moral high ground, she said easily, 'Maybe. It's all going very well at the moment. How about you?'

Johnny grinned and pulled a face. 'Not so great. Temperamental creatures, women. They can be pretty hard work.'

They. Just to let her know how popular he was, subject to the attentions of hordes of besotted females. Cleo smiled politely, registering lack of interest, and said, 'What's going to happen to Ravenswood?'

'Sell it, I suppose. If I can.' Johnny shook his head. 'Just stick it on the market, asap. Not the ideal time, of course, but you never know. Someone might come along and see the potential. And it'd be great if we could find a buyer before Christmas. There's an opportunity to bag the apartment below mine if we can get a quick sale. I could turn it into a fantastic gallery.' He stopped and looked at her. 'Why are you asking? Might you and your chap be interested in putting in an offer?'

Oh yes, that was *so* on the cards, what with Ravenswood being a seven-bedroomed detached house with a garden bigger than a football pitch. Although when it was that size you didn't call it a garden, it was referred to as *the grounds*.

'I could mention it to Will.' And start buying extra Lotto tickets. 'How much will you be asking?'

He shrugged. 'I've got a couple of estate agents coming over tomorrow to look the place over and come up with a valuation. I'm pretty out of touch, but somewhere around two and a half, at a guess.'

Two and a half million pounds. Cleo envisaged the number, all those noughts rolling across the paper if you were to write it down. Did Johnny have any idea what an inconceivably huge

10

amount of money that was? And the casual way he said it, as if it were completely *normal* . . .

Ah well, maybe she and Will would give it a miss after all. 'Well, good luck. I'll leave you to get on.'

As she made to move away, he said, 'This chap of yours. Does he work in private health insurance?'

'What? No! Why?'

'Just curious.' A smile lifted the corners of Johnny's mouth. 'He just looks as if he might, that's all.'

Ooooooh . . .

'Oh dear, look at you.' Abbie greeted her sympathetically. 'I saw you talking to Johnny. Been getting under your skin, has he? Here, have a sip of my Malibu.'

Cleo could always rely on her sister to make her feel better. Abbie was looking lovely today, her fine honey-blonde hair falling in waves to her shoulders and her gentle face glowing, thanks to the subtle application of make-up she generally didn't wear but liked to save 'for best'.

Then again, sisterly sympathy only went so far. 'I've got a better idea. Why don't I have my own drink? Seeing as Lawrence is paying. Which means Johnny is. In fact, let's make it a great big one. Dry white, please.' Cleo signalled to Deborah behind the bar. 'Lovely, thanks. Honestly, he doesn't change, does he?' She knocked back some much-needed wine. 'Two and a half million pounds he's going to be asking for his dad's house. He wondered if Will and I might like to make him an offer. And he's keen to get it sorted before Christmas because he wants to buy another apartment in New York and turn it into a gallery. I mean, does he even *care* that Lawrence has just died? As far as he's concerned, it's a nice little windfall coming along at just the right time . . . God, it's enough to make you *spit*.'

11

'Is this a diatribe?' Tom, Abbie's husband, looked pleased with himself. 'Ha, there's a word I've never used before. But it is, isn't it? Definitely sounds like a diatribe to me.'

Cleo smiled, because Tom was looking so smart in his dark funeral suit and a bright blue shirt that matched his sparkling eyes. It always seemed strange to see him out of his work clothes of dusty polo shirt and jeans. Even his short brown hair had been given a trim in honour of Lawrence's funeral. 'Oh yes, it's a diatribe. Some people just deserve one.' She nodded and took another glug of wine.

'But you liked him once,' said Tom.

'What?' Cleo froze. 'No I didn't!'

'You must have done. If you didn't fancy him, why would you have said yes when he asked you out?'

Oh, for crying out loud. To his left, Abbie was suddenly engrossed in a loose thread on her bronze shirt. Her heart beginning to thud in double time, Cleo said, 'I don't know what you're talking about.'

Tom was actually laughing now, wagging a finger at her. 'Come on, I know it was a while back, but you still did it. Johnny LaVenture asked you out at the school disco and you agreed, then— *hey,* mind my drink!'

'Tom.' Abbie, who had given him a nudge, shot him a warning look. 'Shut *up.*'

Staring at them open-mouthed, Cleo said slowly, 'Oh my God, you *know* about that? *Both* of you know?'

It was her deepest, darkest, most shameful adolescent secret. All these years she'd kept it buried, telling herself that, OK, she'd made an almighty fool of herself but at least her family didn't know.

Except . . . she looked from Abbie to Tom, then back again . . . it rather looked as if they did.

'Honestly, you're such a blabbermouth,' Abbie scolded.

12

'Hey, it was years ago.' Tom's grin spread across his face as Ash approached them. 'What does it matter now?'

'What are we talking about?' Ash, whose nosiness knew no bounds, looked interested.

Cleo blurted out, 'Don't tell him!'

'The time Johnny LaVenture told Cleo he was crazy about her and she agreed to go out with him.'

Brilliant, thanks a lot.

'Oh yeah, at the school's end-of-term disco.' Ash nodded solemnly.

Right, that was it. Ash had only moved into the village three years ago. Facing him, Cleo's voice rose. 'Does *everyone* know about this?'

'Well, yes. Although I thought it was supposed to be a secret. You weren't meant to *know* that we know.'

Cleo swallowed. What had taken place had been enough to mentally scar a girl for life. In fact, she was fairly sure it *had* mentally scarred her for life. She'd gone along to the end-of-year disco with no expectations other than drinking a few alcohol-free shandies, dancing with her friends and having a fun time. When Johnny LaVenture had come up to her and asked to speak to her outside, she had initially refused, but he'd practically begged until curiosity had got the better of her and she'd eventually given in. Then, once they were outside, Johnny had haltingly confessed his true feelings for her. He'd only teased her so much, it transpired, to cover up the fact that he really liked her, but now he could no longer hide how he really felt. And as he'd been telling her this, his beautiful dark eyes had gazed beseechingly into hers, his trembling hands had stroked her shoulders. Cleo, hypnotised by the declaration and scarcely able to take it in, had leaned back against the rough exterior wall of the girls' changing rooms and been unbelievably moved by the admission; he must have been plucking up the courage to say this for months.

Then Johnny had falteringly asked her out on a date the following week and although she didn't really want to go out with him, she'd known she couldn't refuse. It would shatter his confidence. Sixteen-year-old boys had easily bruised egos, it would be too cruel to turn him down . . . just one trip to the cinema, then she'd gently suggest that they'd be better off as platonic friends . . .

So she'd smiled up at Johnny and said yes, of course she'd go out with him, and at the back of her mind she had also taken great satisfaction in the knowledge that, *ha*, all the bitchy girls who'd sided with him and called her Misa would have to be nice to her now.

It had been a heady moment, the kind of turnaround any downtrodden sixteen-year-old could only dream about, but it had actually happened and it felt . . . God, it felt fantastic! Not only was everything going to be all right from now on, but she hadn't retaliated, poked fun at him *when she could so easily have done*, or said something mean. And now he looked as if he was about to kiss her. Well, one little kiss wouldn't hurt, would it? To be honest, she could use the practice. Tilting her face up to his, Cleo closed her eyes, encouragingly puckered her lips and waited for—

A snort of laughter directly above her head *wasn't* what she'd been waiting for, but it was what she heard. Followed by a chorus of muffled giggles, a scuffling noise and the kind of clattering sound you'd get if someone standing precariously on the loo in the cubicle below the open window had just lost their footing and fallen off.

Someone was eavesdropping. Several someones, from the sound of it. This was what the girls in her year were like. Not what you'd call mature. Still, did it really matter if they'd overheard? Putting

14

out a hand to reassure Johnny, Cleo said, 'It's all right, don't worry about them,' and wondered why he wasn't looking at her any more.

The giggles turned to shrieks of hysterical laughter and the head of Mandy Ellison poked through the open window. Crowing with delight, she opened her horrible big mouth and yelled, 'Ha ha, I can't believe she fell for it, you were brilliant!'

Bewildered, Cleo turned to Johnny. 'What does that mean?'

Half smiling and backing away, Johnny said, 'Sorry, she bet me a fiver I couldn't do it.'

Everyone was scrambling up on to the loo seats now; along the row of windows, more heads popped out. Everyone was laughing harder and harder. As the realisation sank in that she'd been well and truly set up, colour flooded Cleo's cheeks.

Johnny shrugged and raised his hands, absolving himself from blame. 'I never thought you'd say yes.'

She was torn between wanting the ground to swallow her up and an overwhelming longing to burst into tears. 'I only said it because I felt sorry for you!'

'Ha ha ha ha ha! Yeah, of course you did,' jeered Mandy Ellison.

'It's *true*. I don't fancy him!'

'But you seriously thought he fancied you,' Mandy sniggered. 'Like that's ever going to happen, *Misa*. Ha, you've just given us the best laugh we've had in months. And all for a fiver.' As she said it, she grinned at Johnny. '*Bargain*.'

By the time Cleo's dad had arrived to drive her home, she'd been hanging around outside the school for over an hour. Inside, the disco was about to end.

'All right, love? Didn't expect to find you out here waiting for me. Had a good night, have you?'

How could she tell him? The last thing she wanted was her

family feeling sorry for her. 'Not bad.' Buttoning up the hurt and humiliation, she said offhandedly, 'Got a bit boring towards the end.'

'Oh, that's a shame.' Her dad gave her a teasing nudge. 'But did you dance with any boys?'

'There wasn't anyone I wanted to dance with. They're just a bunch of losers,' said Cleo.

Now, here in the front bar of the Hollybush, the shame was every bit as acute as it had been all those years ago.

Cleo looked at Ash, Tom and Abbie. She said, 'Who told you?'

Ash shrugged and pointed at Abbie. 'You told me, didn't you? A couple of years back.'

'Tom told me,' said Abbie, 'straight after it happened.'

'Honestly, why do I have to get the blame for everything? Everyone was having a laugh about it in the pub the day after the disco,' Tom protested. 'Stuart Ellison told us about it. His sister Mandy was there when Johnny did it. It was just a bit of fun.'

Cleo resisted the urge to rip every last freshly trimmed hair from Tom's head. So all this time she'd been the laughing stock of the entire village. And like one of those well-kept secrets you never imagine could actually be kept secret, she'd had no idea.

What's more – talk about adding insult to injury – the chances were that if you were to ask him about it now, Johnny himself probably wouldn't even remember that evening at the school disco when he'd earned himself the easiest fiver of his life.

Chapter 3

The For Sale signs had been up outside the house for over a week now. Having instructed his solicitors to take care of everything, Johnny had flown back to the States the day after the funeral. Busy cleaning the windscreen of the Bentley she was due to take out again this afternoon, Cleo paused as, across the green, two cars slowed to a halt outside Ravenswood.

It wasn't nosy to watch them, was it? It was being neighbourly, making sure the place wasn't about to be burgled. Although it had to be said, the couple emerging from the maroon Volvo didn't look like your archetypal burglars. And the other chap, even from this distance, was visibly an estate agent. Of course, where Johnny was concerned, it would be just typical that the first people to view his old family home would fall in love with it at first sight and buy it on the spot.

Cleo was kneeling across the Bentley's back seat, vigorously vacuuming under the driver's seat, when someone pinched her bottom.

'Oof!' She collapsed, rolled over on to her side and pointed the vacuum nozzle like a pistol at Ash. 'Don't *do* that.'

His eyes danced. 'Can't help myself. If I see a cute little backside sticking up like that in front of me, I just have to pinch it.'

He was home from work. The downside of hosting a breakfast radio show might be the inhumanly early starts, but the upside was that it was all done and dusted by ten o'clock and he was back at Channings Hill by eleven. Switching off the vacuum cleaner and picking up her polishing cloth, Cleo said, 'Pass me the beeswax. How'd it go today?'

'Bloody brilliant. If you'd bothered to listen to it, you wouldn't have to ask.' When it came to his radio show, Ash's modesty knew no bounds. Since taking over the breakfast slot three years ago, having been poached from a smaller commercial station in London, he had conjured a seventy per cent increase in listening figures. He was the star of BWR, much loved by his ever-growing audience. As well as local listeners, fans from all over the world were now tuning in to hear him online. On his show he exuded confidence, wit and irresistible charm. Women and girls of all ages adored him and Ash played up to this, reading out his fan mail and regaling listeners with indiscreet stories of his wild, testosterone-fuelled, Hollywood-style love life.

In reality, out of the studios, his confidence melted away. Actually that wasn't true; in the company of friends, people he knew, he was fine. But plant a new and attractive woman in front of him and Ash completely lost it every time. It was like watching a Dementor suck the life out of him. Along with the vanishing confidence went the easy wit and charm, their places usurped by clunky awkwardness as, before the astonished audience's very eyes, Ash Parry-Jones shed a dozen years and reverted to being a cripplingly shy, overweight and unattractive teenager. And no amount of cajoling could snap him out of it, though Cleo had certainly tried. As Ash himself freely admitted, success was the best revenge and career-wise he'd achieved that in spades, but it would have been nice if he could have undergone the kind of physical transformation achieved by Brad Pitt when he'd guest-starred in *Friends* as the once-fat dorky one from school.

Sadly, this hadn't happened to Ash. He may have lost some of the excess weight that had haunted his adolescence but there was still plenty left; he would never be lithe. His solid frame was always going to be chunky. His hair was fairish, messy, unremarkable. And looks-wise, he had the kind of face that gave the impression of having been put together using leftovers – a wonky nose, double chin, wayward eyebrows and slightly asymmetric ears. Cliché it might be, and again Ash was the first to point it out, but his was a face perfect for radio. Of course there were photos of him on the internet for those curious enough to track them down, but the vast majority of his listeners had no idea what he looked like. Which meant that girls, attracted enough to his radio persona to deliberately seek him out, ended up getting a terrible shock.

'I couldn't listen to your show. I was on a job,' said Cleo.

Ash raised his wayward eyebrows. 'On the job?'

'*A* job.' She flicked the polishing cloth at him. 'It was really sweet, actually. A married couple celebrating their golden wedding anniversary. Their children clubbed together to send them on a fantastic holiday as a surprise present. And this morning they thought they were being picked up by an ordinary taxi.' Clients like these, thrilled and excited to be taking possibly the first ride of their lives in a limo, were the kind Cleo loved the most. They made up for the silent high-flying businessmen who took the service for granted, the ear-splitting racket generated by over-excited children leaving junior school for the last time, and having to control groups of wildly inebriated women on hen nights. This morning's lady, bless her, had burst into tears in the back of the Bentley. Through the sobs she'd hiccupped, 'Oh my days, whatever did I do to deserve a family like mine? I'm the luckiest woman in the world!'

'And just think how much more they'd have enjoyed the journey if they'd been allowed to listen to my show.'

'You never give up, do you? You're nothing but a ratings tart. If you want to be useful,' said Cleo, 'you could make me a cup of tea.'

'Excuse me.' Ash tapped his chest. 'This is a future global super-star you're talking to.'

'Nice and strong, not much milk, two sugars.'

He ambled inside, returning five minutes later with the mugs of tea. Classily, he'd given her the one featuring the bikini-clad woman whose bikini disappeared when the mug was hot. As Cleo settled herself on the wall separating their adjoining front gardens from the road, the three visitors emerged from Ravenswood. They stood chat-ting together for a minute before the estate agent jumped into his car and with a cheery wave drove off. The remaining couple surveyed the village before climbing into their Volvo, the tall man opening the passenger door for his alarmingly spindly-legged wife.

'Do you think they'll buy it?' said Cleo.

'Might do. She looks like a flamingo.' Ash narrowed his eyes. 'Not to mention a Radio Four listener.'

The immaculate maroon Volvo pulled away in stately fashion, made its way past the pub then, instead of turning left out of the village, carried on around the green towards them at a menacing ten miles per hour. Watching it, Ash hummed the theme tune to *Jaws*.

Up close, the woman looked even more like a flamingo, her eyes dark and beady, her nose a beaky hook. She needed to tilt her head back in order to gaze down it at Cleo and Ash.

'Morning. Live here, do you?' The eyes registered disapproval of the naked lady mug. 'We've just been to view Ravenswood. Seems like a quiet enough village. Are people generally happy to live here?'

'Happy?' Ash said good-naturedly, 'They're ecstatic. So you're interested in the house, then?'

The woman pursed her narrow lips like a VAT inspector. 'Possibly. But we need to know more about Channings Hill before we make any decisions. My husband and I like peace and tranquillity. Is this a quiet village?'

'I wouldn't say quiet, exactly. We have our moments,' said Ash. 'It's just . . . normal.'

'What does *that* mean?' The woman's husband surveyed him intently. Cleo wondered what it must be like for the two of them, being married to each other.

'Not too many people have parties,' she explained. 'It's more kind of . . . unstructured noise. Like the teenagers on their motorbikes . . . they're good kids really, they just don't think about the noise when they're racing round the green.'

The dual intake of breath was audible. The woman shuddered and said, *'Motorbikes?'*

Lady Bracknell would have been proud.

'Not all of them,' Cleo rushed to reassure her. 'Some just have mopeds. But it all stops at midnight.'

The man's eyes bulged. 'The estate agent didn't mention anything about this.'

'I'm not surprised! But the rest of the village is great!' Cleo nodded with enthusiasm. 'Fantastic pub, loads going on there. You'll make lots of new friends in no time, especially if you're into karaoke!'

The Volvo left the village a lot more speedily than it had arrived. Ash reached for Cleo's hand, gave it a smack and said, 'You are a bad, bad girl.'

'Don't care. I didn't like them. That woman looked as if she wanted to peck my eyes out.'

'If you've put them off, that estate agent's going to hunt you down and shoot you.'

OK, that was something she hadn't actually thought of. Cleo shrugged. 'They wouldn't have fitted into this village.'

'And it's nothing at all to do with wanting to muck things up for Johnny LaVenture.'

Goddammit, how did Ash *do* that? Putting on her most wounded face, Cleo said, 'That's a terrible thing to suggest.'

'But a great opportunity to get your own back. He's desperate for a quick sale. You've probably stopped that happening. Just how fond of your kneecaps are you?'

'Oh come on, somebody else'll come along and buy it. Somebody a million times better, then you'll be glad I did it. Anyway,' said Cleo, jumping down from the wall and handing back her empty naked lady mug, 'Johnny's in New York, so how's he ever going to find out?'

Chapter 4

Something had happened; Abbie's stomach was in knots and she didn't know what to do. Maybe if she had more experience of relationships, like her younger sister, it would be easier to cope. Cleo might have had a dodgy dating history, pre-Will, but at least she'd been out on her share of dates.

But when you'd been married for twenty-three years to a cheerful, uncomplicated, completely relaxed man who had become withdrawn and distant practically overnight, it turned your whole world upside down. There was no getting away from it, Tom had the air of someone with a terrible secret. What's more, he was refusing to admit that anything was wrong, which only made it worse. Usually sunny-natured and able to joke about anything, he was like a different person now. When she had broached the subject again this morning, he had given her a look she'd never seen before and had ended up snapping at her to stop going on, before letting himself out of the house.

It was terrifying. Abbie had spent the last three days eaten up with fear. Since he was a man, top of her list of suspicions was the possibility that, healthwise, Tom knew there was something seriously amiss. Had he discovered a lump? Visited the doctor and been given terrible news? This was her number one fear. Number two, and a suggestion that until this week she would have dismissed as utterly unthinkable, was that he was having an affair. But Tom's behaviour had veered *so* wildly out of character, maybe it wasn't unthinkable after all. And didn't they always say the wife was the last to know? Oh God, what if he *was* seeing another woman? Sleeping with her? What if it was someone she knew . . . the affair had been going on for years, but now her rival was wanting more, putting the pressure on him, threatening to tell everyone in order to force him to take action . . . dump that boring wife of his and start a new life with her . . . *maybe she was already pregnant . . .*

Snap went the stem of the pink and gold glass apple in her hand. Bugger, and these were the expensive ones, three pounds fifty each.

'I don't believe it. *Another* one.' Des Kilgour, who owned the garden centre, spotted the broken Christmas ornament as he loped past. 'I bet it was that little kid in the red coat, he was over here just now—'

'It wasn't, it was me. I broke it.' Tempting though it was, Abbie knew she couldn't let an innocent four-year-old take the blame. 'It just snapped in half, I'm really sorry.'

'Oh hey, that's all right, don't worry about it.' Seeing that she was upset, Des backed down at once. 'No problem, accidents happen.' He paused, raking pale fingers through his reddish fair hair and surveying her with concern. 'You OK?'

Abbie nodded, determined to keep it together. Des was a good boss, and he'd always had a bit of a soft spot for her, which was why he wasn't yelling blue murder now.

'Sorry, I'm fine. It's just been one of those days.'

'Well, don't break any more, will you?' He gave her a jovial pat on the shoulder. 'Those apples don't grow on trees!'

Good boss, terrible stand-up comedian. Summoning a half-hearted smile, Abbie said, 'I won't.'

'Anyway, it's nearly six o'clock. Tom picking you up?'

She shook her head. 'He's working late tonight.' Or busy having sex with his mistress, you never know.

Please don't let him have a mistress . . .

Des's Adam's apple bobbed up and down. 'I can give you a lift home if you like.'

It was kind of him to offer, but Abbie shook her head again. The garden centre was only a mile from home and the walk would do her good.

'Right then, I'd better get on. And you cheer up, eh? It might never happen!'

All her life she'd hated that expression. What if Tom had fallen in love with another woman? What if she was young and fertile and he *did* want to have babies with her? Abbie busied herself sorting the jumbled-up Christmas decorations into their respective colour-coordinated compartments. What if everything she most dreaded was happening now?

You knew you'd got it bad when you tried to cook for someone and pretended it was the kind of thing you did all the time. Uncorking the wine and pouring herself a glassful – just to check it was all right – Cleo huffed her fringe out of her eyes and wondered why she was doing it again. Except she knew the answer to that; it was like seeing a dress in a glossy magazine, rushing out to buy it because it looked amazing on the model then somehow expecting it to make *you* look like her too. And this was all Nigella's fault. She'd watched the programmes. Nigella had made preparing a three-course meal look *soooo* easy. Tricking her, Cleo, into believing it was and, in

25

turn, casually inviting Will to come on over after work and telling him she'd cook dinner for him.

And yes, at the time the words had been spilling gaily out of her mouth, she truly *had* believed it would happen. She'd believed she could do it, that it was actually within her powers to dazzle Will with her culinary capabilities to the extent that he'd realise she was indisputably The Perfect One for Him.

Well, that had been the plan. Instead of which, she was surrounded by chaos, lumpy cheese sauce, worryingly odd-tasting chicken and incinerated parsnips.

'Everything OK?' Will wandered into the tiny blue and white, eclectically furnished kitchen, clearly wondering if they were going to be eating before midnight.

'Fine, fine, I'm just . . . getting everything together . . .' Frantically stirring the sauce, Cleo wondered how on earth you were meant to get the lumps out. 'Won't be long now!' It was one of those sauces that was too thick to sieve. It would just sit there refusing to go anywhere. But if she tried using the vegetable colander the smaller lumps would slide through. The only way to do it was going to be by using tweezers and picking them out one by one, which was going to take *ages* . . .

'What are those?'

'Parsnips.' She knew she sounded defensive. How were you meant to get the fat ends cooked without burning the pointy ends anyway? How did Nigella deal with triangular vegetables?

Eyeing the cheese sauce, Will said valiantly, 'The chicken looks nice.'

Oh God, the chicken. It had tasted too salty so she'd counter-acted it with sugar, then that had been frankly weird so she'd added a coating of satay paste but the sweetness had still been there and now it was all hideously reminiscent of peanut toffee with a renegade dash of Worcestershire sauce. And garlic. It was no good, she couldn't let him taste it, the look of horror on his face would be too much to bear. She was going to have to confess. Taking another glug of wine, Cleo shook her head and said, 'You know what? I've made a—'

The crash of the door-knocker stopped her in her tracks.

'Who's that?' said Will. 'Have you invited someone else for dinner?' There was a note of hope in his voice, as if having another person here to help eat the food might not be a bad thing.

'No. It might be carol singers.' Equally glad of the reprieve, Cleo went to the front door and opened it.

Yeek, not carol singers. Standing on the doorstep, wearing a Barbour with the collar turned up against the cold, was Johnny LaVenture.

'Cleo, I'd like a word.'

Cleo wavered; whenever people said this, she experienced a wild urge to shout, 'Kittens!' or 'Brassiere!' or 'Nincompoop!' But he didn't look as if he'd find that amusing. In fact his expression was bordering on grim.

'Fine.' She stood her ground, wondering what had brought him here. 'I thought you'd gone back to the States.'

'I had. And now I'm here again. What's that diabolical smell?'

Cheek. Then again, he had a point. The broccoli she'd cooked earlier was still sitting in a pan on the hob, waiting to be covered with the cheese sauce just as soon as she worked out how to de-lump it. Offended, she said, 'It's dinner.'

'It's burning.' Stepping into the house *without even being asked*, he headed past her through to the kitchen.

'Excuse me!' Cleo bridled with indignation as she followed him. The cottage instantly seemed smaller with Johnny in it. He'd better not leave mud on her cream hall carpet.

'Bloody hell, can't you smell it?' Johnny went straight to the stove, picked up the blue enamel pan of drained broccoli and dumped it in the washing-up bowl in the sink. A mushroom cloud of steam instantly enveloped the kitchen, along with an ear-splitting hiss.

'That gas ring wasn't supposed to be on.' Defensively Cleo blurted out, 'I thought it just smelled horrible because it was broccoli!'

He tilted the still-steaming pan towards her. The broccoli florets were blackened and stuck to the bottom. Oh well, at least it meant she didn't have to wonder any more how to get the lumps out of the cheese sauce. Raising an eyebrow at the half-charred parsnips, the sauce and the chicken quarters, Johnny said to Will, 'Are you seriously going to eat that?'

Wonderful though it would be if Will were to punch Johnny in the face, there was the danger that he might agree with him instead. Cleo said heatedly, 'Hang on, I don't remember inviting you into this house.' It might not compare with Ravenswood but it was her home, it was where she'd grown up and she loved every cosy, crooked, cottagey inch of it.

'No?' Johnny looked at her. 'Well, do you remember talking to the couple who were interested in buying *my* house?'

Oh. Bugger.

'What?'

'Don't pretend you don't know. Come on, I didn't come over here to sample your cooking.' Pityingly, he shook his head. 'I spoke to the estate agents. Then I called the couple who'd been put off after talking to someone in the village. Before that, they'd been really interested.' His eyes glittered. 'Until they heard about the gangs of Hell's Angels we have marauding around this village every night.'

'And you're saying Cleo told them that?' Will was defending her at last. 'I don't think she did, you know.'

Honestly, why couldn't he have defended her when he was supposed to?

'Well, I'm sure you're right,' Johnny drawled. 'It's just that when I asked them to describe the person they'd spoken to, they said it was a brunette in her late twenties with magenta streaks in her hair and a big freckle under her right eye.' He paused. 'So you can see why I'd jump to conclusions.'

Cleo sensed Will's shock.

'OK, so it was me.' Cleo defiantly straightened her back. 'But you should have seen them. They wouldn't have fitted into the village *at all*.'

'And I expect you thought it would be fun to piss me off,' said Johnny. 'Well, congratulations, you managed it. If I don't find another buyer before Christmas I'm going to lose that apartment I've been trying to buy. So the reason I came over is to ask you not to do it again. Because, trust me, I don't find it funny.'

And that was it. He turned; he left.

When the front door had closed behind him, Will gazed across the kitchen at Cleo.

'I can't believe you didn't tell me.'

Oh God, a man with morals. 'I just hate it that he always gets everything he wants.' She heaved a sigh. 'Are you shocked and disappointed? Have I blotted my copybook and let myself down?'

A slow smile began to spread across his face. 'I'll forgive you.'

Phew, thank goodness for that! And while they were on the subject of confessing their faults . . . 'There's something else,' said Cleo. 'I'm really bad at cooking.'

'You don't say. I'd never have noticed.' Grinning now, Will moved towards her. 'Come here and give me a kiss. Who wants to eat vegetables anyway?'

'Or chicken. That's awful too.' Between kisses, Cleo said, 'We can get something to eat at the pub. What are you doing?'

His hands had slid under her top . . . whoops, and now he was unfastening her lilac satin bra.

'Bed first,' Will murmured in her ear. 'Pub later.'

The smell of scorched broccoli had pretty much spoiled her appetite too. Wrapping her arms around his neck, Cleo said happily, 'That sounds like an excellent idea to me.'

Chapter 5

Abbie, lying beneath a layer of bubbles in the bath on Saturday evening, was listening to a problems phone-in on the radio. Hearing about other people's difficult lives and dilemmas was meant to be taking her mind off Tom but it wasn't having the desired effect. He'd gone away for the weekend on a fishing trip with a couple of friends from work. *Allegedly.* Then again, the trip had been arranged months ago, so maybe it was true.

She no longer knew what to think. His friends might be in on whatever his big secret was, and be covering for him. Every time she thought of Tom with another woman, Abbie's heart gave a lurch of fear and nausea rose in her throat. Then shame kicked in when a sweet lady on the radio broke down in tears because her husband had died and the doctors had just given their profoundly disabled son six months to live. Faithful or not, at least Tom was still alive. Oh God, unless he too had had terrible news . . .

'. . . And now we have Eric on the line,' said the female radio presenter. 'Welcome, Eric. What's your problem this evening?'

'Um . . . well, it's been a problem for years.' Eric sounded incredibly nervous. 'But up until now I've always managed to keep it under control. The thing is, I don't think I can do it any more.

I can't keep it a secret from my wife. I love her, you see. I hate having this . . . this *thing* between us. I've got to come clean, but I'm so scared I'll lose her. I mean, what if she can't handle it?'

'Eric, you sound like a caring husband to me. And *very* well done for having plucked up the courage to make this call.' The presenter's tone was lovely and soothing, like honey being drizzled over warm toast. 'So why don't you tell me what your secret is?'

Abbie waited. He'd had an affair with his secretary. Or he'd gambled away the family's life savings. Or he'd murdered his mother.

'Um . . . the thing is, I'm a transvestite,' said Eric. 'I've been cross-dressing for the last twenty years.'

Is that all? Abbie exhaled with disappointment. After the anguish she'd been going through, she'd be ecstatic if Tom broke down and admitted that the reason he'd been acting all weird lately was because he liked to wear women's clothes. God, Eric's wife didn't know she'd been *born*.

'Oh, Eric, can I tell you something? This is actually a lot more common than most people realise. Many, many men secretly put on their wives' dresses or take pleasure in wearing silky knickers under their work clothes.'

'I do that.' Eric sounded relieved. 'I'm a company accountant. If people knew what I was wearing under my grey suit . . . well, I'd never let that happen. I just want to share it with my wife.' Unable to help himself he added proudly, 'And it's all good stuff, you know. Nothing cheap, no man-made fibres. One hundred per cent silk from La Perla.'

'Oh Eric, La Perla's *lovely*. You have great taste.' The presenter was filled with admiration for him. 'But it must be tricky, keeping it all hidden from your wife.'

'It is, it's a nightmare. I have to wrap them up in polythene and hide them in the loft, in the bottom of a box of old curtains. And I just can't do it any more . . . I want my wife to know what I do and still love me. My dream would be for the two of us to go shopping together.' Eric sounded wistful. 'But what if she finds the idea repulsive? What if she wants a divorce?'

Abbie put down the bath sponge and sat up, two things hammering through her brain. First, highly unlikely though it seemed, what if Tom *was* a transvestite? When they'd been invited to a fancy dress party a couple of years back, he'd gone as a drag queen! It had never occurred to her that he might have done it because he longed to wear a curly blond wig, full make-up and a turquoise satin evening dress in public. Even if he had resembled one of Cinderella's ugly stepsisters and his leg hairs had poked through his fishnet tights.

And secondly, until now it hadn't occurred to her to search for clues. Which just went to show how completely . . . well, *clueless* she was. If she hunted through the house, who knew what might turn up?

And what was she waiting for? Anything would be better than this awful not knowing. With a swooooosh Abbie hauled herself out of the bath, dried herself, threw on her dressing gown. Then, hair dripping, she ran into their tidy, pale green bedroom and pushed up her sleeves. Here first. Office next, where Tom kept all his paperwork. And if neither of those threw up any clues, up the ladder into the loft with the spiders and the dust. OK, if she was Tom with something incriminating to hide, where would she hide it?

Forty minutes later, she found it. Just as she'd been about to give up on the bedroom, there it was. In Tom's sock drawer, of all the unimaginative places. She almost hadn't even bothered to look somewhere so obvious. But the moment she heard a crackle of paper and her fingers closed around the folded-up envelope, she knew this was what she'd been searching for.

Now the nausea came in waves, getting stronger and stronger. Trembling, Abbie pushed the drawer shut and sank down on to the edge of the bed. Oh yes, this was it, no doubt about it. A blue envelope, first-class stamp, postmarked eleven days ago. Tom's name and this address on the front, written in a female hand. If this was from his mistress, she'd taken a risk sending it. Unless that was the whole point and she was pushing for the secret to come out.

Abbie closed her eyes. Once you knew something, you couldn't un-know it. Her life was about to change for ever.

Right, here goes.

She slid the sheet of writing paper out of the envelope. As she unfolded it, a photograph dropped to the floor. Her bare toes scrunched with fear, Abbie left it there and began to read.

Dear Tom,

OK, you haven't been back in touch and you promised you would, so I'm writing again. Were you hoping that if you ignored me, I'd go away? Because I promise you, that's not going to happen! All my life I've wondered who my dad was, and now I've tracked you down, I'm not giving up – *no way*. I'm glad you aren't questioning it, by the way, or trying to say you might not be my father, but Mum says I do look a lot like you. Anyway, here's a photo of me taken last year (during my mad hat phase!), so you can judge for yourself. I'm not too ugly, am I?!

And I'm really sorry if it's awkward for you with your wife but that's not my fault, is it? Please ring me *soon* so we can fix a date to meet. You have no idea how desperate I am to see you! (Mum says hi and she's sorry too, but you already know what she's like!)

Love,

Your very keen to meet you daughter,

Georgia xxxxxx

Abbie bent down, picked up the photograph and turned it over. As if any further proof were needed, Tom's laughing, light-blue eyes gazed up at her out of a teenager's heart-shaped face. A girl, beaming away, with Tom's cheekbones and the unmistakable outline of his mouth. Tendrils of fair hair were escaping from her purple butcher-boy cap. She was wearing big hooped earrings and a white denim jacket.

She wasn't too ugly. She was beautiful. And she looked so like Tom it was ridiculous.

Slowly, Abbie nodded to herself. So that was it; now she knew the truth. Tom wasn't ill. He wasn't having an affair either. But he'd had one, years ago. Her loving, straightforward, utterly trustworthy husband had been unfaithful to her and his mistress had given birth to a girl who was now – understandably – desperate to meet her father.

After everything they had been through together, it was like being stabbed in the stomach, over and over. Clutching her chest, Abbie let out a low-pitched broken wail of grief as her world crumbled. Now she knew, and she couldn't un-know. Life would never be the same again.

The phone rang an hour later. Caller ID told her it was Des from work. Feeling utterly wretched, Abbie answered and mumbled, ''Lo.' Oh God, her throat was so swollen from crying she didn't even sound like herself. Too late, she wished she hadn't picked up.

'Abbie? Is that you?' Des sounded surprised.

'Yes.' She cleared her throat, tried again. 'Hello.'

'Listen, I'm here doing the rota and Magda's got her uncle's funeral on Wednesday, so we're short-staffed. Any chance you could swap your day off to Thursday?'

'Um . . . er . . .' Her brain was like cotton wool; he was talking about four whole days away.

'Are you all right?'

'Yes, yes . . . yes, I'm fine . . .'

'No you're not. What's wrong?'

'Nothing . . .' The fact that he was being kind, sounding as if he really cared, was what finished her off. A huge uncontrollable gulpy sob burst out like a cannonball.

'Right, that's it. Is it Tom?' His voice rising, Des said urgently, 'Is he beating you up?' Like Superman, ready to swoop to the rescue.

'N-no, Tom's not here. He's gone f-fishing.' Another involuntary sob escaped. Her face was tight and salty from all the tears.

'And you're on your own? OK, don't move, wait there. I'll be five minutes.'

'No . . . you don't have to . . .' But it was too late, Des had already hung up. He was on his way.

Abbie just had time to wash her face and gaze miserably at her piggy-eyed reflection in the mirror before the doorbell rang downstairs. If Cleo had been free, she would have asked her to come over. But Cleo was in Bristol with Will, and now that Des was here she was grateful for the company; the urge to talk things through was welling up unstoppably like water in a garden hose and Des, a genuinely kind soul, would be a good listener.

When she opened the front door he took one look at her face and said, 'What's happened?'

'It's Tom. He's had an affair.' As she led the way into the living room, Abbie saw it with fresh eyes. Everything was immaculate, because they had both always taken great pride in their house. From the pale yellow Colefax and Fowler wallpaper and matching curtains to the polished wooden floor and cream rugs, it was all perfect. She looked at the happy smiley framed photographs of her and Tom together, arranged on tables and window ledges around the room. She tipped the nearest one over. 'And a baby.' Saying the word aloud caused her to shudder. *Bang*, went the next photo frame, face down. 'A daughter.' *Crack* went the glass in the lovingly polished silver frame containing a picture of them taken on their wedding day. Oh yes, the happiest day of her life. 'Called Georgia.' *Crash*.

'Oh Abbie, God, I'm sorry.' Des looked appalled. 'And she's just been born?'

Abbie shook her head, pulled the envelope from her dressing-gown pocket and gave it to him. She watched him look at the photograph first, then read the letter.

'Jesus.' When he'd finished, Des said, 'This is pretty major. But she doesn't say how old she is. Maybe it happened before you two got together.'

'Nice try.' Abbie's jaw ached with the effort of keeping the muscles rigid. 'But it didn't. We've always been together. Since we were fourteen, if you can believe that. Childhood sweethearts.' The words curdled on her tongue; everything was spoiled now. 'We lost our virginities together on my sixteenth birthday. All we ever w-wanted was each other, for ever and ever, for the rest of our lives. Ha, and to think I actually believed that!' *Craaaacccckkkk*, glass from the next frame shattered on the floor and she flinched as a shard ricocheted off her bare foot.

'Right, stop it. Come here.' Grabbing hold of her by the hand, Des yanked her away from the glass. 'You're going to hurt yourself.'

'And you think I'm not hurt already?' Hyperventilating with rage and grief, Abbie howled, 'You can't *begin* to understand how I'm feeling! Des, did you ever wonder why me and Tom didn't have children?'

There was bemusement in his grey eyes. It had clearly never occurred to him to question it. 'No.'

'Well, it's because I *couldn't* have children. At all. Ever.' Was she completely losing it now? Abbie didn't care. Possibly not caring that she might be losing it was a sign that she really was. Dimly aware that Des was herding her away from the broken glass – oh great, now he was treating her like a mentally fragile *sheep* – she burst into tears and sobbed, 'Which makes all this quite h-hard to bear, really, seeing as it was all I ever w-wanted in my life.'

Superman took charge, guiding her firmly out of the living room and in the direction of the stairs. 'Tell me where you keep your vacuum cleaner. Then go and get yourself dressed. You're not staying here on your own.'

When you were at the end of your tether and didn't know what to do, being given clear, simple instructions was such a relief. Getting dressed, she could manage that. While the Dyson crackled and roared downstairs, slurping up splinters and shards of glass, Abbie pulled on jeans and an old oversized blue V-neck sweater. Everyone had always said she and Tom had the happiest marriage they knew, and she'd been gullible enough to believe them. Whereas behind her back, whilst she'd been feeling ridiculously happy and loved, Tom had kept the secret of his own infidelity. And once you'd had one affair . . . well, why stop there? For all she knew, he could have had dozens.

It didn't bear thinking about. So she didn't. Having attempted to comb the tangles out of her hair, Abbie gave up and tied it back with a green scrunchie instead.

Were you meant to vacuum up broken glass with a Dyson or would it irretrievably shred the innards and render it useless?

Oh well, she knew how *that* felt.

Chapter 6

Des's flat, above the garden centre, was plainly furnished, decorated in shades of magnolia and tidier than she'd imagined. He was being so kind. When he offered her a drink, Abbie said, 'Wine please, white if you've got it,' and Des said apologetically, 'Sorry, I don't have any wine. I could go to the pub and pick up a bottle, or there's some brandy left over from last Christmas.'

He evidently wasn't a great drinker, which was no bad thing. In the narrow beige kitchen, discovering lemonade in the fridge, Abbie said, 'Well . . . brandy and lemonade then, that'll be fine,' and didn't have the heart to complain when Des, knowing no better, poured equal quantities of each into a half-pint beer mug.

Actually, it kind of grew on you after the first few shudder-making sips. And the spreading warmth in her stomach was definitely helping her to relax. You could see why people in times of trouble turned to drink. Next to her on the faded leather sofa, in front of a real fire, Des was being a brilliant listener, nodding sympathetically and being completely on her side. He didn't interrupt, didn't seem to mind that she was dominating the conversation and passed the box of tissues every time she'd soaked another one right through.

'. . . We found out when I was seventeen. I had to go to the hospital and have all these tests done, then they told me I didn't have a viable womb. And that was it, there isn't anything you can do about that, is there?' Having spared him the gory details, Abbie sank her head back against the slippery sofa cushions. 'I just wanted to die. I thought Tom would leave me. Why would he want to stay stuck with someone who could never have children? Because even then, already, we knew we'd want to have them one day. But he was fantastic.' Tears slid down her face and dripped off her chin. 'He said it didn't matter and he loved me too much to let me go. Of course, he forgot to mention that he'd be taking his mind off things by screwing other women behind my back.'

'It might only have happened the once,' said Des.

Abbie wiped her eyes. 'And that's meant to make me feel better, is it? You're sticking up for him now?'

'No, no, I'm really not.' Covering her hand, Des gave it a squeeze. 'I don't know how he could do it to you.' He shook his head. 'What about adoption? Did you never want to try that?'

'Oh, we did want to. We got married when I was twenty-one and started trying straight away. But everyone kept telling us we were too young to adopt, like we were being punished for it. And I couldn't wait.' Abbie closed her eyes as the painful memories of that time came flooding back. Cleo, their parents' unplanned but happy accident, had been a lively seven-year-old then, and she had loved looking after her little sister, but it had only served to emphasise the gaping, baby-shaped hole in her life. 'All I wanted was a baby of my own. Every day felt like a month, every month felt like a year and they told us to come back in five years when we were more settled. Settled! And if you get upset when they tell you that, as far as they're concerned it just goes to prove how unsuitable you are!' The words were tumbling out of her now.

41

'So then we tried surrogacy but that was traumatic and it didn't work . . . then we couldn't face any more tries after that, so we saved up for a couple more years and investigated adopting from abroad instead. But it was all so complicated and hard and I ended up getting into such a state that my doctor had to put me on tranquillisers. She told me I was obsessed, that it was taking over my life and if I wasn't careful I'd have a complete nervous break-down. And that was when Tom said it had to stop. He put his foot down and told me he wanted a wife, not a gibbering wreck. He said the way things were going, we'd end up tearing each other apart. And you know what? After going through eighteen months of hell, it was almost a relief. We'd tried everything and nothing had worked. So we gave up and told ourselves we'd leave it for another four years. But then every time we started thinking about it after that, Tom saw me getting wound up all over again and said he wasn't going to put me through it. And when I went along to my doctor in a state, she told me I wasn't doing myself any favours, and that with my mental history I might not be considered suitable to adopt anyway.' She paused, turned to look at Des. 'So that was it. We drew a line, gave up for good, told ourselves that at least we still had each other.'

He gave her hand another sympathetic squeeze. 'I never knew. I'm so sorry.'

'It's not your fault.' Frowning at the empty glass in her other hand, Abbie said, 'Did I spill this?'

Des smiled. 'You drank it. Stay there, I'll get you another one.'

By the time he returned from the kitchen, she was in tears again.

'Sorry, I don't know where it's all coming from.' She fumbled for another tissue. 'This must be the most boring night of your life.'

'Don't be silly. We're friends, aren't we?' He sat back down. 'You've had a rotten thing happen and you don't deserve it.'

A rotten thing happen. Well, that was one way of putting it. But he was trying so hard to help. And it was comforting to know that he was on her side.

'I don't know what to do.' Abbie's voice broke. 'I still can't believe he did it. I can't believe this is h–happening . . . I just want to hurt him like he's hurt me . . .'

Oh no. Oh God. The moment Abbie opened her eyes, the events of the night before came flooding back in Technicolor detail.

Every single detail.

Her stomach clenched with horror, she gazed at the unfamiliar curtains and felt the unfamiliar arm draped over her side, the warm breath on the back of her neck. How had she got herself into this situation? Except she already knew the answer to that. Fuelled by the second half-pint mug of mostly brandy with a dash of lemonade, she had carried on ranting and raving while Des had been . . . well, lovely, really. Kind, patient and endlessly understanding. Until finally she'd cried, 'I mean, how would Tom like it if I did it to him?' and Des had gazed wordlessly into her eyes until the penny finally dropped.

If she was honest, there had always been a frisson of attraction between them. Not that either of them would ever have dreamed of doing anything about it, simply because that wasn't the kind of people they were. She was a happily married woman and Des had respected that.

But now, after all this, well, why shouldn't it happen? A combination of alcohol and the desire for revenge was what had propelled her to do it. She had leaned over and kissed him. That was all, just a kiss, but Des had responded with alacrity. They'd kissed some more and it had felt strange, but it was a way of getting back at Tom, so she'd carried on. Then after a while in Des's arms, the slippery leather sofa had become uncomfortable and he'd helped her to her feet, leading her through to the bedroom. By that stage the alcohol had well and truly kicked in. Recklessly, she'd almost made up her mind to have sex with him. *There you go, Tom, see how you like that.* But when it came down to it, she hadn't been able to see it through. Des had taken off his shirt, but by the time he attempted to unfasten her buttons, she was already shaking her head and pulling away, saying no, no, sorry but no. And to his eternal credit, he hadn't pressed her to change her mind. He had stopped at once, comforted her when she started sobbing all over again, and told her that it didn't matter, just being here with her was enough. Not long after that, overwrought and exhausted and unaccustomed to the alcohol she'd drunk, she'd fallen asleep in his arms.

Still fully clothed, thank God.

Abbie blinked and shifted to the edge of the bed. Her mouth tasted sour and last night's torrent of tears had left her eyes sore and gritty, as if they'd been sandpapered by a deranged carpenter. The clock on the bedside table showed that it was ten to six. Outside, the sky was still pitch black; it wouldn't start to get light for another hour.

'Where are you off to?'

Guiltily, she turned and saw that Des had been watching her. If last night had been embarrassing, this morning already felt worse. 'Sorry, did I wake you? I need to get home.'

'You don't have to. You're welcome to stay.'

He was her boss. She had led him on and nearly-but-not-quite slept with him. And he was still being kind. Feeling sick and dreading Tom's return from his fishing trip this evening, Abbie said, 'Thanks, but I want to go.'

'I'll give you a lift.' He began to throw back the duvet and she caught a glimpse of bare torso.

'No, no . . . really, there's no need.' She backed hastily towards the door; anyone hearing a car at this hour on a Sunday morning could look out of their bedroom window and see him dropping her off.

'OK, I know you've got stuff to sort out with Tom.' He pushed back his tousled reddish fair hair with the flat of his hand. 'But . . . I meant it when I said you didn't deserve to be treated like that. You're lovely . . . amazing . . .' He saw her flinch and went on hastily, 'Look, you can call me or come over whenever you want. Anything I can do to help, please, just say the word.'

'Right.' Abbie nodded. 'Thanks.'

He blinked. 'Will you tell him about this? I mean, you spending the night here?'

'Don't worry.' As she shook her head, she saw the relief in Des's eyes. 'I won't. It's just between us. No one else is going to know.' Awkwardly she added, 'And you won't tell anyone either?'

Des's expression softened. 'Whatever you want.'

'Thanks. Well, bye then.'

He cleared his throat. 'I hate to ask, but will you be able to work Magda's shift on Wednesday?'

God, this was what he'd phoned up to ask her last night. If he hadn't, none of this would have happened.

'Yes. Fine.' Abbie nodded helplessly. She'd spent the night in Des Kilgour's bed and nearly ended up having sex with him, and it was all Magda's dead uncle's fault.

Chapter 7

The moment she saw Saskia and Shelley walk into the pub at three o'clock, Cleo knew where she'd be spending the rest of Sunday afternoon.

How could she even have thought her casual offer would slip a determined six-year-old's mind?

'Cleo!' Saskia came hurtling towards her, mittens on strings flapping as she flung out her arms.

'Sass! You came!' Picking her up and swinging her into the air, Cleo pretended to stagger. 'Oof, you're heavier than a house.'

'I'm not. You are.' Saskia had inherited her mother's slender frame, dancing green eyes and infectious giggle. 'When are we going? Soon?'

'Sorry, sorry.' Shelley, her mother, ran her hands over her neatly tied-back dark hair and grimaced by way of apology. 'She hasn't stopped going on about it all weekend. Are you sure you don't mind?'

Of course she didn't mind. Cleo knew how much she owed to Shelley. Following a series of less-than-thrilling jobs – waitressing, office work, tour guide – she had been more than ready for a change three years ago when she'd heard through a friend of a friend about the vacancy for a chauffeur at Henleaze Limos. Grumpy Graham, who owned the company and ran the tiny office from his home just off Henleaze Road in North Bristol, had wanted another male driver. Shelley, in her late thirties and divorced, had persuaded Graham to take Cleo on instead. She had then been the one who'd shown her the ropes and taught her how to stand up to Graham, who took his grumpiness seriously. She and Shelley had hit it off from the word go, and Saskia – three and a bit then, six years old now – was the light of her mum's life. She also had the memory of an elephant; many months ago, Cleo had mentioned in passing that next Christmas Saskia might enjoy a trip to Marcombe Arboretum, where an illuminated path through the woods led to a hut in a snowy clearing where good children got the chance to meet Santa. When she'd said, 'You should ask your mum to take you there,' Saskia had brightly replied, 'Or you could take me,' and when she'd responded with a vague, 'Yes, but I expect your mum would want to go with you,' Saskia had moved expertly in for the kill with, 'Or you and me could go, wouldn't that be good?'

In years to come, when selling double glazing became a recognised Olympic event, single-minded Saskia would surely bring home gold, silver *and* bronze.

As it was, she was doing pretty well. The moment Shelley had mentioned that she had a pick-up at Heathrow on Sunday afternoon, Saskia had announced without hesitation, 'That's fine, Cleo can take me to that tree place to see Santa.'

But never mind, because it *would* be good. Saskia was endlessly entertaining and they'd have a lovely afternoon together. It would be magical.

'You're a star,' said Shelley, heading for the door. 'I'll come and pick her up at seven, is that OK?'

'Perfect.'

'Bye, Mummy! See you later!' Tugging at Cleo's hand as she attempted to finish her Diet Coke, Saskia said eagerly, 'Come on, hurry up, let's *go*.'

And to be fair, once they'd reached Marcombe, parked in the arboretum car park and trudged along the winding, lit-up path through the woods, it *was* magical. People had come from miles around for this, and a serious amount of effort had been put into making it memorable. Strategically positioned uplighters shone differently coloured lights into the trees, others were strung with garlands of twinkling white stars and a snow machine had been brought in to dust the entire clearing with a festive layer of biodegradable snow.

'Is he really in there?' breathed Saskia, gazing in wonder at the gingerbread-style wooden hut with Santa's helpers guarding the entrance and a pair of real reindeer being fussed over by families at the head of the queue.

'He really is.' Squeezing Saskia's mittened hand, Cleo felt her eyes prickle with sentimental tears. There was such a festive feel to the place. This was what Christmas was all about, wasn't it? Creating wonderful memories for children while they were still young and innocent enough to believe in Father Christmas. All around them, happy families were laughing and chattering, clouds of condensation puffing out of their mouths as they stamped their feet and rubbed their hands together.

'Are you cold, sweetie?'

'No.' Saskia, who had been picking bits of white papier-mâché fluff off the front of her pink flowered Wellingtons, said, 'It's not real snow.'

'It's better than real snow. It doesn't melt.'

'But it's the real Santa?'

'Oh yes, definitely the real Santa.'

Saskia did an excited skip. 'Can we see him now?'

'Soon, sweetie. We have to get in the queue.' Actually it was pretty long; they were going to be here for a while. 'Come on, let's line up, shall we? Ooh, look at those lights shooting right up into the sky!'

It was while Saskia was busy twirling around and gazing skywards that Cleo glimpsed something that gave her a jolt. Several feet ahead of them in the queue, someone was wearing a tan leather jacket just like Will's, and for a split second as the man gestured with one hand he even looked like Will from this angle, which was spooky. Wait until she told him she'd thought she'd seen him ahead of her in the queue for Santa's grotto with two small children in tow.

Except . . .

Oh . . .

Oh God, no, *surely not*.

But of course it was him. It was Will, her boyfriend, not in Manchester preparing for the conference that was taking place tomorrow. Instead, unbelievably, he was here, not three metres away, waiting to see Father Christmas.

Cleo's heart was banging so hard against her ribs she could barely hear all the different voices around her. Her ears were filled with the drumming sound of it. Will wasn't married and he didn't have children but somehow, inexplicably, a small girl in a pink coat and a purple sparkly beret was hanging on to his hand and behind her a boy aged six or seven was stealthily filling the pockets of her coat with fake snow.

Cleo became aware of a tugging on her own arm. Saskia was saying urgently, 'How many presents am I allowed to ask for? Can I ask for six?'

'Um . . .' The drums of the massed bands of the Coldstream Guards were still fogging up her brain. It was so hard to concentrate. 'No, just one.'

OK, let's be logical about this. She was here with Saskia, but did that automatically make Saskia her daughter? No, of course it didn't. So it stood to reason that the same went for Will. He was simply doing a friend a favour, bringing the friend's two children along to the arboretum out of the sheer goodness of his heart and . . .

'Mummy? Mummy!' A child in a Postman Pat anorak was pointing an outraged finger at Cleo. 'That lady there just said you're only allowed to ask Santa for ONE present! But you said we could ask for THREE.'

Oh God, get me out of here. Hurriedly, apologetically, Cleo stammered, 'S-sorry, I made a mistake . . . it's three.'

'*Ha.*' The child shot a look of triumph at Saskia.

'Three?' Saskia gazed up at Cleo for confirmation. 'Three *big* presents?'

Distracted, Cleo nodded. OK, it would be useful if Will could turn round now, catch sight of her and break into a huge delighted smile. He'd exclaim, 'I don't believe it, have you been roped into this too?' before going on to explain that the Manchester conference had been cancelled at the last minute and his boss had asked him for this huge favour and, hey, wasn't this fantastic, now they could all queue up together . . .

'Does an X-Box count as a big present or quite a small one?'

'What? Um . . . big.' Reaching for her mobile, Cleo dragged her gaze away from the back view of Will and scrolled through to his number. She pressed Call. Watched, dry-mouthed, as his phone began to ring. Saw Will take it out of his jacket pocket, glance at the screen and calmly switch it off.

Straining her ears, Cleo heard the girl holding his hand say, 'Who was that, Daddy?'

Will smiled down at her. 'No one, darling. Just work.'

Just work.

Of the extra-curricular variety.

Cleo didn't often find herself at a loss, but watching the three of them, she couldn't for the life of her figure out what to do now. If it had just been Will and herself here, she would have confronted him, *obviously*. But how could she do that with his children present?

So confrontation was out.

Ditto, murder. Sadly.

And she couldn't leave, because that would break Saskia's heart.

So basically she was stuck here, while Christmas music piped out from speakers hidden in the trees and fake snow drifted down, watching the cheating, lying bastard who had, up until this afternoon, been her lovely boyfriend . . . then again, hang on, might it be possible that he was a liar but not a cheat? Thinking fast, it occurred to Cleo that he could still be single; he just hadn't plucked up the courage to tell her about the children by a previous girlfriend in case it put her off him. Because if *that* was the case, discovering the truth like this could actually turn out to be quite sweet and romantic, like the heart-warming ending of one of those schmaltzy films you only ever see on TV at Christmas.

It was a fabulous idea, scuppered in moments when a thirtyish woman squeezed past, the sleeve of her navy coat brushing against Cleo's arm as she murmured 'Sorry . . . excuse me . . .' before reaching Will and the children.

'Yay, you're back from having a wee,' sang the girl, beaming up at her.

'Yes, well, thanks so much for sharing that information.' The

51

woman exchanged an amused look with the couple ahead of them in the queue. 'I'm sure everyone's delighted to know where I've been.'

'You're always going to the loo,' the son chimed in. 'Every time we go out. Isn't she, Dad?'

'*All* the time,' the girl agreed.

'She is.' Will nodded solemnly.

The woman mimed outrage and pretended to hit him. Will ducked away and used his son as a human shield. Everyone around them was laughing now. The perfect family sharing a perfect moment, with pretend snow tumbling down, fairy lights twinkling in the trees and Christmas carols being piped out, creating the perfect festive mood.

'Si-lent night, ho-ly night . . .' Saskia sang along, her voice as pure and high as helium.

Ha, chance would be a fine thing. Cleo wondered what Will would do if she were to march up to him and his family and introduce herself. She wouldn't dream of actually doing it, but what *would* he do if she did? Because somehow or other, he had managed to spend the last three months conducting an affair while he was married. The woman was wearing a wedding ring and now she was affectionately brushing fake snow out of Will's hair, which wasn't something you'd do to an ex-husband.

There was no getting away from it, she was his wife.

The nerve, the colossal *nerve* of the man . . .

'Aaaaaalllll is calm, aaaaaallll is bright,' Saskia sang. People in the queue turned to smile at her and that was when it happened. The woman nudged Will and he turned to look at Saskia. Then, like a join-the-dots picture, his gaze travelled from Saskia's face to her arm to the mittened hand holding Cleo's before travelling upwards and finally reaching Cleo's stony face.

Ha, now whose heart was hammering in his chest with shock and fear? She saw it in his eyes, raised an eyebrow fractionally in return but otherwise didn't react at all. Will looked away first, turning back to his children and shoving his hands into the pockets of his trousers. Even from this distance she could see the tension in his shoulders. And his breathing was rapid, each exhalation marked by a telltale puff of condensation.

'Cleo?' Now that the music had stopped, Saskia tugged her hand again. 'Is an iPod a big present or a small one?'

'It's a big present, sweetie.'

'But it's only *tiny*.' Saskia pulled off her green mitten to demonstrate the minuscule distance between finger and thumb.

'They cost a lot.'

'Oh.' Saskia's eyes were huge. 'So . . . would a dog be cheaper?'

'You know you can't have a dog.' Cleo had wondered how long it would be before the D-word was raised; getting a dog was Saskia's latest mission in life. 'Your mum's already told you that. Dogs need too much looking after.'

'And they wee a lot.' Breaking into a grin, Saskia pointed ahead of them. 'Like that lady over there.'

This was unbearable.

'OK, look, how about this for an idea?' Her voice super-bright, Cleo made it sound like the most genius idea ever. 'My feet are frozen and this queue is being really, *really* slow! So why don't we go back to the café, have some hot chocolate and a huge cake each, then come back later when there's hardly any queue at all? Wouldn't that be brilliant, hmm?'

From the look of horror Saskia gave her, you'd think she'd just suggested stringing up a cute little puppy and cutting off its legs. Her lower lip began to quiver. 'I don't want to.'

'But we wouldn't miss Father Christmas, he'll still be here when we get back, I promise! And we wouldn't have to queue, so isn't that better?'

Saskia wavered for a second.

'Scuse me, love,' said the elderly man behind them with his grandson, 'the later you leave it, the longer the queue gets. By five o'clock it's murder. Take it from me, you're best off staying put.'

Helpful old men. Couldn't you just shoot them?

'We're staying,' Saskia said flatly.

Mutely Cleo nodded. Great.

Forty hellish minutes later, it was Will and his family's turn to be led inside the grotto to meet Father Christmas. He hadn't looked round once since discovering who was in the queue behind him, although he was probably aware of the mental knives being plunged into the back of his neck. Cleo wondered if Will was having a go on Santa's knee: 'Dear Santa, I haven't been a very good boy this year, in fact I've been very, very *naughty*. But could I still get a Christmas present anyway? An invisibility cloak would be nice.'

Or . . .

'All I want for Christmas is for my wife not to find out about my mistress.'

Oh God. She shuddered at the word. Up until that moment it hadn't occurred to her that this was what he'd turned her into.

Cleo swallowed the bitter taste in her mouth; technically, albeit unwittingly, she had been his mistress. Just the thought of the word was enough to bring the traumatic memories flooding back. She was nine years old again, feeling sick and filled with fear at the sight of Auntie Jean in another of her states. At the time she hadn't understood what a mistress was, but Uncle David had had one and it was clearly someone vile and repulsive, worse than any mass murderer.

'Cleo? Is it our turn soon?' Saskia's nose was pink with cold but she was still zinging with pent-up anticipation.

'Not long to go now.' Cleo lifted her into her arms for a cuddle to warm them both up and take her own mind off the fact that she may as well have Evil Harlot scrawled in red felt-tip across her forehead.

Then the door of the wooden hut opened and Will and his family emerged. The children were excitedly clutching wrapped presents and their mother was exchanging cheerful words with the next people to go in. Passing Cleo and Saskia, she smiled and said, 'Don't worry, he's worth the wait!'

Meaning Santa, presumably. Not Will.

'Can we open them now, Daddy?' The boy rattled his parcel.

'No, come on, let's get back to the car.' As he hurried both children past Cleo, Will's glance met her unwavering gaze. There was pleading apology in his eyes and with his wife safely behind him his left hand came up to shoulder level, thumb and little finger extended to indicate that he would call her.

Pointedly Cleo looked away. Three whole months of her life, wasted. And to think that she'd actually had high hopes of Will. He had ticked so many boxes that had for years remained resolutely unticked. Apart from the disappointment and the fury at having been strung along, she just felt so used and gullible and *stupid*.

'You look funny.' Saskia, with not a care in the world, beamed and said, 'You've got all pretend snow in your hair.'

Ha, not to mention murder and retribution in her heart.

Chapter 8

Abbie had been going relentlessly over and over the moment of Tom's return, working out what she was going to say, but when it actually came to it, she didn't need to say anything at all.

His key turned in the front door, the overnight case, cool-box and fishing rods were dumped in the hallway and he yelled out, as he always did, 'Hi, honey, I'm home!'

It was their little joke, the way he always greeted her, and every time he did it, Tom varied the accent. Today, in honour of the fishing trip, it was Irish, and just to prove it – because some of his accents weren't instantly recognisable – he added, 'Bejaysus, it's bloddy frayzin' out dare tonight!'

Ironically, he sounded more cheerful than he had done for the last fortnight. Was that because he'd spent the weekend with his daughter?

Then Tom appeared in the kitchen doorway and his expression changed. The moment he saw her sitting there, he knew.

Abbie knew she looked a fright but she didn't care. *He* had done this to her. It was his fault she'd spent the day a trembling wreck, red-eyed, dry-mouthed and with a whole world of pain in her chest.

56

'Oh God.' The colour drained from his face. His hand rasped over his unshaven jaw and he shook his head. 'How'd you find out?'

'About Georgia, you mean?' Abbie barely recognised her own voice; she certainly couldn't believe she was saying these words. 'Your . . . *daughter*?'

Tom exhaled noisily. 'Oh God. Did she turn up on the doorstep? I *told* her not to do that. Abbie, I'm so sorry, I was going to tell you—'

'Were you? *Were you really?* Well, how fucking considerate of you!' As her voice rose, Abbie realised he was moving towards her, arms outstretched. CRASH went the kitchen chair as she leapt up, sending it flying. Backing away, stumbling against the upended chair legs, she shouted, 'Keep away from me! How *dare* you! Do you seriously think I want you *near* me?'

'But—'

'Oh dear, Abbie's a bit upset,' Abbie mimicked viciously. 'Never mind, soon sort that out, a hug and a kiss'll make it all better!'

Tom stopped dead in the middle of the kitchen. 'Look, I've said I'm sorry. And I knew you'd be upset. That's why I didn't tell you before. I was trying to work out a way of breaking it to you gently . . .'

'Wow, what a hero!' She saw the guilt in his eyes and marvelled at his reasoning.

'Abbie, it's been as much of a shock to me as it has been for you. I still can't believe it's happened.' Will shook his head. 'But we'll get over this, I promise. We just have to work through it together.'

'Are you *serious*?' Jesus, had he *no* idea how she felt? 'Tom, how can I ever trust you again? Our whole marriage has been a sham! Maybe some women could put up with what you've done, but I'm not one of them. That's *it* for me. I feel sick just looking at you . . . I never want you to *touch* me again!'

Tom was staring at her. 'That's not fair.'

Not fair? *Not fair?* Rage surged up through her. This morning she'd promised Des Kilgour she wouldn't tell Tom about last night, but maybe she wouldn't be keeping that promise after all. She'd almost slept with Des to punish Tom, by way of retaliation and in the hope that it would make her feel better. OK, so it hadn't happened, but she'd spent the night with him and if it would hurt Tom to hear all about it, maybe it wouldn't have been a completely wasted evening after all . . . yes, and then he'd know how it felt . . .

'So as far as you're concerned, the fact that you had an affair with another woman is something I should just . . . *forgive*.' Abbie's fingernails dug into the palms of her hands as she spat the words out. 'Does that mean you wouldn't mind if I did it? Would you just say oh dear, never mind, I'm sure we can *work through it together*? Because if that's what you think, let me—'

'Hang on. Whoa.' Tom frowned and raised a hand to stop her. '*What* did you say? What are you talking about? There was no . . . *affair*.'

Oh, for crying out loud. 'Fine,' Abbie bellowed, 'like it makes any difference! So she was just a casual fling, a one-night stand, some tart you had sex with . . . however many times you did it with her, the end result was the same!'

'No, no, *no*.' Shaking his head in disbelief, Tom said, 'Is that what she told you? Georgia . . . did she say it was an affair?'

'I haven't seen her! I never *want* to see her!' Abbie wrenched the letter from her jeans pocket and slammed it down on the scrubbed oak kitchen table. 'It's all in there.'

Something altered in Tom's face. He looked at the letter. Then he looked up again at her.

'Not quite all.' Even his voice sounded different now.

'You've got a daughter.' As she said it, Abbie felt her mouth twist with misery. 'What else is there to know?'

'Oh Abbie . . . sweetheart . . . I love you so much.'

'Don't say that.'

'But it's true. And there's one question you haven't asked yet.' Closing his eyes briefly, Tom said, 'The name of Georgia's mother.'

Nausea crawled up Abbie's throat. If she'd thought it couldn't get any worse, she'd been wrong. Now he was going to tell her she actually *knew* the woman he'd slept with behind her back.

Feeling sicker by the second, she said, 'Go on then.'

His Adam's apple bobbed in his throat as he swallowed. 'This is going to come as a shock to you.'

'Just tell me.'

The silence stretched between them until she was ready to scream. Finally Tom rubbed his hands on the sides of his worn corduroy trousers and said, 'It's Patty Summers.'

Patty.

Patty Summers.

What?

Patty Summers from nearly twenty years ago, with her rippling silver-blond hair and her long floaty skirts? Abbie was confused, struggling to take this information in; it was *the* most unlikely name he could have come out with. Had Tom carried on secretly seeing Patty afterwards?

'I've never cheated on you, Abbie. Never wanted to, never have.' Sensing her bewilderment, Tom moved towards her. His voice infinitely gentle, he said, 'Sweetheart, she lied to us. *She lied.*'

Nineteen years ago. Abbie remembered it as clearly as if it were yesterday. She had been twenty-five and frantic, a seething hormonal

59

maelstrom of desperation and impatience. The more everyone had told her to just relax and stop worrying, the more desperate she had become. Surrogate mothers had been in the news and being told by her disapproving doctor that this wasn't something she should even consider had been the final straw. Who needed an official organisation to make the arrangements anyway? Thanks to all the reading up she'd done, Abbie knew it was a straight-forward enough process, and taking matters into their own hands seemed to be the only way to go. Using a box number, she had placed an advert in the local Bristol papers: 'Surrogate mother required for couple unable to have children of their own. Please help us, we want a baby so much!'

Nothing. No response. 'Told you,' said Tom. 'Why would anyone offer to do something like that for a couple of complete strangers?'

So the following week, Abbie placed the amended ad: 'Could *you* be a surrogate mother for a couple unable to have children of their own? Please help! Generous expenses paid.'

Tom was wary but supportive, her overwhelming need over-coming his own natural reticence. And four days later, the letter had arrived from Patty Summers offering herself to them, volunteering to be their surrogate.

It was as if a miracle had been granted; something wonderful was happening at last. They made arrangements to meet up at a café in Clifton, the upmarket area of Bristol where Patty lived. Abbie, who had never been more nervous in her life, changed her clothes five times beforehand, terrified that the wrong style of trousers or not-trendy-enough shoes might alienate Patty and put her off. She'd made Tom wash and polish their red Astra until it gleamed inside and out.

Not knowing what to expect, meeting Patty for the first time was a revelation. She swished into the café, greeted Abbie and

Tom like long-lost family and dazzled them with her warmth and joie de vivre. She was beautiful, like Claudia Schiffer, with dancing eyes and a wide smile. Spotting their ad in the paper, she told them emotionally, had captured her heart. It had reached out and touched her. What better way could there be to help others than by carrying a baby for a couple who weren't able to procreate themselves . . . she would be *honoured* if they would allow her to do this for them.

Abbie was mesmerised, completely entranced by Patty Summers. It was left to Tom to ask the sensible questions. And no, Patty didn't have children of her own – she'd never been the maternal type, never *wanted* any – but she just knew this was something she was capable of doing. She was twenty-six years old, completely healthy, didn't take drugs or even smoke cigarettes. Her last job, working in a bar, had come to a bit of a sticky end when she'd broken up with her boyfriend, who happened to own the bar in question. This was why she'd been flicking through the local paper in search of work. And that was why it all made such perfect sense. Either she could start some boring new job she didn't enjoy, or she could relax, chill out for a year and grow a baby instead!

After an hour, Abbie's mind was made up. In order to pay the rent on her modest flat in Clifton and cover the rest of her bills, they agreed to pay Patty a thousand pounds a month. More than they'd been expecting, but not unreasonable when you thought about what she would be doing for them. And the beauty of going with Patty was her willingness to start straight away – no more interminable hanging about and waiting for appointments and being told for the millionth time to be patient until you wanted to scream at whoever had just said it. Patty was ready to go, fizzing with enthusiasm, as eager to get on with it as they were.

'A thousand pounds a *month*,' hissed Tom when Patty left them to visit the loo. 'For nine *months*.'

But Abbie wasn't to be swayed. Nothing was going to stop them now. They had their savings, Tom could work overtime and she would take an extra evening job. 'We're not going to argue with her. And you're definitely not going to haggle.' She clutched his hand beneath the table and gave it an iron squeeze. 'Tom, think of the beautiful baby we'll have! We're going to do it and it'll be worth every penny. This is the answer to our dreams!'

'I know. I know. But we don't even know her. We only met her an hour ago.'

'Don't you dare spoil this.' Abbie's chest was tight with anxiety; she felt like a child being told her birthday was being cancelled this year.

'She could be anyone.'

'Don't *say* that!'

'He's right.' Patty, back from the loo and overhearing their fraught exchange, said, 'I *could* be anyone, but I'm not. I'm me.' She looked at the pair of them. 'OK, how about if I show you my flat? Would that help?'

So they'd done that, gone along with Patty to her attic flat on the fourth floor of a Georgian house in Cornwallis Crescent. The place was tiny but the views over Bristol were stunning. Photos of Patty with friends and family chronicled her life to date, she'd painted the walls a sunny shade of yellow, and there were books and drawing materials and CDs everywhere. 'Sorry, not very tidy.' She gestured apologetically at the clothes drying on a fold-out wooden airer in a corner of the sitting room. 'I'm a messy pup. Now, how else can I prove you can trust me? Shall I show you my bank statements? Would you like to meet Dilys who lives downstairs, so she can tell you I'm a nice person?'

'We could do that,' said Tom.

'No, it's fine.' Vehemently Abbie shook her head. 'There's no need.'

'Well, if you're sure. But you're very welcome to.' Busy checking her calendar, Patty said, 'So, looking at dates, I reckon next weekend's when we want to make a start. And I'm free on Saturday afternoon.' She looked at them brightly. 'That OK with you?'

'Next Saturday.' In a daze, Abbie nodded. It was February . . . if everything worked first time, they could have a baby by Christmas.

'Brilliant!' Patty's silver bracelets jangled as she clapped her hands together in delight. 'We'll do it here!'

'Hang on.' Reddening, Tom said, 'There won't be any . . . you know, *contact*. I mean, you and me won't be . . . um, doing anything together.'

'Oh bless, is that what you were worried about? All this time?' Patty burst out laughing. 'Of course we won't be having sex! We use one of those baster thingies, don't we? You do your business into a teacup or whatever, then I'll take care of the girly side of things . . . they sell chicken basters in John Lewis.' Shaking her head at Tom, she went on, 'No offence, darling, and I'm sure you're marvellous in bed, but you're really not my type.'

The following Saturday they had gone back to the Clifton flat. They handed over the first cheque for a thousand pounds so Patty could pay her bills, and Tom asked her to sign the legal document he'd had his solicitor draw up, in order to ensure they both stuck to their side of the bargain. It wasn't *actually* a legal document – the solicitor he'd consulted had flatly refused to have anything to do with such a potentially incendiary situation – but it looked official and that was the main thing; anyone who wasn't on the level would surely baulk at the sight of it.

But Patty was absolutely fine about it. She happily added her signature to the foot of the document and offered them tea or a glass of wine. Then thirty minutes later the deed was done and she hugged them both goodbye, taking Abbie's hand, placing it over her flat stomach and exclaiming, 'Just think, it could be happening in there right now, at this very minute! Can you picture that? Isn't it the most amazing idea *ever*?'

The next two weeks crawled by with agonising slowness. All they could do was wait. Abbie barely slept; convinced it had worked and that their longed-for baby was already on its way, she couldn't concentrate on anything else. Was it a boy? Was it a girl? What names would they choose? Would it be wrong to start buying clothes for it? Not loads of clothes obviously, that would be stupid, but maybe just a couple of teeny tiny white babygros?

Sixteen days after insemination day, Abbie phoned Patty's number.

'Hi, it's me. Um, any . . . news?'

'Oh, hello Abbie! No, nothing yet . . .'

'So that's *good* news.' Abbie sent up a heartfelt prayer of thanks and envisaged the foetus, privately convinced that it was all her hours of visualising it that were keeping it in there.

'Well, it's too soon to tell, really. I might just be, you know, a bit late.'

'But you could do a test. I can buy one and bring it over, if you like!'

'Oh, you're so sweet, but I really think it's too early to do an accurate test. Look, I'll call you if anything happens.'

'But—'

'And just to let you know, I'm popping over to France to see my mum for a week, then I'll be back next Wednesday. So if my period still hasn't started, I'll do the test then and we'll really know for sure!'

The coiled spring inside Abbie's chest coiled tighter still; another nine days of uncertainty was almost more than she could bear. But since she couldn't drive over to Cornwallis Crescent and physically force Patty to pee on a stick, what choice did she have?

Somehow she made it through the next week and a bit. At times she was literally counting the minutes. But it was still possible to carry on believing that everything was fine because Patty hadn't called to tell her it wasn't.

And then, on Wednesday evening the phone rang and there was Patty's voice on the other end of the line.

'Oh Abbie, it's me. I'm so sorry, it didn't work. My period started today.'

Abbie slid down the wall until she was sitting on the living room floor. No baby. So sorry. Up until this moment, she hadn't even realised how much emotion she'd invested in this non-existent miracle.

'Abbie? Are you all right? Look, we tried. We did our best. Sorry.'

OK, get a grip, it's not the end of the world. *Although it felt as if it was.* Forcing herself to keep it together, Abbie said, 'Well, we'll just have to try again.'

'Yes.' Pause. 'Except, um, could you use someone else next time? Because I don't think I want to do it any more.'

'Sorry?' Abbie felt as if all the air was being squeezed from her lungs. 'But you *promised* . . .'

'I didn't promise. We *agreed* that I'd keep going if it didn't work straight away. But, you know, I didn't enjoy it as much as I thought,' said Patty. 'So I've changed my mind about doing it again.'

'But we're paying you!'

'Abbie, don't get upset. I'm not trying to con you out of your

65

money. Of course I won't take any more . . . as soon as you find someone else, you'll pay them instead.'

'*Don't get upset?*' bellowed Abbie. 'How do you expect me to feel?'

'OK, now you're shouting at me. And I'm not going to change my mind.' There was an edge to Patty's voice. 'Anyway, it wouldn't be practical,' she went on, 'because I'm leaving Bristol. My mum's asked me to go down to France, move in with her. So even if I did want to carry on trying for you, I wouldn't be able to.'

'Please. Please don't go. Just . . . have a rest for a couple of weeks, then maybe you'll feel better and we can give it one more try . . . please, I'm begging you . . .'

It wasn't dignified and it didn't work. Patty hastily ended the call and Abbie collapsed in a heap on the floor. She then stayed collapsed in bed for the next fortnight, refusing to speak or eat or go to work. In an act of desperation, Tom drove over to Bristol to try and reason with Patty, but she told him her mind was made up. The emotional repercussions were just too great. She should never have said she'd do it for them in the first place. And she hadn't been lying about leaving Bristol either; the flat had been filled with packing cases, all ready for her move to the south of France.

Upon hearing this, Abbie retreated still further into herself. Panicking, Tom admitted the reason for her breakdown to their GP, earning himself the most almighty lecture on how stupid and irresponsible they'd been to even consider advertising for a surrogate; any fool could see that it was a surefire recipe for disaster.

The fact that he was right didn't make it any easier to bear. Abbie wondered why she was even bothering to stay alive, when she was evidently so gullible and pathetic and pointless. The only thing that stopped her taking an overdose was that she couldn't be bothered.

To say she wished she'd never met Patty Summers was the understatement of the year, but at least it had taught her something. Never, ever again would she entrust another woman with her hopes and dreams.

Chapter 9

Now, nineteen years on, Abbie realised Tom was holding her hands in his own. Her brain felt as if it had been taken out, shaken hard like a snow globe and put back in upside down. What he'd told her simply wasn't believable, it couldn't be real. But, deep down inside, she knew it was.

'Patty lied to us,' Tom said again. 'She did get pregnant after that first try. But she realised she wasn't going to be able to hand the baby over. She didn't expect to feel so different, but she did. As soon as the hormones kicked in, she knew she wanted to keep it herself. So she told her mother, who promised to help her . . . and that was it.'

'She took our baby. She stole her.'

'Legally, it wasn't *our* baby.' Tom's voice was gentle but she could feel the pain he was suffering too. This eighteen-year-old girl was half Patty's, half his. She was his biological daughter and he'd been cheated out of knowing her, loving her, seeing her grow up.

And speaking of cheating . . . oh God, Abbie felt sick all over again, at the thought of last night. She might not have slept with Des but it could so easily have happened. And she'd spent the night with him in his bed. It would kill Tom if he ever found out.

Well, he just mustn't, that was all. Anyway, she couldn't even think about that now. The daughter they'd spent the last eighteen years missing out on and grieving for was alive and curious and desperate to meet her father.

'Sweetheart, I'm so sorry.' Tom stroked her hair. 'I didn't know how to tell you before.'

None of this was his fault. She had the best husband in the world and she didn't deserve him.

'Never mind.' Would he and Georgia form a father–daughter relationship? Would she be excluded and left out? Abbie's heart felt as if it was breaking, but the least she could do now was support Tom. Summoning a weak smile, she said, 'Well, I think you should give the girl a ring. I bet you can't wait to meet her.'

Bursting to talk about Will, Cleo was ready to pounce on Shelley the moment she arrived to pick up Saskia at seven o'clock.

'Hi! Sorry I'm late – the client's flight was delayed!' Shelley sped past her into the house at seven thirty, grabbing Saskia's coat from the banister and calling, 'Sass? Come on, darling, we've got to rush home and get you to bed, it's school tomorrow.' Over her shoulder she said to Cleo, 'How was Father Christmas? Did you have a good time?'

'Great. Um, but you can stay for a quick coffee, can't you? Just for ten minutes? You won't believe what happ—'

'Here you go, put your arms in there . . . good girl, now your boots . . . sorry, we really can't stop, I've got to wash and iron Sass's PE kit when we get home . . . forgot to do it yesterday! Got your present from Santa, sweetie? Ooh, isn't that lovely! Right, we're out of here! Bye!'

No one could out-whirlwind Shelley when she was in a rush. Within milliseconds they were out of the door, into the car and whizzing back to Bristol, leaving Cleo open-mouthed like a cod on the doorstep.

Still bursting to share what had happened and tragically minus a sympathetic ear.

OK, fine. She'd just have to tell Ash instead. And threaten to punch him if he laughed his head off.

Nimbly she vaulted the wall separating their cottages and rattled the knocker on his front door. What wasn't a promising sign, though, was the fact that the house was in darkness.

After bellowing his name through the letter box a couple of times and getting no response, she went back to her own cottage and rang Ash's mobile, only to find it switched off. Honestly, was he doing it on purpose? Frustratedly, Cleo tried her sister's number instead and got Tom.

'Oh hi. Abbie's upstairs in the bath. I'll tell her you rang, but she's not feeling that great just now.' Sounding pretty subdued himself, he said, 'So she'll probably call you back tomorrow, if that's all right.'

OK, was this some kind of conspiracy?

Well, she couldn't stay here. She'd explode. After pacing around the living room a couple more times, Cleo reached for her jacket and switched off the TV. Maybe Ash was over at the pub.

Except he wasn't. The pub wasn't that busy at all. Still, now that she was here she may as well make the walk worthwhile. Perching on one of the stools at the bar, Cleo ordered a gin and tonic and debated whether to tell Deborah behind the bar about the evils of married men.

Then the door leading to the loos opened and Johnny emerged, and she realised the half-full pint of Guinness on the bar three feet away from her belonged to him.

'It's OK, no need to move.' He looked amused as she began to slide down, drink in hand, and swung himself back on to the stool next to hers. 'I'm not in a biting mood tonight.'

Cleo, who was most definitely in a biting mood, said tightly, 'I didn't know you were still here. Shouldn't you be back in New York?'

'Well yes, strictly speaking I should. But it seemed safer to stay and keep an eye on the house. Guard it from anyone who might be wanting to put off potential buyers.'

Trust him not to forget that. 'I already told you, I won't do it again.'

'I know you won't. I'm making sure of it. Well,' Johnny amended, 'I would be, if only we could *find* another buyer.'

Was he trying to make her feel guilty? Cleo crossed her legs, coolly examined her drink then took an elegant sip in the style of Audrey Hepburn. The effect was slightly spoiled by her phone bursting into life, her glass slipping and a sloosh of icy gin and tonic dribbling down her chin into her cleavage.

OK, maybe it didn't quite *count* as a cleavage, but that was where it would have dripped if she'd had one.

'Bit of a waste.' Johnny passed her a bar towel. Glancing at the phone lying on the bar, he said, 'It's your boyfriend. Aren't you going to answer that?'

She'd already seen Will's name flash up on the screen. How he had the nerve to call her, she didn't know.

Leave it? Answer it?

What the hell. She picked up the phone on the fifth ring and said, 'Not interested,' before hanging up.

'Oh dear.' Johnny raised his eyebrows. 'Problems?'

'Don't be nosy.' Cleo finished dabbing at the wet patch on the front of her white T-shirt.

'I'm not nosy. Just concerned.'

71

'Well, don't be. Nothing to worry your pretty little head about.'

'I thought you made a lovely couple, that's all. You seemed so happy together.'

Now he was definitely taking the mick.

Bee-eep, chirruped her phone, signalling the arrival of a text: I can explain everything.

Cleo texted back: You're hilarious.

Bee-eep. This time his message read: I'm coming over.

'You know, this is what I love about the good old-fashioned village pub,' said Johnny. 'The sparkling conversation.'

Ignoring him, Cleo texted back: No No No.

Bee-eep: Please. I need to see you.

'The badinage,' Johnny continued, as if to himself, 'the dazzling repartee.'

Oh, for crying out loud. Cleo quickly sent a final text: NO WAY, then switched off her mobile and said, 'Debs? I'll have another drink.'

She may as well, seeing as staying here was preferable to going home and having a pointless argument with herself about how gullible she'd been.

'I'll get that.' Johnny was reaching for his wallet.

'No thanks. I'll buy my own.'

'That's the other thing I love, the friendliness of the locals.'

'Look, I'm not in a friendly mood.'

He shrugged. 'Maybe I could cheer you up.'

'You know something?' said Cleo. 'You really couldn't.'

'So that makes two of us. Me and poor old Will.' Grinning, Johnny said, 'Has it ever occurred to you to wonder if the person at fault might actually be you?'

The pub began to fill up, Johnny played a couple of games of pool with three members of the local football team and Cleo took her mind off Will by chatting to Deborah about salad dressings, Renée Zellweger's love life, and all-time favourite shoes. She was just describing her beloved red boots, bought in a sale and gorgeous beyond belief to look at but sadly a size too small, when the door swung open behind her and she caught a faint waft of Armani aftershave.

It didn't take a genius to know who'd just turned up. Cleo swivelled round on her stool and looked at the man who until a few hours ago had been her boyfriend.

One for whom she'd had *very* high hopes.

'Go away, Will.'

'Cleo, we need to talk.'

'You might need to. I don't.'

'Please.' Aware of interested eyes upon him, he said, 'Can we just go to your place?'

'Um . . . how can I put this? *No.*'

'Look, I'm *sorry*.' Moving towards her, he said pleadingly, 'But I love you.'

Cleo's breath caught in her throat. All her life she'd dreamed of someone saying those three little words to her. In the romantic sense, anyway; of course her parents had said it while she'd been growing up. But somehow she'd managed to reach the age of twenty-nine without ever once hearing it from a boyfriend, what with them all having been a shower of losers who either had a morbid fear of the word, an aversion to commitment or . . . well, basically, they just hadn't liked her enough to say it. And now, finally, someone was telling her he loved her. In public, too. He was announcing it in front of everyone in the pub, not caring who heard him, which would have been *so* romantic, if only the circumstances could have been different.

As it was, Cleo was filled with fury and disappointment that

73

he had ruined it for her; her first I-love-you would always be this one, about as unromantic as it was possible to get.

'You lied to me.'

Will spread his arms wide in desperation. 'Because I love you.'

'That flat in Redland. You said you lived there.'

'I know.' There was a faint sheen of perspiration across his forehead. 'It's Rob and Damon's place. I had to do it; I didn't want to lose you.'

And now he was making it worse. Did he really have no idea how close he was to getting a bar stool brought down on his head? Cleo gripped her drink tightly. 'Go away, Will. Go home.'

'Not until we've had a proper talk. Come outside,' he begged. 'Let me explain.'

'I think she wants you to leave.' When had Johnny abandoned his game of pool and resumed his old position at the bar?

Will eyed him evenly and said, 'This is between me and Cleo.'

'Cleo doesn't want to speak to you.'

'She needs to hear what I have to say. In private.'

Johnny turned his gaze on Cleo. 'Did he hit you?'

'For God's sake,' Will exploded. 'Of course I didn't hit her!'

Ignoring him, Johnny continued, 'Did he hurt you? In any way?'

'No I bloody didn't!'

'Well, you've done something to upset her.'

This was ridiculous; why was she even wondering if she should say it aloud? 'He's married,' Cleo said flatly. 'And he has children.'

'Oh great.' Will's eyes darted around the pub. 'I didn't mean it to happen, OK?'

'He's been lying to me for three months. I just found out today. Doesn't your wife ever wonder where you are?' said Cleo.

'Just come outside,' Will begged. 'For two minutes.'

With a hiss of exasperation, she slid down from the stool. Next to her, Johnny said, 'Sure about this?'

Cleo nodded. Will's wife was the innocent party here; she didn't deserve to be publicly humiliated, even if Will did.

Outside, the temperature had plummeted, a thick frost was spreading across the parked cars and the grass was crisp beneath their feet.

'Nothing you can say is going to make me change my mind.' Cleo wrapped her arms tightly around her shivering torso.

'I love you,' said Will.

Don't say that.

'You're a liar and a cheat.'

'You don't know what it's like. My marriage is over. But it's different with you . . . when we're together, I feel alive again!'

Oh yes, the clichés were really piling up now. 'You're disgusting,' Cleo shot back. 'And how do you suppose I feel? I believed everything you told me! I *trusted* you.'

'That's because we're perfect for each other.' Will took a step towards her. 'We're *meant* to be together. Look, I made a mistake before, I thought Fia was the one for me, but she isn't. My life at home is a nightmare—'

'Apart from when you're out at clubs, picking up girls and pretending to be single.'

'Once. *Once* I did that. And it was the best night of my life,' Will said fiercely. 'Meeting you changed everything . . . it was fate!'

'Don't touch me.' Cleo backed away as he reached out to her. 'Don't you dare.'

'But you have to believe me, it's the *truth.*'

'I'm not interested in believing anything you say.'

'Cleo, when I—'

'OK, time's up.' The door was wrenched open and Johnny

emerged from the pub. 'You can leave now. Head on home to the wife and kids. I'll take care of Misa.'

Will looked at him with loathing. 'She hates you.'

'Maybe so.' Johnny's mouth began to twitch. 'But right now, I reckon I'm the lesser of two evils. So, bye!'

'Don't tell me what to do,' countered Will.

The air was thick with testosterone. Oh God, don't let there be a fight.

'Wouldn't dream of it. Just making a suggestion. Take care driving home now,' Johnny drawled. 'To wherever it is you live. The roads are slippery.' He paused for a moment, then added, 'A bit like you, really.'

There was no fight; it all happened in a split second. Will took a furious swing at Johnny, who simply put out an arm and blocked the punch. Cleo was watching and he didn't appear to do anything else at all, yet somehow the next moment Will was flying backwards through the air as if twanged by a giant elastic band. Then he hit the ground, his feet shot out from under him, and he was sprawled in a daze, flat on his back on the frosty grass.

'Oh dear,' said Johnny. 'Slipperier than I thought.'

Chapter 10

Leaving the pub by unspoken mutual agreement, Johnny beckoned to Cleo and together they started off across the village green. Behind them, Will got to his feet, brushed himself down and made his way back to his car.

The sky was alive with stars. Away from the golden glow of the street lamps bordering the green, the pitch darkness was absolute. As the grass crunched underfoot, Cleo shoved her hands into her jacket pockets and sighed. 'I suppose I've got to thank you now.'

He laughed at her tone of voice. 'Not if you really can't bear to.'

'How did you do that thing, anyway?'

'What thing?'

'Stick your arm out and send him flying.'

Johnny sounded amused. 'Enjoyed that, did you?'

'It was like something out of a comic. *Kerblam, whooof, splat!* But I didn't see you *do* anything.'

'Ah, that's the joy of self-defence. You use your attacker's strength against him. I did Shoto Ryu for a few years. You should give it a go,' said Johnny. 'Never know when it might come in handy.'

It was a nice idea, but Cleo knew what she was like. She'd join the self-defence class bursting with ambition and good intentions, then lose interest a week later because she hadn't been awarded a black belt. As her teachers had so often written in her school reports during her unbothered phase, she lacked application.

Actually, speaking of her traumatic schooldays . . . 'Could you stop calling me Misa, by the way?'

'Sorry, didn't realise I still was.'

'You said it in the pub.'

'Did I? Force of habit. I'll make a real effort,' said Johnny. 'Scout's honour.'

'You never were a scout.' Cleo glanced over her shoulder as they approached the cottage, double-checking that Will had gone. 'Well, thanks for walking me back.' It seemed strange to be on relatively cordial terms with someone you'd disliked for so many years. Taking out her keys, she said, 'Next time I bump into you in the pub, I may even buy you a drink.'

This was her way of signalling goodbye, seeing as a handshake would be weird and she definitely didn't want to give him a kiss on the cheek. Johnny, however, ignored the hint and headed on up the front path.

'He might decide to come back. I'll keep you company for a bit.'

'Honestly, there's no need.'

'You don't know that. Anyway, it's not a problem.'

Cleo fitted the key into the lock. 'For you, maybe.'

'Hey, I'll just stay for a coffee. You can manage that, can't you?' Deadpan, he said, 'It's not as if I'm asking you to cook me a meal.'

At least there was no evil smell of burning this time. In the kitchen, she added an inch of cold water to Johnny's mug of coffee before handing it to him.

'You know, it's almost as if you don't enjoy my company.'

'It's been one of those days.'

'Pretty miserable, I suppose. Finding out your boyfriend isn't the catch you thought he was.'

Cleo reached for the biscuit tin and pulled it across the table towards her. Unlike men, chocolate digestives never let you down. And to think how she'd paraded Will under Johnny's nose, smugly showing off what a fantastic boyfriend she'd managed to end up with, so desperate had she been to prove she wasn't the loser he and his friends had made so much fun of all those years ago.

'You had high hopes for him, didn't you?'

For heaven's sake, there was being sympathetic and there was ruthlessly rubbing it in.

'Not really,' Cleo lied.

'Oh, come on, you did. It was pretty obvious.'

She rolled her eyes at his lack of tact. 'So now you're trying to make me feel *more* miserable about it? Who do you work for, the Anti-Samaritans?'

'Hey, I'm doing my best.' Johnny smiled. 'I thought girls liked talking these things through.'

Cleo nodded and said pointedly, 'With other girls.'

'Oh well, can't help you there. So, can I have a biscuit instead?'

There were only four left. Reluctantly she offered him the tin. He took two.

'Anyway, he's a dick,' said Johnny. 'You're well rid of him.'

'Thanks. I do know that.'

'You'll find someone else. Eventually.'

'You know what?' Cleo shook her head. 'This whole trying-to-be-a-girl thing. It really doesn't suit you.'

He smiled briefly. 'Just trying to help.'

'OK, one, I know I could find someone else if I wanted. Two, Will was *a* boyfriend, he wasn't the great love of my life.' Counting

79

on her fingers and wondering what the third point was going to be, because when you counted on your fingers there always had to be three, Cleo said, 'And three, I don't need another man anyway.'

Johnny leaned back against the fridge. 'Ah, the old don't-need-a-man thing. I love that line.'

She sighed. 'What's *that* supposed to mean?'

'I mean it sounds great, and girls love to say that stuff because it makes them sound all strong and independent. But it's not actually true, is it? Deep down they're panicking, getting more and more desperate, and the next thing you know, they're hurling themselves into a new relationship.'

'That's so patronising!'

'Happens all the time.' Johnny calmly snapped a biscuit in half.

'*I* don't do that. I *wouldn't* do it.' Cleo was indignant.

'Trust me, give it a few weeks and you'll change your mind. I'm guessing you'll go for whatsisname . . .' he indicated the wall on the right, '. . . radio guy . . . the boy next door.'

'*Ash?*' Ha, so much for him always being right. 'No way! He's a friend, that's all. And don't tell me I'm desperate,' said Cleo, 'because I'm not. I'm just fine on my own.'

'Don't get ratty. I'm sure you're right.' His eyes glittering with amusement, Johnny said, 'I'll ask you again in six months, shall I?'

'Fine, do that.' Seeing as it had taken her twenty-nine years to find a man she'd liked as much as Will, the chances of bagging another by then were practically non-existent. But it was hard to argue when you were desperate for a wee. Cleo moved towards the stairs. 'I'll be back in a sec.' Unable to help herself, she pointed to the biscuit tin on the table. 'And those in there are mine, OK?'

When she returned a couple of minutes later, Johnny had found a glossy magazine and was idly flipping through it while he finished his coffee. Which had to be lukewarm by now.

He looked up. 'How long did you say you'd been seeing Mr Married-with-children?'

Oh please, couldn't he give it a rest? 'It was only three months. No big deal.'

'OK, a word of advice. This is a common mistake women make. And, let me tell you, it's a dead giveaway.'

'What are you talking about now?' Cleo checked the contents of the tin; she wouldn't put it past him to replace the biscuits with a couple of satsumas. No, they were still there, *lucky for him*.

'Still, at least you've saved yourself a couple of grand.' Johnny flicked back through the magazine until he found the piece he'd been looking for, a double-page spread entitled 'Make Him Love You More This Christmas!'

Outraged, Cleo said, 'I wasn't going to buy that for Will!'

He gave her the kind of look that signalled she wasn't fooling anyone.

'I *wasn't*.' Honestly, now she wished he'd eaten her biscuits instead. Jabbing her finger at the photo of the Breitling watch she'd circled, Cleo protested, 'I only did that because I liked the style and the shape of it, the steel strap and the dark blue face.' It was the truth, but it sounded like the feeblest of lies. Her own face heating up, she went on, 'I was going to see if I could find something that looked the same but didn't cost so much.'

'Right.' Johnny nodded, evidently still not believing her. 'Well, that's good. Because let me tell you, there's nothing more embarrassing than being on the receiving end of a seriously over-the-top present.'

'But I wasn't *going* to—'

'He buys you a bottle of perfume and a pair of cheap earrings if you're lucky. And then you go and give him . . .' Johnny consulted the magazine, 'Bloody hell, only a three-thousand-pound watch.' He raised his eyebrows in mock horror. 'Awkwardness all round. Unless of course he doesn't find it embarrassing, but then even you must realise what kind of a man that makes him.'

'For the last time, I was never going to buy Will a three-thousand-pound watch! All I wanted was one in the same style that didn't cost more than fifty quid!' Cleo whisked the mug from his free hand, splashing dregs across the table. 'Finished this? Good. And the biscuits? Marvellous. OK, thanks very much for seeing me home, but you can go now. I don't need a bodyguard. Will isn't coming back and I'm going to have a bath.'

Johnny took a pen out of his jacket pocket and scrawled a number on the magazine, beneath the article's headline. 'That's my mobile. If he turns up and you need a hand, give me a call.'

That was *so* not going to happen.

'Bye.' Briskly she ushered him to the door.

Pausing in the doorway, Johnny said, 'I'm flying back to New York tomorrow. So have a good Christmas.'

'You too.' Cleo wondered if she would.

He raised a teasing eyebrow. 'And we'll see if you're still single next summer.'

'I will be.' Did he think he was setting her an impossible task? It was the easiest challenge she'd ever been set. With her disastrous history when it came to the opposite sex, it'd be a doddle.

Johnny strode off across the green. Cleo watched him disappear into the frosty, inky darkness. Then she closed the front door, went back to the kitchen and chucked the magazine into the recycling bin. To be honest, six months without a man in her life would be par for the course.

Chapter 11

How had she managed to get herself into such a mess? Abbie could barely breathe as she arrived at Kilgour's to start her shift on Monday morning. Some people had a great gaping hole where their conscience was meant to be. Being naughty was a huge thrill for them and telling endless streams of lies came perfectly naturally – it was all part of the adrenaline rush, bringing fun and excitement into their lives . . .

Dammit, why couldn't she be like that?

Oh God, and there was Des now, carrying Christmas trees from the shed and stacking them outside for customers to look over and buy.

A different kind of rush, the nauseous kind, overtook Abbie as she approached him. Des was wearing an unfamiliar red sweater and cleaner jeans than usual. When he saw her and whipped off his knitted grey beanie hat she saw that he'd had a haircut. His just-washed, reddish fair hair stood up in a whoosh of static.

Oh God, he'd only gone and given himself a makeover.

Des hefted a six-foot spruce down from his shoulder, then turned to face her with hope in his eyes and a rush of colour to his pale cheeks. 'All right, Abbie?'

'Not really, no.' Now that she was within six feet of him, she could smell the lavishly applied aftershave. Double-checking that there was no one else within earshot, she took a deep breath and said, 'Look, I need to talk to you, it's really important—'

'Des, are we bringing out the rest of the ten-footers?' Huw poked his head out of the shed and Abbie came out in an icy sweat. OK, *this* was why she would be such a useless adulterer, should she ever seriously contemplate it. Huw was married to Glynis, who worked in the shop and *lived* for gossip. It didn't bear thinking about . . .

'No, that's enough for now.' Addressing Huw, Des said, 'Half a dozen of each size is plenty. Give the customers too much choice and they can't make up their minds.' He turned to Abbie and added calmly, 'Is this about your shifts? Better come up to the office.'

Abbie couldn't believe it; there was no trace of a quaver in his voice, not a nanosecond of hesitation. He'd said it like an absolute pro.

Which was just as well, really. At least it meant one of them was on the ball.

'Women wanting to change their shifts. Bane of my life.' Shaking his head in a man-to-man way, Des said to Huw, 'When you've finished here, can you unload the poinsettias? I'll be back in five minutes.'

Upstairs, he firmly closed the door of the office behind him.

'OK, tell me what happened. Did you confront him?'

Were there listening devices hidden behind the radiators? Was someone crouched under the desk? Dry-mouthed, Abbie said, 'I did. And it wasn't what I thought. Oh God, this is so complicated . . .'

'Worse than you thought? Or better?' Des searched her face for clues.

Faltering at first, then speeding up as the words spilled out, Abbie explained everything. The whole sorry, tragic situation. Finally, her eyes filling with tears, she said, 'So at least that's one good thing. Tom didn't cheat on me after all.'

'So . . . you're not going to leave him?'

'Of course I'm not going to leave him! He's my husband and I love him.' Abbie wiped the back of her hand across her face. 'And he hasn't done anything wrong.'

'Oh. Right. Well then, I suppose you wouldn't want to.'

'But now it's more important than ever that he mustn't find out about, you know . . . what nearly happened the, um, other evening.'

'You mean on Saturday?' Des looked taken aback. 'When we spent the night together?'

'Oh, don't say it like that!' It came out as a panicky squawk. Shaking her head apologetically – because, God knows, she needed him to be on her side – Abbie begged, 'We just have to forget about it. *Completely.*'

Des's shoulders slumped. 'OK, don't panic. If that's what you want, it's what we'll do.' She saw it sinking in that the raised hopes and self-administered makeover had been for nothing. Summoning up a regretful smile, he made a clearing gesture with his outstretched hand and said, 'There, forgotten. Gone.'

Having to pretend nothing was wrong, when everything was wrong, was excruciating. By the time Abbie arrived home at six o'clock she was exhausted with the effort of it all. To make matters worse, Magda and a couple of the other women at work had noticed Des's attempts to smarten himself up. All day long they'd been teasing him, asking him if he'd got a crush on someone and trying to guess who the object of his affection might be. They'd expected her to join in, too. And she'd been forced to jokily suggest that it could be the willowy blonde who came into the garden centre every week for a sack of birdseed.

She'd barely stepped into the house before Tom, home early for once, rushed to greet her. His eyes shining, he said, 'She's written back.'

Abbie hid her disappointment. Together they'd composed the message last night and sent it off to Georgia's email address. As she'd watched Tom press Send, a part of her had prayed they wouldn't hear from her again.

But of course *that* hadn't happened, and her punishment for being so sulky and unsupportive had taken the form of a double-quick reply. Following him through to the living room where the computer was set up, she stood behind Tom while he sat down and gazed raptly at the email up on the screen:

Hi Dad!

Oh my God, it feels so amaaaazing to say that! You can't imagine what a thrill this is. Thanks so much for writing back (at last!!). You sound dead cool. Then again, why wouldn't you be? You're my dad! Yee ha, I just said it again! OK, stop panicking, I'm not completely mad, just a bit over-excited, in case you hadn't noticed!

So how soon can we meet up? I'm in Newcastle at the moment but I can come down any time you like. How about this weekend, would that be good for you? Please say yes! I'll catch the train down on Friday and you could meet me at the station, it'll be just like in a film, you have no idea how many times I've dreamed of this! Am I rambling? Sorry Dad, I'll be normal when we meet up, I promise.

Let me know if Friday's OK. CAN'T WAIT TO SEE YOU!!!

Love love love
          Your long-lost daughter
          Georgia

          xxxxxxxxxxxxxxxxxxxx

That was it. The words were practically zinging off the screen.
They sounded as if they should have been flashing and dancing,
strewn with glitter and written in neon. Tom was still gazing at
them, transfixed. Glad she was standing behind him so he couldn't
see her face, Abbie said with forced brightness, 'Well, looks like
you've made her day!'

When they had composed yesterday's email, Tom had told
Georgia about his marriage and had stressed how much they were
both looking forward to meeting her. OK, it hadn't exactly been
the truth, but she wouldn't have wanted to hear *that*, would she?

But in Georgia's excited email there was no mention of her at
all. It was directed solely at Tom. Clearly, as far as she was concerned,
meeting her father was all that mattered.

Abbie swallowed hard. It was as if she didn't exist.

A tear dropped down one cheek. Too late, she realised Tom was
watching her reflection in the computer screen.

Turning, he said, 'She's looking forward to meeting both of us.'

'It's OK. Doesn't matter.'

'She's eighteen, that's all. She dashed it off without thinking.'

'Tom, you don't have to make excuses for her. As far as she's
concerned, I'm irrelevant.'

He looked stricken. 'You're *not*.'

'Look, maybe it's best if you meet her on your own.' Abbie
shook her head; in a parallel universe, Georgia would have been
her daughter and she would have been Georgia's mother. But it
hadn't turned out that way, had it? Instead they were strangers

87

and there was nothing anyone could do about that. 'It'll be easier for both of you if I'm not there, playing gooseberry. She doesn't want to meet me.'

When delicious five-star cooking smells were wafting through the night air, somehow a packet of plain crisps and a bottle of mineral water didn't quite cut it.

Still, that was chauffeuring for you. Cleo was waiting in the restaurant car park and, strictly speaking, she shouldn't even be eating crisps in the car. But she was being ultra-careful not to spill crumbs, and by the time the clients staggered out at the end of the evening, the chances were that they'd be hard pushed to notice a fully grown polar bear in the passenger seat.

She knew this because one of them had been out twice already to apologise for keeping her waiting and to slurrily explain that chances were, they'd be here for a while yet. She'd smiled patiently in return and assured him that it was fine, no problem, she was more than happy to wait.

Well, why wouldn't she be? It was double time after eleven o'clock and it was their insurance company that'd be footing the considerable bill.

Still, they were successful, hard-working executives, this was their annual Christmas party and they were entitled to enjoy themselves. Cleo didn't begrudge them their fun. She had a warm car to wait in, a radio for company and a good book to lose herself in.

And a phone ringing on the seat next to her, at twenty past eleven at night. Probably Grumpy Graham wanting to know if she'd picked up yet.

But a glance at the screen told her it was from an unknown number. Cleo knew other people who simply didn't answer such calls but she could never help herself; they were the telephone equivalent of Chance or Community Chest. And if it was Will again, calling to beg her to change her mind . . . well, she'd just hang up.

'Hello?' Guessing which it would be, that was the thrill. Had she come second in a beauty contest and won twenty pounds? That was her favourite – as a child, when she'd picked this card, it had actually made her *feel* beautiful. Or was she about to get a speeding fine?

'Oh . . . hi. Can I ask who I'm speaking to, please?'

Cleo froze. Maybe it was her guilty conscience making her paranoid, but the voice was female, doing a good job of pretending to be casual but with an unmistakable layer of tension underneath. Oh shit, don't say Will had told his wife everything.

Although if he'd done that, why was she asking for her name?

'Sorry? I can hardly hear you, it's a really bad line.' Scrumpling her crisp packet, Cleo raised her voice. 'Um, who is this please, and what is it you want?'

And prayed the reply wouldn't be, 'I want to shoot the bitch who's shagging my husband. Oh, and by the way, I'm standing right behind your car.'

Instead, still with that faint edge to her voice, the woman said, 'I've been given this number to call. Could you just tell me your name?'

'Sorry, I'm losing the signal here . . .' Cleo scrumpled the crisp packet noisily, right by the phone, and switched it off. Then dropped it on to the passenger seat and stared at it, dry-mouthed with guilt and fear. She wasn't just being paranoid, was she? There was surely no mistaking who the caller was. Somehow or other, Will's wife had got hold of her number and had been suspicious enough to call it, which meant she might not know for sure that her husband had been playing away but she certainly suspected it. Unless, of course, her view was that Will was being chased by some shameless trollop who deserved to be hunted down and punished, because how dare another woman try and steal her husband . . . and how lucky that her brother was a professional hit-man who would love nothing more than to track down and torture the bitch who was trying to wreck his sister's marriage by—

'Aaarrrgh!' Cleo let out a shriek as the rear passenger door was wrenched open. Crisps flew out of the packet as she leapt a foot in the air . . . oh God, never mind contract killers, her own guilty conscience was going to be the death of her.

'Oops, shorry, shorry, were you ashleep there? Ssshh, don't wake her up, she's having a little shleep . . .' Mervyn, the fattest of the insurance execs, put a sausagey finger to his lips as he collapsed with a *whumph* on to the back seat.

'I wasn't sleeping.' Leaping out of the car so she could hold the door open for the others behind him, Cleo hastily brushed crisp crumbs off her navy skirt. 'You just gave me a bit of a start. There, careful, shall I look after that bottle for you? Has everyone had a good evening?'

'Shenshational. You should have come in with us, joined in the fun. We could've shown you a good time.' The dark-haired one flashed her a confident grin.

'Well, that would have been lovely, but one of us has to drive you lot home.' Humouring well-oiled clients was all part of the job description. Ushering them into the car, Cleo said, 'Seatbelts on, everyone.'

'You're a pretty little thing, you know that? Doesn't your boyfriend mind you doing a job like this?'

Cleo smiled. 'Everyone has to earn a living.'

'He'sh trying to find out if you've got a boyfriend,' the fat one explained helpfully.

'Is he? Now, would you like some music on the way back?'

'She'sh playing hard to get. God, I love it when women do that. How old are you, shweetheart?'

'Seventy-six.'

'Really? That'sh amazing – you don't look a day over sheventy-three.'

His friend said sorrowfully, 'You see, Merv, that's where you go wrong, mate. Women definitely don't love it when you say stuff like that.'

The banter continued for a few miles, then petered out as the occupants of the back seat fell into a collective drunken stupor. Relishing the silence – well, apart from the pig-like snores emanating from fat Merv – Cleo drove back down the motorway to Bristol. Forty minutes later she pulled up outside the first address, opened the rear passenger door and tapped the dark-haired one on the shoulder.

Opening his eyes, he smiled blurrily up at her. 'Hey, beautiful.'

'Hey.' Cleo leaned back to avoid the worst of the alcohol fumes. 'You're home.'

He peered through the window. 'Already? That was quick.'

'We aim to please, sir.'

'You certainly please. And it's James,' he said as he clambered with an effort out of the car. 'Not sir.'

He was in his late forties, crumpled and inebriated but still confident enough to be flirting with her. Opening his wallet, he took out a business card and pressed it into her hand. 'There you go, that's me. Now listen, how about you and me getting together some time soon? You give me your number and I'll call you.'

'Actually, thanks for the offer but—'

'Don't say *but*. Ach, I hate it when girls say but.' He pulled a pouting, little-boy face. 'Come on, live a little. We'd have a good time, I promise. What's your favourite restaurant?' He took out his phone and looked expectantly at Cleo, swaying on his feet as he waited for her to reel off her number.

Cleo, pointing behind him, said, 'I think someone's waiting for you.'

James turned and let out a groan. 'Oh God, why isn't she asleep?'

The woman, arms folded against the cold, was wearing a fluffy pink dressing gown. Her big furry slippers went slap slap slap as she made her way down the front path.

'Always has to turn up and spoil my fun,' grumbled James, leaning against the car.

'Hello. Had a good evening?' Eyeing the business card in Cleo's hand, she said, 'What did you give her that for? Have you been pestering this poor girl? Ugh, and you *reek* of booze.' Tilting her head to survey the snoring occupants of the car, James's wife said to Cleo, 'Sorry, love, he thinks he's George Clooney when he's had a few . . . ha, I wish! Come along now, Georgie-boy, haul yourself inside and let her get off.' Shoving him in the direction of the house she added, 'Why in God's name would a pretty little thing like that be interested in an old fool like you?'

Stumbling up the path, James mumbled like a truculent schoolboy, 'Always worth a try.'

Chapter 12

Pink coat – turquoise scarf, pink coat – turquoise scarf, pink coat – turquoise scarf. The words were drumming through Abbie's head in time with her racing heart as the train drew into Temple Meads station and slowed to a halt. The doors opened and passengers spilled out on to the platform, streaming towards the exit.

This was it, this was the one with Georgia on it. Any moment now, a teenager in a pink coat and a turquoise scarf would step down from the train and she would see the girl who should have been her daughter.

And then it happened. Next to her, Tom took an audible breath before saying in a carefully controlled voice, 'There she is.'

Abbie squeezed his hand before releasing it. As the girl scanned the area beyond the gates, Abbie moved away from Tom. He had insisted she came along this evening but the first meeting had to be between father and daughter. Melting into the background, bracing herself, she watched as Tom raised his hand and stepped up to the barrier.

Georgia was gazing at Tom now, a huge smile spreading across her face. The next moment she let out a squeal of excitement, shoving her ticket at the startled ticket collector and barrelling through the gate, before abruptly screeching to a halt six feet away from him and pulling out her phone. She pressed a couple of buttons, held the phone up to record Tom's face, and yelled joyfully, 'Hi, Dad!'

Then she threw down her rucksack and launched herself like an Exocet missile into Tom's arms.

It was hard to watch but impossible to look away. Other people were looking too, nudging each other and smiling and assuming the two of them hadn't seen each other for weeks, maybe even months.

Then father and daughter pulled apart and gazed wordlessly into each other's eyes. Abbie's stomach twisted with envy and emptiness. With her heart-shaped face, slender figure and long, rippling, silvery-blond hair, Georgia resembled her mother but she was also, without question, a part of Tom. As in the photograph, there were those shared cheekbones, that exact same mouth shape. Even from this distance you could see that their eyes were an identical shade of sky-blue.

Abbie watched as Tom said something to the girl then led her over to where she was standing outside the entrance of WHSmith. He was trying so hard not to show it, but the pride he was feeling was inescapable.

'Abbie, this is Georgia.'

'Hiya, nice to meet you.' Politely Georgia held out a hand for her to shake. 'Isn't this amazing? Look, I recorded it all on my mobile! Hang on, let me play it again . . .'

Her throat so tight she could barely swallow, Abbie was forced to stand by and smile and watch as the video clip was replayed on the mobile's tiny screen.

Twice.

And then one more time for luck.

'I'm going to keep that *for ever.*' Georgia clutched the phone to her chest. Then, putting her face next to Tom's, she said, 'Go on, can you take another one of us? Do we look alike? We do, don't we! Look at our eyes!'

Eventually they made their way out of the station to the car park. Having chucked her haversack in the boot of the car, Georgia automatically jumped into the passenger seat, so she could sit next to Tom. Abbie, relegated to the back seat, listened to her chattering excitedly in the front, and felt more left out than ever. She may as well be travelling in the boot.

Back at Channings Hill, Georgia climbed out of the car and surveyed the house, currently in darkness but with the trees in the front garden decorated with twinkling white Christmas lights.

'And this is where you've been living since before I was born.'

'It is.' Tom nodded in agreement. 'We like it here.'

'Pretty.' She followed him up the front path. 'So if Mum had given me to you like she was supposed to, this is where I'd have grown up.'

'You would.' He unlocked the front door, then showed her into the living room and began switching on the lights.

Georgia clapped her hands at the sight of the tree. 'You've got a real Christmas tree! All my life I've wanted a real one. Mum always said they were too messy.'

Eighteen Christmases they'd missed out on. Abbie said, 'I'll put the kettle on, shall I? Make us all a nice cup of tea?'

'No thanks, I don't drink tea. I'll have a coffee.' Grabbing Tom's left hand, Georgia held out her own and exclaimed, 'Hey, our fingers are the same shape! Spooky!'

'Um, do you take sugar?' said Abbie.

'That is so weird! How about cracking your knuckles, can you

95

do that? And how about bending your thumb back until it touches your wrist?'

In the kitchen, Abbie fumbled to undo the packets of biscuits she'd bought specially. As she waited for the kettle to boil, she recited the alphabet backwards in her head. Then tried counting down in sevens from two hundred. These were meant to take her mind off what was happening in her house . . . which was, of course, more painful than any extramarital affair Tom could have had.

Anyway, they didn't work. The lump in her throat grew and grew, and the girl who should have been her daughter carried on laughing and exclaiming and comparing various body parts in the living room with the man who actually was her dad.

Abbie opened the back door and slipped out into the garden. It was a relief to be able to let the tears out. They slid down her cheeks, icy cold within seconds. She must be a truly horrible person to resent all this so much, but just couldn't help herself. It was only now that she truly appreciated how happy and un-complicated and easy her marriage *had* been.

Georgia's arrival had ruined everything. Hopefully, once this weekend visit was over and her curiosity had been satisfied, she would disappear again and leave them to carry on with their lives.

Well, you could always dream.

The kitchen door creaked open and Abbie hurriedly wiped her face before Tom could see that she was upset. But when she turned, she saw that the figure silhouetted in the doorway wasn't Tom's.

'Hello?' Gazing through the darkness, Georgia said, 'Are you OK?'

'Fine, fine! Just . . . fancied some fresh air. Where's Tom?'

'He went up to the bathroom.' There was a pause. 'Are you crying?'

'Of course I'm not crying!' This was now technically true; the embarrassment of being caught had stopped the tears dead in their tracks.

But Georgia was coming across the garden towards her. When she reached Abbie, she peered closely at her face and said, 'Liar.'

Abbie braced herself; she was the grown-up and she didn't feel like the grown-up. 'Really, I'm OK. You go back inside. I'll be in in a minute.'

Georgia didn't move. 'Do you hate me?'

'No. No.' Shaking her head, Abbie said, 'I definitely don't hate you.'

'Mum, then. I bet you hate my mum.'

Oh God, this was difficult. 'I don't think hate is the right word. But yes, she made me . . . very unhappy.' Which was about as inadequate an explanation as you could get, but how else could she put it?

'She didn't mean to,' said Georgia. 'She told me all about it, about everything that happened. The reason she did it in the first place was because she really wanted to help you. But then afterwards, as soon as she knew she was pregnant, it all kind of began to sink in that she was having an actual baby. And her feelings began to change and she started to panic . . . basically, she was falling in love with me, even though I hadn't been born yet, even though I was only *that big*.' Georgia held up her hand, her thumb and forefinger practically touching. 'And she realised she couldn't bear to give me away after all.'

Abbie nodded; how could she dispute that?

'So she told her mother, my grandmother, and they decided they'd raise me between them,' Georgia continued. 'But if they'd told you and Tom, you'd have gone mental and nagged her to change her mind, and you might have got the police involved, and it would have been upsetting for everyone. So it was easier

97

just to lie and say she wasn't pregnant. Which I think was fair enough.' She shrugged. 'Under the circumstances, it was the best thing to do.'

From behind them, Tom said, 'What are you two doing out here?'

'Nothing. Just talking.' Georgia, who was only wearing a T-shirt, said through chattering teeth, 'I can't believe we're standing outside in the freezing cold!'

'Did you miss having a father when you were growing up?' Abbie had to ask.

'I don't really know. A bit, maybe, sometimes. It's hard to know if you really miss something you've never had.' Georgia's teeth gleamed in the darkness. 'Then again, it's pretty cool meeting him now.'

That was the point of all this, Abbie reminded herself. It was happening for Georgia's benefit, not theirs.

'And I'm sorry if I made you cry,' Georgia went on.

'That's OK. It wasn't your fault.'

'If my mum hadn't decided to keep me, you'd have been my mother.' Her blond hair swung as she shook her head. 'That's definitely weird.'

'I know.'

'The thing is, all my life I've been wondering who my dad is, and wishing I could meet him.'

Abbie nodded. 'I know.' God, she sounded like a stuck record.

'So, no offence, but I haven't spent years and years wondering who my mum is,' said Georgia, 'because she's always been there.'

This was stupid, she couldn't say 'I know' again. Searching for an alternative, Abbie said, 'Of course she has.'

'So what's going on?' From the kitchen doorway, Tom called across, 'Are you two planning on staying out there all night?'

Georgia was shivering, her arms wrapped tightly around her midriff.

'I could light a bonfire,' said Tom.

Georgia looked uncertainly at Abbie. 'Is he joking?'

'That's something you'll just have to get used to, your dad's sense of humour.' Smiling, Abbie said, 'Come on, before we get frostbite. Let's go inside.'

Chapter 13

'I just saw them leaving.' Cleo unwound the bright pink scarf from around her neck and gave her sister a hug. 'How did it go?'

Abbie heaved a sigh. It was late on Sunday afternoon and Tom was driving Georgia to the coach station; having spent the last fortnight with friends in Newcastle, she was now heading back to London, to the Paddington flat she shared with her mother.

'Well, I suppose it could have been worse.' At least she could be honest with Cleo. 'She's a sweet girl. But I'm glad it's over.'

'Over?' Cleo looked doubtful. 'You think she'll leave you alone now?'

'Fingers crossed.' Pushing up her sleeves, Abbie began running hot water and Fairy Liquid into the sink; having spent hours cooking an elaborate roast dinner, it would have been nice if Tom and Georgia could have told her to put her feet up and let *them* do the washing up, but of course it hadn't occurred to them to offer.

And just because she was crossing her fingers didn't mean her wish would come true.

'I wondered if she'd want to stay for Christmas.'

'Me too, but it's OK. She's off to Portugal with her mother.

Patty's got this semi-boyfriend who lives out there. He's invited them to stay for a few weeks.' Drily Abbie said, 'He has a massive pool.'

'Well, good. Maybe now she's met Tom, the novelty'll wear off.'

This was what she was hoping too. Something told Abbie, though, that it wasn't likely to happen. Scrubbing hard at a plate, she said, 'How about you, anyway? Any more funny phone calls?'

Cleo shuddered. 'No, thank goodness. Maybe it wasn't his wife after all.'

'It was probably just some wrong number and you've got yourself all worked up about it for nothing.' Even in the midst of her own misery, Abbie could still feel sorry for her sister, who had never had much luck with men; during her late teenage years Cleo had got herself entangled with a number of supposed charmers who'd turned out to be less than charming in the long run. Since then, she had grown wary and ultra-fussy, reluctant to take the risk of getting hurt again. 'Tell you what, how about if we get you a lie detector for Christmas? Then the next time you meet someone, you can give them a good old interrogation first.'

'Oh wow, wouldn't that be brilliant?' Her eyes lighting up, Cleo said, 'God, I'd love one of those! Think of the stuff you could find out, the havoc you could cause!'

Abbie reached for the next plate. 'Like when you had your hair coloured and it turned out bright purple and you asked me if it looked awful.'

'I knew you were lying.'

'I was just trying to make you feel better about yourself.'

'Ooh, speaking of lies, you know what this place is like.' Cleo pulled a face. 'They were gossiping about Georgia in the pub last night. The O'Brien brothers were joking about Tom playing away.

I think some people just don't want to believe the whole surrogate story.'

'Great.' Abbie had expected as much, but it still hurt; the downside of living in a village was the gossip. As soon as Georgia's startling resemblance to Tom had been spotted, they'd been forced to explain her existence and knowing nods had ensued.

'Don't worry, I had a real go at them in front of everyone. I said you and Tom were the happiest couple we all knew, and it was sick of them to even think that, because Tom had never done anything behind your back and he never would. I said the two of you had the perfect marriage.'

Oh God. 'Well, thanks anyway.' Here came the guilt again; she concentrated all her attention on the washing up. 'Was it busy in the pub?'

'Packed! Anyway, I showed up the O'Briens. They're probably just jealous of you and Tom anyway,' said Cleo. 'Everyone knows Barry O'Brien's wife had a thing with that guy from the garage who was always going round there to "fix her car".'

Abbie splashed washing-up suds across the front of her petrol-blue angora sweater and carried on vigorously scrubbing an already clean gravy jug. She could be honest with Cleo about a lot of things but there were limits. She was the older sister, the happily married, *settled* one, the one Cleo still looked up to.

No, there was no way she could tell her about Des Kilgour. Cleo would be shocked. Some secrets you just had to keep to yourself.

'I never thought about it before,' Cleo said dreamily, 'but I could look on the internet.'

'For Barry O'Brien's wife?'

'No, *duh.*' The other thing about Cleo was the way her brain was capable of careering from one train of thought to the next, like a wasp in a bottle. 'To see if there's a company that sells the machines so I could do my own lie detector tests.'

'You know, I really hate to sound like a miserable old killjoy,' said Cleo, 'but if one more person asks me in a jovial manner if I'm *all ready for Christmas*, I might just have to scream and stamp my feet and batter them around the head with a bunch of mistletoe.'

'Or you could sing to them. Christmas carols,' said Ash. 'That'd teach them a lesson they'll never forget.'

Cleo pinched him. It was Christmas Eve and they were in the pub, sitting together in one of the window seats like a couple of Grumpy Old Men. 'Why do people always say it, anyway? What difference does it make if we're all-ready-for-Christmas or not? In two hours' time, it'll *be* Christmas, so it's too late to do anything about it anyway.'

'Bah.' Ash nodded sagely in agreement. 'Humbug.'

'You know what? I'm twenty-nine and I'm sat here with you, and this *so* isn't how I was expecting this Christmas to turn out.' Cleo licked her index finger and dabbed at the last salty crumbs in her crisp packet.

Ash took a gulp of lager. 'You make me feel so special.'

'Oh, you know what I mean. I really thought this year was going to be different.' She'd actually secretly fantasised that Will would produce two airline tickets and whisk her away somewhere glamorous, even if it was just for a few days. Imagine, Christmas in Paris, living it up at the George V, walking hand in hand along the banks of the Seine while showers of stars exploded, *Moulin Rouge* style, in the sky.

Except *that* happy fantasy had exploded when she'd discovered Will had a wife and kids.

'All right then, you two?' Raising a glass in greeting – and not

103

the first of the evening by the look of it – Des Kilgour said genially, 'All ready for Christmas?'

OK, Des was her sister's boss and she couldn't beat him with a bunch of mistletoe. Forcing a bright smile, Cleo said, 'Not really, but never mind!' Then, on the basis that if you can't beat them, join them, she added, 'How about you?'

This was Des's cue to say cheerily: Oh well, the usual chaos, you know what it's like!

Instead he said, 'Not much point in doing anything. It's just me at home, after all.'

Yeek, wrong reply. Oh dear. 'Um . . . well, I expect that's what you prefer, a nice lazy day . . .'

'I wouldn't say I prefer it.' Des shrugged. 'It's just the way it is.'

'Oh. Right.' Fiddling with her empty crisp packet, Cleo felt awful. She didn't really know Des Kilgour that well, but Abbie worked for him. He was evidently a good boss and a nice enough person—

'How's your sister?'

'She's fine, thanks.'

Des nodded slowly. 'Good . . . good.' He paused, then raised a hand in salutation and said, 'Well, just wish Abbie and . . . um, Tom a happy Christmas from me. And I'll see her back at work next week. OK, bye.'

'I know what was going through your mind,' Ash murmured in her ear when Des had wandered off to the other end of the pub. 'You nearly invited him over to your sister's for lunch.'

'I know, I know.' Exhaling, Cleo said, 'I just think it must be so horrible, spending Christmas Day on your own. If I was on my own, I'd want someone to invite me to their house.' But she hadn't invited Des; Abbie wasn't having the easiest time of it lately and having another last-minute guest foisted on her probably wouldn't fill her with joy.

'It's that bloody film's fault.' When he'd called round earlier, Ash had spotted the DVD on the coffee table. 'I'm never letting you watch *Love, Actually* again.'

'Trust me, I never want to watch it again.' It had been her attempt to cheer herself up. Instead, as each of the wonderfully happy endings had unfolded, her own unhappy one had only made Cleo feel more miserable. Because let's face it, the chances were that she *didn't* have a Hugh Grant or a Colin Firth-type character waiting to sweep her off her feet. 'Ash, what happens if I never meet anyone else?'

'You will. Some poor sucker'll come along. It always happens in the end.'

'Yes, but what if it doesn't? What if I end up a Lonely Old Maid?'

'Hey, look on the bright side. You'll be able to wear a crocheted shawl,' said Ash. 'And pince-nez!'

'So could you. And a frilly bonnet. OK, here's an idea. We could be like *When Harry Met Sally*.' Inspired, Cleo grabbed his arm. 'We're friends, aren't we? So we'll make a pact! In ten years' time . . . no, better make that five years, if neither of us has met the perfect partner, we'll get married.'

Ash frowned. 'What, to just anyone?'

'No! To each other, you dipstick.'

He pulled a horrified face. 'But I don't fancy you. At all.'

'All right, all right.' It was actually quite hurtful, having to hear him say it. 'I don't fancy you either.'

'And you call me a dipstick.'

'I wonder why.'

'But you still think we should get married.'

'Why not? Wouldn't it be better than nothing? You'd be lucky to have me! Plus, I don't want to end up on my own,' said Cleo, 'in a rocking chair and a bonnet.'

'Fine, then. If it'll shut you up, that's what we'll do. In five years, if we're both still unattached, we'll get married. To each other.'

'Good.' Cleo gave a nod of satisfaction; OK, now at least she had a safety net to fall back on. It might not be romantic but it was practical.

'And if that's not an incentive for me to hurry up and find myself a girlfriend,' said Ash, 'I don't know what is.'

Chapter 14

Bristol Airport was busy, packed with people arriving, leaving and waiting to meet other people. Cleo, her greetings board tucked under her arm, waited at the back of the scrum and watched as the doors slid open to disgorge the latest stream of arrivals.

She was here to pick up a client flying in from Amsterdam, a Mrs Cornelia Van Dijk, which she wasn't altogether sure how to pronounce. Well, hopefully she wouldn't need to. Anyway, she was taking her to the Hotel du Vin, where she would be having lunch, then chauffeuring her wherever she wanted to go after that, until six o'clock. And, as always when all she had was a name to go on, she had a fully formed picture in her mind of Mrs Van Dijk; she would be tall and grey-haired, in her sixties and as thin as a whippet. Her nose would be long and pointy, she might be wearing an unusual hat and could even have a pointy beard and moustache . . .

OK, probably not. But her art teacher at school had been a big fan of Van Dyck the painter, and once you had an idea lodged in your head it was hard to—

Oh my God, look who was coming through the glass doors!

Cleo experienced that jolt of shock you always got when you

saw someone out of context. Johnny LaVenture was wearing a sand-coloured suede jacket, white shirt and black jeans. He was also pushing a trolley piled high with dark blue cases. Glancing up at the arrivals board, she saw that he'd just flown in from New York.

There was no need to duck down; she just automatically found herself doing it. But the crowd was clearing around her, there were no handy pillars or enormous fat people to hide behind and what did it matter if he saw her anyway?

As she straightened up, Cleo discovered that he already had.

Breaking into a smile, Johnny came towards her. 'Misa! Sorry . . . *Cleo.*' He shook his head, correcting himself. 'Look at you in your uniform, all smart and efficient. Have you come to pick me up and take me home?'

He was wearing a new aftershave, lemony and intriguing. Different smell, same old deliberately provocative manner.

'Not unless you're in the middle of having a sex change.' She showed him the name on her greetings board.

Johnny pulled a face. 'No, that's not me. Shame. How do you pronounce it, anyway?'

'Van Dyke,' said Cleo breezily.

He frowned slightly. 'Really? Sure it's not Van Deek?'

Damn, he'd been testing her. Trust him to know. Changing the subject, Cleo nodded at his mountain of cases and said, 'That lot must have cost a fortune in excess baggage.'

'All my worldly goods.' He gave the uppermost case a pat. 'Why?'

'Why d'you think?' Johnny raised a meaningful eyebrow. 'Ravenswood still hasn't sold. *Somebody* managed to scare off the only serious buyers. And it's not the kind of place you can leave standing empty. So I'm getting out of New York and moving back to Channings Hill. For the foreseeable future.' He paused, noting with amusement the look of dismay on her face. 'I know, and it's all your fault. So you don't have anyone to blame but yourself.'

Ouch. Well, that served her right. She'd done a bad thing and now she was being punished for it.

Wasting no time in pointing this out, he went on, 'Anyway, what's happened with your married guy? Mr Oh-so-perfect New-man?'

Because that was the thing about Johnny, he never had been able to resist taking the mickey out of other people, reminding them of their own imperfections and failures.

'I haven't seen him since that night.' Glancing up at the arrivals board, Cleo saw that the Amsterdam flight had landed.

'Found yourself another chap yet?'

'No. I don't need another man.'

'That's the spirit.' He half smiled.

As patronising as ever. But . . . what *was* that aftershave he was wearing? Breathing in surreptitiously, Cleo inhaled the herby lemoniness and attempted to commit it to memory. Mrs Van Dijk would be emerging soon. She looked at Johnny and said, 'Are you waiting to be picked up?'

'Always.' His dark eyes glittered. 'Sorry. Yes, I am, thanks. So, do you like it?'

Deliberately cryptic. He probably enjoyed the sense of superiority it gave him to have the upper hand. It was slightly puzzling, though, that he should seem so cheerful about coming back to live in Channings Hill when he'd been so keen to sell the house. Patiently she said, 'Do I like what? Being single? Waiting to be picked up? Snails in garlic?'

'My aftershave. Actually,' Johnny amended, 'it's not mine. I tried it in Duty Free and I think it might be OK.' He leaned towards her, inviting her to smell his neck. 'Here, what do you reckon?'

How on earth did he know what she'd been thinking? Had she been snuffling the air like a truffle-hunting pig? No, she definitely hadn't been doing that. Cautiously Cleo moved forward an inch and breathed in again. 'It's . . . fine.'

'Fine?' He looked disappointed. 'You mean it's not great, it's not awful, it's just . . . bearable?'

Oh, this was ridiculous. 'Actually, it's really nice,' said Cleo. 'What is it?' At least now she could find out without it sounding like some cheesy chat-up line.

Johnny frowned. 'Damn. I can't remember.'

'Well, think.'

'I am thinking! There were hundreds of bottles. I picked up loads of different ones and smelled them . . . then this one seemed good so I gave it a go . . . and now I have *no* idea which one it was.'

'That's just stupid, then, isn't it?' More people were beginning to emerge through arrivals; Cleo kept an eye out for Mrs Van Dijk.

'It's annoying, I'll give you that.' Frowning again and tugging at the collar of his shirt, he offered her another sniff. 'Don't you recognise it? I thought girls were experts when it came to after-shave. They always seem to know what you're wearing.'

'Sorry, not this girl.' There was a tall, beaky-looking woman in her sixties coming through now; stepping away from Johnny, she held up her greetings board and assumed a smiley, welcoming expression.

'Ah good, you are hjere!' The client approached her and, not for the first time, Cleo's preconceptions flew out of the window. As the beaky woman strode towards the exit, a curvaceous, sultry brunette in her late thirties, with cushiony crimson lips and smoky eyes, offered her the handle of her expensive-looking case-on-wheels. 'I am hjere too!'

Which just went to show, you never could tell. Oh well, never mind, she seemed fun anyway. Cleo said cheerfully, 'Welcome to Bristol, Mrs Van . . . ?' This was how she handled tricky names; if in doubt, let the client tell you themselves.

'Van Dijk.' It was Johnny's voice chipping in, pronouncing it Van Dyke. He broke into a broad smile. 'Or as I call her, the wonderful Cornelia.'

Excuse me?

'Johnny! You beautiful man, I didn't know you were there behijnd the sign!' Exclaiming with delight, Cornelia threw her arms around him and kissed him extravagantly on both cheeks.

OK, this clearly wasn't a coincidence. Cleo watched as the woman made a production of wiping the lipstick imprints from Johnny's face.

Still smiling, he told Cornelia, 'Looking rather spectacular yourself. And is this a new bracelet?' Diamonds glittered as he held up her arm, turning it this way and that.

'Just a little Christmas gift.' Her eyes bright, Cornelia confided, 'From me to myself.'

'When you live in Amsterdam, it'd be a crime not to.' Johnny regarded her with affection. 'It's so good to see you again.'

'Oh, dear Johnny, it ijs wonderful to see you too! Well, Ij am hungry! Shall we go?'

Cleo nodded. 'Absolutely. I'm taking both of you, then? To the Hotel du Vin?'

'That'd be great.' Steering his trolley towards the exit, Johnny said easily, 'I booked the car just for Cornelia, originally. I was planning to fly in yesterday. Then I had a last-minute meeting,

111

switched my flight to today . . . and we've actually managed to arrive at the same time, which is a bit of a miracle. Still,' he beamed at Cleo, 'it was good of me to use your limo company, wasn't it?'

Hmm. As far as she was concerned, it had less to do with generosity and more to do with his eternal bid for one-upmanship. But Cleo smiled and nodded and said obediently, 'Very good. Thank you.'

With the luggage stowed in the boot of the car – today she was driving the midnight-blue S-class Mercedes – Cleo pulled out of the short-stay car park and headed towards Bristol, still with no clue as to who Cornelia Van Dijk actually was.

Apart from absolutely loaded, if the diamonds were anything to go by, and in possession of a stupendous pair of gravity-defying breasts.

'Right,' said Johnny. 'We'll be a couple of hours. Will you be OK out here?'

They were parked outside the Hotel du Vin where he and Cornelia had a table booked for lunch.

Cleo nodded. 'No problem. It's my job to be OK out here.'

'I can send out a cup of coffee if you want.'

'Thanks, but I'm fine.'

He hesitated. 'You will wait here, won't you?'

The cheek of it! 'Don't worry,' said Cleo, 'I'm not planning to go off shopping and dump the car in some NCP with all your worldly goods in the boot.'

'Darling, don't worry, Ij am sure she'll keep everything safe.' Shaking back her glossy hair, Cornelia said, 'Shall we go inside now? Ij am gasping for a drink!'

Johnny reappeared shortly after three.

'See?' Cleo climbed out of the driver's seat, indicated the car. 'Still here. I didn't even sell your stuff on eBay.'

He inclined his head. 'Excellent. Cornelia's just freshening up. She'll be out in a moment.'

'Good lunch?'

'Great, thanks. So, are you curious about Cornelia?'

What a question – of course she was curious. She spent her whole life being curious . . . not knowing the answers to questions drove her *insane* . . .

Aloud, Cleo said, 'No, why would I be?'

'Oh, OK.' He shrugged, shoved his hands in his pockets and kicked at a stone on the road.

Pause.

Longer pause.

Oh, for heaven's sake. 'Go on then,' said Cleo. 'Who is she?'

'A client.' Johnny smiled briefly at her capitulation. 'A very wealthy one. Her husband died last year.'

'Really?' She was shocked. 'How awful.'

'Not really. He was eighty-six.'

Euw. Careful not to pull a face, Cleo gulped and said, 'And she's how old . . . ?'

'Think of a number, then double it.' Amused, he explained, 'She has a great plastic surgeon. But that's beside the point. She isn't my girlfriend, if that's what you were thinking. Cornelia bought two of my pieces last year while she was over in New York and now she's interested in commissioning a third.'

Cleo nodded, because this was how the other half lived. In her line of work she'd experienced it before. If normal people wanted to treat themselves, they ordered something off the internet or popped down to the local shops to see what caught their eye. Whereas when Mrs Van Dijk fancied a new sculpture for her drawing room, she hopped on to a plane to meet up with the artist.

And here she came now. Crikey, was she really in her sixties? Smiling fondly at Johnny as Cleo held the car door open, she trailed the back of her hand along his cheek and said, 'Darling, you do smell delicious. Acqua di Parma, am I right?'

A flicker of recognition crossed Johnny's face as the name rang a bell. 'In a bright yellow box? I think that's the one. Clever you.'

'Colonia Intensa.' Inhaling appreciatively, Cornelia purred, 'I'm always right. Cary Grant used to wear it, you know. And David Niven.'

Cleo didn't dare look at Johnny. Crikey, Cornelia was older than they thought.

It was five o'clock. Having dropped Johnny and Cornelia at Ravenswood an hour ago, Cleo was now back to take Cornelia on to Cheltenham, where she was due to spend a couple of days with an old friend before flying back to Amsterdam.

Johnny answered the door and said, 'We'll be a few more minutes, is that OK?'

'Absolutely.' She took a couple of steps back but he opened the door wider. 'No need to wait in the car. Come along in and see my new studio.'

Curiosity got the better of Cleo. Having never seen inside a proper artist's studio before, she followed Johnny across the oak-panelled hall.

'Well,' he amended, 'it'll be my new studio when I've finished with it.'

They were in the drawing room, a vast, high-ceilinged space with tall sash windows and French doors that opened on to the garden at the back of the house. Given that Lawrence LaVenture's priority in life had been socialising in the pub and not interior design, the décor was on the tired side. The wallpaper was stripy and peeling at the edges, the carpet was a riot of swirls and none of the sofas matched. There were hunting prints on the walls, bookcases crammed with books, and the TV, Cleo saw with a start, was balanced on the back of a three-foot-high, bright red clay statue of an elephant.

'I know.' Watching her reaction, Johnny said drily, 'but this was how Dad liked it. The estate agents were marketing the house as an excellent opportunity for the buyer to stamp their own personality on the place. Meaning basically that it needed a total refurb.'

'I love the elephant!' Cleo moved towards it, unexpectedly entranced. There was a quirky, cheeky glint in the creature's eye.

'So did Dad. It's the first piece I did that he ever really liked.'

She looked at the elephant again. 'You made this?'

He nodded. 'When I was sixteen.'

Back when they'd been enemies. But he'd had real talent, even then.

'Anyway,' said Johnny, 'now that I'm going to be living here, there are going to be some changes. And this room will be perfect to work in.'

Cleo could see that it would be. She headed over to an octagonal dining table, across which were strewn oversized sheets of paper covered in sketches. As she studied the charcoal drawings of horses grazing in a field, Cornelia burst into the room and said, 'Hjere I am, all ready to leave now! Ah, you are admiring my beautiful horses? Johnny is going to make them for me. He's brilliant, isn't he? I'm such a lucky, lucky girl! Thank you, thank you,' she exclaimed as Johnny helped her into her long velvet coat. 'There, all sorted, I have everything now. Shall we go?'

Chapter 15

A week later, Cleo was on her way home from a job when the
first snow of the year began to fall. Tiny dissolving snowflakes
at first, followed by faster, fatter ones that stuck to the windscreen
and whitened the fields on either side of the motorway. The married
couple she'd picked up earlier this morning and dropped at
Southampton docks were sailing to the Caribbean on a luxury
cruise ship; envying them, Cleo turned off the M4 and headed for
Channings Hill. Just enough snow to settle and look picturesque
would be nice. But not enough to bring Gloucestershire to a grinding
halt, especially when she had another pick-up this afternoon.

Her stomach rumbled loudly as she neared the village. A mug
of tea and a plate of hot buttered currant buns, that was what she
wanted right now. Which was frustrating, seeing as she didn't have
any at home, but not an insurmountable problem because unless
there'd been a mad rush on buns this morning, she'd be able to
grab some from the village shop.

Oh yes, toasted currant buns dripping with butter. The more
Cleo thought of them, the more badly she needed to have them.
Finally reaching Channings Hill, she pulled up on the forecourt
outside the shop and jumped out of the car.

God, it was *freezing* outside . . .

But at least the shop was warm. Waving at Myrna behind the counter, Cleo hurried round the central aisle towards the bread section and screeched to a halt when she saw Johnny ahead of her. With his dark hair tousled and his jeans and sweatshirt spattered with paint. And two cellophane packets of currant buns in the crook of his left arm.

Stiffening in disbelief, she stared at them, then at the empty shelf where *no more packets of buns sat*.

This was ridiculous. Was he doing it on purpose? Had he been reading her mind again?

'Morning! Sorry,' Johnny checked his watch and corrected himself. 'Afternoon!'

Never mind about that. Cleo pointed to the buns. 'Are you having both packets?'

He looked surprised. 'Well, yes. That's why I'm holding them.'

'So you're buying . . . *all* the buns?'

'Not for my own personal use,' said Johnny. 'I've got a crew of painters and decorators waiting back at the house. If you're working undercover for Weight Watchers,' he added, 'and worried I might be guzzling the lot myself, I can promise you I'm not.'

It was no joking matter. The thought of not being able to have currant buns was sending Cleo's blood pressure sky high. She blurted out, 'How many in the crew?'

'Five. Plus me. That's two each.' Johnny frowned. 'Is that a problem?'

Could she say it? Yes, she could. 'OK, here's the thing. I came into the shop because I really, really want toasted currant buns with butter.'

'Oh.' He nodded in amused recognition. 'I've just realised why.'

'Why?'

'Mrs Clifford.'

Heavens, he was right. Mrs Clifford, the lovely cuddly cook who had been in charge of the kitchen at Channings Hill village school all those years ago. Whenever the snow had fallen, she had made currant buns and brought them into the classroom heaped up on huge plates, halved and toasted and laden with butter. It had been a tradition that everyone would eat two halves before piling outside to pelt each other with snowballs. How funny that she'd forgotten that.

So, the fact that Johnny was here buying them too wasn't such a coincidence after all. More of a Pavlovian reaction to snow.

'We could have one packet each,' Cleo offered reasonably.

He raised an eyebrow. 'Have you *seen* my team of decorators?'

'Look, there's Scotch pancakes! I bet they'd prefer those.'

Johnny gave her a look. 'Nobody in their right mind would rather have a boring Scotch pancake than a toasted currant bun.'

OK, he was doing it deliberately now.

'There are crumpets.' She picked a packet off the shelf and waggled it persuasively. 'Crumpets are the *best*.'

'Are they?' said Johnny. 'Why don't you have them, then?'

Ooh. 'Because I want a bun!'

He shrugged. 'You could buy plain bread rolls and poke currants into them.'

'Or,' said Cleo, 'I could poke currants into you.'

Johnny laughed, thinking she was joking. He didn't know her at all.

'OK,' he said finally. 'You aren't having a whole packet, but I'll give you two.'

If he'd been Ash, she'd have made some bawdy quip about it being better than him giving her one.

But he wasn't Ash. Instead, Cleo went along with Johnny to

the counter and watched him pay for both packets of buns. Then he tore open the cellophane on one of them, asked Myrna for a paper bag and handed it over with two of the buns inside.

'Here.' In return, she tried to give him a fifty-pence piece.

'Have them on me,' said Johnny.

'Thanks.' Much as she'd have preferred not to be beholden to him, Cleo wasn't going to get into an undignified grapple over fifty pence.

As they left the shop, Johnny paused next to the ancient Land Rover he'd driven down in. 'You could come up to the house if you want. See what's being done to it. We can have a communal tea break, all toast our buns together.'

A flurry of snowflakes swirled around them. Cleo shivered in her thin uniform. 'No thanks. I've only got an hour before my next job.' And nothing, *nothing* was going to spoil her enjoyment of the hard-won buns.

Apart from anything else, in his house they might be tainted by the smell of paint.

Even if she wanted to go there, which she didn't.

Johnny reversed the Land Rover across the shop forecourt and roared off up the hill. Hungrier than ever and practically salivating by now at the prospect of toasting the buns, spreading them with Lurpak and biting into their crunchy, curranty, butter-soaked heavenliness, Cleo followed suit.

At the top of the hill, Johnny gave her a wave and turned right at the village green. She took the left-hand fork and made her way between the avenue of chestnut trees, passing a metallic-blue Fiesta parked up by the play area before pulling up outside the cottage.

There was someone sitting at the wheel of the Fiesta. Just sitting there, not speaking on a phone or anything. Which was slightly

119

unusual, given the weather. When it was warm and sunny, parents often brought their children to the play area, but today it was empty. Mildly curious, Cleo glanced over as she climbed out of her own car. Was it a man or a woman? She couldn't even tell. And what were they *doing*, sitting there? Reaching the front gate, she stopped and turned again. Were they lost, or ill, or—

Rurr-rurr-rurr-rurr went the engine of the Fiesta as the driver turned the key in the ignition. Rurr-rurr-rurr.

The engine wasn't firing. So that was why the car was there. It had broken down. The driver was trying to get it started. What a rotten time for it to happen, in weather like this.

Rurr-rurr-rurr-rurr-*rurr*. As the driver banged the steering wheel in frustration, Cleo saw that it wasn't a man with short hair, it was a woman with her hair tied back in a ponytail.

Oh God. Her stomach was rumbling like a cement mixer, her feet were cold and in less than an hour she had to be out again. The very, *very* last thing she wanted to do now was see if she could help a stranger in trouble.

Offer to push a car and hopefully get it bump-started? And more than likely get mud and slush sprayed over yourself when the wheels broke through a frozen puddle?

Or make a cup of tea, watch TV and eat two hot buttered currant buns?

Oh *God*. With a sinking heart, Cleo took her hand off the wooden gatepost. Sometimes she really wished she didn't have a conscience. Life would be *so* much easier if she could just waltz into the house and not feel an ounce of guilt. But she couldn't bring herself to do it. Slowly she made her way across the street, blinking snowflakes out of her eyes and flexing her already icy fingers. As she approached the car, the woman behind the wheel stopped turning the key in the ignition. She was looking at Cleo, waiting for her.

120

Oh fuck, oh no, please don't let this be happening. Cleo's heart lurched up into her throat as her eyes met those of the woman and recognition hit her like a brick. This was Will's wife – *Jesus, his actual wife!* – and she was here in Channings Hill, parked less than fifty yards from her house.

OK, had Will told his wife about her? Was she here for a confrontation? Or was this . . . please God . . . simply the most bizarre coincidence ever? And did she know who she was about to speak to? Cleo had recognised her because she'd spent forty minutes queuing behind her to see Santa, but Will's wife definitely wouldn't be able to remember her from then. That was impossible.

Which meant there was still the faintest of possibilities that she didn't know who was standing in the snow beside her car.

The woman opened the driver's window. She had a clear complexion, huge amber eyes and glossy gold-brown hair pulled back from an oval face to reveal exceptionally pretty ears. *The stupid things you notice when you're in shock.*

'Hi. Um, problem with the car?' Cleo had never felt more ridiculously British. She even sounded all clipped and nineteen-fifties. Plus, it was a completely idiotic question.

'Er, yes. I don't know what's wrong. It just . . . died on me.'

Was that a hint of things to come? Well, at least she hadn't bellowed accusations or leapt out of the car and started beating her up.

Dry-mouthed, Cleo said, 'I could give you a push, if you like. See if we can bump-start it on the slope.'

Will's wife was still gazing at her intently, as if she wasn't sure whether Cleo was the one or not. She was also shivering.

'OK, we'll give it a go. Thanks.'

'No problem.' Slinging her bag satchel-style over one shoulder,

Cleo braced herself against the back of the Fiesta and gave it an almighty shove. She was strong, she could do this . . . *heeeavvve* . . .

Nothing. The car didn't move an inch. Stopping and making her way round, she said to Will's wife, 'You have to take off the handbrake.'

'*Oh*. Sorry!'

They tried again. This time the car began to roll slowly forward. Pushing hard, then harder still, Cleo yelled, 'Try now!' but the engine didn't catch and they ran out of downward momentum. Brilliant, now the car was stuck right outside her cottage, which was *worse*.

'Hang on, I've got some WD40.' Fetching the can from the Mercedes, she flipped up the Fiesta's bonnet and sprayed every available lead.

Still no joy. Her hands were numb by now, her nose pink and stinging with the cold.

'Oh well. Thanks for trying, anyway.' The woman's teeth were chattering. 'I'd better call the RAC.'

She took out her mobile. Cleo stood next to the car like a lemon and listened to the brief exchange on the phone. Finally Will's wife hung up. 'They've had loads of calls. It's going to be at least an hour before they can come out.' She shivered. 'Typical.'

Oh God, here we go again. Cleo swallowed hard. This entire situation was surreal. Because she knew who this woman was and she suspected that this woman knew equally well who *she* was, yet neither of them was saying it and she certainly wasn't going to be the one to make the first move, because . . . well, what if Will's wife *didn't* know?

But the thing was, if anyone else were to have been stranded in a freezing cold, broken-down car, she wouldn't think twice about inviting them into her house.

Which meant she was going to have to invite Will's wife in, because otherwise it would look suspicious and give the game away, and it would become blazingly obvious to Will's wife that she *was* the one who'd been having an affair with her husband . . .

OK, this was too confusing. Stamping her icy feet and blowing on her hands, Cleo said, 'Well, you can't wait out here. You'd better come in.'

'Are you sure?' Will's wife blinked and looked startled, then relieved. Recovering herself, she reached for her bag and jumped out of the car. 'OK. Thanks.'

If the situation had been surreal before, it became even more so once they were inside the cottage. Cleo put the kettle on, sliced the currant buns and popped them into the toaster.

While she buttered the buns, Will's wife was making the tea, spooning sugar into mugs. Cleo, with her back to her, jumped a mile when a teaspoon clattered on to the flagstoned kitchen floor.

Will's wife smiled as she picked up the dropped spoon. 'Nervous?'

'Sorry.' Perspiration prickled under her armpits. 'It just made me jump.'

'It's kind of you to invite me in. What's your name?'

Did Will's wife know her name? Had Will told her? 'Uh, Cleo.'

'Hi. And I'm Fia. Short for Sofia.'

'Right. Um . . . bun?'

'Thanks.' Fia paused, taking the plate and gazing at her. Then she looked directly at Cleo and said, 'So, do you know who I am?'

Chapter 16

Cleo's heart launched into overdrive. 'No.'

'Sure?'

Breathe, *breathe*. 'Why would I know?'

'Just thought you might.' Fia shrugged. 'You're having an affair with my husband, aren't you?'

Shit. Cleo's hand flew to her mouth. Collapsing on to a stool, she said, '*Did* have. Past tense. I didn't know he was married, I swear.'

'How did you find out?'

'I saw him with you and the children. Queuing at the arboretum to see Father Christmas.' Feeling awful, Cleo said, 'As soon as I found out, that was it. I finished with him that same night.'

Fia thought back for a moment, then nodded and shrugged. 'Will's a good liar. It's always been one of his special talents.'

Cleo was still finding it hard to believe they were having this conversation. 'I felt terrible. You all looked so happy together.'

'We probably thought we were.'

'Was it you who phoned me the other week?'

Another nod. 'I got hold of a copy of his mobile phone bill. Your number cropped up quite a few times. Of course, it could

have been completely innocent, just something to do with work.'
She half smiled and took a sip of tea. 'Then I called you and you
sounded so guilty and panicky . . . well, that was when I knew for
sure that it wasn't.'

'You frightened the life out of me. I didn't want to get dragged
into anything. I definitely didn't want you to find out.' Of the
two of them, Cleo realised she was the one finding this more of
an ordeal. Her buttered toasted bun was growing cold in front of
her and she could no longer even face eating it, which was something that had *never* happened before.

'Oh, I wouldn't call it the surprise of the century.' Making short
work of her own bun, Fia shook her head and said, 'He did it last
year too.'

'He *did*?'

'With a girl from his office. When I got to hear about it, he
begged me to forgive him. On his knees.' Her lip curled at the
memory. 'And he swore he'd never do it again. Silly me, I believed
him. Decided to give him one more chance.'

For the sake of the children. Cleo felt another surge of guilt
followed by a wave of anger; Will's selfishness was wrecking his
family, threatening to destroy his children's lives.

She didn't want to ask, but she had to. 'And now?'

'Well, he's blown it, hasn't he? I'm not a complete doormat,'
said Fia. 'And he's never going to change. So it's all over.'

'Oh God. I'm sorry.'

'You didn't know. Anyway, I'm sure I'll get over it. Will liked
to put on a great show of us being happy in front of other people,
but it hasn't actually been that much fun being married to him.'
She eyed the untouched bun on Cleo's plate. 'Are you going to
eat that, or can I have it?'

Cleo pushed the plate across the table. Those poor kids, how would they cope with their parents' divorce? 'So why did you come here today?'

'I just wanted to see you. Find out what you looked like. I wasn't even going to speak to you.' Wryly Fia said, 'The car breaking down wasn't part of the plan.'

'And how did you know where I lived?'

'Ah well, that was a teeny bit illegal.' Fia pulled a face. 'You're on the same network as Will. And I happen to have a friend whose brother works for the phone company. He was the one who got me the copy of the bill. Then I persuaded him to look up your address. But it's OK, he made me promise not to set fire to your house.'

Twenty minutes later, Cleo looked out of the living-room window and saw that the snow was still falling in flurries.

'Look, I can't be late for my next job. I'm going to have to leave early.'

Fia flipped open her phone and rang the RAC again. She frowned, listening to them. '*How* long?'

OK, this was going to be awkward. Cleo wondered what she was supposed to do now.

'Another two hours.' Hanging up, Fia said with heavy irony, 'Apparently they're snowed under.'

'Um . . .'

'It's OK, I know. I'll wait in the car.'

Damn. Cleo was torn; turfing her out was going to be even more embarrassing now. But how *could* she go off, leaving a complete stranger in her house? Except Fia was *worse* than a complete stranger; she was Will's emotionally tortured, cheated-on wife. Who was to say she wouldn't go completely ballistic, cut up all her clothes and smash everything she could get her hands on?

126

Cleo hesitated, still suffused with guilt. *On the other hand, I did have an affair with her husband.*

Plus, two hours outside in her car and she'd freeze to death.

'Hang on.' Picking up her own phone, she speed-dialled Ash. 'Hi, it's me, what are you doing?'

'Nothing much. Googling myself, seeing how popular I am. You know, I can't believe how much everyone loves me, they—'

'Come round,' Cleo interrupted. 'I need a favour.'

She opened the door to him twenty seconds later. Ash, wearing a torn checked shirt over a faded Superman T-shirt, struck a pose and said, 'Damsel in distress? I'm here to help. What is it, something electrical? Or another jam-jar lid you can't get undone?'

'I have to get back to work. Can you look after someone for me? Her car broke down.' Cleo pointed to the Fiesta, wonkily parked by the gate. 'Just keep her company until the RAC turns up.'

'OK, no problem. Do I smell toasted buns?' Breezing past her, Ash headed into the living room and stopped dead in his tracks. 'Oh. Hi.' He stared at Fia and promptly flushed an unbecoming shade of red.

She gave him a curious look in return, taking in the uncombed hair, blotchy complexion and scruffy outfit. 'Hello.'

'Fia, this is my friend Ash.' Cleo didn't have time to play nursemaid; if he was going to be shy, that was his problem. 'Ash, this is Fia.' Having rapidly introduced them, she grabbed her bag and keys. 'And I need to go.' She waved goodbye to Fia. 'Hope your car gets fixed soon. And good luck with, you know . . . the other stuff.'

'Thanks.' Fia nodded and smiled. 'Bye.'

The front door slammed behind Cleo and Ash felt his hands go clammy. This was it, the story of his life. On the outside everyone thought he was so confident and cheerful. And a lot of the time they'd have been right, he *was* confident and cheerful. Until the moment he found himself in the company of a girl he fancied, and his entire personality shrivelled and dried up like a grape.

He was used to it. It had been happening for years. If he were American, no doubt he would have spent countless hours and thousands of dollars in a therapist's office by now, learning the expensive way that he had issues with low self-esteem. As it was, he already knew this and preferred to spend his money on fast cars, skiing holidays and all manner of electronic wizardry instead.

Fia was covertly watching him. She was wearing a plain black V-necked sweater and grey jeans tucked into boots. Her hair, a kind of shiny, chestnutty brown, was pulled back in a ponytail and she had really nice ears. And he couldn't think of a single solitary thing to say to her. OK, now she was going to start thinking he was some kind of retard, but he just couldn't help it. God, she was gorgeous.

Say something, you plank.

Ash cleared his throat. 'What other stuff?'

She looked taken aback. 'Sorry?'

This was what it was like, every time. He gazed out of the window, praying to see an RAC van pulling up outside. 'Cleo said good luck with the other stuff.'

'Oh, right.' Fia nodded. 'Well, she was seeing this guy, Will Newman? Did you ever meet him?'

Blinking fast, Ash said, 'No.' Jesus, what was going on here?

She gave him a look. 'It's OK. You're allowed to say yes.'

See? He'd even lost the ability to lie. Usually he was world-class at it. He shrugged. 'Yes.'

'Well, I'm his wife,' said Fia.

'Shit.'

'Yes, he is.' Her half-smile only made her more irresistible.

128

Ash felt himself become correspondingly more tongue-tied. She was probably thinking how ugly he was. When he'd been young, the pretty girls had told him outright that he was ugly. They'd giggled and made sick-noises at the very thought of having to kiss Fat Ash. So that was one good thing; at least they were old enough now to keep their opinions to themselves when he was within earshot.

Although he knew they were still thinking it.

The awkward silence lengthened. Ash examined his hands, checked again that there was no sign of the RAC van. 'Tea?' It came out like a frog's croak.

Fia looked puzzled. 'Sorry?'

'Cup of tea?'

'Oh right!' She got that relieved look people get when they manage to make out what some deranged foreigner is trying to say to them. 'No thanks, we just had one.'

'OK.' It was his biggest fear that one day this would happen while he was live on air; some girl with whom he was secretly besotted would walk into the studio during one of his brilliant comedy rants and his listening audience would hear him grind to a halt and turn into a monosyllabic moron.

'Are you all right?' said Fia hesitantly.

Humiliation made him defensive. 'I'm fine. Just, uh . . . never mind.' The TV remote control was balanced on the arm of the sofa. Seizing it with relief, Ash said, 'Shall we watch TV?'

Cleo pulled up outside the cottage and stared in disbelief at the snow-covered blue Fiesta still parked in front of her gate. This was ridiculous, it was eight o'clock at night. How could Will's wife still be here? She should have been gone hours ago.

More to the point, where was she now? Because both Ash's cottage and her own were in darkness.

Oh well, ask a silly question.

'We're in the pub.' Ash had to raise his voice to be heard above the racket. 'Coming over?'

'Did the RAC not turn up?' Cleo was outraged.

'Oh yeah, they did. They fixed the car,' said Ash.

'Oh, for God's sake! So why's Fia still here?'

There was an edge to his voice that she couldn't identify. 'I don't think she wants to go home.'

Chapter 17

Cleo changed out of her uniform into combats and a hoodie, then set off across the green. As she crunched through the snow towards the lit-up pub, she heard a chorus of cheers and whistles emanating from within, followed by someone who didn't sound a lot like Elvis launching into 'Hound Dog'.

Looked like they were having an impromptu karaoke night.

A rush of warmth and noise greeted her as she pushed open the door. She'd guessed right about the singer. Frank, the landlord of the Hollybush and a lifelong Elvis fan, was clutching the microphone and swivelling his hips. His audience was applauding and yelling encouragement. There was Ash, observing the proceedings from the safety of the bar. A little way away, Fia was clapping wildly. And next to her, holding a pint of Guinness and grinning at Frank's more extravagant pelvic thrusts, was Johnny LaVenture.

'What's going on?' Joining Ash, Cleo gave him an accusing nudge.

'I didn't know what to do with her, did I?' Ash wasn't looking too thrilled either. 'We sat and watched TV for ages. Then it got to five o'clock and she saw the lights coming on outside here and there was still no sign of the RAC, so I thought why not, it'd be something to pass the time. Then just after we arrived, Johnny and his crew came piling in.' Drily he said, 'That's when she perked right up.'

'But eventually the RAC did turn up.'

Ash nodded. 'They did. And they got the car going in five minutes flat. But then Johnny persuaded her to stay for one more drink . . . then another . . . and she's been here ever since.'

'Oh God.' Cleo groaned and looked over at their unwanted guest. 'Is she completely wellied?'

'Not yet. But give her time.'

Frank's moment in the spotlight had come to an end and he was now shamelessly milking the applause. Leaning across to whisper something in Johnny's ear, Fia confidingly clutched his arm.

'So what did she tell you about Will?'

'Not a lot.' Ash shrugged. 'He's a dickhead, it's over, she's leaving him. That's pretty much it.'

Yet again, Cleo felt the weight of a responsibility she didn't deserve. 'Those poor kids.' Flinching, she said, 'Oh help, and now she's going to sing . . .'

A roar went up as Fia took Frank's place on the tiny raised stage. Call it instinct, but Cleo guessed at once that this was her first close encounter with a karaoke machine. Seizing the microphone and blasting everyone's ears with high-pitched feedback, Fia announced, 'My husband cheated on me and as from today my marriage is *over*. But guess what? Life goes on and he's the one who's going to be missing out. Because I can promise you one thing. I-I-I . . . wiiiiiillll . . . surviiiiiiiiive!'

More cheers as the opening bars of the great Gloria Gaynor classic filled the pub. Fia's singing voice was way worse than Frank's, but what she lacked in vocal skills she made up for with reckless alcohol-fuelled enthusiasm. Johnny's painters and decorators all joined in the chorus, everyone was clapping and stamping their feet and Fia carried on singing her heart out.

At last the song was over. Having soaked up the applause, she jumped down and returned to Johnny who was looking after her drink. Cleo watched as he put a reassuring arm around Fia's shoulders and gave her a congratulatory you-did-it hug.

'Right, I'm off.' Finishing his own drink, Ash said, 'I'll leave you to it. Good luck.'

Moments later, spotting Cleo, Fia came over.

'Hi! Did you see me up there? I've never sung karaoke before in my life!'

And if she knew what she sounded like, she'd never do it again. But that was mean, and it was beside the point – it had been the very *act* of singing that had been cathartic – so Cleo said, 'You were . . . incredible.' Because she'd certainly been that.

Joining them, Johnny said easily, 'Didn't she do well?'

'Gosh yes. Really brave. So!' Cleo turned brightly to Fia. 'Your car's all fixed!'

'Yeah, the chap was really nice. He couldn't stop apologising because of the wait, but I told him it didn't matter. If he'd turned up two hours earlier, I'd have just driven straight home. We wouldn't have come over here to the pub.' Fia was still flushed from her exertions. 'And I'd never have met all these fantastic people!'

No prizes for guessing which fantastic person in particular she was so delighted to have met. Honestly, weren't people whose marriages had just broken down meant to be miserable for the first six months at least? Fia appeared to be having trouble stringing it out for six *hours*. And as for those two innocent children . . . shouldn't she be at home comforting them, gently preparing them for the imminent upheaval in their young lives?

'Another drink?' said Johnny.

'Ooh, let me buy this round!'

'Absolutely not.' He reached for Fia's empty glass. 'I'm getting them. Cleo, what'll you have?'

'Actually, it's half past eight already.' Cleo looked at her watch; surely it was time for Will's wife to leave now. 'Shouldn't you be going home?'

Fia looked appalled. 'Home? You mean, where Will is? I don't think so.' Pulling out her phone, she glanced at the screen and said with satisfaction, 'Seven messages from him so far. Ha, good. Let him wonder where I am for a change.'

Was she for real? 'But what about the children?'

Puzzled, Fia said, 'What about them?'

OK, she was now officially heartless.

Cleo said pointedly, 'Won't they be expecting you home?'

'Oh lovely, thanks so much!' Fia smiled up at Johnny and took the brimming glass from him before turning her attention back to Cleo. 'No. Because they're not there.'

'But you still have to drive back at some stage. Is that a soft drink?' Cleo indicated the glass of what looked like Coke.

'Most of it is, yes.' Still beaming, Fia said, 'And the rest's Bacardi.'

'So who's looking after the children?' Cleo couldn't help herself, she had to know.

Fia gave her an odd look. 'Well, their mother of course. Will only sees them every other weekend.'

Clannnggg, the penny finally dropped.

'You mean . . . they're not yours?'

'God, no! Did you seriously think they were?' Shaking her head vigorously, Fia burst out laughing. 'No, no, no, the kids are from his first marriage. I mean, they're really sweet and I've always got on well with them, but they're definitely not mine.

They live with their mum and her second husband in Birmingham. I only met Will three years ago and he was already divorced by then.'

Good grief, this country was littered with Will's wives. Up on the stage, one of the painters was belting out 'Do Ya Think I'm Sexy?' Every time he sang the question, his work colleagues yelled back, 'Nooooo!'

'Sorry. I thought they were yours,' said Cleo.

'I wondered why I was getting interrogated. So anyway, that's that sorted out.' Waving her hand in a forgiving manner, Fia said, 'But you're right about me not being able to drive home. Look, seeing as it's kind of your fault I'm here, I couldn't crash at yours tonight, could I?'

Yet another favour? Honestly, hadn't she already done enough? Cleo hesitated. While she was prevaricating, Johnny passed her a glass of white wine.

'Please? I wouldn't be any trouble,' Fia wheedled. 'I promise.'

'Um, the thing is, the spare bed isn't made up . . . and I have to be at work *really* early tomorrow morning . . .'

'DO YA THINK I'M SEXY?'

'NOOOOOO!!!'

'Don't worry about making up a bed, I can just sleep on the sofa.'

'Er . . .'

'Tell you what,' said Johnny. 'You can stay at my place.'

Cleo saw the way Fia's eyes lit up and something in the pit of her stomach tightened. No, no, this wasn't the answer.

'Really? Gosh, *thanks*!'

Hastily backtracking, Cleo said, 'Look, it's fine, we can make up the bed. Of course you can stay with me.'

'But you have to be up *really early*.' Evidently overjoyed by

Johnny's Far Better Offer, Fia did a poor job of pretending to be grateful to Cleo. 'And you've helped me so much already.'

'But you can't stay at Johnny's house . . .' It wasn't Fia's fault; she didn't know what he was like. Cleo did her best to discreetly signal with her eyes that she could well be risking life and limb.

'Hey, it's OK, I'm not a serial killer.' Intercepting the look, Johnny said with amusement, 'She'll be safe, I promise.'

'That's really kind. And you won't even know I'm there,' Fia promised him. 'Just leave me with a blanket and I'll sleep on the sofa.'

'No need for that. There are plenty of spare bedrooms.'

'Plenty?' Fia giggled. 'What do you live in, some kind of *mansion*?'

Chapter 18

Frank the landlord, handing Johnny his change, said, 'Biggest house in the village, love. Gives Buckingham Palace a run for its money.'

Fia did an astonished double take. She turned to Johnny, still wearing his paint-splashed sweatshirt and torn jeans. 'Is he serious? But . . . sorry, and you're a painter and decorator?'

Cleo raised her eyebrows and took a big glug of wine.

'It was my father's home. He died before Christmas and now I've moved back in. We did try to sell it,' Johnny said innocently. 'But no luck.'

'Um, yes.' Nodding, Fia continued to look dumbfounded.

Johnny indicated the team clustered around the stage, still heckling their unsexy co-worker. 'So that's why we've been working on the house. But I'm not a decorator by profession.'

Her forehead creasing, Fia said, 'But I asked Ash. He *said* you were a painter.'

'I do paint.' Johnny nodded in agreement. 'But canvases, as a rule. Not walls.'

'You mean you're an artist? Oh wow, that's amazing!' She was now gazing at him as if he'd sprouted celestial wings. 'What kind of work do you do?'

'Well, all sorts.' Looking suitably modest, Johnny said, 'But my main thing these days is wire sculpture.'

'You mean . . . like making figures out of wire? Oh my God,' breathed Fia, recognition slowly dawning. 'Don't tell me you're the one who does those huge great ones . . . you're not Johnny LaVenture . . . ?'

Cleo couldn't believe Fia even knew his work, let alone his name. It wasn't as if he was as famous as Damien Hirst or Banksy.

'I'm impressed.' Johnny smiled slightly. 'And flattered.'

'Are you kidding? I love your sculptures!' exclaimed Fia. 'They're *brilliant*.'

Cleo's jaw ached from smiling. This was Will's *wife*. She didn't want her staying here in Channings Hill any longer than necessary.

'Well, this is a treat. Compliments are usually pretty thin on the ground around here.' Evidently enjoying himself, Johnny said, 'I'm glad you turned up.'

'Me too.' Her eyes shining, Fia visibly came to a decision and scrabbled in her bag for her phone. 'Right, well, if you're sure I can stay . . .'

Rod Stewart had been replaced by Amy Winehouse; Deborah had come out from behind the bar and was performing 'Rehab', with three of the decorators singing and dancing in unison behind her.

'Hi, yes, I'm fine. Sorry? Oh, because I didn't want to. Anyway, this is just to let you know I won't be home tonight.' Moving the phone away from her ear, Fia said, 'No need to shout. I've met an extremely good-looking man and he's invited me to spend the night with him.' She smiled up at Johnny, enjoying being in control for possibly the first time. 'Well, I can do whatever I like. Same as you always have. No, it doesn't matter where I am, and it's not actually any of your business anyway.'

Cleo watched her. Fia's eyes were bright, her mind made up. She was tipsy but not that drunk, galvanised by adrenaline rather than alcohol. Would she wake up tomorrow morning and regret it?

Having listened to Will at the other end of the line, Fia replied, 'Because you've been shagging another girl behind my back, and that means our marriage is over, that's why. Yes, you have. No, she didn't tell me.' Catching Cleo's eye, she winked. 'If you must know, you've had a private detective following you for the last three months. Oh yes, cost a fortune but he was worth every penny. Anyway, I have to go now. Sleep well.' Cheerily, Fia concluded, 'I'll be home some time tomorrow, we can talk about solicitors and stuff then. Byeeee!'

She switched off the phone with a flourish, dropped it into her bag and exhaled.

Johnny surveyed her. 'Are you OK?'

'I think so.' Fia pulled a shaky-scared face. 'Phew, who knew so much could happen in one day?'

Cleo glanced over at Johnny. *Not to mention one night.*

'I haven't had anything to eat.' Fia sounded surprised. 'Not since those currant buns ages ago. Do they serve food in this place?'

'No.' Cleo shook her head.

'Oh. Damn, I'm starving.' Pleased, Fia said, 'And my marriage just broke up. That has to be a good sign, doesn't it?'

'They sell crisps,' said Cleo. 'And nuts.' She was hungry too. At home in the fridge was a sausage casserole ready-meal for one; not easily split between two famished people, but if she didn't offer—

'OK,' Johnny raised a hand as Cleo opened her mouth to speak. 'How about we have one more drink here, then head back to my place? I can do you steak and chips or a mushroom risotto, or there are pizzas in the freezer.' As an afterthought he added, 'And there's blackberry crumble too.'

Honestly, who did he think he was? Jean-Christophe Novelli?

'Wow!' Clearly thinking the same thing and wildly impressed, Fia exclaimed, 'Not only a world-famous artist, but you can cook as well.'

'Well, not quite.' Johnny shrugged. 'Chips and risotto out of the freezer. But I can chargrill a mean fillet steak.'

Fia looked as if she'd been shown a stupendous magic trick. 'That's good enough for me!'

Ten minutes later, up on the stage, a couple of new arrivals were being Elton and Kiki, making a surprisingly good job of 'Don't Go Breaking My Heart'. Taking advantage of Johnny's visit to the loo, Cleo managed to take Fia to one side.

'Listen, you don't know Johnny. I really don't think you should go home with him. You can stay at my house, it's no trouble. We'll have sausage casserole!' Sausage being the operative word, seeing as there was only one of them; she'd have to cut it in half, add a can of tomatoes and maybe tip in some baked beans to make the casserole stretch to serve two. Cleo gave her a winning smile. 'Honestly, it'd be better.'

She could see the thought processes going on in Fia's head. Hmm, fillet steak and chips versus sausage casserole. Tiny cottage versus stonking great mansion. Husband's somewhat grumpy ex-girlfriend versus flirtatious, seriously attractive sculptor . . .

So all in all, it would be better in what way, *exactly*?

Fia searched for the right words. Finally she came out with, 'Thanks, but I've already said I'd stay at his place. It'd be rude to back out now.'

Surprise, surprise.

On the bright side, she'd have a whole sausage to herself. Cleo nodded. 'OK, but can I just say? Johnny has a bit of a reputation, so don't do anything you might regret.'

Fia considered this for a bit. Then she replied, 'You know, I never thought I'd be getting moral advice from my husband's mistress.'

That was below the belt. 'I wasn't a mistress! I didn't even know he was married!'

'Well, exactly. So you're hardly an expert, are you? Sorry, not being rude, but you've kind of buggered up my life already.' Fia made placatory, don't-be-offended gestures as she spoke. 'So why can't I just go with the flow now? Because who's to say what'll happen? This could be fate, couldn't it? I've come here today for the first time in my life. I came to see you, and I've ended up meeting Johnny. And he's been incredibly kind and he seems *really* nice . . .'

Cleo wondered how to respond. Should she explain that the whole point of men like Johnny LaVenture was to make you *think* they were really nice?

'In fact what I'm starting to wonder,' Fia waggled a mischievous index finger at her, 'is if you might not be a little bit envious because you're secretly quite keen on him yourself.'

Ew, what a thought. 'Johnny and I grew up in this village. We went to school together. I'm kind of the opposite of keen,' said Cleo.

Cleo was in Cardiff by six thirty the next morning. She picked up a middle-aged actress who snored all the way to Chichester and dribbled all over her emerald-green Hermès scarf. On TV she was the epitome of glamour.

Back home by two in the afternoon, Cleo saw that Fia's car had gone. At last. The snow had almost disappeared as well. Later she would pay a visit to the supermarket and stock up on food – last night's sausage casserole dilemma had shamed her – but first she wanted a long hot soak in the bath.

Which was interrupted twenty minutes later – nooooo! – by the doorbell.

But ignoring someone at the door was as impossible as not answering a ringing phone, so Cleo hauled herself out of the tub, pulled on her white fleecy dressing gown and wrapped a fetching orange towel around her head.

This had better be worth it. Ewan McGregor at the very least, Hugh Jackman at a push. Anyone else would be a crushing disappointment.

Her heart sank when it wasn't either of them.

And frankly, having this one back on her doorstep wasn't much of a consolation prize.

'Hi!' Fia was still wearing yesterday's clothes, together with fresh make-up and a beaming smile.

'Hello.' Cleo clutched her dressing gown tightly around herself, shivering as a blast of icy air attacked her wet legs.

'Oh sorry, I saw your car was back! Were you in the bath?'

No, just frolicking naked in the kitchen sink.

'It's fine. Um . . . come in.' Was Will's wife looking so ecstatic because she'd spent the night in Johnny's bed?

'Actually, I need to get home. Start sorting everything out with Will. I just popped over to say thanks. For yesterday . . . trying to help me with my car . . .' Fia shrugged and said, 'Not to mention having an affair with my husband.'

'I told you, I didn't *know*—'

'It's OK, I believe you! And I'm really glad you did!' Fia nodded vigorously. 'It's the best thing that could have happened. I can't tell you what a weight it is off my mind. I feel . . . free at last!'

'Right. Well, good.' What had gone on last night? Cleo knew she mustn't ask, but thought she could probably guess.

'So that's it, I just wanted to say thanks to you and your friend . . .

142

thingie . . .' A vague gesture in the direction of the cottage next door.

'Ash.'

'That's right.'

'He's in there,' said Cleo, 'if you want to tell him yourself.'

'Oh no, it's fine.' Fia pulled a conspiratorial face. 'He's a bit . . . strange, isn't he?

'No. Not strange at all.'

'Not like that! I just meant he's very quiet.'

'He isn't usually. He's a DJ.' Cleo felt she needed to defend him.

'A what?' Laughing, Fia said, 'You mean, he does the disco in the village hall, that kind of thing?'

'He has his own radio show.'

'Wow, that's . . . excellent!' From the look on her face Cleo could tell Fia thought she meant a thirty-minute slot on hospital radio, once a fortnight. Opening her mouth to explain, she was beaten to it. 'Anyway, I'd better shoot off before you get frostbite.' Backing down the path, Fia waved and said gaily, 'Back to Bristol to get everything sorted!'

'It's really over with Will?'

'Too right it is! He's all yours if you want him. You're more than welcome!'

'No thanks. Hang on, though.' Cleo was baffled. 'Yesterday you were ready to drive off without even speaking to me. You didn't even know for sure I'd *had* an affair with Will. And now all of a sudden you can't wait to dump him.'

'I know! Isn't it brilliant? But it's the right decision.' Fia pressed the flat of her hand to her sternum. 'Like Johnny said when we were in the pub yesterday, we only get one life. So why waste it?'

'Right, but—'

'He says Will doesn't deserve me and I owe it to myself to find someone else who does.'

'Well yes, but when—'

'And he's so right!' Shaking her head as she reached the gate, Fia glowed with self-confidence. 'I just needed to hear someone else say it. I *do* deserve better.' And she raised her hand in a final wave. 'So, wish me luck! Bye!'

Cleo watched as the blue Fiesta disappeared from view. Will's wife had definitely had sex with Johnny LaVenture last night.

Well, good luck with waiting for him to call.

Chapter 19

Ten women, one of them celebrating her thirtieth birthday. Ten metallic pink helium balloons. Ten sparkly fluorescent pink cowboy hats. The question was, however was she going to manage to spot them in the crowds?

Oh look, fancy that, there they were! As she reached the bottom of Park Street in Bristol's city centre, Cleo slowed down and pulled up outside the Hippodrome. When you were at the wheel of a bright pink stretch limo, other people in turn tended to take notice. All around, they were swivelling to stare at the car. Some might call it naff but it was just a bit of fun. If it was what the customers wanted – and were paying good money to be driven around in – where was the harm in that?

Well, apart from the damage it threatened to do to the driver's eardrums.

Bracing herself, Cleo climbed out of the car and the stiletto-heeled, Stetson-wearing, balloon-toting party advanced in a great high-pitched squealing pack. Age-wise, they sounded more thirteen than thirty, but that was the effect a Barbie-pink stretched Chrysler 300C tended to have.

'Good evening, ladies.' Cleo opened the doors and allowed them to pile in. 'All set to enjoy yourselves?'

'Yayyyy!'

'Yee-haaaaa!'

'Oh my God, will you look at this!'

Shrieks of excitement filled the inside of the limo as they discovered the glittery indigo carpeting, the strobes and multi-coloured lighting ropes, the TVs and DVD players. They swarmed over the seats like magpies, exclaiming over the stars on the ceiling, the ice buckets, the box of DVDs.

'*Pretty Woman!*' The birthday girl gave a yelp of delight, snatched the disc out of the case and shoved it into the DVD player.

Honestly, why did they even bother offering a choice? It was *Pretty Woman* every time. If Cleo could choose this film as her specialist subject, she'd win *Mastermind*.

'Bloody hell, I don't believe it.' The next moment, one of the Stetsons was tipped back and the woman wearing it began to laugh. 'It's you, isn't it? Misa!'

Oh, please. Her heart plummeting, Cleo met the heavily made-up gaze of the woman she hadn't noticed until now.

Many, many layers of mascara. Burnished gold eyeshadow, perfectly plucked eyebrows, beige lipstick and darker lipliner. Bright blond swept-up hair, French-manicured nails, clinging gold dress and strappy sandals.

New hairstyle, same old knowing, better-than-you smile.

And to think that it had been a toss-up which of them would take this job tonight. Shelley had said, 'Your call. Birthday bash in Bristol or hen night in Weston?'

So purely because she'd done a hen night last week and it was always good to ring the changes, Cleo had said, 'OK, I'll do the birthday bash.'

If she'd gone for the other one, this unhappy encounter could have been avoided.

The birthday girl, whose name was Jen, was looking interested. 'What's this, then? You two know each other?'

'From years back.' Mandy Ellison smirked. 'We were at school together.'

And we hated each other.

'Misa, that's an unusual name! Is it Spanish?'

'That's just what we used to call her,' said Mandy. Raising her hand and mimicking fifteen-year-old Cleo, she chirped eagerly, 'Me, sir! Me, sir!'

The others fell about laughing. *Be professional, be professional, don't react.*

'Do you remember that?' Mandy was in her element. 'You were such a swot! We used to make fun of you all the time.'

Cleo smiled distantly, as if she could barely recall those days. 'Everyone comfortable? Excellent. Could you all fasten your seatbelts, please?'

'And after that, you ended up as a driver. So a fat lot of good all that swotting did you!'

OK, she'd stopped being swotty at school practically as a direct result of the merciless teasing. Plus, was there anything *wrong* with being a chauffeur? Cleo said politely, 'Are we ready to go now, ladies?'

The others let out a cheer and yelled, 'Yaaaaaaaaaaaaaaaaaaayyyy!!!!'

The point of hiring a stretch limo for the evening was so you could impress as many of your friends and acquaintances as humanly possible. This meant driving around Bristol as *noisily* as possible, stopping off at endless pubs and wine bars, showing everyone what you'd arrived in, then knocking back a quick round of drinks before getting back into the car and setting off to the next on the list.

They were a very shrieky crowd and the decibel level rose with each port of call. By the fifth, everyone was on an unstoppable roll.

'So, Misa. Still not married then?' Sitting behind Cleo, Mandy opened the sliding window that separated them.

'No. And my name's Cleo.'

'Clee-oh.' Mandy emphasised the word to humour her. 'No kids? No bloke?' She waited until Cleo briefly shook her head. 'God, aren't you worried about getting left on the shelf? Me and Gary have been married for eight years now. Shania's five and Brad's three. Gary earns shedloads of money, so I don't have to work. And you should see our house. Five-bed detached in Bradley Stoke. We've got matching BMWs with personalised plates. Pretty good, eh?'

'Very good.' They were heading up Whiteladies Road, making for Henry Africa's bar. Smiling to herself, Cleo realised how ridiculous Mandy was making herself sound with her need to boast, and how inevitably her list of achievements would have to include personalised plates.

'Yeah, we're really happy. So where are you living now?'

'Channings Hill.'

'Oh God! Noooo! *Still?*' Mandy cackled with incredulous laughter. 'Have you never thought of getting a life?'

Why, *why* hadn't she chosen the hen night in Weston?

'Clearly not,' said Cleo. 'I like living there.' And she *usually* liked her job. 'OK, here we are, Henry Africa's.'

By midnight they'd visited Clifton Village, Park Street, Berkeley Square and the Waterfront, before returning to busy, bar-strewn Whiteladies Road. This was the last stop of the evening and Cleo was counting down the minutes. The other members of the party had been fine but Mandy Ellison had carried on bragging and making digs at every opportunity.

Except she wasn't Mandy Ellison any more, was she? She was Mandy Ross now, married to perfect Gary, mother to two perfect angels, living the perfect life . . .

Unlike poor old Unloved Spinster Cleo Quinn, yet to acquire any of the above.

Waiting behind the wheel of the limo, Cleo watched as a boisterous group of staggering studenty types attempted to gain entrance to Callaghan's across the road, where Jen and the others were currently ensconced. The security guys on the door sent the students packing. Then she did a double take as a couple stumbled out, arms wrapped around each other. Clearly well away, their intentions were plain. The man pushed the girl up against the wall, his hands roaming over her body and his mouth fastening on hers.

The girl enthusiastically kissing him back was Mandy.

Hee! Cleo stared at the pair of them, enthralled. They had their tongues down each other's throats and were writhing together as enthusiastically as a pair of teenagers. Moments later, as if realising they might be spotted, Mandy pulled away and, with the logic of only the completely plastered, drew him five metres along the road into a shop doorway.

And proceeded to grope her conquest with all the subtlety of an army medic examining a squaddie. Prompting him, in return, to plunge his hand down the back of her gold dress and unfasten her bra.

Ooh dear, so much for Mandy's so-called perfect marriage.

Youch, wasn't she uncomfortable in that teeny thong?

And here came the rest of the party now, looking for her. As they spilled out of the bar, one of the students who'd been refused admittance made a playful grab for Jen's Stetson. Jen chased after him, clattering along the pavement in her high heels. Spotting the

149

writing couple in the shop doorway, she skittered to a halt and let out an ear-splitting shriek.

Cleo watched as Mandy jumped guiltily and, in her tequila'd-up state, attempted to conceal the identity of her companion by shoving his head against her chest. From here, it looked as if he was having a coughing fit. Maybe he was suffocating in her cleavage. Then Mandy leapt back in horror, shoving him away from her so hard he went crashing back against the shop door. She was screaming, repulsed, staggering all over the pavement with her arms outstretched and her fingers like claws.

Oh dear God, he'd only gone and thrown up on her.

Equally appalled, the rest of the party floundered. The next moment, spotting the limo across the street and panicking like a family of ducklings in need of their mum, they made a beeline for it.

Well, they were all steaming drunk, so it was a wobbly, zig-zagging kind of beeline. With Mandy, still shrieking, bringing up the rear.

Cleo was out of the limo in a flash. Up close, the front of the gold dress was liberally decorated.

'Let me in, let me in!' Mandy was shuddering with revulsion. 'That bastard . . . look what he's *done*.'

'You can't get into the car like that.' Shaking her head, Cleo said, 'No way.'

'You have to let me in!'

'Sorry, I don't.'

'So how else am I supposed to get home?'

One of the other girls said slurrily, 'How 'bout a taxi?'

Jen wrinkled her nose. 'No taxi's going to take her.'

'FOR FUCK'S SAKE,' Mandy bellowed. 'JUST GET ME HOME!'

'She could phone Gary, ashk him t'come and pick her up.'

'Yeah,' Mandy snorted, 'like he'd do that.' She turned to Cleo, her face the picture of misery. 'Please, OK? Let me in.'

'Only if you take the dress off.'

'What?'

'If you take it off carefully,' said Cleo, 'and don't get any of the sick on you, I'll let you into the car.'

Swaying, Mandy frowned. 'So how would the dress get home?'

'It wouldn't. You'd put it in that litter bin over there.'

'Are you having a laugh? This thing cost three hundred quid!'

'Fine.' Cleo shrugged. 'Keep it on then. But you'll have to walk home.'

Across the road, the man who'd caused all the trouble staggered off up a side street. Mandy, mascara-smeared and sobering up fast, heaved a sigh of frustration and hissed through gritted teeth, 'Go on then, someone undo me.'

Gingerly, Jen stepped up and unfastened the zip at the back. The gold dress slid off Mandy's shoulders and fell to the ground around her feet. Mandy let out a howl as she realised her bra was undone and her boobs were swinging free.

Passers-by jeered and whistled at the sight of her shivering in her high heels and flowery thong. Cleo, delighted to spot a bit of cellulite too – thank you, God! – opened the door of the limo and said cheerily, 'OK, everyone in. Time to go home!'

'Gary's going to go mental,' Mandy whined. 'He bought me that dress for Christmas.'

'Just tell him it wasn't your fault.' Jen gave her a disapproving look. 'You didn't know when you stuck your tongue down that bloke's throat that it was going to make him puke.'

Mandy's eyes narrowed. 'OK, OK. No need for Gary to hear about any of that.'

Cleo's conscience finally got the better of her. Sometimes, just sometimes, she really wished she didn't have one. With a sigh, she went round to the back of the car and opened the boot. Prepared for all eventualities – well, almost all – she kept a supply of heavy-duty black bin bags in the side pocket. Resignedly she handed one to Mandy and pointed to the bin. 'Go on then, get it out of there and put it in this.'

'Thanks,' muttered Mandy when the deed had been done and the tightly knotted bin bag had been stowed in the boot.

Was this a moral victory? Cleo shrugged and said, 'I shouldn't really be doing this. It's against company policy.' She paused then added with an innocent smile, 'But what else are old school friends for?'

Chapter 20

'Abbie, we need to start thinking about the Easter promotions. Come on up to my office and let's have a chat about it.'

Abbie brushed flecks of dry, crumbly compost off her hands and followed Des upstairs. The last thing they needed was a repeat of last year's debacle when the Easter egg hunt had been scuppered by blazing sun. All the chocolate eggs had turned to puddles of goo and the garden centre had reverberated to the sound of wailing, inconsolable children.

'OK, I've had a couple of ideas,' she said as Des closed the door behind him. 'It might not be sunny. But if it is, how about those mini-eggs in crispy shells? Or we could make little straw nests in bowls, then put them into bigger bowls filled with ice cubes—'

'Fine, we'll do that.'

'*Or*, I thought we could hide tokens of some kind, and when they find the tokens they can come inside and exchange them for the real Easter eggs—'

'Look, I didn't bring you up here to talk about Easter.' Des spoke urgently, as if he'd just pulled the pin out of a grenade set to detonate in ten seconds. 'I've tried to forget what happened, OK? Kissing you like that . . . being with you . . . I've tried my best, I really have, but it won't go away. Everything changed. I can't stop thinking about you.'

Abbie's heart began to thud. 'Des, no, don't say that.' Rapidly she shook her head. 'You don't mean it.'

'I do.'

'No, no, I'm *married*.'

'I know.' His shoulders slumped. 'And I wish you weren't.'

'But I'm happy with Tom.' She couldn't believe he was doing this.

'I don't want to feel this way,' said Des. 'I just can't help it.'

'Well, you're going to have to! Des, I'm sorry, but this is my life we're talking about!'

He rubbed the side of his face, visibly torn. 'It's my life too.'

'But nothing's going to happen.'

'Just give me a chance,' Des pleaded.

'No,' Abbie backed towards the door, 'and you promised you wouldn't do this. Tom means everything in the world to—'

The phone rang on the desk and they both jumped. For a moment they stared at each other. In desperation Abbie blurted out, 'Just stop this now, Des, OK? I mean it. Pull yourself together and leave me alone. Because this is just . . . stupid!'

Heart pounding, she let herself out of the office and left Des to answer the phone. This was a nightmare threatening to get out of control and it terrified her. She'd trusted him to keep their secret . . . but what if she shouldn't? And how could she make him understand how badly she needed him to?

How was it that her quiet, settled, uneventful life had come to this?

'Wow!' Hurrying into the pub on Saturday lunchtime and screeching to a halt when she saw Ash, Cleo pointed at the table in front of him. 'You're eating!'

'I don't know how you do it,' Ash marvelled. 'It's like a gift, some kind of spooky sixth sense. You should be a psychic detective. Oi, give me that back.'

Cleo dug his fork into the lasagne and sampled a mouthful to see if it tasted as good as it smelled. Her eyes widened. 'Mmm . . . mmmmm!'

'Oh no you don't.' He snatched the fork back before she could steal any more. 'Get your own. Actually, have the fish pie, then I can see what that's like.'

'Fish pie? I *love* fish pie!' Whirling round, Cleo saw that a menu had been chalked up on the blackboard that had remained menu-less for the last six weeks, ever since Tony-the-temperamental-chef had broken up with his boyfriend and stropped off in a huff to work in a restaurant in Malaga. In all honesty, Tony's cooking hadn't been that great but he was so hot-tempered, Frank had never been able to pick up the courage to tell him.

Then Cleo's mouth dropped open as the new chef emerged from the kitchen carrying a tray of food.

Fia Newman, wearing a blue and white striped apron and with her hair tied back in a high plait, made her way over to one of the other tables. As Cleo stared in disbelief, she greeted the customers and deftly unloaded the plates. Finally, spotting Cleo, she waved and came over.

Just as if she belonged here.

'Hi! What about this, then?' Fia's amber eyes danced. 'Surprised to see me?'

Cleo had spent the last four days and nights chauffeuring a visiting American businessman around the country. She felt as if she'd been away for four months. 'Are you the new chef?'

'Morse,' murmured Ash. 'Marple. Holmes. You're up there with all the greats.'

'Well, I really wanted to be the resident karaoke queen, but Frank said no to that. So I thought I'd give this a go instead!'

'But . . . how . . . ?' When Fia had called to say goodbye last week, Cleo hadn't expected to see her again *ever*.

'I know! It's like fate, isn't it? That night I stayed at Johnny's house, I was saying how crazy it was that this place didn't serve food, and he told me what had happened with the chap who used to work here, Mad Tony. I didn't think any more of it, but then I went home the next day and had my big showdown with Will. That was when I realised I'd have to find somewhere else to live, because there was no way he'd move out of his precious house.' Fia pulled a face. 'And I was definitely going to have to find a new job, because I was working for Will's mother, and as far as Vivien's concerned, her boy can do no wrong. If he had an affair, I must have driven him to it.'

'God . . .'

'Oh, I never liked her anyway. Walking out of that fancy china shop of hers was a joy. Now I'll never have to listen to the old witch banging on about her perfect son again. So then I thought about this place,' Fia said cheerfully. 'And I knew everyone was friendly, so I gave Frank a call. Well, he seemed keen on the idea, so long as I really could cook. So I came over with some of my food. He liked it, I liked the flat upstairs and bingo, here I am!'

'Well, gosh, that's . . . great.' Mixed emotions didn't begin to describe how Cleo was feeling. Logically she knew she wasn't the one responsible for wrecking Fia's marriage, but she'd been inadvertently involved and the guilt was still there.

'How's that lasagne?' Fia looked over at Ash.

Ash nodded, chewed, swallowed. At last he said scintillatingly, 'Um . . . nice.'

156

'Good-good.' She turned to Cleo. 'How about you? Can I get you anything?'

'I'll have the fish pie.'

Fia gave a nod of satisfaction. 'You'll love it.'

Twenty minutes later, Cleo called her back over. She said, 'You know what? You're right, I do love it.'

Not being entirely thrilled about having Will's wife living here was one thing, but she cooked like an angel.

'I don't do fancy food.' Fia looked pleased. 'Just the basics. But they're the *best* basics.'

'Which is just what we need. This is amazing.' The fish pie was indeed sensational, made with cream and wine and topped with a thick layer of grilled cheese. 'Mad Tony was forever trying out new stuff that didn't work. Chicken with marmalade sauce, curried peas and mango, that kind of thing. And last summer he was serving everything with rose petals and tarragon.' Cleo looked over at Ash. 'Remember that?'

'Uh . . . yes.'

Oh, for heaven's sake. As soon as Fia had disappeared back into the kitchen, Cleo said, 'You fancy her, don't you?'

'No.'

She gave him a gleeful prod. 'You do! You've gone all stupid again!'

Ash put down his drink and heaved a sigh. 'OK, now listen to me. If you were fourteen years old, you might think it'd be funny to blurt it out in front of everyone. But you're *not* fourteen, so I'm sure you can understand that it wouldn't be funny for me. It would be embarrassing all round. What's more, I'd never forgive you. So, seeing as you're supposed to be my friend, I'd really appreciate it if you'd keep this to yourself and just let me get it out of my system in my own time.'

'You're no fun.' Cleo pulled a face.

'But I mean it.' She could tell he did by the look in his eyes. 'This isn't just someone I've met at a party. She's living here now, which means I'm going to be seeing her practically every day.' Ash leaned further across the table. 'And if you tell her, it'll make it unbearable. So you need to keep that . . .' he made a zipping gesture in front of Cleo's mouth '. . . shut. Or we won't be friends any more. And I will be your vengeful neighbour from hell, I promise.'

Crikey, he did mean it. 'OK, I won't say anything. Cross my heart. How long, d'you think, before you get over it?'

'Oh, a couple of hours.' Exasperated, Ash said, 'How the bloody hell do I know? I just wish it wouldn't happen, it's a complete pain. Apart from anything else, she's only just left her husband.' He shook his head. 'So it's going to be months before she's even ready to look at another man.'

Which just went to show how naïve Ash could be. The very next moment, as if to prove it, Johnny came into the pub and Fia was out of the kitchen in a flash.

'Hi, I was wondering when you'd be in!' Her whole face was lit up, her body language unambiguous. 'It's all going *really* well!'

Fia clearly subscribed to the theory that the best way to get over one man was to meet another. Preferably in less time than some people took to hoover their carpets. Eagerly she said, 'What are you going to have?'

'Sorry, busy, can't stop.' Holding up a carrier bag, Johnny offered it to one of the lads standing at the bar. 'Dave, you left your brushes behind – I found them in the sink in the utility room. Thanks for finishing up last night. Great job.' Turning, he grinned and said, 'Cleo, hi! I tell you, it's going to be weird not having that lot around any more. I came downstairs this morning and made six mugs of tea before remembering I was on my own.'

He hadn't called her Misa. It was like a miracle from heaven. To show that she could be civil too, Cleo said, 'So the house is all done now, is it? How's it looking?'

'You wouldn't believe the difference. Come on over if you want. See for yourself.'

'Oh, um . . .' Now she didn't know what to say. She hadn't been expecting an invitation. Next to him, Fia was also looking taken aback.

'I'll show you what I'm working on too,' Johnny added. 'For Cornelia.'

OK, now that was something she'd definitely like to see. Not that Johnny would ever know this, but she'd been Googling him on the quiet and had – even more secretly – fallen in love with his work. Some of the larger-than-life sculptures were breathtaking.

'One of her horses? I'd love to.' Aware of Fia's gaze on her, Cleo said, 'Great.'

His grin broadened. 'Come round when you've finished your lunch. I'll be the one wrestling with a mile of wire.'

All of a sudden the mental picture this conjured up seemed quite exciting. Oo-er, what was *that* about? Was this how it felt to fall under Johnny LaVenture's spell? Returning to the real world, Cleo got a mental grip. Like tipping over the edge from dabbling to addiction, from social drinking to alcoholism, the trick lay in being aware, realising what could happen and stepping back on to safe ground before it was too late. Johnny was an inveterate charmer who loved to flirt for his own amusement. Only a fool would believe he meant it.

Or a Fia.

'Fine, yeah, maybe later.' Cleo waved her fork and went back to her meal. Johnny said his goodbyes to Dave and the boys at the bar and moved towards the door.

Fia, her face falling, called after him, 'Will you be in this evening?'

'Who knows? Never say never.'

When he'd gone and Fia had once again vanished into the kitchen, Ash echoed, 'Fine, yeah, maybe later,' mimicking Cleo's casual tone.

'Behave yourself.' Having jabbed the back of his hand, Cleo wiped her fork on a napkin. 'Would you rather Fia went over there again instead?'

'So that's what you're doing, is it? Selflessly offering yourself in her place, like some kind of noble sacrifice? Don't take her, take me.' Ash shook his head. 'I had no idea you were so brave, so heroic.'

'And I had no idea you were such a philistine. He's an artist. I'd love to watch him at work.'

'Why? You've never wanted to watch *me* work.'

'He's creative!'

'Bloody hell, so am I! I create a radio show,' Ash retorted. 'Which is *also* art, and is a damn sight more difficult than bending bits of wire in this direction and that direction. Any idiot could do that.'

Cleo smiled. 'Are you jealous?'

'Maybe. Just a bit. OK, of course I'm bloody jealous.' He jerked his head in the direction of the kitchen. 'She's crazy about him. It's so obvious.'

Bless. Cleo's heart went out to Ash. 'I know, but I'm going to talk to him about that, tell him not to get involved.'

Ash nodded slowly, acknowledging that this made sense. 'Well, be careful. He probably works with his shirt off.'

OK, delete that thought before it could take hold. Chasing the last fat prawn around her plate, Cleo shrugged and said, 'Don't we all?'

Chapter 21

'Hey, you came.' Answering the front door and thankfully not topless, Johnny looked pleased to see her. He was wearing faded jeans and desert boots, and a white T-shirt with a diagonal reddish-brown smear across the front.

'Is that paint?' Cleo pointed to it; hardly a cheerful colour for a room.

'What?' He glanced down at the smear. 'Oh, right. No, it's blood.'

'Did somebody stab you?'

'Ever the optimist. No, I've just been having a fight with a horse.' Lifting his T-shirt, he showed her the cause of the bleeding, a long, freshly inflicted scratch. 'Occupational hazard. You wouldn't believe how many T-shirts I get through in a year. So,' he led her into the house and gestured around the hall. 'Is it looking better in here?'

It was. Better, fresher, cleaner. The smell of paint still hung in the air but all the clutter had gone. There were new rugs on the polished wooden floorboards, the light fittings had been replaced and the windows glittered.

'Much,' said Cleo.

'Just as well. It's cost a fortune.'

She kept a straight face. 'You poor thing. I'm welling up.'

'OK, sorry.' Johnny smiled briefly. Then they reached the drawing room and he threw open the double doors.

'Oh *wow* . . .'

No more worn, threadbare carpet. No more peeling outdated wallpaper. The entire room, including the floorboards, had been painted white. Sunshine streamed in through the full-length windows. Lined up against the far wall were huge bales of wire and in the centre of the room stood the current work-in-progress, a half-completed, four-metre-high sculpture of a horse.

It was an arresting, magnificent sight. No wonder Cornelia was such a fan of Johnny's work. Looking at photographs of the creations on his website gave no inkling of the emotional impact to be gained by viewing them in the flesh. So to speak.

Watching her with a faint smile on his face, Johnny said, 'You like it?'

Cleo nodded, barely able to tear her gaze away from the horse. Stepping over the coils and lengths of wire strewn across the white dust sheet upon which it stood, she moved towards it. 'Am I allowed to touch?'

'Go ahead. It's not as fragile as it looks. Watch out for sharp edges – I haven't turned them in with pliers yet.'

It was just as well he'd given his permission; not reaching out and touching the sculpture would have been the worst kind of torture. She ran the flat of her hand wonderingly over the horse's flank. How could something silvery and made of lengths of galvanised steel seem so alive? It was extraordinary. Finding herself smiling in disbelief, Cleo moved round to the front and stroked the proud curve of its neck. Imagine being able to create something as – yeesh, that windswept mane was *sharp*.

A bead of blood grew on the end of her finger. Stepping up and taking hold of her wrist, Johnny examined the wound.

'Oh dear. We're going to have to amputate.'

Cleo retrieved her hand and sucked the blood from her finger. She moved back. 'Show me how you do it.'

'How I amputate? Well, I generally get a big old electric saw . . .' He picked up a pair of safety glasses, then nodded at the only piece of furniture in the room. 'Go and sit down. You'll be safe over there.'

The sofa was long and sleek, upholstered in deep purple velvet. Sitting on it, the view was of Johnny and the sculpture, then the French windows behind him, then the terrace and the grounds beyond that. As he worked, illuminated by the afternoon sunlight flooding into the room, Cleo was able to see the play of tendons and muscles in his body. No wonder he had broad shoulders and a washboard stomach; the galvanised steel wire needed to be strong enough to bear the weight of the piece when it was completed. Johnny flexed and stretched as he bent and sculpted each section into place. Perspiration gleamed at his throat and on his forearms. Behind the safety glasses his eyes were narrowed, constantly judging and gauging and checking that every new addition was exactly right. You could see the intensity of his concentration as he moved around the figure, making endless additions and improvements. Every so often a length of wire whipped through the air, catching the sun like a flash of mercury. A couple of times the sharp end of the wire caught Johnny's arm.

Watching Johnny at work was a magical, mesmerising experience. When he finally stopped, Cleo would have guessed she'd been sitting there for fifteen, maybe twenty minutes. But the shadows in the room had lengthened and when she looked at her watch she saw that it had been an hour and a half.

'I can't believe it's four o'clock.' She shook her head in amazement. 'This is definitely how time travel should be. Just think, if airlines supplied wire-sculpture demonstrations on long-haul flights, you'd find yourself on the other side of the world in a flash!'

'It's like that for me too.' Pushing his fingers through his hair, Johnny stepped back to survey his work from a distance. 'Once I start, I lose all track of time. I can go through the night.'

Now there was an image to conjure with.

He flexed his shoulders. 'Come on, let's get a coffee.'

'OK, *oof.*' Her left leg, which had been tucked under her on the sofa, had gone dead. Gingerly uncurling it and levering herself upright, Cleo shook her head when he offered a hand. 'It's fine, I can manage.'

'Stubborn as ever,' Johnny remarked. 'Either that, or you're scared of my irresistible animal magnetism.'

'Or your incredible modesty.' Cleo limped into the kitchen after him and leaned against the polished granite worktop as her foot began to fizz and prickle back to life. 'Listen, what's going on with Fia Newman? Was it your idea for her to move here?'

He began making the coffee. 'No. She was trying to figure out what she could do. At one stage I happened to mention that a live-in job would kill two birds with one stone, but I didn't suggest the Hollybush. I just dropped in yesterday evening and there she was, carrying her stuff into the flat upstairs.'

Her foot was really zinging now, like Alka-Seltzers dropped in water. 'And the other night?'

'The other night what?'

'When she stayed here with you.'

He turned to look at Cleo. 'What are you asking?'

'Nothing.' They were two consenting adults and it was none

of her business what they might have got up to, but she felt it only fair to warn him. 'It's just . . . she spent the night in your house. You were kind to her. And now, bam, she's moved into the village! I don't know if you realise this, but you're probably the reason she's done it.'

Ha, she caught the flash of genuine surprise in his eyes. So he hadn't cottoned on. 'Me?'

'Oh yes.' Cleo rotated her recovering ankle. 'She's just left her husband. You flirted with her in the pub, invited her back to your place for dinner, let her spend the night here.' She paused. 'And now she's back.'

'Riiight.' Johnny nodded slowly. 'OK, I see what you're saying.'

Men, honestly. They had no idea. 'You're her sticking plaster.'

A quick grin. 'I'm even more irresistible than I thought.'

Cleo reached for the mug of coffee he was holding out to her. 'She's vulnerable.'

'Because you had an affair with her husband.'

She gave him a look, but he was right, she did feel responsible. 'You don't want to mess her around. That wouldn't be kind.'

'OK, spare me the lecture. And you should have a bit more faith in me,' said Johnny. 'I'll have you know I can be a gentleman when I want to be. When Fia stayed here the other night she slept in the spare room.' He paused. 'And I slept in mine.'

'Well, good.' Cleo smiled, relieved to hear it.

'Do I get a reward for that?'

'Yes you do. You get a nice warm glow from knowing you did the right thing.'

'Fantastic.' He nodded. 'A nice warm glow. Who could ask for more?'

Cleo drank her coffee. 'Getting involved with her would just be asking for trouble.'

'Fine, I get the message. Sounds like you're not too thrilled about having her here.'

'She seems nice. Normal enough. Apart from having a major crush on you.'

'Touché.' He acknowledged the dig with a brief smile.

Cleo sighed; did he think she was a complete bitch? 'But it's just . . . difficult, you know? Every time I see her, I'm going to be reminded of Will. And I'll keep on feeling guilty.'

'It wasn't your fault, though.'

'I know that logically. But I'm still the reason she left him.'

Johnny said, 'Sooner or later it would have happened anyway. You've done her a favour. And at least the children weren't hers.'

Cleo nodded. 'That's true.'

'If she'd stayed with Will for a few more years, chances are they'd have had kids of their own. And she'd have ended up a single parent. So you've saved her from all that.'

'You're right.' It was Cleo's turn to look modest. 'I'm practically a heroine.'

'A heroine with terrible judgement when it comes to picking a man. I mean, there's me,' he tapped his chest, 'pretty much perfect in every way, and you're not remotely interested.'

She dipped her head in agreement. 'So true.'

'But a complete arse like Will Newman comes along and you think he's the answer to your prayers.'

'OK, you might find this hard to believe, but he did actually do a pretty good job of hiding his complete arsiness. He's like a lot of people.' Cleo's tone was meaningful. 'They can give the impression on the surface of being really nice. But deep down, they're capable of all sorts.'

Johnny raised an eyebrow. 'Are we talking about you now? Because I have to tell you, you aren't often nice to me.'

'Actually, I was thinking of someone else. When did you last see Mandy Ellison?'

He looked blank. 'Mandy? God, not for years. Ten years, I suppose. Why?'

'I saw her last weekend. She's been married for ages. Two kids, wonderful husband, great life.' Cleo said playfully, 'She told me *all* about it. They even have personalised plates.'

He sounded mildly interested. 'Does she work?'

'You're joking. Gary earns tons of money. No need to.'

'Sounds like Mandy.' Amused, Johnny said, 'She never was the grafting kind.' He paused, watching Cleo finish her coffee and reach for her bag. 'You haven't seen the rest of the house yet. I was going to show you upstairs.'

Hmm, there was an offer.

'Not like that.' He tut-tutted, demonstrating his unerring ability to read her mind. 'Well, not unless you really want me to.'

'Very generous of you, but no thanks. I do have to go now. But it's been fun.' Cleo made to leave. 'And remember what I said about Fia, OK? Don't do anything . . . you know.'

'Fine. For now.' Johnny's eyes glinted with mischief as he showed her out. 'Although it still feels like you're the one who wrecked her marriage and I'm the one getting punished for it. Seems a bit harsh.'

She smiled up at him. 'Just concentrate on that nice warm glow.'

Chapter 22

Abbie was in the bath waiting for her face pack to set when the doorbell rang downstairs.

And Tom was still at work.

She waited for whoever it was to give up and go away. No way was she answering the door with a pale blue clay mask slathered over her face. Also, since the sachet of blue gloop had cost two pounds fifty, she absolutely wasn't going to wash it off before it had had a chance to do its refining, beautifying, drawing-out-the-impurities thing.

But like a dog that never tires of chasing and retrieving a stick, the person on the doorstep kept on ringing the bell. Again.

And again.

And agaaaaaain—

'OK, I'm coming, just *stop* it.' Sloshing water, Abbie climbed out of the bath and pulled on her towelling robe. If it was Tom and he'd lost his keys, she'd slather pale blue gloop all over his face and it would jolly well serve him right.

She padded downstairs and paused in the hallway before calling, 'Who is it?' through the front door.

Then she heard, 'Hiya, it's meee!' and felt her stomach turn to concrete.

Oh God. Without even any warning. Completely forgetting the face pack, Abbie opened the front door and gazed at Georgia, very tanned and blonder than ever. And with a huge battered grey suitcase at her feet.

'Hi, Abbie! Euw, look at you! Dad's not home from work yet, then?'

She didn't mean for her breezily worded question to hurt, but the effect was like fingernails scraping down a blackboard. Actually, the setting face pack came in handy, keeping Abbie's features immobile and her true feelings hidden. While inwardly her brain screamed, *No, go away, leave us alone and don't even think of bringing that case into this house.*

Aloud, Abbie said, 'Not yet. Does he know you're here?'

'No, it's a surprise! I called him this afternoon and told him I was sunbathing on the beach in Praia de Rocha, and he said lucky old me. But I'm not there, and when he comes home I'm going to go whoo-hoo, I'm back!' Georgia beamed at her. 'It's going to be brilliant! Won't he just love it?'

'Well, it'll definitely be a surprise.' The drying clay meant she sounded as if she were speaking through clenched teeth. And of course she couldn't stop Georgia bringing the case into the house. Abbie stepped to one side as the girl lugged it past her over the front step and into the narrow hallway. 'Have you come straight from the airport?'

'No, we've been in London for the last couple of days. I've left Mum clearing out the flat, packing everything up before she flies back to Portugal.'

Abbie followed her through to the living room. 'Why?'

'Because she's doing another of her flits, surprise surprise.'

Georgia peeled off her coat to reveal a stripy top and lime-green shorts. 'We've had a bit of an argument about it. She's dumped Christian, right, and now she's met this new guy, Ted. I mean, this is a middle-aged woman we're talking about, d'you know what I mean? She can't keep chasing men for the rest of her life. It's not dignified.'

'So Ted lives in Portugal too?'

'Lives and *drinks* in Portugal.' Pulling a face, Georgia said, 'And he's made it perfectly clear he doesn't like me. Which is fine, because it's absolutely mutual. I was in the way there and he wanted me out of the picture. So I said that was cool, I'd live in the Paddington flat by myself, but then *Mum* said she couldn't afford to keep it on if she wasn't going to be there . . . so then, well, we ended up having a bit of a falling out about that.' She paused to examine the beaded leather bracelet on her left wrist. 'Actually, quite a lot of a falling out.'

'Oh dear.'

Georgia looked at her. 'Can I make a cup of tea, is that all right?'

'Yes, yes . . . sorry, I should have offered.'

'It's OK. You know, it's weird trying to talk to you with all that gunk on your face. Why don't I make the tea while you go upstairs and wash the blue stuff off?'

Abbie didn't ask the question that was uppermost in her mind and Georgia didn't answer it. Instead, like the elephant in the room, it remained unmentioned for the next seventy minutes while they talked instead about Portugal, their respective Christmases, the annoying way jumpers went bobbly at the sides and how weird it was that people would gag at the sight of mouldy yogurt but would happily tuck into blue cheese, the mouldier the better.

Basically, she didn't need to ask the question because she already knew the answer. Even a chimp could guess.

Then Tom arrived home and Abbie saw his face light up at the sight of his daughter. Georgia yelled, 'Surprise!' and almost sent him flying, wrapping him in an exuberant hug. The little knives were out in force in Abbie's stomach, twisting with envy and dread.

'So is that all right then?' said Georgia when she'd finished explaining the story of how she happened to be here. 'It's OK if I stay with you?'

This was it, this was the question. Abbie carefully kept her expression neutral, while inside her head she shouted, no no no no no.

'Well . . .' Startled but hopeful, Tom had turned to look at her. 'That sounds . . . um, what do you think, Abbie?'

Cruel. Cruel and unfair. He had to know what she was thinking.

Georgia was looking taken aback too, as if it hadn't occurred to her that she might have to beg. 'Oh God, is this really awkward? I'm sorry,' she blurted out to Tom. 'I thought you'd be pleased!'

'Sweetheart, sit down, don't get upset.' Tom was mortified. 'Of course we're pleased . . . it's just all a bit sudden, and how long were you thinking of—'

'Don't worry, Dad, it's fine, I'll go back to London.' Georgia's blue eyes swam as she backed away. 'Sorry to bother you . . . I'll find someone to put me up . . .'

'Wait, you can't go, of course you can stay!' Tom turned to Abbie and blurted the words out in a panic. 'That's all right with you, love, isn't it?'

Cleo was painting her toenails when the phone rang.

'Hello?' Whoops, she managed to blob cyclamen pink polish on to the side of her foot as she clasped the phone between shoulder and chin.

'Hi, it's me.' Abbie's voice. 'Come over to the pub.'

'Hm? Oh, no thanks, I'm having a lazy night in. Actually, I'm just doing my toes and you've made me—'

'It wasn't a question,' Abbie cut in. 'I'm telling you to come over because I need you.'

'What? Why?' Putting the lid back on the bottle of Rimmel polish, Cleo straightened. 'And why are you sounding all weird and echoey?'

'I'm in the loo. Hiding. How soon can you be here?'

Whatever was happening? 'Well, it says this stuff dries in sixty seconds. So all I've got to do is put some clothes on. Oh, except I've just plucked my eyebrows. As soon as the redness goes down, I'll—'

'Never mind your eyebrows,' Abbie blurted out. 'Get yourself over here *now*.'

Which was easy for her sister to say, but Cleo knew from experience that after a vigorous plucking session, the skin around her eyebrows glowed neon red and stayed red for ages. Then again, Abbie had sounded desperate. Heroically, Cleo got herself dressed, roughly dried her hair and spent a couple of minutes applying minimum-level make-up plus white highlighter under the eyebrows to disguise the worst of the damage.

Cleo surveyed the end result in the mirror. She still looked ridiculous but never mind. In a way, it was nice to be wanted. And since Abbie didn't make a habit of needing her company in such dramatic fashion, she could even hazard a guess as to what this might be about.

The guess was confirmed when she arrived at the pub and saw the blonde girl with Tom's eyes standing with Tom and Abbie. She hadn't met Georgia last time, but the girl had evidently turned up again. Poor Abbie, hopefully it was only a flying visit. Even now, she was looking wan and left out, like the wallflower nobody wanted to dance with.

'Oh look, it's Cleo.' Feigning surprise, Abbie beckoned her over. 'Georgia, meet my younger sister. Cleo, this is Georgia. And you'll never guess what? Georgia's come to stay with us! Isn't that lovely?'

Bloody hell. No wonder Abbie was looking a bit wild-eyed.

'Hi. Great.' Wondering how to greet the girl who under other circumstances would have been her niece, Cleo stuck out her hand before realising that Georgia was going in for the air-kiss so they ended up like novice Morris dancers, doing an awkward bit of both. 'So how long are you staying?'

'Who knows? I'm moving in!' Leaning towards Tom – oh God, it was so weird to think he was her father – Georgia said cheerfully, 'I could still be here when I'm seventy!'

So that was why Abbie had sounded frantic on the phone.

'Drink, Cleo?' Tom already had his wallet out.

'Yes please.'

'Actually, I hope you don't mind me saying.' Georgia peered more closely at her. 'But are you allergic to your eyeshadow? Only your eyes are, like, really *red*.'

'What could I do?' Abbie murmured thirty minutes later when they visited the loo. 'How could I say no? She doesn't have anywhere else to go.'

'Oh God, it's not fair on you.' Cleo gave her a hug.

'And Tom's thrilled; it's like a dream come true for him. He's trying to hide it, but he can't. And every time I think about it I just feel sick.' Abbie shook her head. 'But then I tell myself it's not her fault and I hate myself for being so horrible. I must be some kind of monster . . .'

'Look, you're in shock. And you're definitely not a monster. It'll get easier. Everything'll settle down and you'll all get used to each other.' Cleo knew she was probably spouting rubbish, but what else could she say? 'And this is Channings Hill we're talking about. She's used to living in London. A couple of weeks here and she could be going out of her mind with boredom. She'll be begging to leave.'

'That'd be too much to hope for,' Abbie sighed.

The door was pushed open. Georgia said brightly, 'Talking about me?'

She hadn't heard them. 'No,' Abbie managed a smile.

'We were a bit,' said Cleo.

'Of course you were. I'm not completely stupid. It's OK, I don't mind.'

'Actually, Abbie's got a headache, but she was worried you might think she was just using it as an excuse to leave. She's feeling pretty rotten,' Cleo went on, 'so really she should go home and take some painkillers.'

'Oh poor you, you should have said! Of course you must go,' Georgia exclaimed, over-sympathising in that way people do when the least popular member of the party says they might leave. 'Me and Dad'll be fine.'

'And I'll be here too.' Cleo nodded at Abbie, who was so obviously not enjoying herself. 'Go on, off you go.'

Grateful for the excuse, Abbie left and Georgia and Cleo rejoined Tom at the bar. Georgia said interestedly, 'Who's that, over there?'

While they'd been in the loo, Johnny and Ash had both arrived and were setting up a game of pool. Johnny was looking handsomer than ever tonight in a white cotton shirt and jeans, with his hair falling into his dark eyes. Ash, never the most sartorial of dressers, was wearing a baggy red sweatshirt that made him look like an off-duty Father Christmas.

'Just a couple of locals.' Changing the subject, Cleo said, 'So, what are you going to be doing job-wise? Any ideas?' This was the girl who had just spent several weeks lazing by a pool in Portugal; she really hoped Georgia didn't think she could just move in with Tom and Abbie, eat them out of house and home and generally sponge off them like . . . well, OK, like millions of bone-idle teenagers the world over, but that was beside the point.

Chapter 23

'Absolutely!' Leaning forward, Georgia said eagerly, 'How funny, I was just about to ask you about that. Now, my plan is to start up a business. Minimum outlay, maximum profit, flexible working hours, how does that sound?'

'Like I've fathered Richard Branson.' Baffled, Tom said, 'Blimey.'

'What kind of business?' said Cleo.

'Ironing.'

So, not *exactly* like Richard Branson. 'Seriously?'

'Why not? I love ironing. I've always done all our stuff since I was eleven.' Dreamily Georgia said, 'It's brilliant, taking something crumpled and messy and making it all smooth and perfect. Like creating order out of chaos. And you can charge one pound twenty a shirt! How long does it take to iron a shirt? Five minutes. Easy peasy. And you can watch telly while you're doing it.' She looked pleased with herself. 'All I need is an iron!'

'And an ironing board,' said Cleo.

'That too.'

'And hangers. Lots and lots of hangers.' Oh dear, was she raining on the girl's parade?

'Fine. They're cheap.'

'And leaflets to advertise the business.'

'Okaaay.'

'And transport.'

'Not if I tell people to just drop the stuff off at the house and pick it up again once it's done.'

Tom shook his head. 'That won't work. Ironing services collect and deliver. You'd definitely need a van.'

'Fine then, forget the ironing.' Georgia puffed out her cheeks, exhaled noisily and shook back her hair. 'I thought it was a good idea, but it wasn't. *And* I was going to subcontract work out to pensioners. But never mind, I'll just go on benefits instead.'

'Hang on—' began Tom.

'I'll be unemployed and sponge off the state. Far more restful.' Her interested gaze wandered over to the pool table.

'Look, I'm sure we can—'

'Or I could become a pole dancer. That pays well, doesn't it? Then I can save up for a van. Look, they've finished playing now. Shall we challenge them to a game of doubles?'

'No.' Cleo glanced briefly across at Johnny, who was laughing, and at Ash, who was juggling pool balls and being generally boisterous. 'Anyway, he's too old for you.'

'Why? How old is he?'

'Thirty.'

Georgia's eyes widened. '*Is* he?'

Sensing that they were being watched, Ash turned round to look at Cleo and demanded, 'What's going on over there? Are you ogling my irresistible backside?'

Cleo opened her mouth to retort that she could think of prettier sights but was beaten to it by Georgia who said, 'Cleo was just telling me about you. I can't believe how old you are.'

What? Cleo did a double take.

'Bloody cheek. So how old do you think I am?' Ash demanded. 'Sixty-five?'

Beaming, Georgia said, 'I'd have said mid-twenties.'

'But I *am* in my mid-twenties.' Ash raised his eyebrows. 'What has that witch been telling you?'

'She said you were thirty!'

Cleo was stunned; so much for jumping to conclusions. 'I didn't. I meant *Johnny* was thirty.'

'Who's Johnny? Oh, I suppose that must be you.' She briefly acknowledged Johnny before turning back to Ash. 'So what's your name?'

And within moments she was over at the pool table, chatting away to Ash, the two of them getting along together famously. Cleo heard him tell Georgia that she, Cleo, was in fact fifty-seven years old.

'She's too young for Johnny, surely.' At her side Tom was panicking, having made the same assumption. 'Oh God, how am I supposed to deal with all this? I'm missing out on eighteen years of practice.'

'I'll have a word with her.' Not that it had done much good with Fia Newman, but she had to try her best for Tom's sake. Cleo took a gulp of her drink; if things had been different, she would have been Georgia's aunt. Fabulous, trendy, brilliant Auntie Cleo who was always fun, never nagged about boring stuff and had taught her how to carry off a trilby with style.

OK, who was she kidding? Any attempt to wear a hat made her look like a care-in-the-community patient out on a day trip. Her head was the wrong shape or something. But she could still be an aunt-by-proxy, couldn't she, who might be rubbish at hats but was still great company and gave really excellent advice when it came to men and relationships.

Particularly the ones you shouldn't even consider—

'I'll buy her a van,' said Tom.

'What?'

'Just a cheap one, so she can set up the business.' He'd obviously been mulling it over in his mind. 'Can't have her going into pole dancing.'

'Well, no.' Georgia had pretty obviously only said that to terrify him into buying her a van, but he couldn't take the risk that she might do it.

'So, you've met her now.' Tom tried and failed to keep the pride out of his voice as he watched his newfound daughter from a distance. 'What's the verdict?'

Cleo touched his arm and said gently, 'I think she's a character, and she's going to change your life. But this isn't as easy for Abbie as it is for you. Don't let her feel left out of all this, will you?'

He looked surprised. 'She isn't left out. We're all in it together.'

Cleo nodded slowly. She'd always loved Tom but he wasn't necessarily brilliant at understanding how women might feel. 'OK. I'm just saying it might not feel that way to her.'

He shook his head; this was clearly beyond him. 'Look, I know, but give it a few days and everything'll be fine.'

Three games of pool later, Georgia said, 'Where's whatsisname gone? That friend of yours?'

'Johnny. I wouldn't call him a friend,' said Ash. 'He's just the bastard who beats me at pool. Anyway, he left twenty minutes ago. Which means it's my turn to beat you.'

'That's what you think, is it?' Dimpling, Georgia waggled her finger at him. 'Excellent, bring it on. You're going to be so humiliated when I win *again*.'

Cleo, watching them, marvelled at Georgia's apparent lack of concern about Johnny's departure.

At ten thirty Ash left too.

'Wow,' said Georgia when he'd gone. 'I *love* him.'

Cleo smiled; the two of them had definitely hit it off. 'Good, I'm glad.'

'And is it true that he's single? I mean, he said he doesn't have a girlfriend but you know what men can be like. I'd hate to make a play for him, then discover he's got some on-off female stashed away.'

A *play*? Cleo did a double-take. 'When you say you love him . . .'

'I mean I fancy the pants off him! That is my idea of the perfect man. OK, I know,' Georgia's chin tilted with teenage defiance, 'but that's the way I am. As far as I'm concerned, personality is *way* more important than looks. Give me someone who can entertain me every time. Trust me, I've been out with my share of pretty boys. You soon get bored with looking at them, gazing into their beautiful eyes and admiring their perfect . . . ooh, I don't know, *teeth* and stuff. If they don't have what it takes to make me laugh, I'm not interested. It'd be like going out with a poster on your wall.'

Her lip curled with derision as she said it. God, she really was serious. Cleo finished her drink in silence; and to think she and Tom had both spent the evening assuming it was Johnny her nearly-niece was interested in.

'Do you think he likes me?' said Georgia eagerly.

'Um, well I'm sure he does.' Cleo looked at Tom, who was clearly bemused by his daughter's upfront attitude.

'Good. Because I *really* fancy him. A *lot*. Even if he is a milkman. So, do you think I should just ask him out, or should I wait for him to ask me?'

The milkman line was one Ash habitually used as his reason for leaving early.

'I'd wait,' said Cleo. 'It's a pride thing. Men generally like to be the ones to make the first move.'

'As long as he hurries up and *does* make it.' Georgia's slim fingers were already tapping impatiently against the side of her pool cue. 'I hate it when people play hard to get. It's such a waste of time.'

Blimey. If Georgia had her way, she and Ash would be married by Easter.

Tom had already headed off for work. Abbie, busy buttering toast and drinking tea, was due to leave in ten minutes. Having crept around upstairs in order not to disturb their new house guest, she got a shock when the door was pushed open and Georgia came padding into the kitchen in a green and purple striped nightie and with her hair askew.

'Hi!' Abbie knew she sounded over-bright but she couldn't help herself; it just kept happening. 'Did you sleep well?'

'Yeah, thanks. I was having the most amazing dream before I woke up.' She paused. 'Was someone else down here just now?'

'No. Unless you mean Tom. He left at eight.'

The look of hope in Georgia's eyes faded. She raked her fingers sleepily through her tangled hair. 'Oh, right. Is it OK for me to have a cup of tea?'

What did she expect the answer to be? *No you can't?*

'Of course you can! Help yourself to anything you like!' Abbie cringed inwardly; here she was, off again and drowning in a forest of exclamation marks. 'Cereal, toast . . . we've got Marmite, honey, apricot jam, blackcurrant jam, eggs . . .'

'Thanks, I'll just have tea for now. Is your head better?'

'Oh!' She'd forgotten about last night's fictitious headache. 'Yes, thanks, all gone! So, what are your plans then for today?'

Georgia shrugged and dropped a tea bag into a mug. 'Don't know. Just have a rest and watch a bit of TV, I suppose.' She wrinkled her nose at the radio on the window sill, currently playing a Neil Diamond track. 'Is that Radio Two?'

She made it sound like Radio Born-in-the-Ice-Age. Was this Georgia's way of telling her that from now on they would be listening to a station that was hip and happening? Feeling about a hundred years old, Abbie said defensively, 'No, it's—'

'Actually, d'you know what time milkmen finish work?'

'Sorry?' Was this a trick question?

'You know, people who do a milk round. They start work dead early so they must finish early. I just wondered if you knew when.'

'No idea. Midday, possibly.' Surely Georgia wasn't considering that as a job? In a hurry now, Abbie took a big mouthful of toast and checked her hair in the mirror. She liked Neil Diamond. If she'd been alone in the house she'd have sung along, maybe even had a bit of a dance around the kitchen. Having a hyper-critical teenager *in situ* was going to change her life in more ways than she'd imagined. She chewed, swallowed, took a swig of too-hot tea then another bite of toast. The chances were that Georgia wouldn't share her taste in TV programmes either, would flinch at the prospect of having to watch a wildlife documen-tary or chatter distractingly all the way through a vital episode of some series she wasn't interested in but which she, Abbie, was addicted to.

Oh God, listen to me, I'm just a horrible human being who—

'Hang on!' Georgia held up a hand. 'Sorry, can you shush a minute?'

OK, this was too much. Now she wasn't even allowed to eat

toast in her own kitchen? But ridiculously, despite her indignation, Abbie found that she'd stopped chewing. Georgia was listening intently to something. Had she heard an intruder trying to break in through the back door? A mouse skittering across the floor-boards? A bird singing in the garden? Maybe she was interested in wildlife after all.

'What is it?' Having listened for several seconds, Abbie said, 'I can't hear anything.'

'Him.' Georgia pointed in disbelief to the radio on the window sill. 'I know it can't be him, but . . . God, that voice! It sounds just like the person I was talking to yesterday in the pub . . . wow, that is so *spooky* . . .'

Realisation dawned. She'd been asleep by the time Georgia and Tom had come in last night. 'Oh, did you meet Ash?'

'Ash! Yes, yes!' Georgia gestured wildly at the radio. 'Can you believe it? This guy sounds *exactly* like him!'

Everything belatedly became clear. Abbie said, 'That could be because it's The Ash Parry-Jones Show.'

Georgia's teaspoon clattered on to the worktop. 'Get out of here.' Her head swivelled between Abbie and the radio, where Ash was now exchanging banter with his newsreader. Her eyes widened 'But . . . but he told me he was a milkman!'

'It's kind of a running joke. He uses it on the show too, pretends he does a milk round before coming into the studio. He lives next door to Cleo. Look, I'm going to have to go—'

'He's an actual DJ! That's amazing! God, is he good?' Completely recovered from the earlier musical assault on her ears, Georgia was now turning up the volume, gazing in wonder at the radio. 'OK, stupid question, of course he is. I just can't believe this. I thought he was brilliant before, but now he's even *better.*'

Abbie moved towards the door. 'Will you be OK? I'll see you later.'

'I'll be fine,' Georgia said absently. Her eyes were shining, her attention elsewhere. 'This is so cool! It's like I'm going to have my very own Chris Moyles!'

Chapter 24

Fia marvelled at the difference a month could make. Just a few weeks ago, her morning routine had involved getting up at eight, starting work in her mother-in-law's shop at nine and, in between being polite to customers, listening patiently to her mother-in-law's non-stop stream of gossip, criticism and social commentary. Regularly interspersed, needless to say, with paeons of praise for Will.

Which had been pretty boring, not to mention repetitive. Vivien liked to replay her waspish opinions on a more or less permanent loop and especially loved waiting until customers had left the shop, then criticising their hair, their voices, their peculiar taste in clothes. It had been like being trapped for eight hours a day with Trinny and Susannah. Fia would have found another job months ago but each time she'd mentioned it, Will had been upset; she'd be letting both him and his mother down.

And like a complete pushover she'd believed him. Whereas in reality he'd been controlling her, keeping her mentally tethered to him and Vivien while he conducted his own life as he pleased.

Looking back on it, she couldn't believe she'd been so gullible. That was the payback for having a trusting nature. Well, she'd put all that behind her. Will and his bossy nightmare of a mother could take a running jump; this was the next phase of her life and from now on she wasn't going to take any rubbish from anyone.

From now on she was going to decide what she wanted and go for it.

Who dares wins, and all that. What's more, it was all working out really well. She had been daring and she was definitely winning so far.

Best of all, she was loving her unexpected new job. Even if it did mean getting up at six in order to go and buy the food she'd be cooking that day, then bringing it back and spending the next three hours doing all the prep.

'La la la, laaa laaaaa.' Humming along to her CD, Fia finished peeling and quartering the King Edwards for the shepherd's pie and slid them into the pan of water on the hob. From the kitchen window she was able to look out over the pub garden, where wild rabbits hopped about and birds swung like acrobats from the trees, feeding on berries and seeds. She loved the utter peacefulness of the mornings, then the contrast of the buzzy conviviality of the pub when it was open. Of course it was hard work, but everyone was so appreciative of her cooking, it more than compensated. Never before had she been on the receiving end of so many compliments. Maybe the novelty would wear off one day, but it hadn't yet.

Frank, the landlord, came into the kitchen as she was frying the sliced onions in butter and oil.

'Morning, pet. Smells good. Coffee?'

'Hi, Frank. Yes please.' She sprinkled caster sugar on to the onions. 'I'm doing shepherd's pie, mushroom stroganoff, beef curry, and chicken and leek casserole.'

'Great. We've already got twelve booked for lunch. Bunch of

women who usually eat at the Bear are coming over because they've heard good things. Word's spreading, pet.' Frank clapped her on the back. 'You're turning out to be a bit of a star, aren't you? Our very own Hugh Fearnley-Whittingstall.'

Fia didn't burst into tears. He meant it as a compliment.

'Hey up.' Frank glanced out of the window. 'Rabbits at two o'clock. Where's my shotgun?'

And sometimes he thought *he* was Hugh Fearnley-Whittingstall.

'Don't kill them. I love watching them jump around out there.'

'Spoilsport. Little buggers aren't so sweet when they're jumping all over your vegetable patch.' Frank sloshed boiling water into two mugs and nodded at the CD player on the shelf above the fridge. 'What's that you're listening to?'

'*Carmina Burana*. By Carl Orff. Like it?'

He grimaced. 'Never really bothered with all that classical stuff. It's Elvis for me, every time.'

Could she win him round? 'It's relaxing. I just like to have it playing in the background.'

Frank listened for a few seconds, clearly underwhelmed. Finally he said, 'You should listen to the radio. Wouldn't that be more cheerful?'

Cheerful? Now it was Fia's turn to pull a face. Will's mother had been a huge Radio Four fan and had always had it on in the shop. When she wasn't critiquing her customers, Vivien was disagreeing with practically everything on the radio and conducting pointless one-sided arguments with the presenters. Having to stand by while her opinionated mother-in-law screeched, 'Oh, will you just *listen* to yourself, you silly little man,' day in and day out, had succeeded in putting her off talk radio for life.

'You want to give BWR a go,' Frank persisted. 'Have a listen to Ash's show. He's a right laugh, that lad.'

Fia's hackles rose instantly. A right laugh. Except, hard though it was to believe, it actually appeared to be true. Last night while she'd been working away here in the kitchen, she'd heard Ash laughing in the bar. When she'd carried food through, she'd even seen him laughing with her own eyes; Ash had been playing pool with Johnny, joking around and generally being the life and soul of the party. Yet when she'd squeezed past and smiled at him he'd practically cut her dead, turning away as if she didn't exist. And this wasn't the first time it had happened either. Everyone else in Channings Hill had been welcoming and friendly, but Ash Parry-Jones invariably treated her like some unwanted intruder. At first she'd assumed he was simply the quiet, stand-offish, keep-himself-to-himself type. Discovering over the course of the last fortnight that he was actually completely confident and outgoing with everyone else had come as a shock, not to mention a slap in the face. Because that meant he was being cold for a reason. He just didn't like her.

And if he was going to be such an unfriendly miserable sod, she was buggered if she was going to listen to his precious radio show, no matter how hilarious it might be.

Frank left the kitchen. Fia powdered the frying onions with flour, then added a glug of red wine. Ten minutes later, curiosity got the better of her and she switched off the CD. If BWR hadn't been one of the pre-set radio stations she wouldn't have found it. As it was, she jumped at the sound of Ash's voice. God, it was weird to hear him being himself, playful and good-humoured and utterly relaxed.

'. . . and that was Katie Melua, for those of you who like that kind of thing. Although if I had to be buried in my coffin with an iPod and only one artist playing on it, I'd want to kill myself if it was her. Or George Formby.'

188

'Who?' He had a young-sounding female in the studio with him. 'The boxer guy who sells lean mean grilling machines?'

'Do you know what? You're thinking of George Foreman who I'd love to have on my iPod in my coffin because he's a legend, even if he doesn't sing. But *I'm* talking about George Formby who played the ukulele and sang in a *really* annoying way. And I wouldn't want Lonnie Donegan either. The King of Skiffle. Because I don't like skiffle music,' said Ash. 'Although I have to say, the actual word *skiffle* is one of my all-time favourite words. It's right up there with knickerbocker and lollygagging.'

'You just made that last one up!'

'I didn't. It's a real word,' Ash protested. 'It means hanging around. Which is a lot nicer than you might think, because you'd *think* it meant gagging on a lolly.'

The girl said, 'I like pernickety.'

'That's our producer's favourite word,' said Ash. 'Can't imagine why. Probably because he wears knitted pullovers and lets his mum spit on her hankie before she cleans his face—'

Footsteps sounded outside the kitchen, signalling Frank's return. Before she knew it, Fia's arm had shot out and switched from radio back to CD. OK, maybe it was childish, but she wasn't going to give Ash the satisfaction of even hearing that she'd listened to his show.

If he could be cold and unfriendly for no apparent reason . . . well, that was fine. So could she.

'I bet you couldn't believe your luck, could you?'

Cleo glanced in the rear-view mirror at her passenger and nearly got dazzled by his teeth. 'Sorry?'

'When you found out who you were picking up. Not just your lucky day either. Your lucky three weeks.'

189

'Right. Absolutely.' She nodded and flashed a professional smile of assent. Oh joy. Five minutes into the first of many journeys and already the client was proving himself to be a dickhead.

And to think Grumpy Graham had thought, in his own grumpy way, that he was doing her some kind of favour when he'd allocated her the job.

'Here you go, you can take this one.' Graham had actually winked – winked! – as he'd handed her the booking sheet last week. 'Nice and regular, and a bit of a looker by all accounts. Don't say I never do anything for you.'

'Ooh, Casey Kruger!' Coming into the tiny cluttered office to drop off some keys, Shelley had peered over Cleo's shoulder. 'I used to have a poster of him on my bedroom wall when he was in *On the Beach*.'

Cleo hadn't watched *On the Beach*, one of Australia's most successfully exported soaps, but she knew who Casey Kruger was. Like Kylie and Jason and so many other soap stars, he had gone on to have a career in music.

And now here he was, lounging in the back of the car in an unbuttoned black shirt and super-tight black jeans, drinking Diet Coke and autographing a pile of publicity photos of himself. For the next three weeks he was starring at the Bristol Hippodrome in a new musical called *Beach Party!* It was her job to pick him up every afternoon from his hotel on the outskirts of Bath and deliver him to the theatre, then collect him again after each performance and return him safely to the hotel.

'Here.' Casey leaned forward and tapped her on the shoulder as they waited at a junction.

Turning, Cleo saw that he was presenting her with one of the photos he'd just signed.

'Oh thanks. That's really kind.'

Well, what else could she say — no thanks, that's really nauseating?

'See what I've put on it?' Casey looked pleased with himself. Glancing at the words, Cleo read: 'To Cleo, You're a babe and you're driving me crazy! All love, Casey Kruger xxx.'

Which was less flattering than it sounded, because 'You're a babe!' was Casey's catchphrase and he said it to everyone he met. Several years back, while appearing at a charity event, he'd even said it to Princess Anne, and if that didn't confirm his dickhead-edness beyond all shadow of a doubt, Cleo didn't know what did.

'Pretty good, eh? And I put "Driving me crazy" because you're my driver and that's what you're going to be doing for the next few weeks!'

She smiled and nodded. At this rate it was going to feel like the next few years.

'You know what? We're going to have fun, you and me.' Chuckling and taking a sip of Diet Coke, Casey lowered his darkened window so the people waiting at the bus stop could recognise him. He nodded and waved graciously before buzzing the window up again. 'So, Cleo, tell me all about yourself. Were you a big fan of *On the Beach*, back when I was in it?'

Oh dear, it was already feeling like the next few years. Maybe she could persuade Shelley to swap jobs.

Chapter 25

Lunch with his producer followed by an uncharacteristic urge to go shopping for new clothes meant it was four o'clock by the time Ash arrived home. As he hauled a load of carrier bags out of the boot of the car, he heard footsteps behind him. Purposeful footsteps at that. For a split second his heart leapt at the thought that it could be Fia. Turning, he came face to face with . . .

OK, not Fia. It was Georgie – no, *Georgia*, Tom Wells's eighteen-year-old, sperm-donated daughter. What a weird situation *that* was.

'Hey, how are you doing?' She was looking and sounding exceedingly perky. 'I thought you'd have been home earlier than this!'

Straightening up and slamming the boot shut, Ash said, 'Well, now I don't have to wear my electronic tag any more, I'm allowed to stay out pretty much as long as I like.'

For a moment her bright blue eyes widened like saucers. 'Did you really have one?'

'No.'

'Oh, phew!'

'I know. Curfews are the pits.'

Georgia grinned at him. 'I've been waiting for you. Guess what?'

He shrugged. 'No idea. You're my long-lost sister?'

'Shut up! No, listen, I am your biggest fan! I can't believe you didn't tell me last night that you're a DJ!'

'I'm very modest,' lied Ash.

'Seriously, I heard your show this morning . . . and you were *brilliant*. And all that stuff about the online listeners, getting them to email in from all over the world and making up that song about them . . . that was just brilliant! You know what, you're *way* funnier than Chris Moyles.'

'I happen to agree with you there.'

'Can I come in?'

'Sorry?'

She nodded at his front gate. 'To your house. You can show me what you've been buying. It's funny, isn't it? If I'd grown up here with my dad, we'd have known each other for years. And I only met you yesterday but it feels as if I *have* known you for years! You know when two people just seem to click and get on really well together? Well, that's what I reckon it's like with us. Come on, let's have a look at your new things. If you went out and bought a load of stuff to impress me, I'll tell you if it's worked.'

Ash had bought them in an attempt to impress Fia, but was aware that his taste in clothes was decidedly dodgy. In the absence of Cleo, he may as well solicit advice while it was being offered. Even if the person making the offer was currently wearing a purple denim jacket, emerald-green corduroy shorts over black tights, and a multicoloured spotted scarf.

'Don't look at me like that,' Georgia scolded. 'I have great personal style. I'm very eclectic.'

Ash jangled his keys. 'Come on then.'

In the living room, she wasted no time in making herself at home. 'Ooh, that's a big one!' She was pointing at the TV. 'And I like how you've done this room.' She gazed around, taking in the chalk-white walls hung with black and white photo prints, the pale grey carpet and black suede sofa and armchairs. 'Not too tidy, but not a complete mess.'

'Thanks.' In the process of picking up the magazines and newspapers strewn across the coffee table, Ash let them drop back down.

Georgia laughed, revealing pearly teeth. 'I'm going to listen to your show every day. Now, try on your clothes. It's OK, you don't need to go upstairs—'

'Oh yes I do. Jesus, what are you like?' Ash kept his overweight body to himself, thank you very much; even on beaches he stayed covered up. Stripping to the waist in front of a skinny, straight-talking eighteen-year-old simply wasn't going to happen.

'I'm like me.' Unperturbed, Georgia said, 'I'm unique.'

'I can tell.'

When he came back downstairs she surveyed him through narrowed eyes.

'What does that mean?' Ash glanced down defensively at the shirt and jacket.

'It's all wrong.'

'Bloody hell, I spent hundreds on this lot.'

'Calm down, the clothes are OK. It's the way you're wearing them.' Jumping up from the sofa, she began briskly unfastening buttons, turning back cuffs, tweaking collars and loosening the shirt he'd tucked too tightly into the waistband of his jeans. 'You need to relax. Just keep things fluid and casual. And take *this* thing,' she picked a bright, zig-zaggy sweater out of one of the bags as if it were a dead snake, 'straight back to the shop.'

The zig-zaggy sweater from Ted Baker was his favourite. 'No, no,' Ash shook his head. 'I'm keeping that one.'

'Oh dear,' said Georgia soothingly, 'are you starting to regret asking me to help you now?'

'Actually, I didn't ask you. You just came barrelling in here and started barking orders like a sergeant major.'

'I'm sorry, I know I can be a bit full-on. I just really want to help you.' She dumped the Ted Baker bag on the sofa and went back to adjusting the turned-up collar of his jacket. 'There, that's much better. Although I don't know why I should, because it's only going to make more girls chase after you.'

Ash eyed her with suspicion. 'Are you taking the mickey?' Because if she was, he wouldn't like it.

'God, no. Why would I do that? You're fantastic.' She fixed him with her unblinking vivid-blue gaze. 'Don't you understand why I'm here? I absolutely completely fancy you rotten.'

He exhaled. 'OK, who put you up to this?' If it was Cleo, he'd wring her neck.

'No one!' Raising her hand, Georgia reached out and gently brushed the backs of her fingers against his face. When he leaned away, she said, 'I felt it last night. I kind of hoped you did too. And that was *before* I knew you were on the radio. Which proves I'm not some kind of screaming groupie.'

Ash shook his head. 'This is a trick.'

'It's not. OK, you're not pretty. But that's not what I go for,' said Georgia. 'Never have done. It's character every time for me. When all my friends were drooling over Zac Efron, I had pictures of James Corden on my wall. And now I've met you.' She moved a couple of inches closer. 'I just think we'd be perfect together. And you must want me.'

This was surreal. 'Why must I want you?'

'Because I'm pretty *and* I have a great personality.' She grinned. 'What's not to like?'

'But—'

'Hey, don't look so stunned. This is a good thing! I'm so glad I came here now.' Reaching up on tiptoe, she planted a quick kiss on Ash's unsuspecting mouth. Then, pulling away a fraction of a second before *he* could pull away, she said, 'And you're going to be glad too.'

Jesus, she really meant it. Ash wiped his mouth, now sticky with melon-flavoured lipgloss. 'OK, stop right there. I don't know what you think you're playing at . . .'

'Come here, then, and let me show you.'

'No. Get *off*.' It was like trying to wrestle an octopus. Unpeeling her hands, he said firmly, 'This isn't going to happen. No way.'

'Why not? You can't tell me I'm not pretty enough.' Georgia was indignant. 'Not being big-headed or anything, but I do know what I look like.'

He could understand her confusion. On the scale of physical attraction, she was stratospherically out of his league. Ash said, 'Look, you're stunning. But you're eighteen.'

'So?' Her voice rose.

'That's too young for me.'

'For God's sake, I'm not some little kid! I'm an *adult*.'

'I know, I know, but it's the way I am. I've always gone for girls my own age or older. It's just . . . personal preference.'

'So you're not interested in me. You'd prefer someone older and uglier. And probably way fatter too.' Her hands on her narrow hips, Georgia said, 'Do you have any idea how . . . *wrong* that is?'

Ash broke into a smile. 'Yeah, I suppose it is.'

'Not to mention frustrating. Oh well, I'll leave it for now. But don't think I'm going to give up,' she warned, 'because I'm not. I can still try and win you over with my dazzling personality.'

'Of course you can try.'

'I'll be your number one fan. And the age thing doesn't matter, you know. That's nothing. What are you, anyway? Twenty-seven? Twenty-eight?'

'Twenty-six,' Ash said gravely. 'And a half.'

'Well, there you go, that's nothing at all! Right, I'm definitely not giving up now.'

'Good luck then, because it's not going to happen.'

Unperturbed, Georgia changed tack. 'I'd be great on the radio. Can I be on your show?'

'No you bloody can't!'

'Spoilsport.'

'I know, too bad. And I have calls to make, business to take care of.' Inching her towards the front door, Ash said, 'So I'm afraid I'm going to have to ask you—'

'To leave, yeah yeah. You're getting rid of me. But I know what I want and I don't give up until I get it.' She flashed him a dazzling smile as he ushered her out of the cottage. 'And there's something else about the age thing.'

'What's that, then?'

'When you're eighty-two, I'll be seventy-four.'

Why, *why* couldn't he be shamelessly lusted after and chased by Fia?

'Trust me,' said Ash, 'when I'm eighty-two, I'll be dead.'

'You see? That's such a defeatist attitude. I could definitely help you work on that,' said Georgia.

Chapter 26

'I had a call from Ash this morning.' Back from transporting a clutch of corporate types to a conference in Manchester, Cleo dropped in on Abbie after work. 'He's being sexually harassed by Georgia. She threw herself at him!'

'Lucky old Ash.' Abbie carried on basting the chicken she'd just taken out of the oven.

Cleo switched on the kettle. 'Except he's not the least bit interested. She's not his type. He says—'

'Not that one,' Abbie blurted, stopping her in her tracks as she took a carton of milk from the fridge. 'That's the full fat.'

'It's OK, I like full fat.'

'But it's Georgia's. Use the other one, the semi-skimmed, otherwise there won't be enough for her cereal and it'll be my fault.'

Abbie was clearly stressed. Her hair was escaping from its scrunchie, her cheeks were flushed and she was spooning melted butter over the chicken at warp speed. Putting back the wrong milk, Cleo said carefully, 'Where is she?'

'Out with Tom. Looking at vans. She needs a van for her ironing business so he's buying her one.' Baste, baste, baste.

'He said he might. So, she can drive, then? I mean, she has a licence?'

'Oh yes. Passed her test first time, last October. One of her mother's boyfriends was a driving instructor. So that was handy.'

'Abbie, sit down.'

'I can't, I'm making the dinner.' Prodding the chicken with the basting spoon, Abbie said, 'Except we can't have the stuffing *in* the chicken because that makes it *claggy,* apparently. So we have to cook it in a separate tin and make sure it's all crunchy on the outside, because doing it the other way is just *gross.*'

Oh dear. Cleo debated whether to remind her older sister about the endless arguments their family used to have over the optimum shape for chips, straight or crinkly, thick or thin . . .

'And I daren't get it wrong,' Abbie rattled on, 'because I've already blotted my copybook today. God knows, you'd think I'd done her washing for her out of spite. I even hand-washed her little white top because I wanted to make sure it stayed white.'

'What happened?'

'I put it in the tumble dryer and it shrank. And of course it was Georgia's favourite. So I apologised because I could see she was upset, and she told me it said on the label that it *shouldn't* be tumble-dried.'

'Oh.' Cleo's sympathies were by this time yo-yoing between Abbie and Georgia. A favourite top was a favourite top.

'So I said I'd looked for a label to see what the washing instructions were, and there wasn't one on it. And Georgia said there *had* been a label, but it had been all scratchy on the back of her neck so she'd had to cut it off, but if I'd asked her if it was OK to go in the tumble dryer, she could have told me it wasn't.'

Again, Cleo wondered whether this was the moment to recall the time she had added her school shirt to the white wash in the washing machine, forgetting the ink cartridge in the top pocket. When Abbie had seen the disastrous blue splodges all over her best white jeans, she'd hit the roof. Which was completely understandable, but the fact remained that it had *been an accident*.

'Poor you.' Instead, she gave Abbie a hug. 'Things'll settle down, though. You'll get used to each other.'

Abbie shook her head. 'I'm trying my best, but I feel like such a spare part. And we were planning to go on a cruise this summer, remember? It's always been my dream. But when I asked Tom about it yesterday, he said it might be a bit awkward now. He doesn't think we can just swan off, the two of us, and leave Georgia here on her own. But if she came along too, we'd have to book another cabin just for her, and that would almost double the price of the holiday, which would mean we couldn't afford it anyway, so basically that's that. We're not going anywhere. But hey, it's probably for the best, because who needs a lovely cruise around the Mediterranean anyway when they can stay here and spend all their hard-earned savings on some crappy old van instead?'

Her voice had spiralled up to bat-squeak level; it was almost painful to hear. Cleo's ears were saved by a car pulling up outside. She glanced out of the window. 'They're back.'

'Right. OK, calm, *calm*.' Taking deep breaths and vigorously fanning herself with the tea towel, Abbie said, 'Sorry, just having a bit of a moment. I'll be fine.'

The front door slammed and there was clattering and a squeal of laughter out in the hallway. The next moment, two voices chorused, 'Hi, honey, I'm ho-me!'

Which was what Tom always said in his jokey way, but before Cleo could smile at Abbie to signal that everything would be OK, they heard Georgia exclaim, 'Oh, wow, you live here too? That's amazing, so do I! Oh, honey, look at us, we're both *home*!'

'Home!' echoed Tom. 'And honey, do you smell cooking?'

'Honey, I do! In fact I think I smell . . . chicken!'

The next moment they burst into the kitchen together, but not before Cleo had seen the look in her sister's eyes. Once, she had been the person Tom called honey. Now, Georgia had managed to hijack that shared endearment and she and Tom were calling each other by that name. And if they hadn't meant to make Abbie feel even more left out, they'd managed it anyway. She minded a lot.

So much for telling Tom last night to be a bit more sensitive. He was clearly besotted with Georgia and unable to help himself.

'Hiya! Is it crunchy stuffing?'

'Yes, I've—'

'But you won't undercook the carrots, will you? I can't stand crunchy vegetables.'

Abbie shook her head and summoned a cheery smile. 'No, don't worry, I won't—'

'Ha! Guess where we've been?' Clapping her hands and hopping from foot to foot, Georgia blurted out, 'To look at vans! And guess what we've done?'

Abbie opened her mouth to guess. 'Did you—'

'WE'VE BOUGHT A VAN!' Launching herself at Tom, Georgia hugged him and kangaroo-jumped around the kitchen. 'Well, my dad bought me a van! Isn't that just the coolest thing ever? Tomorrow morning as soon as we've got the insurance sorted out, I'm picking up my very own van! And it's blue!'

Abbie was like a nervous bride posing for the photographer, forced to hold her smile for too long. 'Blue! How *lovely* . . .'

OK, enough. 'It wasn't just your dad, though, was it?' Cleo couldn't help herself; she had to say something. 'It was Abbie too. That money came from both of them.'

'Did it? Oh right, I didn't realise.' Shaking her head, Georgia said gaily, 'Thanks, Abbie,' and let go of Tom just long enough to give Abbie a quick embrace and a kiss on the cheek.

Well, an air-kiss close to her cheek.

'No problem, sweetheart. It's our pleasure.' Abbie gave her an affectionate hug in return, but within seconds Georgia was back at Tom's side, clutching his arm and chattering excitedly about how early tomorrow morning they'd be able to collect the van.

Cleo glanced across at Abbie, longing to say something, but Abbie was already shaking her head.

Never before had she had to work so hard to bite her tongue.

Chapter 27

Out of all the cars, the 1985 Tudor red Bentley Continental convertible was Cleo's favourite. Although she preferred it when there weren't a million bits of red and silver confetti scattered across the ivory leather seats and cream carpets.

But it was hard to be churlish when being picked up this morning had been a complete surprise for the bride, who had expected to be driven to the church in her uncle's Mazda. She had burst into tears of joy and Cleo had had to blink back a few of her own as the girl's uncle carefully lifted her out of her wheelchair and into the back of the Bentley. She'd looked beautiful too, in a crimson velvet bridal gown.

And then after the ceremony she'd driven the girl and her new husband back to the uncle's house in Downend where the modest reception was being held, and their happiness had known no bounds. Hundreds of photos had been taken in, out and in front of the Bentley and blizzards of confetti had been flung into the air in celebration. The girl's parents had died three years ago, Cleo learned, in the car crash that had put her into a wheelchair. It had always been the father's dream to take his beloved daughter to church in a red limousine on her wedding day.

Well, you'd have to have a heart of stone not to be affected by that, wouldn't you? So much unimaginable tragedy, yet today the girl and her young husband had shown it could be overcome. Sitting together, holding hands in the back of the confetti-strewn car, she'd said, 'You know what? I'm just the luckiest girl in the world.' And Cleo had believed her.

So no moaning about the confetti, even if it was the metallic sparkly kind that built up a static charge and jumped around like delinquent popping corn rather than disappearing up the vacuum cleaner nozzle like it was supposed to. It just needed a bit more effort and—

'Hi there!'

'*Ow.*' Startled by the unexpected tap on her shoulder, Cleo banged her head on the door frame and saw stars. Switching off the vacuum cleaner, she backed out of the car and turned to see who'd been the cause of her self-inflicted injury.

'Ooh, sorry, didn't mean to startle you! Are you OK?' The girl was tall, with emerald-rimmed rectangular spectacles of the arty-farty kind, and her bony frame was encased in weirdly styled grey clothes that probably cost ten times more than you'd ever guess.

'I'll live.' Cleo rubbed the back of her head. 'Can I help you?'

'Well, I do hope so. We were wondering if we could borrow your car!'

A watery sun was breaking through the clouds and the village green was deserted. Double-checking that there was no one else in the vicinity, Cleo said, 'We?'

The girl beamed. 'I work for Schofield? We've been spying on you! Well, *he* has, and once Schofield sets his mind to something there's no stopping him, so I really hope you're going to say yes. We're just over there,' she added, gesturing vaguely behind her.

'Johnny's house?' Cleo hadn't the foggiest who Schofield was, but it was an educated guess.

'That's right! We're doing a photo shoot . . . I'm Terri, by the way, Schofield's assistant . . . and he spotted your car from the upstairs window. So he's sent me over here to see if you'd lend it to us, just for a couple of hours.'

OK, it was half past one. Cleo thought fast. She didn't have to pick Casey up until four o'clock, so it was technically possible. 'Where would you want me to take you?'

'Oh, nowhere! We want the car to feature in the shoot, that's all.'

'It's for hire. I can't lend it to you.' Well, she could, but she wasn't going to. 'A hundred pounds,' said Cleo.

Terri nodded earnestly. 'Oh God, yes, of course, that's no problem at all!'

Bugger, should have asked for more. This was why she'd be rubbish working as a market trader in a Moroccan souk.

Schofield resembled a wiry little gnome. He was wearing a tartan baseball cap, crumpled black linen suit jacket and tight-fitting custard-yellow jeans. Greeting Cleo like a long-lost relative, she could only be grateful he wasn't.

'Darling, you're a life saver. I was having a *nightmare*.' He even sounded like a gnome. And his baseball cap was too big for him. Behind him, Johnny's raised eyebrows signalled that Schofield wasn't the only one having the nightmare. They were clearly in the presence of An Artistic Type.

'You see what I was aiming for? Silver, grey, white . . . all mono-chrome.' Schofield was now leaping around, framing the scene with his hands: Johnny, in a white shirt and grey combats, working in the huge white room on the silver steel sculpture of a stallion rearing into the air. And in the background, through the French windows, a grey and white garden utterly devoid of colour and iced with . . .

Hang on a minute.

Snow?

Observing her double-take, Johnny said drily, 'We had a snow-making machine here earlier. They sprayed the whole garden. It's papier mâché.'

'I know that.' Honestly, did he think she was stupid?

'White . . . grey . . . *monochrome*,' intoned Schofield. 'But then we started the shoot and there was something missing. Something crucial . . . *vital* . . . and I couldn't figure out what it was that I needed. Until I looked out of the upstairs window and saw . . .'

'My Tudor red Bentley Continental convertible.'

'Yes! *Yes!* You're going to park it over there, behind those trees . . . and it's the juxtaposition of the horse,' Schofield indicated the rearing steel stallion, 'and the horse*power*,' he flung his arms out to indicate where the car would be. 'You see? D'you see it now?' His too-big baseball cap slid sideways over one ear as he nodded excitedly. 'Do you *see*?'

Cleo nodded. He was barking mad. 'Yep.'

It took ten minutes of driving back an inch, forward two inches . . . 'No, no, back again, just a *smidge* more,' before the Bentley was finally parked to Schofield's satisfaction and the shoot was able to recommence. Discovering that she was required to stay in case it needed moving again, Cleo was secretly delighted. She'd never seen a photo shoot in action before. This one, for a feature in a glossy magazine, was set to continue for hours and the attention to detail was mind-boggling. In addition to Schofield-the-hyperactive-gnome there was his assistant Terri, a stylist called Lorna (orange jumpsuit, turquoise hair, chainmail tank top), a hair and make-up artist called Mike (shaven head, no make-up) and the journalist conducting the interview, whose name was Roz.

Coming over to join her during a break in proceedings, Johnny murmured, 'Can you believe this? I thought they'd turn up, take a few snaps and it'd all be over in five minutes.'

'Oh no no no.' Cleo kept a straight face and shook her head slowly, à la Schofield. 'It takes longer than that to find the right . . . juxtaposition.'

'You're so right. I had no idea. Why are you looking at me like that?'

'Are you wearing hairspray?'

'No!'

She peered more closely. 'Make-up?'

'Bugger off, no I am not.'

'So why do you have a hair and make-up artist?'

'I don't. He's here for Roz. She wants to be photographed interviewing me.'

Mike, sorting through his boxes of cosmetics, glanced up and saw them looking over at him. Reaching for a brush and a pot of loose powder he said hopefully, 'Ready for some of this?'

'No thanks,' said Johnny.

'Sure? Just to take the shine off?'

'Quite sure, thanks.' While Schofield was scampering up and down a stepladder checking potential angles, Johnny said to Mike, 'Is he always like this?'

'God, yes. He's pretty chilled today. The last shoot I worked on with him, we ended up in Regent's Park with three supermodels in couture gowns surrounded by a dozen pissed-up old tramps glugging cans of Tennants Extra.' His lip quivered at the traumatic memory. 'And they *all* wanted make-up.'

'Ha.' Roz perched on a chair next to Johnny. 'We did one last year and he made Terri go and bribe a female traffic warden to come back to the studio. Next thing she knew, he had the woman lying on the ground with this Oscar-winning actor holding a steering wheel and standing over her with one foot on her chest. He even had a title for the picture. Driving Over Miss Daisy.'

'I heard about that!' Cleo remembered reading something about it in the paper. 'Didn't the woman end up losing her job?'

Roz nodded. 'Which was really sad, of course. And completely unfair.' She paused. 'Except, hey, she was a traffic warden, so who's bothered?'

'Right, everyone back in position.' Schofield was now dangling from the stepladder like a monkey. 'Johnny, over to the right of the horse, darling, then I'll tell you just where to go.'

'Snap,' Johnny murmured under his breath.

'Only a couple more hours,' Roz consoled him.

'You know what?' Mike gave his pudgy stomach a slap. 'I'm starving. Terri? Terri! We need food.' Just in case Terri didn't understand, Mike cartoon-mimed eating with a knife and fork.

'OK, right, no problem.' Pressing a button on her phone, Terri said efficiently, 'Hi, Terri here, we're ready now.' She switched off the phone, looked over at Cleo. 'Are you a vegan?'

'No.'

'Oh phew, thank goodness for that.'

Ditto, thought Cleo.

Five minutes later the doorbell went. Terri, holding up a reflector board for Schofield, called out, 'That'll be the food. Can someone get it?'

Cleo was watching the shoot, enthralled by the process. The lighting was all-important. Schofield was working away, capturing every twist and turn as Johnny manipulated the wire. It was actually fascinating, observing the way he captured the angles as—

'Someone *please*?' bellowed Schofield as the doorbell rang again.

OK, fine. Cleo rose to her feet.

'Hang on.' Schofield abruptly stopped snapping and narrowed his eyes at the Bentley through the French windows. 'We need a . . . a . . . chauffeur.'

'Fabulous idea,' breathed Terri.

'You.' He swung round to Cleo. 'Do you have a chauffeur's hat?'

'Um . . . yes. At home.' Yay, he was going to ask her to be in the photos, she could have her hair and make-up done, people she knew would actually see her in a glossy magazine . . .

'Be an angel and go and fetch it,' said Schofield.

Cleo opened the front door and saw Fia standing there with a huge covered tray. Behind her, holding another tray, was Georgia.

Fia was visibly taken aback. 'What are you doing here?'

Ha, this felt so good. 'They're using me in the photo shoot.'

'Oh God, you lucky *thing*,' squealed Georgia. 'Can we stay and watch?'

'Terri came over and ordered a load of food earlier.' Fia, who didn't normally wear make-up during the day, was wearing a ton of it today. 'They're ready for it now; shall we take it on through?'

'Go ahead. I just need to pick something up from home.'

'Is Johnny looking hot?'

Cleo did a double take; the question had come from Georgia. '*Excuse* me?'

'Fia wants to know. She's been piling on the mascara like nobody's business.' Giving Fia a nudge, Georgia added mock-lasciviously, 'She's really hoping it's a naked photo shoot.'

Chapter 28

Honestly, talk about shameless. It took Cleo less than five minutes to fetch the seldom-worn chauffeur's cap from the top shelf of her wardrobe, give it a quick dust with her sleeve and hurry back across the green to Ravenswood. Letting herself in, she found the food laid out in the kitchen, Mike and Roz piling fajitas, crostini and triangles of frittata on to plates and Fia and Georgia in the drawing room, avidly observing the shoot.

Cleo said, 'Don't you have to get back to the pub?'

'It's two thirty. We've stopped serving.' Fia could barely tear her eyes away from Johnny. 'Anyway, I asked the photographer guy if we could stay and he said it was fine. He likes an audience.'

Honestly, she was ogling Johnny like some kind of groupie. Where was her pride? 'Yes, well. Just make sure you don't get in anyone's way.' Cleo turned to Georgia, her nearly-niece. 'And how come you were in the pub anyway? I thought you were supposed to be setting up a business.'

'I *am*.' Georgia was indignant. 'Yesterday I got a thousand cards printed. I've been out delivering them since seven o'clock this morning. I popped into the Hollybush to give out some more, and Fia needed a hand carrying the food over here. Plus, I thought

Johnny might be interested in my service.' Delving into her denim jacket pocket, she produced a fat envelope and took out two blue and white business cards. 'Here, you can have one too. Aren't they great?'

Cleo scanned the card, which stated:

> Never fear, Georgia the Ironing Genie is Here
> To grant all your Ironing Wishes!
> You won't believe how cheap I am!

This startling pronouncement was followed by a phone number and web address.

'You see, people throw flyers away, but they're far more likely to keep a card, pin it up on their cork board. And I set up the website yesterday.' Modestly, Georgia said, 'It's brilliant.'

Oh God. 'You can't put that,' said Cleo.

'Yes I can.'

'Sweetheart, you can't.'

'She can't what?' Johnny joined them while Schofield set up the next shot.

Wordlessly Cleo handed him the card.

'See?' said Georgia when Johnny burst out laughing. 'He gets it!'

'He doesn't *get* it. He's laughing at what you've written.'

'And he's paying attention to it. Far more than if it was just some boring old *ordinary* business card. It stands out from the crowd,' Georgia explained. 'And it's going to make some people think I'm probably a bit thick, so if I say I'm doing the ironing on the cheap, that means it's going to be *really* cheap, which in turn makes them think they'll be getting a bargain.'

'Excellent.' Johnny nodded, clearly impressed. 'Smart move. Well done you.'

'They're going to be phoning up asking what other services you provide,' said Cleo.

'And I'll tell them I only do ironing.'

'Right, where's the girl with the hat? Ah, there you are.'

This was it, her big moment. As Schofield made his way over, Cleo put the cap on and struck a modest pose. She'd never had her make-up done by a professional before. If she sucked her cheeks in, would it give her face that classy, sculpted look?

'Perfect.' Removing the navy peaked cap from her head, he examined it from all angles. 'Perfect, perfect, *yes*.'

'Shall I go and see Mike?'

'What for?'

'So he can do my face?'

Schofield said blankly, 'Why would he want to do that?'

'Well . . .' Honestly, was he *that* artistic? Had he forgotten already? 'You wanted a chauffeur in the shoot, remember? You asked me to go and get my cap.'

'I know I did. But I don't want you to be the chauffeur.' He looked at her askance as if she'd just sprouted a unicorn's horn, and over his shoulder Cleo saw hope flare in Fia's amber eyes. Before Schofield went and spoiled it all by announcing, 'I want Mike.'

Mike raised an eyebrow and carried on stuffing tortilla into his mouth. It evidently wasn't the first time he'd been corralled into a shoot. 'Two hundred, cash in hand.'

Damn, she knew she should have charged more for the Bentley.

'Unless, hang on . . .' Schofield was gazing out at the car, lost in thought. 'Or we could try something else, we could *add another layer* . . .'

'No more snow,' Terri interjected worriedly. 'They've taken the snow-making machines away.'

'Not snow. I'm talking about adding another layer to the story.'

212

He narrowed his eyes at the Bentley and slowly began to nod. Then he turned to look with fresh interest at Cleo.

Yes, yes, he wanted her to be in it after all! Her heart was still racing in her chest when she saw the interest fade and his intense gaze switch to Fia. Cleo saw Fia react in exactly the same way. Then at last . . .

'*You*,' Schofield pronounced, abruptly seizing Georgia by the shoulders. 'We see the chauffeur in the limousine, being seduced by a beautiful young girl. But the sculptor is so involved, so . . . lost in his own world of creation that he's *oblivious* to what's going on in the car behind him . . . ha, yes, perfect!'

'I'm not seducing anyone,' said Georgia flatly.

Fia blurted out, 'I will!'

Ignoring her, Schofield focused on Georgia. 'I'm not asking you to have sex with the man . . .'

'Thank Christ for that,' murmured Mike.

'Look, he's sitting back in the driver's seat and you're about to kiss him. You'll be arching over him, your mouths a few inches apart.'

'Clothes on?'

'Oh yes. Clothes definitely on.'

'Three hundred pounds.'

'Two hundred.'

'No way.'

'OK, three.'

'Deal.' Georgia beamed and high-fived him. 'Cool! That's, like, the same as ironing two hundred shirts!'

For the next forty minutes Cleo and Fia sat and watched Schofield take hundreds more shots of Johnny at work while Mike and Georgia cavorted and nearly-kissed in the background.

'It's her hair,' Fia muttered. 'That's the only reason he chose her, because she's so blonde.'

Which could well be true, but it was still galling to have yearned to be involved in something, then spurned in favour of someone else. Like being picked last for hockey.

'God, don't you just love watching him work?'

Cleo helped herself to another slice of frittata. 'Who, Schofield?'

'Johnny.' Fia exhaled. 'He's just . . . so amazing.'

'He definitely thinks he is.'

'Ooh dear.' Roz, waiting to interview Johnny and with her hair in rollers in readiness for their photos together, said, 'Is there a history between you two?'

'No. I'm just talking about men like him.' He might have been away from Channings Hill for years, but they had all heard the stories about Johnny's escapades from his father; never one to shy away from an entertaining anecdote and wickedly indiscreet, Lawrence had kept the village up to date in that respect. Glancing at Fia, Cleo said, 'Like Will too. They're the same type. Men who think they can have anyone they want, do anything they like.'

Fia was still fixated on Johnny. 'He can do anything he likes to me. I wouldn't complain.'

'But that's exactly what I mean. He *would*. And you *wouldn't* complain. And you'd end up getting hurt.'

'So?'

Roz said playfully, 'I think she's trying to say, it doesn't always have to be the romance of the century. Sometimes all a girl wants is a bit of fun.'

'You're exactly right.' Fia nodded vigorously. 'And God knows, after the time I've had, I reckon I deserve some.'

Roz laughed. 'Good on you! If I wasn't happy with my chap, I'd be tempted myself.'

Honestly, Fia was a lost cause. Cleo jumped as her phone beeped. Three thirty.

'Ten more minutes,' she called across to Schofield, 'then time's up.'

Schofield finished in five. He paid Georgia in cash and she almost exploded with happiness. 'I could do this for a living!'

'No you couldn't.' He was busy poring over the photos on his laptop.

'Look, if you ever need me again just give me a call. Seriously.' She handed him one of her business cards. 'I can come up to London. Or anywhere you like. I could be your muse!'

Schofield glanced at her over the top of his glasses. 'Don't take this the wrong way, but you're too short to be anybody's muse. But you did a good job today,' he flashed her a brief smile. 'Thanks.'

'I'm five foot six. Kate Moss is only five seven. I could *think* myself tall.'

'I think you'll find she's Kate Moss. And you're not.'

'It's OK, I know what you're saying. My knees aren't knobbly enough. Ooh, that's a good one.'

Cleo, behind her, peered over Georgia's shoulder at the photo currently dominating the screen. In it, Johnny's face was half in shadow, his hair falling over his forehead, and he was looking particularly menacing and hawk-like.

'Yep.' Schofield nodded approvingly and tagged it.

'Not very flattering,' observed Cleo.

Joining them, Johnny slung an arm across her shoulder. 'I'm not interested in being flattered.' He gave a squeeze. 'But it's sweet of you to care.'

She flushed. 'I don't care. I'm just saying.'

'And flattery's not my thing. It's all about character for me,' said Schofield. 'If anything, the good-looking ones are the hardest to shoot because their looks are a distraction. You have to work to get people to see past the outer layer.'

'And they're usually rotten underneath, because they've never had to try to be nice. Sorry.' Georgia realised her gaffe then defiantly tossed back her hair. 'But it's true. Trust me, all my life I've watched my mum chase after good-looking men with crappy personalities. They just treat her like rubbish and she ends up getting kicked in the teeth every time.' She paused, saw the looks on their faces. 'OK, not literally kicked in the teeth. But you know what I mean.'

Which went some way towards explaining why she was so mad keen on Ash. And who was to say she wasn't right to be? Well, apart from the slight drawback that Ash didn't appear to reciprocate her interest, possibly because he was in the grip of a crush on Fia.

Who, in turn, only had eyes for the star of today's photo shoot.

And as for *herself* . . . oh, forget it. Cleo jangled the keys to the Bentley; she had an annoying Australian has-been to pick up. Honestly, life would be so much less stressful if only getting people successfully paired off didn't have to be so complicated.

Chapter 29

Ash stared at his reflection in the mirror. Jesus, what was the matter with him? What was happening to his *face*?

Perspiration prickled at the back of his neck as he psyched himself up to try again. It had been bad before, but never this bad. OK, he might not have many best features in the physical sense, but his smile had been one of them. And most of the time it was fine. It wasn't something you even thought about doing, was it? You just smiled at someone and it improved your face. He even had photographic proof, for God's sake. He was perfectly capable of smiling in a normal, natural fashion.

That is, so long as Fia Newman wasn't anywhere in the vicinity. In which case the muscles refused to contract in their usual way and went into some kind of awful rictus serial-killer grimace instead.

Ash took a deep breath and had another go. The prickling increased; there it was again, as he'd known it would be. Like impotence, once you'd experienced failure, the fear of it recurring never left you and the more likely it was to happen the next time, and the next . . .

OK, stop. Thinking about impotence when you hadn't yet

worked out how to smile in an acceptable manner was like worrying about your first triathlon before you'd even learned to swim.

'Great show this morning,' said Frank, taking his order for chicken curry. 'Loved all that stuff about the nun.'

'Thanks.' See? When it was Frank he could smile away, no problem. Then Deborah joined them and he did another one. Practice made perfect.

Deborah said cheerfully, 'Did Frank tell you about the nun thing? He was laughing so hard he snorted coffee out of his nose.'

'You could go on *Britain's Got Talent* with that,' said Ash.

'Chicken curry for Ash, love.' Frank waylaid Fia as she emerged from the kitchen and Ash felt the muscles in his face begin their familiar contortion. Jesus, this must be how it felt to turn into the Incredible Hulk. OK, just ignore it, ignore it and power on through, distract her with something else . . . yes, that's it, distract her with your trademark lightning wit and dazzling charisma . . .

'How about you? Did I make stuff come out of your nose too?'

Fia stared at him. So did Deb. There was a stunned silence that probably lasted a second or two but felt more like twenty. Great; probably the largest number of words he'd managed to string together while directly addressing her and *this* was what he'd come out with.

'Sorry, sorry.' Ash felt a great whoosh of heat shoot up his neck. 'I didn't mean that. We were talking about something on my show this morning . . . the stripping nun . . . don't know if you heard it . . . ?'

'No,' said Fia evenly. 'I didn't.'

'Oh. Well, it was funny.' He didn't mean to sound so defensive; it just came out that way, probably as a result of his clenched muscles.

She gave him a cool look. 'Was it?'

Frank said, 'Fia doesn't listen to your show. She's into Carmen Miranda and all that malarkey.'

A happy mental image flashed into Ash's mind, of Fia scantily clad and dancing saucily towards him with an explosion of fruit on her head.

'*Carmina Burana*,' Fia corrected him. She smiled slightly. 'I like classical music.'

God, bloody classical. Ash nodded. 'Yeah? Me too.'

Her look of surprise said it all. 'Really?'

What, did she think he was too thick to appreciate it? Too much of a heathen? 'I do,' said Ash.

'How about opera?'

'*Love* opera.'

Fia looked as if she didn't believe him. Ash shrugged defiantly, as if he didn't care whether she did or not.

'What's your favourite?' There was a note of challenge in her voice.

'*Madame Butterfly*.' Ha, take *that*.

'By?'

'Puccini.' *And that.* 'Giacomo Puccini,' he casually added for good measure.

'What else did he compose?'

'*La Bohème. Tosca. Manon Lescaut.*' With knobs on.

'Wow.' Grudgingly impressed, Fia said, 'Didn't have you down as an opera lover.'

Keeping a straight face was so much easier than trying to execute a smile that wouldn't frighten the horses. In the same vein, pretending to be someone else was definitely easier than trying to be himself. Channelling Roger Moore as James Bond, Ash raised one eyebrow and heard himself drawl, 'Oh, I'm full of surprises.'

Another stunned silence. Frank frowned and said doubtfully, 'Are you trying to sound like . . . Roger Moore?'

For fuck's sake. 'I could give you the answer to that question,' said Ash. 'But then I'd have to kill you.'

The smiles were uncertain. It wasn't remotely funny. Maybe he should kill himself and put them all out of their misery.

'Anyway, I'd better get on!' Breaking the silence, Fia said brightly, 'I'll bring your chicken curry out in a few minutes. Rice or chips?'

Ash loved chips. Only heathens ate their curry with chips. *Telegraph*-reading, opera-loving, sophisticated men of the world – and the women who found them attractive – turned their noses up at people who ordered chips with their curry.

'Rice please,' said Ash.

'Bloody hell,' Frank barked with laughter, 'there's a first. What's up with you, lad? Trying to shift some of that flab?'

By the time Fia arrived with his food, Ash had formulated a plan.

'There you go. Chicken curry with basmati rice.'

'Thanks.' There was an awkward pause while he watched her place a bowl of poppadoms and a ramekin of mango chutney on the table. 'So the thing is, sometimes we get given tickets to . . . er, things.' Roger Moore had evidently done a bunk; Ash realised he was back to being his clumsy tongue-tied self. 'At the radio station. So if I got some for . . . you know, something classical, would you be interested, d'you think?'

Fia paused, as if struggling to work out what he was actually saying. Finally she said, 'Well, that sounds . . . brilliant. Yes, I would. Thanks.'

'Great!' Ash did his best to keep the adrenaline surge under control. 'Thanks . . . I mean, right, I'll see what comes in! Probably we'll have some in the next few days . . . because we get sent these things a *lot* . . .' Uh oh, he'd gone from tongue-tied to full-on burble in under ten seconds. 'And if you think it's something you'd like to see, that'll be great.' OK, stop *saying* that word. 'Better than us giving the tickets away in some stupid phone-in like we usually do. They always end up going to complete idiots anyway, like the drunk guy last week who won seats for *Don Giovanni* and thought he was going to see Jon Bon Jovi . . .'

'Right, well, food to cook, people to serve.' Backing away with a look of bemusement, Fia said, 'Enjoy your curry!'

Casey Kruger was on the phone in the back of the car, loudly discussing offers for a potential book deal with his agent.

'Jace, Jace, don't let *them* dictate terms! What are you, a man or a mouse? Tell them if they don't give us what we want, they can take a running jump, right? This is my story we're talking about and I know what I'm worth. Tell 'em we can always go elsewhere.'

Cleo tuned out and slowed to let a lorry pull in front of her. This morning while she'd been getting ready for work, she'd listened to one of the nation's best loved veteran actresses being interviewed on TV about her blissfully happy fifty-two-year marriage to her knighted actor husband.

'Love at first sight? Oh, good Lord no, the absolute opposite! When we first met I thought he was the most ignorant, obnoxious, awful man on the planet! If anyone had told me we'd end up marrying each other and actually staying together for the rest of our lives . . . well, I think I'd probably have thrown myself under the nearest bus!'

Which had made the interviewer laugh because as a love story it was both funny and a salutary lesson. But an about-turn like that had to be rare, surely. Cleo inwardly winced; the thought of it happening to her and Casey was too horrible to contemplate . . . that you could loathe and detest every aspect of someone's personality, then somehow change your mind and eventually discover that you loved them after all . . . well, that was downright scary. And what did it say about your judgement?

'Jace, are they the ones being difficult or is it you? Because I'm telling you now, mate, I can always find myself another agent.' Pause. 'OK. Yep. Glad to hear it.' Ending the call and closing his phone with a click and a flourish, Casey said with satisfaction, 'Ha, that shut the fucker up.'

To pass a bit of time and mildly torture herself, Cleo imagined actually *being* his other half. No squirming allowed. Physically Casey didn't do it for her, but there was no denying he was an attractive male specimen still lusted after by many, many women. And maybe, beneath the surface, he had his good points. Well, he might have them. Very tiny and well hidden beneath a hefty layer of smug-gittishness. He could turn out to be incredibly kind to animals, devoted to his frail grandmother, the kind of thoughtful man who never forgets to send birthday cards . . . he might cry at sad films, be wonderful with small children, rescue baby birds when they fell out of nests and lay cheeping piteously on the ground . . .

'Holy crap, will you look at the size of the arse on that? And she's got kids! That means some poor sod actually had sex with her! Must have been pissed out of his head!'

Cleo persevered. Maybe, deep down, he was shy and insecure and terrified of revealing his true feelings because he'd been hideously bullied at school.

'Ha, geriatrics ahead! Quick, put your foot down, extra points for the one with the tea cosy on her head!'

Or his mother had fed him on stale bread and dandelions, and kept him locked day and night in a box.

'Do you read much, Casey?' Catching his eye in the rear-view mirror, Cleo smiled pleasantly and said, 'What's your favourite book?'

There were so many ways he could confound her expectations and impress her. He could tell her he loved anything by Charles Dickens.

Or Tolstoy.

Or the biography of Nelson Mandela.

Or that book by the amazing Irish woman who'd devoted her entire life to building and running an orphanage in Vietnam.

'OK, it's the one I take with me wherever I go. My favourite book,' said Casey, 'is the little black one I keep all my favourite phone numbers in.'

He was grinning like an idiot. He *was* an idiot. If there was an iota of niceness in Casey Kruger's body, it was buried very deep down indeed.

Chapter 30

Absolutely typical. Just when you needed free tickets, the radio station turned into a ticket-free zone. The ones for this weekend's big concert at the Colston Hall had already been given away in a competition to a farmer who insisted he was a huge fan of Prokofiev. Another pair, to see the opera world's latest heart-throb tenor in London, had been awarded to an avid female fan whose winning chat-up line, should she ever be lucky enough to meet him, had been, 'Hello, does this cloth smell of chloroform to you?'

Ash sat back in his chair and tapped a ballpoint against his teeth. The sensible thing to do, clearly, would be to hang on and wait for the next lot of freebies to arrive in the office.

But patience had never been his strong point. And having managed to inveigle himself into a situation that could almost call itself a date, waiting was now out of the question. Which meant buying the tickets himself. Fine, he'd do that.

Five minutes of web-surfing later, the deed was done. The expensive deed, what with the event being sold out and having to resort to eBay. Two tickets in the stalls had just set him back over a hundred pounds. Not that he cared, but it was going to be slightly frustrating having to pretend he'd got them for free.

Oh well, couldn't be helped. Because it wasn't a proper date, was it? If Fia thought he'd paid for the tickets, she would never agree to go along with him. More to the point, he wouldn't have had the nerve to invite her in the first place. Because she thought he was an ugly, awkward, undesirable lump and he couldn't blame her. He was stuck in mental quicksand, liking her more and more and becoming progressively more troll-like and dumbstruck in her presence. Apart from those brief, even more humiliating interludes when he was burbling rubbish.

Oh well, that was the joy of going to a classical concert. At least you were meant to sit in silence while all the action was going on. And when it came to the interval, he could write a script for himself beforehand, learn it off by heart and stick to it. Yes, a script, that was the answer.

Sorted.

Frank greeted Ash and poured him a lager. 'Eating here tonight?'

Ash glanced at the menu up on the blackboard. Even the thought that it had been written there by Fia in her own hand-writing made it seem special and gave him a thrill. On the minus side, he wasn't remotely hungry. Then again he didn't want Fia to think her food wasn't good enough and feel rejected.

'She's done the steak and mushroom pie again.' Frank gave him an encouraging look. 'Your favourite, isn't it?'

What if she'd made it *because* it was his favourite? Ignoring the feeling of fullness in his stomach — dammit, he knew he shouldn't have stopped for that KFC on the way home — Ash patted his stomach and said expansively, 'How can I say no to world-beating steak and mushroom pie? Bring it on, Frankie boy, and don't spare the gravy!'

So much for looking his best in order to impress Fia. Since

she'd started working here in the kitchen he'd put on half a stone. Oh well, some sacrifices were worth making. It was a matter of give and take. From now on, he'd give breakfast a miss.

His heart physically missed a beat when Fia emerged from the kitchen carrying two plates and looking more gorgeous than ever.

'One gnocchi Dolcelatte, one steak pie.' She gazed around the tables and Ash experienced a pang, instantly wishing he'd gone for the gnocchi instead. The kind of men who ordered pie were plain, dull, stodgy and unadventurous. A man who chose gnocchi Dolcelatte was mysterious, exotic, debonair and sensational in bed.

'Yes, over here.' Gnocchi man raised a weedy arm; he looked like a put-upon civil servant who'd been overlooked for promotion his whole life.

Ash exhaled. So much for stereotyping. Feeling fractionally better, he signalled to Fia that he was the pie. By allowing her to serve gnocchi man first, he'd be able to tell her about the concert. Oh yes, it was all in the planning.

'There you go.' She flashed him a smile – polite? friendly? shy? – and put the plate down in front of him.

'Hi.' The muscles around his mouth flew into a mass panic at the prospect of smiling back and he felt them bunch themselves into a Munster-style grimace. OK, call in the distraction technique . . . 'Gnocchi sounds good.'

'Oh.' Fia paused. 'Don't you want the pie?'

'No . . . I mean *yes* . . . I just meant it *sounds* amazing . . . *gnocchi Dolcelatte* . . .' Shit, he was doing it again. And this time, unbelievably, in a ridiculous exaggerated Italian accent. Hurriedly he concluded, 'But that doesn't mean it tastes any good, does it?'

She looked at him. 'There's nothing wrong with my gnocchi.'

'I know, I know there isn't, I didn't mean it like that.' Ash shook his head and rushed on. 'Anyway, good news, I've managed to get hold of a couple of tickets for Richard Mills at the Colston Hall.'

At least he was capable of getting something right. Fia's eyes widened and she let out a squeak of excitement. 'Oh my God, for *real*?'

'For real.' Her whole face had lit up. Even her pupils had dilated. Why couldn't that happen when she looked at *him*?

Fia held her breath and clutched her chest. 'Which night?'

He might be a lot of things but he wasn't stupid. Ash said, 'Tuesday.' Because Tuesdays were her night off. This, believe it or not, was why he'd bought tickets for Tuesday night.

'Yay, fantastic! Two tickets to see Richard Mills, I can't believe you got them. You are such a star!'

Ash experienced a warm glow. This could turn out to be the best hundred and twenty quid he'd ever spent.

'You're going to get a free pudding for this.' Fia was still beaming at him. 'Cherry crumble, chocolate mousse, peach tart . . . take your pick.'

'Well, I'm just pleased you're pleased.' Truthfully, her enthusiasm had exceeded expectations. Feeling himself relax fractionally, Ash said, 'It should be good.' Good? It had been a stroke of genius. He was already envisaging the evening, picturing them together having a drink beforehand, chatting together in the crowded theatre bar, all awkwardness forgotten as they bonded in a way he hadn't—

'Oh my God, it's going to be so brilliant! Whoops, customers waiting. I'd better get back to work!'

By the time Ash had cleared his plate, he and Fia were practically married. And to think he'd imagined having to endure an evening of Richard 'Look at me, I'm such a smouldering stud' Mills would be a form of torture. They'd probably end up having the first dance together at their wedding reception to his overblown version of 'O Sole Mio'.

Which, for someone whose all-time favourite song was The Prodigy's 'Firestarter' was quite an achievement.

But that didn't matter. Because it would be *their* song, a permanent reminder of the night they'd first got together, when he'd paid a fortune for two tickets and pretended he'd got them for free . . . how she'd laughed when he finally came clean about that little ruse . . .

'Here you go.' Deborah appeared, removing his empty plate and replacing it with a bowl of hot cherry crumble. 'We've got one very excited girl in the kitchen. You've made her day.'

Confidence surged through his veins. Winking at Deb, Ash said, 'That's good to hear.'

'I didn't know you could get free tickets like that, through work.'

'Well, every now and again. These just happened to come along at the right time.'

'You're so lucky. The only perks we get in this job are crisps once they're past their sell-by date.' Deb looked hopeful. 'If you ever have any tickets for Take That going begging . . .'

'Don't hold your breath,' said Ash.

Full to bursting though he was, he somehow managed to plough through the crumble. He'd just finished it when Fia came out again, a huge grin on her face.

'Have your ears been burning? I've just called my friend Aaron to tell him what you've done. I can't believe it. I've never heard him so excited. And he says thank you so, so much.'

Ash experienced a momentary flashback to the English grammar tests that had been the bane of his life at school: Describe what is wrong with the above paragraph.

He shook his head fractionally. 'Why's he saying thank you?'

'Because I've asked him to go with me and he's completely *besotted* with Richard Mills. I mean, seriously, you have no idea. Aaron is his biggest fan!'

OK, he knew what was wrong with that one. As the words ricocheted around Ash's brain like sprayed bullets, he mentally rewound to the original conversation. Somehow a misunderstanding had arisen and—

'Which is what makes it so perfect,' Fia rattled on, 'because imagine the waste if I took someone along who thought Richard Mills was just . . . you know, OK. And then I'd end up not enjoying it as much either. But having Aaron there is going to make the whole night even more fantastic, because he loves him so much.'

Ash wanted to knock Aaron's head off his besotted, Richard-loving shoulders. Aloud he said with an edge to his voice, 'If he's that keen, I'm surprised he hasn't already bought a ticket himself.' *Tight bastard, sponging off other people, hoovering up freebies . . .* ha, except they hadn't been free, had they? Right, that was it, no way was he going to stand by like a mug and let—

'Oh, but that's the other reason it's so great, because normally he'd have been there like a shot, first in the queue. But there's no way he could afford it now,' said Fia. 'He's totally broke.'

Hmm, wonder why. Hang on, might that be because the bloke's a complete loser?

'And he so deserves to have something nice happen,' she carried on. 'It'll really cheer him up after the nightmare year he's had.'

Ash briefly closed his eyes. 'Who is this guy anyway?'

'He used to run the little picture-framing place across the road from Will's mother's shop. Aaron's lovely, always helping other people with odd jobs they can't manage to do themselves. He lived with his mum, then she got Alzheimer's and he had to spend all his time looking after her because she didn't want to go into a home. So he ended up losing the business and running up debts . . . they had to sell their bungalow and move into a tiny flat. Anyway, Aaron's mother died on Christmas Eve and he was devastated. I've been keeping in touch with him since then, just calling him every week or so to see how he is, making sure he's all right. But this is the first time he's actually sounded happy.' Fia leaned forward and for a moment grasped Ash's hand. 'Thank you. Really, you've no idea what a difference it's going to make. And it's so fantastic to be able to do something nice for him for a change.'

Oh, for *fucking* fuck's sake.

'Don't mention it.' His heart lay like a lump of cold dead meat in his chest; Ash could barely bring himself to say the words. 'My pleasure.'

Chapter 31

Parked in the side street, Cleo watched from a distance as Casey Kruger worked his way through the crowd of fans gathered on the pavement by the Hippodrome's stage door.

Although to call them a crowd was pushing it. At ten thirty on a cold and rainy evening in March, there were barely enough to form a gaggle. Cleo counted eleven and most were fans she'd seen before, the diehards who congregated there night after night and revelled in the knowledge that Casey recognised them, sometimes even greeting them by name and making them feel loved in return.

'I'm a celebrity,' Casey announced, falling into the back seat eight minutes later. 'Get me out of here.'

He made the same 'joke' every night. Weaving past the fans as they dispersed, Cleo said, 'Good night?'

'Pretty good.' He heaved a sigh. 'We sang, we danced, they applauded, they cheered, we sang some more.' Pause. 'I tried calling my ex and she hung up on me.'

'Oh dear.' *Good move, ex.*

'Then I tried to call my parents back home, but no reply.'

'Oh.'

'My dad's bald. I mean, completely.' Casey shook his head. 'Like an egg.'

'Is he?' Where was this heading?

'Yup.' He nodded morosely, rubbed his hand through his hair. 'And guess what I saw when I looked in the mirror tonight?'

Cleo negotiated the car through the city centre traffic. 'Well, if you were looking in the mirror, I'm guessing you saw . . . you?'

'Funny.' Clearly, her attempt at a joke was on a par with his. Sinking back against the leather upholstery, Casey said, 'I saw a bald spot. At the back of my head. Not totally bald.' His hand explored his scalp, searching it out. 'But it's thinning. Definitely starting to go.'

'Well, I can't see anything.' Poor guy; she had to say something to try and cheer him up.

'It's there.' Casey sounded resigned. 'Nature's way of telling you your time's up, you've had your fun, your heart-throb days are over.'

'Oh, come on, it doesn't have to be that bad.'

'No? Eight years ago I was mobbed in the streets. I had a double platinum album and sold out Wembley. And now I'm thirty-four.' Catching Cleo's eye in the rear-view mirror, he said, 'OK, thirty-*six*. And it's all downhill from here.' He paused. 'Shall I tell you how that feels? It feels like shit.'

The journey from Bristol back to Casey's hotel took twenty minutes. Cleo pulled into the courtyard and he said, 'Sorry, sweetheart. I've been a miserable sod tonight, haven't I?'

'It's allowed.' Who would have thought she could feel this sorry for Casey Kruger? He was usually so full of himself.

'It's my parents' wedding anniversary today. That's why I wanted to get hold of them.' He held up his mobile. 'Oh well.'

'You're just feeling a bit homesick. That's normal.'

'Just because it's normal doesn't make it any easier.' Switching on the interior light and twisting round so he was facing away from her, Casey tilted his head back and said, 'Have a look, will you? Can you see the bald spot? Does it really notice?'

'It doesn't. And I'd tell you if it did,' said Cleo. 'I'm very honest.'

'Ah, you're a star.' Visibly relieved, he broke into a wry smile. 'I don't suppose you'd like to come in for a drink?'

Cleo hesitated. Which would be the best way to say no?

'Go on. I promise to stop being a miserable sod.'

'It's nearly eleven. Isn't the bar about to close?' There was no way she was going up to his room.

'As long as there are people buying drinks, they stay open.' Indicating the full car park, Casey said, 'And it looks like there's plenty in there tonight.'

'I have to drive.'

'Look, if you leave now, I'm going to sit on my own in a corner of the bar, feeling homesick and crying into my beer. But if you stay for one drink,' said Casey, 'just to keep me company for twenty minutes, I'll feel better.'

The windscreen wipers swished back and forth. Rain fell out of the blackness and drummed on the roof of the car.

'Please,' said Casey.

There was a lucky parking space right next to the hotel entrance, with an overhang of honeysuckle that would shield them from the rain on their way in.

'OK.' Cleo executed a swift three-point turn and reversed into the space. 'Just the one drink.'

Except it never worked out that way, did it? One drink was never enough. Certainly not for Casey, who was now on to his fifth bottle of beer and third whisky chaser. Keeping him company,

Cleo had drunk orange juice, sparkling water, still water and an Appletize. It was thirsty work having to sit and listen to a former superstar, now relegated to being just your average bog-standard star, complain to you about how crap his life was.

But it was kind of fascinating too. And it made a change to glimpse beneath the brash, super-confident exterior. The longer they sat there in a corner of the hotel bar, the more of Casey's insecurities spilled out.

'. . . see, I should be settled down by now, married with kids, the whole shebang. I'm thirty-four . . .'

'Thirty-six,' Cleo reminded him.

'Jeez, don't say it, that's even worse. And I want to be married, I *do*.' He shook his head sorrowfully. 'But I just can't find the right girl. I don't know where I'm going wrong. Everyone I get involved with ends up selling stories about me to the papers. It's just so bloody . . . predictable.'

This was true. Then again, Casey didn't do himself any favours when it came to selecting girlfriends. The ones he went for were invariably blonde, perma-tanned, micro-skirted and pouty-lipped. Furthermore, if you were to line up a whole row of identikit pouty blondes, Casey would unerringly choose the one with 'I Sell Stories to Newspapers!' painted on the placard she was waving above her head.

'You need to find yourself a nice girl.' Cleo swirled the ice cubes around her tumbler.

'I know.'

'Who does tapestry, and flower arranging, and knows how to cook.'

'And has a hot body.'

'You see? This could be where you're going wrong.'

Casey looked offended. 'Hey, I have my standards. I don't want some ropey old dog with fat ankles and saggy tits.'

'Is that what the women in your world are divided into? WAGs with boob jobs and ropey old dogs?'

He frowned. 'That's a bit harsh. It's just a case of women I fancy and the ones I don't.' He half smiled. 'Does that sound terrible?'

'So, just out of curiosity, am I a WAG or a dog?'

He looked confused. 'Um . . .'

'OK, would you go out with someone like me? In theory?'

'God . . . well, no. S'pose not. No offence.'

'That's fine, none taken. So that makes me a dog,' said Cleo.

'No, no!'

'But you wouldn't class me as attractive, would you? Because I don't have dyed blond hair and extensions.'

Casey said defensively, 'I went out with a brunette once.'

'Relax, I'm not looking for compliments. You're not my type either. But this is interesting,' said Cleo. 'Come on, give me a few more reasons why you wouldn't be interested in me.'

He finished his beer, wiped his mouth, sat back and slowly appraised her.

'You haven't had a boob job.'

'Well spotted.'

'You should really consider it, you know. You're completely flat-chested.'

'Not completely.'

'It'd make all the difference, I'm telling you.' He indicated her shirt and jacket. 'And your clothes are pretty dull.'

For heaven's sake. 'These aren't *my* clothes, they're my uniform!'

Casey raised a sceptical eyebrow. 'So when you're off duty, do you wear skirts up to here, really low-cut tops and PVC outfits that you have to be laced into?'

'Funnily enough,' said Cleo, 'no, I don't.'

He spread his arms. 'I rest my case. Your clothes are dull.'

Why was she even bothering? He was a lost cause. Also, a thirsty one.

'Back in two minutes.' Excusing himself to visit the gents', Casey said, 'Can you be an angel and get another round in?'

'A frumpy angel?'

He grinned. 'You're not frumpy.'

'I'm quite tired though. It's late.'

'Just one more. It's good to have someone to talk to.' Sensing her reluctance, he added, 'I'll pay you if you like.'

'That's OK. I'll stay for one more.' When he'd left the bar, Cleo called the barman over. 'Fizzy water for me, please. And another whisky for Mr Kruger.' It was turning into a long tab; thank goodness she wasn't the one footing the bill.

'Double?'

'God, no.'

The barman hesitated. 'It's just that all the others have been doubles.'

Blimey, had they? Talk about packing it away. 'Just a single this time,' said Cleo. 'Stick in a bit of extra ice. He'll never notice the difference.'

Fifteen minutes later she rose to leave. Following her out to the wood-panelled reception hall, Casey said, 'You know what, babe? I've enjoyed this, being with you tonight.'

Babe. Cleo let it slide. 'You mean I'm not bad company for a frumpy girl.'

'I told you before. You're not frumpy.' Catching hold of her elbow, he swung her round to face him. 'There's something about you, babe. You've got . . . character.'

'Shall I let you into a secret? *I* don't mind being told that, but most girls would be really insulted.'

236

'I wouldn't say it to most girls. Because their characters don't tend to be that important. But you're different.'

'Yup. I don't wear PVC and I don't have gravity-defying E-cups.'

Casey laughed. 'See? You're good company. Entertaining.' Abruptly leaning back against the wall, he pulled her with him. 'Maybe I've been getting it wrong all these years . . . come here, babe . . .'

His right arm grasped her waist. For a split second his mouth clamped down on hers and alcohol fumes stung the inside of her nose. Damn, she should have seen this coming. Cursing herself for letting it happen, Cleo jerked her face away, slid sideways and ducked under the left arm propped against the wall.

And saw Johnny LaVenture watching her from the other end of the reception hall with a faint, unreadable smile on his face.

'Whoa, hey, where'd you go?' Casey took a steadying step forward and did a bewildered double-take.

'Cleo.' Acknowledging her with a nod, Johnny said, 'Fancy bumping into you here.'

Mortified at the thought of what he'd just witnessed, she straightened her jacket. 'I'm just leaving.'

'Someone you know?' Glancing over his shoulder at Johnny, Casey said, 'She's a great girl, this one. A real character.' He gave Cleo a nudge. 'Even if you do have to pay her to keep you company.'

Johnny's eyes glittered. 'How much does she charge?'

Hilarious. Ignoring him, Cleo turned back to Casey. 'Bye. I'll pick you up at four tomorrow.'

'I'd have paid more,' said Casey. 'You only had to ask.'

Chapter 32

Casey reeled back into the bar, trailing a cloud of whisky fumes in his wake. OK, time to go. Cleo left the hotel, ran down the stone steps and splashed through the puddles to the car.

The tap on the passenger window came as she was pulling out of the parking space under the dripping honeysuckle. Through the rain-dappled glass, his face looked as if it were melting.

She buzzed the window down and Johnny said, 'Hey.'

'Hey.' In the glimmering darkness he had cheekbones like Johnny Depp's.

'Off home?'

'Amazingly, yes.'

He didn't say anything, just steadily held her gaze.

'Go on then, get in,' said Cleo.

'Thanks.' He jumped into the seat next to her.

'I'm not a taxi service, you know.'

He grinned. 'You're a friend. That's even better.'

'Hm.' Cleo's stomach curled like a prodded oyster. A friend. Was she really?

'I tried four cab companies but they were all booked up for the next couple of hours. It's my own fault; should have called earlier.' Johnny raked his fingers through his damp hair. 'Never mind. You came along at the perfect time.'

'I have my uses. And just so you know, I don't charge Australian soap actors for my company.' As they drove out through the hotel's impressive iron gates, Cleo said, 'He was drunk.'

'I guessed that, when I saw him kissing you. Sorry,' Johnny raised his hands in self-defence. 'That came out the wrong way. Of course he'd want to kiss you. Who wouldn't?'

OK, what was *that* supposed to mean? 'If you're going to start taking the mickey now, you can jolly well get out and walk.'

'I'm not.' The corners of his mouth twitched. 'Anyhow, you can do better than him. What was all that about the PVC and the E-cups?'

'Nothing that would interest you. Well,' Cleo amended, 'it probably would, but never mind. What were you doing at the hotel anyway?'

'Having dinner with the Hart-Berkeleys. They want to commission a piece for their stud farm.' He paused. 'You wouldn't want to be an E-cup.'

For crying out loud. 'I know I wouldn't! How much did you overhear of our conversation?'

'Oh, a fair amount. We were sitting right behind you in the bar.'

Damn those high-backed wooden booths.

'So just out of interest, were you angling for compliments back there?'

'No.'

'Do you secretly have a thing for Casey Kruger?'

'No!'

'Sure?'

'Weren't you watching? I *escaped* when he kissed me.'

239

Johnny shrugged. 'Could have been playing hard to get.'

'Trust me, I wasn't.'

'Shame. I'd have won my bet.'

So he hadn't forgotten.

'Well, you haven't won.' Cleo's insides were back doing the squirly oyster dance and she had a horrible feeling she knew why. She didn't want Johnny to think she had any designs on Casey Kruger. If she was completely honest, and this was something she wouldn't tell another living soul, there was only one person she'd be interested in having designs on and he was currently sitting beside her in this car.

Oh God, there, she'd admitted it to herself at last. Cleo swallowed with difficulty. Her confused feelings about Johnny LaVenture had settled into something recognisable. He'd always been seriously attractive and charismatic but it had recently begun to dawn on her that personality-wise, he was also actually a lot nicer than she'd always thought. She took shallow breaths, genuinely scared by the turn events had taken. She liked him. A lot. But that still didn't mean it was a sensible idea; he might have good qualities but he was also a—

'Fox,' Johnny observed as a blur of reddish-brown fur darted across the road before diving into the undergrowth and disappearing from sight.

Which was apt, because he and the fox shared so many traits. They were both clever and confident, rapacious and sly. They knew what they wanted and they didn't stop until it was theirs. With their who-dares-wins attitude, they exerted a kind of hypnotic fascination on other, less single-minded types.

And they usually left a trail of headless chickens in their wake.

Cleo concentrated on the road ahead, dark and slick with rain. If she'd learned anything while she was growing up, it was that you didn't get involved with the human version of a fox. You didn't allow yourself to get into that situation. Because if you did, it could destroy you.

From when she was really little, she'd adored her mother's younger sister. Auntie Jean, with her dancing brown eyes and strong resemblance to the young Audrey Hepburn, had showered her with love and affection. She was always happy, laughing and carefree, like a princess living the best possible life. Cleo had vowed to be exactly like her when she grew up.

She didn't remember Auntie Jean and Uncle David first getting together, but one of her favourite childhood memories was of herself at the age of six, being a bridesmaid at their wedding. It had been a hot sunny day, she'd been wearing a shiny pink dress and matching silk rosebuds in her hair, and she'd been told off by Abbie for pretending to be a pony and galloping around the churchyard after the service.

The only other thing she really remembered about that day was cantering out of the village church hall during the reception and discovering Uncle David down the side alley kissing a woman she'd never seen before. Although he seemed to know the woman pretty intimately. Well enough, at any rate, to be investigating her bra.

Then, as she'd grown older, and without anyone actually saying anything about it, Cleo had instinctively learned that when you came home from school and Auntie Jean was sitting in the kitchen with your mum, you steered well clear. Because Auntie Jean wasn't so happy-go-lucky these days; in fact she hardly smiled at all. Instead she quite often got upset and talked on and on and on in a mixture of whispers and coded references to things that weren't for children to hear. Then she'd start crying, quietly at first, then louder and more messily, getting through tissues at a rate of knots and not even caring that her nose was running and she looked a complete mess. These were the times Cleo had most hated. Even if she'd been really desperate for a biscuit or a drink of squash, she'd refused to go into the kitchen while Auntie Jean was in one of her states. And that had been before she'd started bringing those little bottles of medicine along with her, taking them out of her handbag and adding the contents to her cups of tea.

Teacher's. That had been the name on the bottle. At the time, Cleo remembered, she had often wondered whether her Auntie Jean, who *wasn't* a teacher, should really be drinking it.

Next to her in the car, Johnny said, 'You've gone quiet.'

'Just thinking.'

'What about?'

'Foxes.' Uncle David had been a fox; good-looking, flirtatious, a real player. Back then, she had liked him because he was fun and always laughing. Now, all these years later, she recognised that he had been selfish and irresponsible, only interested in pleasing himself and not remotely bothered about the pain he inflicted on others along the way.

And God knows, he'd inflicted plenty. Uncle David liked to share himself around; affair followed affair and Auntie Jean crumbled under the pressure. Her drinking escalated and she discovered mix and match pills, knocking back tranquillisers and anti-depressants with un-gay abandon. Anything to get her through the day. Apart from the obvious solution, which would have been to leave her charming, unfaithful husband.

But leaving him didn't feature on Auntie Jean's radar. She loved him more than anything in the world. He was her life. If she didn't have Dave, she'd want to be dead.

Cleo, passing the kitchen, had overheard her saying this once, followed by her mum replying, 'Don't say that, Jean. Nobody wants to die.'

To which Jean had announced in a slurry voice, 'No? Sounds like a pretty good deal to me.'

That exchange had taken place when Cleo was ten. Just over a year later, her mother had suffered a catastrophic brain haemorrhage and had died in hospital three days later without regaining consciousness.

It had seemed so unfair that Auntie Jean, who wanted to die, was still alive. Whereas her mum, who loved every aspect of life and whom Cleo still so badly needed, was now gone.

And Auntie Jean hadn't comforted her, not even once. She'd just carried on drinking and trembling and crying. But not over the tragic loss of her sister. Oh no. About *David*.

This was when Cleo had stopped liking her once-joyful aunt and had begun to resent her instead. And at the same time she had experienced the first flickerings of fear, because this was what happened when you loved someone too much and they didn't love you back. They grew stronger and you grew weaker and more helpless. They humiliated you and you let them do it. And you ended up with no self-respect, not even caring that other people were pointing and laughing at you as you stumbled down the street with your shirt undone and your tatty underwear on show.

Which was undoubtedly entertaining for everyone else, but a lot less funny when it was your own auntie they were mimicking and laughing at.

They'd reached Channings Hill. Right, stop thinking about Auntie Jean now.

Seeing as it was still bucketing down, Cleo pulled in through the gates of Ravenswood and drove up to the house.

'Door-to-door service,' Johnny observed.

'Only because it's raining.'

'You're a star. I owe you one.'

The security lights had come on; he was giving her that indecipherable look again. Wiping her cheek, Cleo said self-consciously, 'What's wrong? Do I have something on my face?'

'Yes, you do.'

As she'd climbed into the car a great swathe of wet honeysuckle had brushed against her hair. *Oh God, please don't let it be a slug . . .*

'This.' He raised his hand and with the back of his index finger touched the big freckle beneath her right eye. 'Your beauty spot.'

Phew, not a slug then. 'It's a freckle.'

'D'you know something? I've always really liked it.' Johnny nodded slowly. 'That's a great freckle you have there. Makes you look like Pierrot.'

Oh God, he had *no* idea what he was doing to her insides when he touched her face like that.

Either that or he knew exactly what he was doing. Which, let's face it, was infinitely more likely. She concentrated on keeping her breathing even, not betraying her emotions. Letting Johnny know how she felt about him would definitely be a terrible idea.

'OK. Well, bye.'

'Thanks for the lift.'

She managed an easy smile. 'No problem.'

Johnny climbed out of the car, then leaned back in through the open door and said, 'I'd have given you a goodnight kiss, but you didn't seem to enjoy the one you got earlier.'

'Not much, no.'

He grinned. 'I couldn't cope with the rejection.'

Cleo's mouth was dry; her lips were actually tingling at the thought of what she'd just missed. Aloud she said, 'Good job then that you didn't try.'

Chapter 33

The doorbell rang while Abbie was in the kitchen. Answering it, she found Fia Newman on the doorstep.

'Hi.' Fia held up a black bin bag. 'Frank's rushed off his feet so he asked me to bring his stuff over for Georgia. Is she in?'

'Yes, I'm here! Come on through!'

Abbie bit her lip; she knew she should be glad Georgia was working, but she was beginning to feel like an intruder in her own home. Showing Fia into the living room, she breathed in the steamy smells of Lenor and spray starch. Freshly ironed shirts, trousers and dresses were festooned around the place, arranged on hangers and dangling from picture rails and pieces of furniture. The radio, tuned to BWR, was blasting out. Piled up on the sofa were bags of clothes still waiting to be dealt with. In the centre of the room, wearing a Snoopy vest top and a pair of stripy pink and white shorts, was Georgia, working away like a thing possessed. True to her word, she had indeed turned out to have a talent for ironing; her work was speedy and meticulous.

'Wow, look at you.' Fia was visibly impressed. 'How much stuff have you got there?'

'Loads.' Beaming, Georgia expertly flipped over the shirt on the ironing board and smoothed out one of the sleeves. 'I'm under-cutting all the other ironing services in the area, so it's all flying in. Isn't it great?'

It was great, thought Abbie, so long as you didn't want to sit down with a cup of coffee and watch the TV in peace. The living room was pretty much off limits these days. If there was a programme she or Tom particularly wanted to see, they had to watch it on the temperamental portable upstairs.

'Isn't she amazing?' Fia was in a chatty mood. 'To be honest, I never thought she'd do it. Most teenagers wouldn't be bothered.'

'Oh, she's a hard worker.' Abbie wondered how Fia would feel if Georgia were to set up her ironing board in the middle of the pub.

'Right, where shall I put Frank's stuff?'

'Over there by the fireplace. I'll have it all done by tomorrow night. Abbie, can you do a label?'

Abbie reached for the roll of sticky labels, scribbled Frank's name on one and slapped it on to his bag.

'You're going to be working all day and night at this rate.' Fia watched as Georgia finished the shirt she'd been ironing, lovingly hung it up and pulled the next one from the basket at her feet. 'Oh, I know who that belongs to!'

Georgia gave the crumpled shirt an ecstatic hug. 'It's Ash's new one. His body has been inside it. This material has had actual physical contact with his *chest*.'

Abbie said by way of apology, 'She has a bit of a thing about Ash.'

'I know.' Fia looked baffled. 'Everyone in Channings Hill knows.'

'It's not a "bit of a thing".' Georgia lovingly wrapped the arms of the shirt around her neck and dreamily began to dance along to the radio. 'It's true love.'

'One-sided love,' Abbie pointed out. 'Ash isn't interested.'

'Yet. But I'm going to win him over. With my wit and my charm and my dazzling skill with an iron.'

Fia was clearly amused. 'It's not as if he's even good-looking. He can't afford to be too picky.'

'Exactly.' Georgia nodded vigorously in agreement. 'I've already told him that.'

Poor Ash. Abbie wondered how he'd feel if he knew he was being discussed like this.

'I mean, who's he holding out for?' demanded Fia. 'Angelina Jolie?'

'He'd better not be. Because if she does turn up,' said Georgia, 'I'll fight her for him.'

'Angelina Jolie has more muscles than Rambo.' Abbie couldn't help herself. 'She'd win.'

Waiting in the car for him, Cleo saw that Casey Kruger wasn't pining for her too desperately. He had company tonight. When he finished signing autographs after the show, he reached for the hand of a woman who'd been lurking in the shadows and brought her over.

'Heya, Cleo, how ya doing? Bringing a friend back with me tonight.'

A blonde friend, naturally. If a little older than she'd have expected. Discreetly studying the woman as they settled themselves into the back seat, Cleo guessed that she was in her mid-thirties. She also noted the low-cut top, the spectacular cleavage, the acrylic nails. Undeniably attractive, Casey's new friend was without doubt the best of the bunch that had been hanging around the stage door this evening. And she hadn't seen her there before. She could have been sitting in the front row tonight and Casey had spotted her during the show. Maybe he'd caught her eye a few times, then winked and smiled and indicated discreetly that should she want to meet him afterwards, her luck would be in.

He'd probably done it hundreds of times over the years.

Then the woman caught Cleo's eye in the rear-view mirror and she smiled, a charming friendly smile. Cleo was instantly ashamed. Who was to say she wasn't a genuine old friend of Casey's? They might have known each other for years and she wasn't a groupie at all.

Before they reached the outskirts of Bristol, Casey said, 'Can we pull over at those shops up ahead? Outside the off-licence?'

'No problem.' *What a skinflint.*

'Not being tight,' Casey went on, 'but the room service charges at that hotel are just mental.'

Cleo stopped the car beneath a street lamp and he touched his companion's thigh. 'Won't be two minutes. What would you like to drink, um . . . ?'

'My name's Maria. And white wine would be lovely, thanks. New Zealand Sauvignon if they have it.'

Casey nodded and clambered out of the car. Looking through the shop window, Cleo saw that the off-licence was busy and there was a queue at the till. Oh well. It wasn't up to her to start up a pass-the-time conversation with Casey Kruger's 'friend'.

Except, had he really scanned all the females in the front row of the stalls, picked her out and persuaded her with a wink and suggestive tilt of his head to spend the night with him?

From the back of the car, Maria said easily, 'So what's this hotel like? Pretty nice, I'd imagine.'

'*Really* nice.' Cleo shifted sideways in her seat, noted the absence of a wedding ring. 'Fourteenth century. And the grounds are beautiful too.'

She was met with an engaging grin. 'Don't suppose I'll be getting to see much of the grounds, will I?'

There wasn't really any answer to that. 'Well, anyway, the hotel's great.'

Maria said drily, 'Although the room service is expensive.'

You couldn't help warming to her. And Casey, still busy selecting wine, would be a while yet. Indicating him with a tilt of her head, Cleo said, 'Is it the first time you've seen him in the show?'

'Who, Casey? I haven't seen the show. Can't stand musicals. So how long have you been doing this job?' Smoothly the subject was changed.

'Three years.'

'And is it good fun? Boring?'

'Some of each.'

'Like any job, I guess.'

'It has its ups and downs.' Cleo wondered what she did for a living.

'And you live here in Bristol?'

'Actually, no. I'm not too far from Casey's hotel. It's a village called Channings Hill—'

'Oh, I know that place!'

'Yes?' Casey could do a lot worse than this one; she might be ten years older than the girls he usually went for, but she was actually really likeable. 'Have you been to the Hollybush?'

Maria shook her head. 'I knew someone who lived there, a friend of mine. His name was LaVenture.'

Oh God, not another one. Was there anyone he hadn't '*known*'? Deflating, Cleo said, 'Johnny.'

'No, Lawrence.'

'Oh! Johnny's dad!' That was so much better. 'How d'you know Lawrence?'

Maria shrugged. 'We were friends.'

'He was quite a character. Everyone loved him.' Cleo stopped abruptly; maybe she hadn't heard. 'Um . . . OK, I don't know if you know this, but I'm afraid Lawrence died a few months ago.'

'Yes.' Maria was already nodding. 'I knew.'

It was on the tip of Cleo's tongue to find out if she'd heard about the circumstances of his death, when something about the set of Maria's mouth stopped her.

The penny slowly . . . finally . . . dropped.

Oh my God.

Their eyes met for a prolonged moment. At last Maria tilted her head and said cheerfully, 'Got there in the end, then.'

'It was you!' Cleo couldn't believe she'd been so slow to catch on.

'Dear old Lawrence. He didn't suffer.' Maria's eyes danced. 'Mind you, he gave me a bit of a fright.'

In the off-licence, Casey was now handing over his credit card at the till.

'I thought you were a groupie!'

'Casey Kruger's biggest fan? Give me a break!' Maria looked appalled. 'The Kaiser Chiefs, now they're my kind of music. Anyway, groupies don't get paid.'

She had a point. Fascinated, Cleo longed to talk money. How much was Casey paying for the pleasure of her company tonight? A fair amount, presumably, if he was reduced to buying their alcohol from Threshers.

But no, that was a question she couldn't ask. Instead she said tactlessly, 'We wondered if you'd turn up for Lawrence's funeral.'

Maria shook her head. 'I was invited. I'd have liked to, really. Lawrence was a regular client of mine, and I was very fond of him. But it would've caused a stir.'

'It would. Who invited you?'

'Lawrence's son, Johnny.'

'You met him, then?'

'No, but he phoned me. After my interview with the coroner. He sounded really nice.' Interested, Maria said, '*Is* he nice?'

Cleo paused. OK, this was a potential scenario she definitely didn't need to envisage. 'He has his good moments. And his bad ones.'

'Bit of a looker, is he? Like his dad?'

Cleo said casually, 'He's all right. Then again, lots of people think Casey Kruger's gorgeous.' Relieved, she saw that Casey was heading towards them, bulging plastic carriers in each hand.

'Phew, sorry about that. Took longer than I thought.' The carriers clanked as he climbed in. 'Had to sign a load of autographs.'

'No problem.' Crikey, how much had he bought? There had to be a dozen bottles in there.

'Thought I might as well stock up. Don't you just hate it when you run out of stuff to drink?' Settling himself into the back of the car and giving Maria's knee a seductive squeeze, Casey said, 'Well, that's not going to happen to us, is it? We're going to have a *grrrreat* night, yes sirreee!'

He was already unscrewing the top of a bottle of Scotch and noisily glugging it back. Cleo restarted the engine. For a split second, her eyes met Maria's in the mirror.

God, imagine having to submit to the sexual demands of someone who made your skin crawl.

It didn't bear thinking about.

However much Maria was getting paid, it wasn't enough.

Chapter 34

'There you go. Enjoy!' As Fia put the plate down on the table in front of him, Ash caught a waft of faint but delicious perfume. 'And don't forget, this is on me.'

It was a bowl of spaghetti Bolognese. Normally a statement like that would provoke a joke from him, but he was too busy being tongue-tied and awkward in Fia's presence. Just for a change. Not to mention thinking that his on-the-house spaghetti Bolognese had in fact cost him one hundred and twenty pounds.

It was Wednesday lunchtime. Last night Fia and her oh-so-deserving friend Aaron-the-do-gooder had gone to the Colston Hall *on his tickets*, and so far she had told him seventy-three times that it had been the best concert she'd ever seen in her life.

OK, maybe not seventy-three. But she was certainly rubbing it in.

'You know, he was just so . . . *fantastic*.' Fia shook her head, lost in admiration for Richard Mills's talent, good looks and captivating stage presence.

Ash wondered how it would feel to hear her say those words about him.

'Even my hands are sore.' She held them out to show him the palms. 'They're still burning from clapping so much.'

He forced a smile, willing himself not to imagine those warm hands roaming over his body . . . no, no, now he was just torturing himself, don't even go there, she'd probably leap away in disgust and run a mile.

'And Aaron's still on cloud nine. He's phoned me up three times today already!'

'Good. That's . . . good.' Ash twirled a mound of spaghetti around his fork, raised it to his mouth and leaned forward, managing to catch a single spaghetti strand between his teeth while the rest promptly unravelled and dropped back on to the plate. '*Shit.*' He snatched up his paper napkin and rubbed at the orange splashes on the front of his shirt.

'You've got a bit on your chin too,' Fia said helpfully.

'Oh. Thanks.'

She pointed. 'And your ear.'

'Right.' *Fucking* uncontrollable spaghetti.

'Well, I'd better get back to work.' Gaily, Fia turned and swung into the kitchen, singing a line from one of the arias Richard Mills had performed last night.

Ash exhaled and put down his sauce-spattered napkin. Was this rock bottom? Had he finally hit it?

Because if he had, maybe it was time to take that step and call Losers Anonymous.

Hi, my name is Ash Parry-Jones and when I'm at work I'm funny, smart and super-articulate without even trying . . . I have thousands upon thousands of fans who tune in to my show every morning because they know I'll entertain them and brighten their day.

And outside work I'm a complete dick.

★   ★   ★

The trouble with having a bit of a clear-out downstairs and hauling three bin bags of assorted clutter up into the loft was that you never actually dumped them and came straight back down again. While you were there, you always somehow managed to spot something you hadn't seen for years and get sidetracked.

Cleo, sitting cross-legged with her back to a bundle of blankets, had been up in the loft for the past two hours. She'd looked through a suitcase of her dad's favourite clothes. Losing her mum at eleven had been devastating, but she knew how lucky she'd been to have her loving, gentle father, who had become two parents rolled into one and done such a good job, along with Abbie, of bringing her up. One day she'd feel able to donate his old woolly jumpers and faded checked shirts to the charity shop, but not quite yet.

She had then examined a cardboard box containing all the books she had adored as a child; OK, the charity shop definitely couldn't have these because one day she planned on reading them to her own children, whether they wanted to hear them or not.

And there was another box filled with jigsaws, which she really should chuck out; God knows, no twenty-first-century child would be seen dead doing a jigsaw.

She'd also been through a tin of her mother's costume jewellery, a shoebox filled with old postcards and a box file of graffiti-strewn school exercise books and end-of-year reports. Reading them had brought the memories – not all of them great – flooding back. Mr Elliott had written, 'If Cleo were to pay more attention to History and less to Boyzone, progress might be achieved.' Miss Barlow had put, 'On the tennis court, Cleo is enthusiastic.' Which was a polite way of saying unable to hit the ball over the net, but good at picking it up again. And Mr Haines, her maths teacher, had described her as, 'Easily distracted during lessons, usually by herself.'

Which was just sarky. It wasn't her fault she hadn't been able to get to grips with quadratic equations.

Anyway, karma had come good in the end. Two years later, Mr Haines had been stopped in his car by the police and charged with driving without due care and attention. Whilst wearing nothing but a satin corset, stockings and lacy suspenders.

Ouch, her foot had gone numb. Cleo shifted position, bent forward and reached for the next packet of photos in the trunk in front of her.

This was what had kept her up here for the last hour. Her father had never gone anywhere without a camera. He'd taken endless photographs throughout her childhood and at the time she'd quite often wished he wouldn't. Back then, it had been a source of embarrassment and shame.

But almost two decades later, the embarrassment factor had faded and she was glad he'd done it. Village life had been captured to a T and it was brilliant to see everyone looking as they'd looked all those years ago. Sorting through the snaps, she came to one of herself with an ill-advised high fringe, showing off her new lemon-yellow dungarees in the back garden. And here were a whole load taken at the village summer fete . . . there was Welsh Mac when he still had hair . . . and Glynis from the shop, wearing a white crimplene trouser suit and high heels that were sinking into the grass as she manned the hoopla stall. Flipping on through, she came to one featuring Abbie and Tom looking young and in love, and another of Glynis's husband Huw looking hot and half-cut outside the beer tent. And – ha! – there was Johnny in the background, in jeans and a dodgy striped T-shirt, fooling around with a couple of friends in front of the coconut shy. Next was one of herself – oh, good grief – wearing a homemade hula skirt and crepe flowers in her hair for the fancy dress competition.

Then another of Johnny stretched out on the grass, feeding crisps to the vicar's yappy Jack Russell terrier. And here was one of Huw sprawled in a chair and fast asleep now, oblivious to the fact that, behind him, his young nieces were gleefully sprinkling daisies and bits of grass on his head.

She smiled at the pictures. The next one showed Wayne Carter, who had always been the wild boy of the village, snarling at the camera and brandishing a can of lager. His hair was dyed black and gelled into aggressive spikes and he was wearing a Sex Pistols T-shirt, strategically ripped to reveal a nipple ring that, back then, had sent shock waves through the community. He was a chartered accountant now.

Her mobile burst into life and she answered it.

'Hi, it's me.' Her pulse quickened; there was no mistaking Johnny's playful drawl.

'This is a coincidence. I've just been looking at old photos of you!' Hastily Cleo added, 'Not in a stalkery way.'

'How did I look?'

'You've had better hairstyles.'

'And how did you look?'

'Stunning, of course.'

He laughed. 'Listen, remember you liked my new dining room?'

'Um . . . yes.' When he'd shown her over his house the other week, she'd fallen in love with the shade of paint he'd chosen for the walls, a rich, velvety topaz yellow.

'Well, I've just been sorting through junk in the garage and I've found another ten-litre tin of the stuff. I knew we'd ordered too much, I just didn't realise how much. And you said you were thinking of redoing your living room, so I wondered if you wanted it.'

'Great, thanks!' Ten litres of good quality paint, for free? Brilliant.

'If you're at home, I can bring it on over.'

'I'm in the attic. It's easier to get into than it is to climb out of,' said Cleo, 'so you'll have to give me five minutes. But the door's on the latch.'

Johnny didn't hesitate. 'In that case, just stay where you are. I'm on my way.'

Chapter 35

Three minutes later Cleo heard the front door open and close, then footsteps on the stairs. Peering over the edge of the hatch, she said, 'Where's the paint?'

'I left it in the hall. What are you doing up there?'

'Looking at old stuff.' Cleo let go of the photo in her hand and watched it twirl down towards him like a leaf. Catching it, Johnny studied the snap of himself in front of the coconut shy and shook his head.

'I was fourteen. God, look at the state of me.' He grinned and climbed on to the chair beneath the hatch, then expertly – impressively – hauled himself up into the loft and gazed around. 'You've got a lot of stuff to look at.'

'I've been here for ages.'

'I can see why. It's nice up here. Cosy.'

'I think I have abandonment issues. I can't bring myself to throw anything away.' Bending her head to avoid the slanted beams and the forty-watt lightbulb, Cleo made her way back to where she'd been sitting before. She patted the rolled-up blanket next to her. 'Come and have a look at the photos. I daren't take this lot downstairs; they'll never get back up here again.'

'Bloody hell, I don't believe it. Welsh Mac with hair!'

Cleo loved it that he was as entertained by the photographs as she was. The next thirty minutes flew by. She and Johnny may not have been friends during their teenage years but they'd known all the same people. He exclaimed with delight as he recognised places and events from their shared-but-separate pasts. There were assorted Christmases, bonfire night parties, school sports days, Badminton Horse Trials . . .

'There's your Auntie Jean.' Next to her, Johnny picked up a photo that had slipped out of its pocket. Older than the ones they'd been looking at, it showed a young Jean, in her mid-twenties and still healthy, glowing with joie de vivre. In this picture she was wearing a pink and green dress and flowers in her long dark hair. She was sitting on a gate, holding a small lop-eared mongrel and laughing into the camera. Cleo felt her stomach contract with longing for the happy auntie she'd lost.

'Look at her,' Johnny marvelled. 'Pretty stunning, wasn't she? In her day.'

Cleo nodded.

'Those eyes.' He held the photo at arm's length, then turned to survey her. 'She looks just like you.'

'I know.'

'Hey, stop it, don't cry.' Johnny's hand covered hers. 'What's wrong?'

All the old memories had been stirred up like mud in a bucket. Cleo recalled the hideous afternoon when Auntie Jean, off her head and barely able to stand, had said, 'Hey, baby, look at us, don't we look the same, eh? You an' me?' She'd flung an arm around Cleo before she had a chance to escape, and had planted a wet kiss on her face. 'You're goin' to be just like me when you grow up!'

Which, when you were twelve, wasn't the cheeriest of thoughts.

And stupidly, Cleo hadn't been able to dismiss it from her mind. Maybe it was ridiculous, but for years after that she'd been haunted by the fear that she would one day turn into Auntie Jean.

'Here.' Johnny wiped her wet cheeks with his thumb. 'Don't cry. I'm sorry.'

'It's OK, I'm fine.' She must be hormonal. Cleo exhaled, steadied herself. He must think she was a complete wuss.

'I don't suppose it was easy, growing up with Jean as your aunt.' As he said it, he gave her a reassuring pat on the back. He wasn't wearing aftershave today, but the clean, natural smell of him was, if anything, even more hypnotic. 'There was no need to feel ashamed of her, you know.'

Cleo nodded. 'She was embarrassing, though. You never knew what she'd do next.' Her shoulders began to unbunch as he rubbed the flat of his hand in soothing circles over her back. 'I was ashamed of being ashamed. Does that make sense? She was showing us all up and I wished she'd go away.'

And she scared the living daylights out of me, because if it could happen to Auntie Jean, who was to say it couldn't happen to me too?

'Nobody would blame you for feeling like that.' Johnny's voice was consoling; it was still weird, him being this nice to her.

'Anyway.' Reaching for another packet of photographs, Cleo said, 'I ended up getting my wish, didn't I? She went away for good.'

He nodded. There was no need to say any more. Auntie Jean's liver had held out, heroically, for a few more years. She'd stumbled from crisis to drink-fuelled, chaotic crisis before finally succumbing to hepatic cirrhosis. She was forty when she died, and Cleo had been eighteen.

'Now that's what I call style,' said Johnny, changing the subject.

Cleo looked at the photograph of herself on her thirteenth

birthday, proudly cutting a star-shaped, Smartie-studded cake and evidently delighted by her choice of puff-sleeved purple blouse and green-and-purple checked waistcoat.

'I dread to think what I had on the bottom half.' In the photo she was standing behind a table but Cleo had a distinct memory of orangey-brown cotton trousers from C & A. Oh well, he didn't need to know that.

'Ha!' Johnny spluttered with laughter as the damn things were revealed in the next photo.

'Fine, you weren't always so sartorial yourself.' Retaliating, she flipped through an earlier batch until she found the one of him leading the fancy dress parade at the summer fete. Aged ten or eleven, he was wearing dark brown tights, a brown turtleneck jumper and a hat decorated with huge branches and swathes of greenery.

Pointing to them, Cleo said, 'Tights.'

'I was a *tree*.'

'With transvestite tendencies.'

'I try to keep those under control these days.'

'You looked ridiculous.'

'But I came third. I won a book token.' Pause. 'And I got to keep the tights.'

She groaned aloud at the next photo of herself eating candyfloss, with pink gunk around her mouth and bits of it attractively stuck in her hair. 'Look at the state of me there.'

'Ah, but you've improved with age.' Johnny was half smiling. 'In fact you've scrubbed up pretty well.'

'Shut up.' Cleo squirmed; for some reason he still had his hand on her back.

'You don't take compliments very easily, do you? But it's true.'

And she'd been doing so well up until now. Hopefully he

261

couldn't tell how fast her heart was beating. Casually she said, 'Maybe it depends on who's giving them.'

'You're a beautiful girl. That's a fact. Trust me.' His green eyes glittered with amusement. 'I'm an artist.'

Ha, a smarty-pants con artist, more like. But even as she was thinking this, her body was reacting to his voice, his physical proximity, the warm hand on her back. And she wasn't moving away.

She wasn't moving *at all*.

'Listen to me.' Johnny's voice softened. 'I mean it. I don't think you have any idea how attractive you are.'

For the life of her she couldn't speak.

'Seriously.' He was nodding now. 'And I've only just realised this, but I think I know why too.'

'Why?' It came out as a croaky whisper.

'OK, let me ask you something. What do you see when you look in the mirror?'

An infinitesimal shrug. 'Me.'

'I don't think you do, though. I think you see your Auntie Jean.'

It felt like being punched in the stomach. Cleo's eyes grew hot. He had caught her completely off guard. She'd kept those feelings bottled up inside herself for so long, and no one else had ever guessed. Yet just from her reaction earlier, Johnny had intuitively worked it out. He knew that every time she studied her reflection, she wished with all her heart that she didn't have Auntie Jean's eyebrows, Auntie Jean's chin, Auntie Jean's freckles . . .

The only thing she had that Auntie Jean hadn't was the Pierrot beauty spot beneath her right eye.

And the ability – thank God – to say no to the offer of just one more drink.

'You don't have to worry.' Johnny shook his head. 'You're nothing like she was.'

He was right. It was time to put the fear behind her. Cleo relaxed and said, 'I know.'

He paused, then frowned and said slowly, 'You know, I have this horrible feeling . . . oh God, did I *tease* you about her when we were kids?'

So he'd remembered. After all these years. Cleo smiled slightly. 'Maybe.'

'Oh God.'

'It was just stupid stuff at school. Everyone gets teased about something. If it's any consolation,' she said drily, 'you weren't the only one.'

Johnny exhaled. He looked mortified. 'No wonder you hated me. I'm sorry.'

She nodded. 'I know.'

'*Really* sorry.'

'OK.' Cleo smiled. 'No need to grovel.'

'I feel as if I should.'

'Fine, then. Go ahead.'

'I'm sorry. I was a complete idiot. I'm sorry, I'm *sorry*.'

'That's enough. You can stop now.' Was it her imagination or was he moving fractionally closer?

'Stop what?'

'Apologising.'

'Oh right. Sorry.'

Now he was definitely teasing her. And if he were to reach out and kiss her at this moment in time, Cleo knew she would kiss him back. Last time, in the car, it hadn't happened. But now they were teetering on the brink of the next stage. Every centimetre of her skin was prickling with adrenaline, she wanted it to happen and there was only so much anticipation a girl could take. Up here in this shadowy, dusty, cobwebby attic, it seemed as if he was about to make his move at last. And she wasn't going to stop him. OK, maybe it wasn't the most romantic of locations but—

Dee-de-deee, da da da deeee dah!

Cleo froze. Sometimes, just sometimes, didn't you just wish mobile phones had never been invented?

In her ear, Johnny murmured, 'You could always not answer it.'

Which was a tempting thought, but today of all days she couldn't do that.

'I have to. One of the other drivers wasn't well this morning, so I'm on standby.' Cleo winced when she saw Grumpy Graham's name pop up on the screen. She pressed reply, crossed her fingers and said, 'Hi, what's happening?'

'Don's gone down with food poisoning, big time. He can't do the Edinburgh trip. And they need picking up in forty minutes so you'll have to get your skates on.' Graham's tone was brusque.

Her heart sank. There was no point arguing or trying to wriggle out of it. She had a job to do and that was that. 'Fine, no problem.'

Next to her, Johnny mouthed, 'Job?'

Cleo nodded.

'Shame,' he said under his breath.

Which was just about the understatement of the year. Cleo said, 'Where are the clients now?'

'The Marriott Hotel. Don't be late whatever you do, they're fussy buggers.'

The Marriott was the five-star hotel in the city centre, which at this time of day meant she had roughly five minutes in which to shower off the dust and change into her uniform. Scrambling to her feet, not even daring to signal regret with her eyes, Cleo glanced at Johnny and said into the phone, 'I'm on my way.'

Chapter 36

It wasn't the Colston Hall but at short notice it was all he'd been able to manage. Sometimes you just had to make the best of what you could get.

'I've been given a couple more tickets,' said Ash, 'for *Madame Butterfly* next Tuesday at the Pargeter Theatre in Clifton.'

'Are you serious?' Fia's face lit up. 'Oh my God, that's my favourite opera!'

He'd had an inkling it might be. Weeks ago, Frank had announced with relish that Fia didn't listen to his radio show, she was all into that warbly *Madame Butterfly* stuff.

'It's a touring production. They're supposed to be pretty good.'

'That's *fantastic*. Ash, thanks so much, this is really kind of you!'

Oh no, he wasn't falling for that one again. Do-gooder Aaron was on his own from now on. Bracing himself, Ash said, 'The thing is, I have to review the show for the radio station, that's why they've given us the tickets.'

'Oh.' Fia's change of expression was like a knife between his ribs. 'Oh right. I see.'

'But it's still *Madame Butterfly*.' His mouth was dry; he couldn't fall to his knees and beg her to go with him. But it was so obviously not what she wanted to do.

She hesitated and he could see her wrestling with her conscience. Thankfully good manners won out and Fia didn't blurt out, 'But I'd rather cut off my own *feet* than go to the theatre with a fat loser like you!' Instead, mustering a brave smile, she said, 'Well, that's fine, it'll be great. Thanks for inviting me.'

'Yes.' Ash mentally kicked himself; once he got tongue-tied, he couldn't get even the simplest response right. Belatedly he said, 'No problem.' Jesus, what was *wrong* with him? This was his big chance; he'd actually managed to trick Fia into going out on a date with him. Even if it wasn't a real date and she was only agreeing to do it because otherwise he might never supply her with free tickets again.

Despite everything, Ash couldn't help experiencing a squiggle of excitement and hope.

It might not be much. OK, it *wasn't* much.

But it was a start.

There was a jolly feature on dance aerobics on the TV and Abbie joined in as she vacuumed the carpet. Turning up the volume so she could hear the music above the roar of the Hoover, she danced and sang along with the instructor and knocked the Hoover against the metal legs of the ironing board that had now taken up more or less permanent residence in the living room.

And if she was being noisy, well, so what? When Georgia had first moved in, she'd been conscious of her presence and had made every effort not to disturb her in the mornings. But carpets still needed to be cleaned, she *liked* singing along to her favourite songs and you couldn't tiptoe around for ever.

Besides, it was almost lunchtime. Georgia should be up by now.

'And stretch and *bend* and stretch and *bend*,' yelled the fitness instructor on TV. 'And *reach* and twist and *reach* and twist those hips, that's it! Now *stretch* and *reach* and *bend* and—'

'WAAAH!' Abbie let out a shriek as a hand touched her shoulder.

'Sorry, sorry, I didn't mean to frighten you.' Georgia pulled an apologetic face as Abbie pressed the mute button on the TV.

'I thought you were still in bed.' Abbie flushed; had she looked completely ridiculous? Did her bum look big? Had Georgia been laughing at her?

'I've got loads to do. I was up ironing till three o'clock this morning.'

Hadn't they all known it; the irregular clunk-clunk of the iron and the burble of the TV had driven Abbie demented when she'd been trying to get to sleep.

'Anyway, just to let you know I'm off now. I've got deliveries, pick-ups and a trip to the printers for more business cards, so I won't be back before teatime.'

'OK, fine.' Was it wrong to feel this delighted at the prospect of having the house to herself on her day off?

'Oh, and we're out of milk, so you might want to get some more. Bye, then. See you later!'

Abbie bit her tongue until Georgia had packed the completed ironing into the van and driven off. *This* was what drove her insane, the lack of concern and utter thoughtlessness. In the kitchen, she found the empty two-litre milk carton on the counter and a drained glass sitting in the sink. This was teenagers for you. And she knew she should probably be grateful that Georgia had bothered to tell her, because otherwise she wouldn't have discovered the lack of milk until she'd come through to make herself a cup of tea.

Oh well, she'd finish the cleaning first, then change out of her tracksuit bottoms before heading on over to the shop. Reaching for the remote control, Abbie de-muted the TV and switched the Hoover back on. The dance aerobics section had finished but vacuuming still used up plenty of calories, didn't it? Seeing as it now promised to be an extra-nice, home-alone day, she might treat herself and see if Glynis had any toffee doughnuts.

Conditions were getting crowded beneath the sofa. Abbie found three empty crisp packets, several magazines, a glittery eyeliner, seven coat hangers and an unopened peach yogurt. Straightening up after clearing them out and hoovering under there, she glimpsed a flash of dark red through the front window as a car pulled up outside.

Her stomach did a little flip because it was Des's car and the faint awkwardness between them was still there, even if no one else was aware of it. She switched off the vacuum cleaner and watched him climb out of the driver's seat. OK, there was absolutely no need to be nervous. He'd dropped by to ask her to swap shifts with someone, that was all. They saw each other at work every day and it had been weeks since he'd even mentioned the . . . the *thing* that had happened.

Forcing herself to sound and behave in a completely normal fashion – and God knows, she should be used to doing it by now – Abbie opened the door and said cheerfully, 'Hi, Des! Let me guess, Magda wants me to do Sunday for her so she can have loads to drink at her neighbour's party on Saturday night.'

'No.' Following her into the house, Des ran his fingers through his reddish fair hair and shook his head. 'I just needed to see you. We have to talk.'

The fading anxiety did an abrupt about-turn. 'What about?'

A muscle was twitching in his forehead. 'I love you.'

The vacuum cleaner nozzle dropped from her hand. 'What?'

'I'm sorry, I can't help it. I can't stop thinking about our night together.' He moved towards her. 'I've tried, but I just can't. I've never felt like this before, about *anyone* . . .'

'Des, I'm married!'

'I know, I know, but he doesn't love you as much as I do. He *can't*. Abbie, I dream about you all the time. I just want us to be together. Just give me a chance and let me prove it to you.'

'No, no, I've told you before, that was just one night.' The fear had her by the throat now, but it was mixed with annoyance. 'You know why it happened, and it's never going to happen again, *ever*.'

'Look, you're not even giving me a chance.' Desperation made him reckless. 'I can make you happy, we could live—'

'*Shhh!*' Abbie froze and held out a hand, her skin prickling with terror. Something had just creaked upstairs. But how could there be anyone up there? Until Des had arrived she'd been alone in the house. It must just be one of those random noises, like when the water pipes start clanking in the night . . .

Oh shit, shit, there it was again. And this time Des had heard it too. Nausea rose in her chest and perspiration broke out as she turned and went out into the hall.

There was no one on the stairs. Nor on as much of the landing as she could see from this angle.

But the shadow on the landing wall was human-shaped.

Never before had Abbie prayed so hard for a burglar. Oh God, please let the figure on the landing be a criminal, a complete stranger who'd climbed up the drainpipe and broken into the house . . . he could take her jewellery, her camera, as many electrical items as he could carry. If he needed a hand she'd even help him. Her voice tight with fear, she said, 'Who's that up there?'

The shadow moved and a voice said, 'Me.'

Chapter 37

Abbie gazed up the stairs at Georgia. Georgia in turn looked first at her, then at Des standing in the living-room doorway.

Abbie said, 'Des, you can go.'

He shook his head. 'I'm sorry.'

'I bet you are.' Georgia's expression was stony.

'Look, this isn't what it sounds like.' So many explanations and excuses were tumbling around inside Abbie's head, she couldn't coherently voice any of them.

'Isn't it? Really? Well, that's a relief, because from where I'm standing it sounds like you're having an affair with your boss who's in love with you.'

'Des. Tell her it's not true.'

Des looked like a rabbit caught in headlights. 'But she heard me say it. I *do* love you.'

'*Out.*' Trembling all over, Abbie yanked open the front door. When he'd gone, she closed it behind her and eyed Georgia again. 'And what are you doing here anyway? You left the house twenty minutes ago. I saw you drive off.'

'Right, listen, I wasn't spying on you, OK?' Georgia's arms were tightly folded, her tone defiant. 'I was a couple of miles down the road when I realised I'd left the drop-off list on my bed. And on the way back I thought I'd stop in at the shop and pick up a carton of milk, to save you the bother. So that's what I did. I actually thought I was doing a nice thing.' As she carried on, she stomped down the staircase. '*Then* I thought how about if I parked behind the house, sneaked in through the back door and left the milk out by the kettle so you'd get a huge surprise when you went into the kitchen? Because you wouldn't have a clue how it had got there and it'd be like the fairies had left it for you! So I did that too, and you were still busy hoovering away, you didn't hear me come in, and then I went upstairs to pick up my list.' Pausing for breath at last, she concluded evenly, 'Which is when it all started to go wrong. And I'm sorry, but how was I supposed to know your boyfriend was going to turn up?'

Abbie had never felt more sick. 'He's not my boyfriend, you don't—'

'Oh please, are you seriously going to tell me I don't understand? I've spent my whole life watching it happen! My mother was either cheating on men or having them cheat on her. That's why I loved it that you and my dad were so happy together. You were a proper married couple who didn't do any of that horrible stuff. You trusted each other and I thought that was fantastic. Well, more fool me.' Georgia's blue eyes, so unnervingly like Tom's, registered disdain. 'Because you aren't like that at all, are you? You're exactly the same as my mother, keeping secrets and lying through your teeth. You're cheating on my dad behind his back. And that is just . . . *disgusting*.'

'OK, stop.' Abbie's voice rose in panic. 'Stop right there. I *haven't* cheated on Tom and I'm *not* disgusting!'

'Hello? I heard it with my own ears . . . you and your boss spent the night together!' On the attack now, Georgia said, 'Was that in a bed, or are you going to tell me the two of you were in a canoe?'

'Nothing happened!'

Georgia looked repulsed. 'Dad's going to be devastated.'

Oh God. 'Could we go into the kitchen?' If she didn't sit down, she'd fall down. Stumbling past her, Abbie said, 'I'm going to explain everything and you're going to listen. Because I never meant any of this to happen and it's not my fault.'

'You're sounding more and more like my mum.'

'If this is anyone's fault,' Abbie retaliated, 'it's your mother's.'

Ten minutes later, Georgia knew everything. And while she was less angry than before, she was nowhere near ecstatic. Frankly, Abbie couldn't blame her. She'd been forced to share information neither of them was comfortable with. There had been kissing, yes. In a double bed, yes. But no sex, God, no, none at all, absolutely not. So no actual physical betrayal, surely.

Except Georgia didn't appear to be convinced of this. And she looked utterly repulsed, as if she was being forced to picture the hideous scene in close-up, high-definition detail.

'OK, so if you came home from work and you went upstairs and found Dad in bed with some other woman, you'd be absolutely fine with that, would you?'

'No, no, of course I wouldn't. But it only happened because I thought Tom had been unfaithful to me. I was distraught. And I wouldn't *ever* have contacted Des.' Abbie was vehement; how could she persuade Georgia to believe her? 'He just happened to phone . . . and I was in such a state, he came over. But I didn't cheat on Tom. And he doesn't need to know what happened that night. I love him. More than anything. And he loves me. It would break his heart.' Her fingers digging into her palms, she pleaded, 'It's best if you don't tell him.'

Georgia twirled a strand of hair round and round her thumb, tightening it like a noose then letting it go. She studied Abbie in silence for several seconds before finally speaking.

'You'd better be telling me the truth.'

'I am.' Scarcely able to breathe, Abbie nodded then shook her head. 'I never wanted any of this to happen.'

'What are you going to do about your boss?'

'Nothing. You heard what I was telling him earlier. Des knows I'm not interested in him. He'll get over it.' She prayed Des would be discreet.

Georgia gazed down at the floor. Finally she looked up. 'OK, I won't say anything to Dad.'

A lump expanded in Abbie's throat. 'Good.' Good was the under-statement of the year. 'Thanks,' she added, even though she knew Georgia was doing it for Tom's sake, not hers.

Georgia's don't-thank-me shrug was a nerve-wracking echo of her father's. 'Anyway, I'd better get going. Lots to do.' Still clutching her van keys, she moved towards the door.

'See you later.' Spotting the condensation-dotted carton next to the kettle, Abbie said hurriedly, 'Oh, and thanks for the milk, that was really thoughtful of you. Um, so what would you like for dinner tonight? Tell me what you're in the mood for and I'll cook it. I could do steak! Or how about that spicy prawn thing with rice? What d'you think?'

Georgia gave her a pitying look. 'I think you have to learn that the first rule of lying is to act normally. Because if you suddenly start being extra-nice to me, Dad's going to be suspicious.'

'Sorry.' It was both a salutary lesson and a slap in the face. Abbie glanced down at her hands, which were still shaking.

Pausing in the doorway, Georgia turned and said, 'We'll have the spicy prawn thing.'

'Come in. Oh, hello.' Des coloured when he saw who had knocked on the door to his office. 'Come on in.' He waited until she'd closed the door behind her then said, 'Look, I'm sorry about yesterday.'

He looked as if he hadn't slept all night. Well, welcome to the club. Abbie said, 'So you keep telling me. But you have to promise you won't come to the house again *ever*.'

'I promise.' He nodded unhappily. 'What happened with you and the girl?'

'She's not going to say anything to Tom. For now. But last night was just . . . horrible.' A sob escaped Abbie's chest without any warning; the strain of pretending everything was normal had been agonising. She'd spent the evening cooking dinner, washing up afterwards, then cleaning the kitchen. When Tom had innocently asked, during the meal, if she knew if Des was signing up for the cricket team this year, Georgia's stony gaze across the table had caused her stomach to clench with fear. How was she going to keep this up for the next week . . . month . . . year?

'Don't cry.' Hurriedly patting his pockets and failing to come up with a handkerchief, Des yanked open the desk drawer and pulled out a Burger King serviette instead. 'Here, use this.'

'I can't b-believe she found out like that. It's just a nightmare.' Abbie wiped her eyes with the thin, scratchy paper. 'She said she thought me and Tom were happy together, she couldn't believe I'd done something like that to him. She's on his side all the way.'

'Do you want me to talk to her?'

'God, are you mad? No way! She heard what you said, all that stuff about . . . you know . . .'

'Loving you? I said it and I meant it.' Des stayed calm. 'But I won't tell Tom. And I won't tell him about our night together either. Whatever happens from now on, it's up to you. If he hears it from anyone, you'll know it won't have been me.'

Was she stupid to trust him? Abbie decided she knew Des well enough to believe what he said. He was an honourable man who wouldn't betray her.

'We're just going to carry on as if nothing's happened.' She wondered if this was actually possible, but what other choice did they have? 'I was going to hand in my notice here, but then everyone would want to know why, and I can't think of a reason.'

'Good.' Des shook his head. 'I don't want you to leave. We'll get through this, you'll see.'

Chapter 38

Ow.

OK, this wasn't funny. As if he didn't have enough to contend with already.

Ow, ow, fucking *ow*.

Right, just breathe slowly. That's it, in and out, you can do it— OWWWW!

Ash caught sight of his reflection in the mirror and clutched the shower door for support. He looked like Quasimodo. A fat, pale, pathetic Quasimodo. Worse, in fact, because in all the pictures of Quasimodo he'd ever seen, he'd at least been wearing clothes.

Carefully, inch by inch, Ash eased himself out of the shower cubicle in a stooped, Neanderthal way. You saw the government health warnings on packets of cigarettes and on all those drinks ads on TV, but it never occurred to the bloody government, did it, to slap stickers on bottles of shampoo?

Warning: dropping this in the shower and bending down to pick it up could seriously damage your health.

Not to mention your bendability.

And it had to happen today of all days, less than four hours before embarking on the date of a lifetime. At seven thirty he was due to pick Fia up from the Hollybush, drive her into Bristol and sit next to her through a two-hour performance of *Madame Butterfly*. He'd been counting down the minutes, so excited he hadn't even been able to eat anything today.

Well, somebody had to be excited about it. Last night in the pub, Tom had suggested getting a group together to go and see the new James Bond film at the Vue this evening. Fia, collecting plates from their table, had said eagerly, 'Ooh, I love James Bond, can I come along too?'

Appalled, Ash had been forced to blurt out, 'But we're going to the Pargeter Theatre tomorrow night, remember?'

And Fia, who had clearly forgotten all about it, had summoned up a smile and exclaimed, 'Oh yes, that's right, so we are.'

And now this. To cap it all, he'd gone and put his bloody back out. Typical. Gingerly wrapping himself in his dressing gown, he made his way ultra-slowly downstairs. Every step was agony. Right, just keep moving and maybe things would improve, the muscle spasm would ease or somehow loosen up.

After twenty minutes the pain was, if anything, worse. It felt as if the Incredible Hulk had jammed his spine into a giant vice and was sadistically tightening it.

Speaking of sadists . . .

Already aware of the outcome of the conversation he was about to have, out of desperation Ash gave it a shot anyway.

'I'm sorry,' drawled the receptionist who answered the phone, 'if you want to see the doctor, you have to phone this number between eight thirty and eight fifty in the morning.'

She didn't sound remotely sorry. She sounded as if nothing gave her more pleasure than to make grown men cry.

'But something just went in my back.' Shit, it even hurt to *speak*. 'At eight thirty this morning I was fine.'

'In that case, try calling us tomorrow morning and we'll see if we can fit you in then.'

Try being the operative word, because the line was usually jammed with desperate sick people dialling over and over again.

'But I need to see someone today. It's urgent.' Ash spoke through gritted teeth. 'How about if I come along to the surgery and just wait until everyone else has been seen?'

'Don't be ridiculous, you can't do that! The doctor's a very busy man.' Irritably, the receptionist said, 'His list is full. We don't have people just turning up here.'

'But I need to be seen!'

'Can you move at all? Or are you completely immobile?'

'I can move a bit. But it's very painful.' *And I have a date tonight, you hideous old bag. When did you last have one of those, eh?*

'If you can move, you can wait till tomorrow. Or if you really want to be a nuisance, get yourself off to Casualty. We can't help you.'

Which kind of made you wonder why she'd bothered picking up the phone in the first place. And now she'd ended the call, not even allowing him the satisfaction of hanging up on her. Hissing air out between his teeth, Ash inched his way over to the kitchen drawer that doubled as a medicine cabinet. He searched through the jumble of antacids, Elastoplasts, cans of Deep Heat and antiseptic spray, assorted Sinex inhalers and sachets of Lem-sip. Painkillers, where were the painkillers? Don't say he'd used them all without realising and— OK, right, two ibuprofen, that'd have to do. At least they were better than nothing, they'd take the edge off.

Thirty minutes later the pain was as ferocious as ever. The Incredible Hulk showed no signs of easing the pressure. It was four thirty and driving a car would be a physical impossibility.

Ash thought the situation through. If he called for a taxi to pick him up and take him to Casualty, there was no telling how long he'd have to wait before being seen. So that was out of the question, because if it killed him he wasn't going to miss out on his big date.

And at this rate it might well kill him. OK, not literally. But he was definitely going to need something else to get through this. Back at the medicine drawer, Ash did some more searching. Packets of Tunes. Micropore tape. Strepsils. Cod liver oil capsules the size of grapes, that got stuck in your gullet and gave you fish breath. Hayfever tablets. Night Nurse. Sun cream that must be at least three years old . . . hang on, Night Nurse? That had pain stuff in it, right? He scanned the side of the bottle. Contains paracetamol. Brilliant, you were definitely allowed to take ibuprofen with paracetamol.

Negotiating the child-proof top took some doing and increased the spasm in his back but he breathed through the pain – God, this had to be worse than childbirth – and glugged down a couple of mouthfuls.

By five thirty he'd ordered a cab to take them to the theatre, taken another *small* sip of Night Nurse and spent fifteen minutes getting his boxer shorts on. With the help of a hoopla throwing action and a wire coat hanger. One final desperate trawl through the medicine drawer came up with a lone orange tablet left over from his mother's last visit when she'd been over here recuperating from her neck-lift, eyebag-reduction and whole-body lipo. His mother, who had moved to Cape Town six years ago, had embraced self-improvement in a major way. In her view, a year without plastic surgery was a year wasted. She was a mass consumer of painkillers. Ash peered at the tablet, badly in need of help.

But since he wasn't stupid, he phoned his mother first.

'Mum? Those orange tablets you were taking when you were over here last year. What were they for?'

'Hello, darling! Goodness, let me see, orange, orange . . . were they oval or circular?'

'Oval.'

'Glossy or matt?'

'Um, glossy.'

'Oh, I know, something beginning with B . . . God, listen to me, memory like a thing with holes in! Darling, why do you want to know?'

'There's a leftover one here. And I've done my back in,' said Ash. 'I'm desperate.'

'Oh, go on, darling, take it. Those things got me through post-op. So how are you otherwise? Lost any weight yet?'

'No.' He swallowed the tablet.

'Thought any more about liposuction?'

'Funnily enough, I haven't.'

'Now, now, darling, don't get huffy, you should give it a go! They sucked *gallons* of fat out of me!'

'Bye, Mum.' Ash hung up the phone before she could start interrogating him about girlfriends. Some women got evangelical about religion but these days his barely recognisable mother preached the gospel of plastic surgery. She was also convinced that if he followed her example, his love life would improve no end.

And who knew? Maybe she was right.

God, no wonder he was messed up.

Chapter 39

'Poor you.' Fia winced in sympathy as the taxi bounced over a speed bump and he sucked in his breath. 'Are you sure you don't want to cancel?'

'No, no, I'll be fine. Can't let the radio station down.' Ash shook his head. 'They need the review. Anyway, nearly there now.' In truth, the pain was less than it had been earlier. The various pills had done a good job of numbing it. They appeared to have numbed his brain too; he felt slightly as if he were swimming underwater, but it was quite a nice sensation. Relaxing. Which helped. He was actually thinking of witty things to say to Fia, which was a first. He couldn't always be bothered to *say* them, mind you, but at least they were there in his head.

And sometimes he thought of things that weren't remotely witty but they came tumbling out anyway.

Oh well. Never mind, at least they were having a conversation of sorts, which had to be better than sitting in awkward silence. Another bump in the road made him flinch. 'I really hope this isn't the early stages of labour. I don't want to give birth in the middle of the theatre.' Damn, that wasn't funny. Why had he said that?

Humouring him, Fia said, 'Could be messy.'

'And I'd have to call it Butterfly. Which would be awful,' said Ash. 'Especially if it was a boy.'

When they reached the theatre he eased himself out of the back of the cab with Fia's help.

'Here, hold on to my arm,' she offered, which was an excellent idea.

'God, I should have thought of this ages ago!'

Fia looked perplexed. 'Thought of what?'

'Nothing.' The swimmy feeling was back, as if his brain was slooshing around inside his skull. Together they made their way verrrrry slooooooowly up the steps. 'We're like a couple of geriatrics. Which probably means I'm not about to have a baby. Don't worry,' said Ash to the couple ahead of them who had turned round to look at him, 'I used to be a woman, had a sex change, but now I'm thinking of going back again. That's the trouble with us females, eh? Can't make up our minds.'

'Look, we don't have to do this.' Fia stopped in her tracks. 'You seem a bit . . .'

'Thingy. I seem a bit thingy. I know, and I apologise, but I promise you I'm OK to do this.' He turned and winked at the elderly woman behind him. 'And I'm not drunk, if that's what you're wondering, madam. It's probably just the drugs.'

Now it was the elderly woman's turn to look shocked. Fia said firmly, 'He's not on drugs.'

'Hey, I like it when you defend me. Very masterful. Ha, or mistress-ful! Quite sexy, in fact.' Dimly aware that he'd meant to only think this but appeared to have said it out loud, Ash made amends by nodding at the woman and patting Fia's sleeve. 'She's a very good cook, you know. Oscar-winning roast potatoes.'

When they finally reached their seats, Fia whispered, '*Are* you on drugs?'

She was looking beautiful tonight. 'No no no no no . . .' Once his head started shaking from side to side, it wouldn't stop. 'Just, you know, painkillers.'

'Strong ones?'

'I think so. But I'm fine.'

The man in the seat beside him said, *'Sshhhh.'*

'What? Excuse me?' Gesturing to the crimson velvet curtains, Ash said, 'The show hasn't even started yet.'

'You're being a bit loud,' Fia murmured in his ear.

God, that felt fantastic. She could murmur in his ear for ever and it wouldn't be long enough. OK, maybe he was being a bit loud, but as soon as the show began he'd be quiet. Turning to the man on his right, Ash said loftily, 'I'm allowed to be loud. I'm the arts critic for the *Sunday Times*. So basically,' he added, 'I can make as much noise as I like.'

Distant music soaring in the distance . . . high voices warbling . . . and emotion, lots and lots of emotion . . . *ow* . . .

. . . more music . . . different voices . . . heart-rending . . . *aaargh* . . .

. . . drums . . . rolling . . . desperate grief . . . people sobbing . . . *ouch* . . . and now the faraway music was reaching a crescendo . . . *give it a rest* . . .

. . . the sound of clapping . . . cheering . . . getting louder . . . oh for God's sake, *shut up* . . .

'What? What's going on?' His eyes snapping open, Ash attempted to jerk upright in his seat. A spasm of pain gripped his spine, hurling him back. Bewildered by the applause, he said, 'Is it starting now?'

'It's finished.'

'What?'

Fia was busy clapping. 'Wasn't it fantastic?'

Ash's befuddled brain sorted through the clues. Oh no, don't say he'd missed the whole thing, *please* don't say that. But then why was Fia asking him if he thought it had been fantastic?

Then he saw that she'd been addressing the woman on her left, not him at all. Giving her a nudge, Ash said, 'Did I . . . um, fall asleep?'

'Yes.'

'Oh *God*.'

'And you snored.'

'No!' He went hot and cold with shame.

The man to his right said drily, 'Oh yes.'

Ash wanted to die. 'Much?'

'Do your ribs hurt?' said Fia.

'What?' Experimentally pressing his ribs, Ash discovered that actually, yes, they did.

'Every time you started to snore,' Fia explained, 'we gave you a poke.'

'We?'

The man on his right said, 'We took it in turns.'

'Oh no.' Ash's heart shrivelled further still when he saw the small wet patch on the shoulder of Fia's cream jacket. 'Don't tell me I did that to you.'

Fia looked down at the damp mark. 'Oh yes, you dribbled a bit. Doesn't matter.'

He'd leaned against her and rested his head on her shoulder. It was practically his lifetime's ambition. And he hadn't even been aware of it.

'I'm so sorry.' To add insult to injury, the pain that had been effectively numbed earlier was now back with a vengeance. He needed Fia's help to stand upright as the audience began to make their way out of the theatre.

Fia wasn't bothered about her jacket; it was machine washable and the production of *Madame Butterfly* had been excellent. It might not have been Ash's finest hour, but it wasn't his fault he'd fallen asleep. And he'd been so funny before the performance, completely different from the way he usually was with her. Usually he was taciturn, distant and unfriendly—

'Now she tells me.' They'd reached the foyer and Ash had switched his phone back on. Having briefly scrutinised it, he showed Fia the text on the screen: 'Remembered at last – the orange one is a tranquilliser. VV strong!!! Love, Mum xx.'

'Is that what you took?' Fia laughed at the expression on his face. 'Serves you right for pinching other people's tablets.'

'She told me it would help with the pain.'

'Well, it certainly did that. You slept right through it.'

'Fia? Is that *you*?'

Fia stopped dead, the little hairs at the back of her neck prickling at the sound of a voice she instantly recognised. In an ideal world she would have preferred never to hear it again.

Slowly she turned to face her mother-in-law. 'Hello, Vivien.'

'Well, well, small world! Fancy bumping into you here!'

Which was somewhat ironic, Fia felt, considering that she was the one who loved opera and classical music, whilst Vivien had never been remotely interested in it. But to be polite she said, 'How are you?'

'Pretty good, pretty good. Busy training up the new assistant in the shop.' This was one of Vivien's Pointed Remarks, emphasising the inconvenience Fia's departure had caused. 'And Will's doing *very* well, all things considered. Got himself a lovely girlfriend, she's an absolute joy!' This meant that she, Fia, had always been hard work and probably unworthy of her beloved son. Vivien's miss-nothing, lilac-shaded eyes flickered over Ash and widened in recognition. 'Are you the person who fell asleep during the performance? The one who was snoring?'

'I may have dozed off once or twice,' said Ash. 'During the boring bits.'

Vivien gazed at him askance. 'Gracious me, and you two are together? Fia, is this your new . . . boyfriend?' As she said it, she took in every detail, from Ash's slightly glazed expression to his crumpled jacket, from his in-need-of-a-comb hair to the straining buttons on his shirt. Her nostrils flared and her mouth began to twitch, as if she couldn't wait to contact Will and tell him what a physically inferior character his wife had hooked up with. The clear inference was: *After my son, is this really the best you can do?*

And Ash, who had never even met her before, knew exactly what was going through her mind.

'Actually, Fia just came along as a favour to me. My dear wife couldn't make it tonight.' Having assumed a very upper-class drawl, he now stuck out his hand for Vivien to shake. 'How d'you do? My name's Humphrey Twistleton-Jakes. Pretty dull production this evening, didn't you think?'

'We should go,' said Fia. 'Our car's going to be waiting outside.' Smiling at Vivien as they moved past her, she indicated Ash and said proudly, 'He's the arts critic of the *Sunday Times*.'

'Right, well, sorry again.' By the time they reached Channings Hill, the swimminess was back in Ash's brain. 'Pretty disastrous all round.'

'It wasn't. I had fun.' Way more fun than she'd expected to have, if she was honest. Fia said, 'Vivien's face as we were leaving. She absolutely believed you. That was one of my all-time favourite moments.'

Leaning across and giving Fia a proper goodnight kiss would have been one of his. But he (a) couldn't physically reach her without inflicting unimaginable pain upon himself and (b) still wasn't brave enough to try. Instead he said, 'I never liked that husband of yours when he was with Cleo.'

'I know, she told me. All I can say is that he puts up a good front and we both fell for it. Or maybe we've both just got rubbish taste in men.' Fia was smiling slightly, her fingers restlessly tapping the door handle. 'So I'm looking to change that, get myself sorted out.'

Inside Ash's head, a voice cried out, 'I could help you with that, let *me* change you!'

'Actually, you might be able to help,' said Fia and for a split second he thought he was dreaming, or she'd read his mind, or he'd accidentally said it out loud . . . 'You know Johnny, don't you? He must talk to you about . . . you know, *stuff*, while you're playing pool together. What kind of girls does he usually go for?'

Ash exhaled slowly. What was that noise? Oh yes, the sound of his hopes crashing down to earth.

He shook his head. 'I don't know. Sorry.'

'Oh.' Fia looked disappointed. 'Well, thanks for tonight anyway. And when you have to do your review, just say the girl who played Butterfly is a star of the future, the guy who was Pinkerton really owned the role and the staging was a triumph.'

'Thanks.' Ash nodded. He didn't have to review the performance; no one had asked him to.

'And I hope your back's better soon. Good luck with it!'

He couldn't kiss her. And it didn't even occur to Fia to kiss him. Watching as she let herself out of the back of the taxi and gave him a little wave, Ash said, 'Bye.'

There was more than one kind of pain.

Chapter 40

Passing the village shop on her way to work, Cleo saw Johnny's car parked outside it. He was back from wherever he'd been. Oh God, the feelings hadn't gone away; if anything, they were stronger than ever. Jamming her foot on the brake, she pulled up and gave her pounding heart a moment to calm down.

Well, calm down a *bit*. OK, just be casual. Walk into the shop, pick up a newspaper or a packet of mints or something, then glance over and spot Johnny and look surprised. Easy.

Pushing through the door just as it was pulled open from the other side, she catapulted into Johnny's chest and let out a squeak like a mouse caught in a trap.

'Whoops.' Steadying her, he said, 'Cleo, hi. How are you?'

'Fine! You? Been busy? Somewhere nice? Oh look, milk!' *God, had she ever sounded more like a complete cretin?*

'I've been away in—'

'Away? Oh, fantastic!'

'Not really. One of my aunts has had a stroke.'

'Oh no!' She'd last seen the aunts teetering around on walking sticks at Lawrence's funeral. They were both in their late seventies and had looked incredibly fragile back then. And they both occupied the same nursing home. Remembering that their names were Clarice and Barbara, Cleo said, 'Which one?'

'Barbara. She's the older sister.' There were dark shadows under Johnny's eyes, as though he hadn't slept for a week. 'She's still unconscious in the ITU at the NNUH. Norfolk and Norwich University Hospital,' he explained when Cleo looked blank. 'It's touch and go at the moment. They don't know if she'll pull through.' He looked exhausted but seemed pleased to see her. 'Look, you couldn't spare ten minutes, could you? Come over for a quick coffee and a chat?'

'Of course I can!' Cleo checked her watch, did some rapid calculations in her head. 'I've just got to pick up Casey Kruger and get him to Bristol. I can be back in an hour and a half.'

But Johnny was already shaking his head. 'I'll be gone by then. This is just a flying visit to pick up some things. I need to get back to Norfolk as soon as I can.'

Bugger. Cleo briefly considered persuading Casey to get off his lazy celebrity backside and make his own way to the Hippodrome, but some requests simply weren't feasible. He was the client and she couldn't let him down. 'Sorry, I can't come over now. I have to work.'

Again.

Johnny's smile was rueful. 'Shame. Oh well, never mind. I'll see you when I see you.'

A quick pat on the arm and he was gone, the car roaring off up the hill. Cleo watched him disappear from view. Poor Johnny. Poor Aunt Barbara.

But on the bright side, at least it meant he hadn't been away conducting a torrid affair with someone infinitely more gorgeous than the freckly female chauffeur from across the green, whose idea of a seductive location was a dusty, cobwebby attic.

*   *   *

'I'm going to make you an offer you can't refuse,' said Georgia.

Her eyes were bright and she was wearing a tight purple T-shirt with 'Dyslexics of the world, UNTIE!' emblazoned across the chest. She was also holding something behind her back.

'Or I'll end up swimming with the fishes?' Switching off the ignition, Ash slowly slid his legs out of the car. He was on the mend but it still hurt. A lot.

'Fishes?' Georgia wrinkled her nose as she jumped down from his garden wall. 'You don't say fishes. It's *fish*. Anyway, I was listening to your show this morning. And I've got something for you.'

'Oh yes?'

'Something you're going to *love*.'

'This doesn't bear thinking about.'

'Don't be so grumpy! OK if I come in?'

'Can I stop you?' Ash clutched the fence for support as she followed him up the path.

'Shouldn't think so, not in your state.' When he'd unlocked the front door she danced past him into the house and said triumphantly, 'Ta–daaa!'

She was holding up her surprise, a small bottle of liquid.

'If that's white wine, it's not nearly enough.'

'It isn't wine. Take off your jacket.'

'Excuse me?'

'And your T-shirt.'

'Why?'

'Because I heard you going on about your bad back. And I am brilliant at giving massages. Not the mucky kind, strictly above board. But I promise you, you won't regret it. I'm fabulous.'

Ash dropped his car keys on to the table. It sounded like the worst idea he'd ever heard.

Then again, his back was still killing him and there was no denying a massage would be nice.

Plus he'd been too busy presenting a radio show this morning to phone his GP's surgery and book an appointment to get seen. And beggars couldn't really be choosers. If you can't be examined by a medical professional, why not let yourself be pummelled by an enthusiastic amateur instead?

'Go on then.' He took off his jacket. 'Where do you want me?'

'Upstairs on the bed.'

He caught the glint in her eye. 'Not a chance.'

'Spoilsport.' Georgia said, 'Fine then, we'll do it on the living room floor instead.'

She brought a bath towel downstairs, laid it on the carpet and fastened her hair back in a loose plait. In too much pain to even contemplate sucking his stomach in, Ash cautiously lowered himself on to the towel and lay face down, still fully clothed.

'You have to take your T-shirt off,' said Georgia.

'No way. I'm not getting semi naked in front of you.'

She rolled her eyes. 'I won't be able to use the oil now.'

'It's this way or nothing at all.'

Grinning, she said, 'Prude.'

To give Georgia her due, it turned out she did know what she was doing. Kneeling beside him, she rubbed her hands together to warm them. Then she began moving her fingers over his back in gentle rhythmical circles.

'Let me know if I hurt you.'

'You're all right,' Ash mumbled.

'I told you, I'm better than all right. I'm genius at this.' Her hands slowly pressed each vertebra in turn, then fanned out on either side of his spine. She stretched and kneaded the muscles and patiently worked her way over every inch of his back.

291

'So how long does this last?' mumbled Ash. He could actually feel it doing some good. The tension was seeping out of his knotted, damaged muscles.

'Fifteen minutes, twenty. For as long as you like.' Playfully, Georgia said, 'So will I get a mention on tomorrow's show after this?'

He smiled. 'You might.'

'Cool! Could you also slip in a bit about me doing ironing at really reasonable rates?'

'Is that all I am to you? A source of free advertising?'

'No, but I wouldn't mind if you just happened to mention it.'

'Well, I can't, because—'

TAT-TAT.

'Ooh, who's that?' Springing to her feet, Georgia bounded to the door before he could even lift his head. Stuck there on the floor, all Ash could do was listen to the sound of the front door being opened and her exclaiming, 'Hi! Oh, isn't that good of you? You must have been listening to the show this morning too!'

Was it too much to hope that his GP, overcome with remorse at not having been able to fit him in yesterday, had decided to grant him a home visit instead?

And had *apparently* brought along some kind of takeaway?

Then the wafts of herbs and garlic grew stronger and Ash heard Fia say, 'Um, yes, that's right. How's his back?'

Oh God . . .

'About to get *much* better.' Cheerfully Georgia led their visitor into the living room. 'Just as soon as I've finished working my magic!'

Having finally managed to turn his head, Ash saw Fia giving him a startled look from the doorway. Hardly surprising, considering she was seeing him lying on his front like a beached walrus.

Thank God he hadn't let Georgia bully him into taking off his T-shirt.

'Oh, sorry, I just thought you might not feel up to coming over to the pub for lunch.' Indicating the basket she was holding, Fia said uncertainly, 'I brought you a dish of cannelloni.'

'Th-th-thanks.' The word juddered out of his mouth as, without warning, Georgia dug her knuckles into his ribs. He'd always been hopelessly ticklish.

'Just leave it in the kitchen,' she told Fia between kneadings. 'I'll heat it up for him later when we're finished. Now, just relax and stop trying to hold your stomach in.' She gave his flabby bits an affectionate prod. 'I can't help you if you're all tense!'

Ash felt her fingers pressing into his sides, only too clearly able to imagine the unattractive view Fia was being presented with. His scalp prickled with shame.

'Ooh, you're so *lovely*,' Georgia burst out, clutching handfuls of flesh through his T-shirt and waggling them like dough. 'Like a great big cuddly seal!'

Chapter 41

Abbie was helping a dithery woman choose from the various types of solar-powered garden lighting on display when she heard Magda say playfully, 'Oh my, who's that handsome hunk coming in now?'

It was Tom. Even after all these years, the unexpected sight of him made Abbie's heart soar. Breaking into a smile, she lifted her arm to wave before realising he wasn't looking in her direction. Instead his attention appeared to be focused elsewhere.

Oh, good grief . . .

Approaching Des in the middle of the shop, not slowing for a second, Tom drew back his arm and unleashed a mighty punch that would have done Ricky Hatton proud. Des went down like a sack of gravel. Screams rang out from women in the vicinity; nothing like this had ever happened before in Kilgour's Garden Centre.

Tom didn't utter a word. Without so much as a glance around the shop, he turned and left. Everyone was in a state of shock, eyes like saucers and mouths agape. People gasped as Des hauled himself into a sitting position and blood dripped from his nose on to the tiled floor.

Then slowly, one by one, faces began to turn in Abbie's direction. Fear squeezed her stomach and bile rose in her throat as she saw their expressions alter, slide from astonishment and confusion to suspicion and then realisation that, logically, the chances were that this had to be something to do with her.

The stunned silence gave way to kerfuffle, a rising babble of voices. Assorted bystanders helped Des to his feet and tissues were produced to staunch the bleeding and mop the mess from the floor.

'Has anyone called the police yet?' This came from dithery solar-powered woman in a high-pitched, panicky voice. 'We have to call the police!'

Fresh blood spattered over Des's grey checked shirt as he shook his head. 'No, no, don't do that.'

Abbie felt more people turning to look at her with varying degrees of accusation and disbelief. Des's reaction confirmed what they'd previously only suspected.

Magda said, 'Abbie? What's this about? What's been going on?'

'I . . . I don't know.' Her cheeks were so hot they felt as if they might burst into flames.

Huw's overgrown eyebrows were bristling as he helped Des to his feet. 'D'you need an ambulance, lad?'

'No, really, there's no need.'

Abbie tried to swallow but her mouth was too dry. Her hands were shaking. She needed to talk to Tom, needed to explain.

'Come on, lad, let's get you cleaned up.' Huw had taken charge now, leading Des towards the stairs.

'Um . . . I'll go and see Tom.' Was that her own voice, calling across the shop after them? It didn't sound like her at all.

Des turned and nodded. Like an automaton, Abbie headed for the door. Somehow she had to sort this out, explain that she hadn't—

'I'm coming with you.' Magda's hand grasped her arm.

'It's OK, you don't have to.'

'What are you going to do, walk home? Come on, I'll give you a lift.'

Back in Channings Hill, Tom's dusty silver-grey van was parked outside the house.

'I'll come in too.' Magda was firm.

'No, please don't.' The last thing they needed was an audience.

'Has he ever hit you?'

'No!'

Magda said grimly, 'There's a first time for everything. He's never hit Des before either.'

'Tom's not like that.' As she stumbled out of the car, Abbie belatedly realised that if she'd been innocent she would have said, 'Why would Tom hit me? I haven't done anything wrong.'

Too late now. Taking a deep breath, she opened the front door.

Ironing, ironing everywhere. The living room was awash with it; there was even an ivory lace wedding dress in the window, hanging from the curtain rail. No Georgia, thank God. Just Tom standing with his back to her, his arms tightly folded and his whole body radiating fury.

This was what she'd been dreading for months. Now it had happened. And it was fairly obvious how he'd found out.

'How could you?' Tom's voice vibrated with emotion. Slowly he turned to face her. 'How *could* you?'

Abbie saw red. Without warning, fear turned to defiance. 'How could I? Look what you've just done!' The words came spilling out, a desperate form of retaliation. 'If you wanted to talk about it, you could have just asked me and I'd have told you everything. It would have been just between us.' Her nails dug into her palms and she felt sick, because from now on her life would be different.

'But oh no, you had to come into work and cause a scene, and now everybody knows!'

'I DON'T CARE.' Tom, who never raised his voice, roared, 'I WANT EVERYONE TO KNOW! YOU AND DES KILGOUR . . . YOU AND HIM TOGETHER . . .'

'I haven't had sex with him.' Abbie blurted the words out, terrified by his fury. 'It was just one night, I thought you'd had an affair and I was upset—'

The front door swung open and Georgia called out, 'Why's there a woman trying to hide in the bushes under our front window?' Then she appeared in the living-room doorway and her expression altered as she took in the scene. Her gaze flickered between them and Abbie knew then who had told Tom.

'Thanks.' Abbie shook her head at Georgia.

Georgia said indignantly, 'What? It wasn't me. I didn't tell him.'

Tom looked at his daughter in disbelief. 'Hang on. You mean you knew about it? You *knew* about Des Kilgour?'

'He turned up here once, and they didn't know I was in the house. I heard everything. Abbie made me promise not to tell you. Oh Dad, I'm sorry . . .'

Could Georgia make it sound any worse? And she was lying; she had to be behind this. Abbie demanded, 'So who was it, then? If it wasn't you?'

Georgia stood her ground. 'How should I know? Maybe it was the woman hiding in the bushes.' Striding over to the window and flinging it open, she said bluntly, 'Well? Was it you?'

Eavesdropping on other people's conversations had long been Magda's forte. Rising slowly to her feet, she brushed leaves from her hair. 'Of course it wasn't me. None of us knew anything about it before today.'

'That's because there isn't anything to know about,' said Abbie.

Tom was curt. 'Magda, get out of here.'

'Just don't hit her,' was Magda's warning shot as she turned to leave.

When she'd driven away and Georgia had closed the window, Abbie looked at Tom and said again, 'So who told you?'

Tom took a folded sheet of paper out of his jeans pocket. 'This was left on my windscreen.'

Her legs still trembling, she crossed the room and took it from him. In capital letters, the anonymous note said: FROM A FRIEND WHO THINKS YOU SHOULD KNOW THAT YOUR WIFE IS HAVING AN AFFAIR WITH DES KILGOUR. P.S. THIS ISN'T A RUMOUR. IT'S FACT.

'Except it isn't true.' Abbie swallowed hard; how many more times did she have to say it? 'Nothing happened, I *swear.*'

'You spent the night with him,' Georgia butted in. 'In his bed. You can't say *nothing* happened.'

Had she written the note? So that Tom would find out, but she could insist she hadn't been the one to tell him?

'There was no sex.'

'But you kissed him.'

'Look, I'd like to talk to Tom about this. Could we have some privacy, d'you think?'

Any normal person would instantly leave. But Georgia, who wasn't any normal person, shook her head. 'No, I'm staying. Look what you've done to my dad.'

Tom was barely recognisable, his face gaunt and his eyes dead. Of course Georgia was siding with him, protecting him.

'Let me explain everything.' Abbie pleaded, but he held up his hands.

'You've lied to me. You've been keeping secrets, doing God knows what, so why would I believe anything you say now?'

This wasn't an argument, this was her whole world slipping away. Abbie blurted out, 'It was when you were off on that fishing trip and I found the letter from . . . her.' She indicated Georgia, who reacted as if she'd been slapped.

'So it's all my fault, is it? Oh no, you're not going to pin the blame on me, just because you've been caught out!'

'Look, I'm just trying to tell you what happened.' Abbie's voice rose. Georgia's interference was the last thing she needed.

'Well, don't.' Tom surveyed her with disgust before turning away. 'Don't bother. Because I don't want to hear.'

'You're sure you don't mind?'

'Of course I don't!'

'You're really sure?'

'Really.' How could she mind her sister moving in with her? Cleo carried a cup of tea over to Abbie, who was in a terrible state. Apart from anything else, it had been a fait accompli; by the time she'd arrived home from work this evening, Abbie had already let herself into the cottage and taken over the spare bedroom. Because staying in her own house was no longer an option.

When she'd heard the reason why, Cleo had been stunned. It was surreal, on a par with Abbie announcing that she was becoming an astronaut and going off to train with NASA.

But it was true. Beyond belief though it seemed, her sister had managed to get herself entangled, however briefly, with Des Kilgour. Who was now, somewhat inconveniently, in love with her.

And possibly also suffering from a broken nose.

It just went to show.

'I couldn't stay there. I *couldn't*.' Distraught and repeating herself,

Abbie rattled on. 'Not with the two of them ganging up on me. Oh yes, this is Georgia's dream come true. She's got her wish. From now it'll just be her and her dad together, and no more moaning misery-woman to rain on her parade. You know, she definitely put that note on Tom's windscreen. I tried so hard to be nice to her and this is the thanks I get. And to think I *trusted* her.'

It was eleven thirty. Cleo was shattered after a long day. 'But what if it wasn't her?'

'Who else could it be? Des hasn't told another living soul. And neither did I. Because I knew it was the only way to be safe.'

'Maybe somebody saw you.'

'But that's just it, they *didn't*. They couldn't have, because there hasn't been anything to see!'

There was no answer to that. Cleo said, 'Well, I can't guess how it happened, then. But I'm sure Tom'll come round. You know how much he loves you.'

'I didn't tell him about Des because I didn't want to hurt him. And now I've made things a million times worse.' Tears were leaking out of Abbie's eyes, dripping down on to her forearm. 'He doesn't believe me any more. The trust has gone. And you know how proud Tom is. God, *sorry* . . .'

'Doesn't matter. Let me do it.' Bending to retrieve the smashed sections of her favourite teacup, Cleo managed to kneel in a puddle of tea and simultaneously slice her finger on a shard of china. Blood oozed out and dripped on to the floor.

'Sorry, I'll help you clear up . . .'

'No, really, it's fine.'

'I just can't believe it's happened.'

'Abbie, it's only a cup.'

'I didn't mean that. I'm talking about my life. My stupid hopeless l-life . . .'

Eleven thirty-five. Cleo grabbed a handful of tissues from the box Abbie was working her way through, and began to mop up the mess. It was going to be a long, long night.

Chapter 42

It was the final performance of *Beach Party!* at the Hippodrome and the Casey Kruger fan club had turned out this evening in force. There were probably fifty-odd in total, and some of them were, without question, odd. Crimplene abounded. And overweight bodies crammed into slightly-too-small I Love Casey! T-shirts. There were even a few men.

At least it wasn't raining. They had a nice night for it. Which was just as well really, seeing as the show had ended fifty minutes ago and they were still waiting with their cameras and autograph books for their hero to emerge from the theatre. But no one seemed to mind. Apparently he'd been fantastic tonight. It had been a performance to remember.

Cleo was having to wait too, but at least she was getting paid for it. And when she'd dropped him at the stage door earlier he had warned her that he'd more than likely be late out tonight.

'Bloody better be anyway,' he'd added. 'There'll be big trouble if the management don't crack open a few bottles of bubbly.'

Settling back in the driver's seat, Cleo turned her attention away from the excited fans and picked up her phone. She'd already called Abbie to let her know she wouldn't be back before midnight. Earlier, too, she'd spoken to Tom and discovered him in no mood to forgive his wife for almost-but-not-quite sleeping with another man. Nor had he taken kindly to being lectured (his choice of words) on the subject of love and trust by someone who'd never even *had* a proper relationship in her life.

Which had hurt, but Cleo had for once stoically refrained from retaliating. Apart from anything else, he had a point. And he was currently very hurt, feeling cruelly betrayed and let down. Because the greater the love, the more devastating the sense of betrayal. Which was why she hadn't been nearly as emotionally shattered when she'd discovered Will's deception.

Well, she'd leave Tom alone for the moment. But still she fidgeted restlessly with her phone; yesterday's bombshell regarding Abbie and Tom had affected her in more ways than one. Because theirs had always been the ultimate perfect relationship, the one against which all others were held up, measured and invariably found wanting.

Call it warped female logic, but if things could fall apart for Abbie and Tom, what hope was there for the rest of them?

Which in turn meant that all the effort she'd made over the last few years to protect herself from being hurt might not have been the smart move she'd thought.

Basically, if you were going to end up sooner or later getting your heart broken anyway, why not stop agitating about it and just let yourself go with the flow? If this was the case, at least have your bit of fun with the most gorgeous man you could think of.

Ooh now, hmm, let's see, and who might that be? Cleo smiled inwardly, mocking the fact that she was a girl with a guilty secret. Because like it or not, Johnny LaVenture appeared to have taken up more or less permanent residence inside her head.

But it wouldn't be out of order, would it, to give Johnny a quick call, just to find out how things were going with his aunt? That would be all right, surely. If he was going through a difficult time, wouldn't he be glad to hear a friendly voice?

The stage door burst open at last and Casey emerged to a rousing cheer from his fans. They clustered around him as if he were a conquering hero. And he was waving a bottle of champagne in each hand, which was only increasing their excitement. By the look of him, it wasn't the first champagne he'd encountered tonight.

Cleo gazed down at the electric-blue screen of her mobile, still trying to decide whether to phone Johnny.

'Wa-heyyyy!' A cork flew into the air and another ecstatic cheer went up. If the fans thought they might be sharing the champagne, their hopes were soon dashed. Casey tipped his head back and glugged it down as if he'd spent the last month in a desert. One of the women screamed delightedly, 'Ooh, he's spilling it down his front. Casey, let me lick it off your chest!'

Since she was in her sixties and barrel-shaped, it wasn't tremendously likely to happen. Cleo scrolled through the numbers stored in her phone and felt her breath catch in her throat as Johnny's name came up. Which was kind of a giveaway. OK, all she was doing was calling *as a friend* to see how things were going in Norfolk.

Or maybe not. His phone was switched off, which probably meant he was at the hospital. Debating whether or not to leave a message, she was distracted by another chorus of squeals as

Casey ripped open his red silk shirt and thrust his bare chest at the sixty-something woman. Oh God, that was so gross. Cleo ended the call; she'd try again tomorrow. Buzzing down the window, she watched as the woman enthusiastically snaked her tongue across Casey's hairless, fake-tanned chest . . . surely this had to contravene some obscenity law or other. *Eugh,* please don't let him invite her to come back with him to the hotel . . .

Ten minutes later Casey reeled over to the car. Shaking his head to stop Cleo opening the rear door for him, he threw himself into the front passenger seat instead.

'I can't talk to you properly from back there. C'mon, let's go, my work here is done. Put your foot down before that fat old bird throws herself on to the bonnet.' He took a messy swig from the second bottle of Moët. 'Jesus, what an octopus, she kept trying to unzip my jeans.'

'I noticed. I thought maybe after the fourth or fifth time you might have asked her to stop.'

Casey gave her a nudge. 'Hey, s'just a bit of fun. I've brightened their day. S'what it's all about, yeah?' He glugged back more champagne as she put the car into gear and pulled away from the kerb. 'You know what? I'm gonna miss this place. Gonna miss you too.'

'Thank you. That's nice.' Cleo turned her attention to navigating the busy multi-laned city centre. Moments later she saw that Casey's eyes had closed and his mouth fallen open. Hooray, just pray he didn't snore like a warthog all the way back to the hotel.

Before long they'd left Bristol behind them. Cleo drove while Casey slept, his head lolling sideways on to his shoulder, the half-empty bottle cradled like a baby in his arms. She was three miles from the hotel when he woke up with a whole-body jolt and said, 'How 'bout you, then?'

'How about me what?'

'Gonna miss me, babe?'

Oh please. Aloud she said politely, 'Of course I will.'

'Ha, knew it!' He slapped his leg. 'Changed your mind about me now, haven't you? Don't want to miss your chance with Casey Kruger. Stop the car, babe.'

'Listen, we'll be at the hotel in five minutes—'

'No no no no *no*! C'mon, babe, pull over, just do it for me, eh?'

He was absolutely plastered. Cleo had no intention of slowing down. 'Let's just keep going, shall we, then—'

'Babe, for crying out loud, stop the fucking car NOW!' As he said it, Casey launched himself without warning across the car and grabbed the steering wheel, wrenching it from her hands. The car swerved wildly to the left as the narrow country lane bent to the right. In slow motion, with Casey's belated yell of, 'Oh fuck a duck!' ringing in her ears, Cleo jammed on the brakes too late to prevent the car crashing through a fence and assuming a sideways momentum of its own as it hurtled down a steep slope on the other side.

It was like being trapped against your better judgement on the world's scariest rollercoaster. Flung left then right then upside down, Cleo gave herself up to the rolling. Was this it, was this how she was going to die? Would everyone blame her for the accident? Would Casey Kruger fans disrupt her funeral and call her names? Oh no, poor Abbie, as if she didn't already have enough on her plate. And what about Ash? Would he be distraught with grief? Damn, and did this mean she'd never find out what Johnny was like in bed? That was so unfair, why hadn't she just . . . oh, hang on, stopping now . . .

Stopping . . .

Stopped now.

Slowly Cleo opened her eyes. Was she still alive or did she just think she was, like Patrick Swayze's character in *Ghost*?

'Oooooh fuuuuck,' groaned a voice next to her.

OK, if they were both dead, this could mean she was shackled to Casey Kruger for all eternity. That would definitely be too much to bear, stuck with the world's most irritating ghostly sidekick.

No, they were still alive. Cleo croaked, 'Are you all right?'

'Fucking stupid question. What did you do?'

Hello? What had *she* done? 'You grabbed the steering wheel,' Cleo reminded him.

'What? No I didn't!' Casey was outraged. 'It was you.'

OK, now wasn't the time to get into a fight. They were trapped in complete darkness, hanging upside down in a smashed-up car on a steeply sloping wooded escarpment. Cleo felt blood trickling down her face. There was shattered windscreen glass all over her. Her neck hurt. So did her legs. Her left hip *really* hurt. Oh God, this was serious. The driver's side of the car was buckled in. Who was to say the petrol tank wouldn't ignite? Fumbling for the door handle with her right hand, she attempted without success to open the door.

'Look,' Casey complained, 'not being funny, but can we stop mucking about now? Just get me back to the hotel, yeah?'

'We need an ambulance.' Cleo tried to work out where her phone was.

'Fine then, tell 'em to hurry up. I need to get back before they close the bar . . . wha's happened to this bottle anyway? S'empty.'

Fingers trembling with the effort, Cleo managed to reach her mobile. It almost slipped from her grasp and the back of her neck prickled with panic because if she'd dropped it, they'd really be stuck. Right, got it, all she had to do now was press nine nine nine and—

'Cleo? Hey, how are you!'

What?

Confused and in a state of shock, Cleo wondered how she could possibly be hearing Johnny's voice. Was he working on the switchboard for the emergency services? Hang on, no, she hadn't called them yet. Belatedly she realised she must have pressed last number redial when she was making a grab for the phone.

'Cleo? Are you there?'

Tears welled up in her eyes because he sounded so close, when in reality he was two hundred miles away. 'Yes, I'm here . . . Johnny, we've had an accident . . . we're trapped in the car and my neck hurts . . . I need to call an ambulance but the battery's almost gone on my phone . . .'

He didn't hesitate or waste a moment. 'I'll call them. Where are you?'

'Pennywell Lane, we came off at the bend opposite Parson's Barn . . . Casey's with me . . . I'm frightened to move and we're stuck here . . .'

'Tell 'em to bloody hurry up,' Casey bellowed. 'I don't want to miss last orders.'

'Right, I'm calling 999. Hang up now,' Johnny ordered. 'And don't panic, OK? Everything's going to be fine.'

He'd gone. Cleo closed her eyes. All they could do now was wait. Next to her, Casey mumbled, 'God dammit, I've wet myself.'

'Never mind.'

In the darkness she heard him shift in his seat. 'S'all *cold . . .*'

'Did you spill champagne on your trousers?'

More shifting around, followed by the sound – *ew* – of Casey smacking his lips. Relieved, he said, 'Yeah, it's the Moët.'

A fresh trickle of blood slid across Cleo's forehead into her ear. It felt horrible but she couldn't turn her neck to stop it happening. There was glass in her hair too. Somewhere nearby, an owl hooted. She started to shiver as shock set in. How long would it be before the ambulance turned up?

Not long at all, thank God. Within minutes they heard a vehicle racing along the lane, coming closer and closer. No sirens though. Maybe when there was no other traffic on the road they didn't bother with them. Cleo listened to the ambulance pull up, followed by the sound of a door slamming and footsteps racing towards the car.

Then she opened her eyes again, and there was Johnny, which was so clearly impossible that she had to be hallucinating.

'About time too,' slurred Casey. 'Get us out of here, mate. Got any whisky on you?'

'Johnny?' His name came out as a croak. 'Is it you?'

'You're OK. Don't try to move.' He managed, finally, to wrench open the buckled driver's door. Crouching beside Cleo, he stroked her hair out of her eyes. 'Can you feel your legs?'

She managed with some difficulty to wiggle each foot in turn. 'Yes. How can you be here?'

'I got back to Channings Hill earlier this evening.'

'Your aunt?'

'Barbara died last night,' said Johnny.

'Oh no. I'm sorry.' Cleo tried to shake her head and winced with pain.

'Keep still. The ambulance'll be here any minute. I can't believe

309

I beat them to it.' Johnny was stroking her hand. 'Then again, I was only three miles away. And I drove like a maniac.'

His presence was such a comfort. 'I'm glad you came.' A tear leaked from Cleo's right eye and she felt him wipe it away. 'How's your other aunt?'

'Clarice? Not too bad, considering. She's back at the nursing home now.'

'Got a can of lager, mate? Not being funny,' Casey complained, 'but all this waiting around's starting to get on my tits.'

Johnny gave Cleo's shoulder a reassuring squeeze. In the distance they heard the wail of a siren – so it was being used after all. He stayed with her, gently picking bits of shattered windscreen glass out of her hair, until help arrived in the form of two police officers and two ambulance crew.

While they checked her over, the paramedics asked Cleo questions. When they heard where she lived, the older one chuckled and said, 'Oh yes, I know Channings Hill. Used to have a regular customer there. Jean, her name was. Thirsty girl! Reckon she used to have us on speed-dial. Used to get herself in some right old states.' As he measured Cleo's blood pressure he added jovially, 'You must have known her. I'm trying to think of her surname.'

Did the sense of shame ever go away? Cleo looked at him and said, 'She was my aunt.'

'Oh, sorry, love.' During the awkward moment that ensued, Cleo saw him sniffing the air, taking note of the alcohol fumes. Casually he said, 'Yeah, now you come to mention it, you look like her. So how about you then, love? Had anything to drink this evening?'

'No.'

'Ha, don't you believe it,' said Casey. 'She's been knocking back the vodka shots all night, saucy minx.'

The second paramedic raised an eyebrow and said drily, 'And how about you, sir?'

Casey waved an airy hand. 'Nothing at all, officer. Completely teetotal, me. Never touch a drop.'

Chapter 43

'How can I put this?' said Ash. 'You've looked better.'

'Thanks.' Cleo would have retaliated, but she knew it was true. Plus, she needed a lift home from the hospital.

'So what's happening with the other chap? Going to sue the pants off him?'

Hmm, that was a tricky question. She'd already been visited by Casey Kruger's manager, his agent and his lawyers. Casey, miraculously unhurt himself, was emphatically denying having caused the accident. According to his statement, a muntjac deer had leapt out in front of them and Cleo, panicking, had swerved off the road. If she didn't agree with this version of events, he would be forced to accuse her of dangerous driving. The publicity for Henleaze Limos would be dreadful, the repercussions potentially horrendous.

Or they could keep the matter out of court and he would pay for the considerable damage to the car.

Just as well it hadn't been the Bentley Continental.

'It's complicated.' Grumpy Graham was currently seeking legal advice on the matter. Easing herself off the bed, Cleo said, 'Ow, *ouch.*'

Ash shook his head. 'You have to go one better, don't you? Just because I hurt my back, you have to deliberately crash a limo and end up in hospital. Has anyone ever told you you're a copycat and an attention-seeker?'

Cleo took his arm. 'Yes, but you're better now. So you can help me out to the car.'

'So long as people don't see us like this and think we're a couple.' Grinning, Ash said, 'I do have my standards, you know.'

The discharge forms had been filled in and she was free to leave. Cleo knew she was lucky; battered and bruised she might be, but no serious damage had been done. The X-rays had been clear. She had cuts to her face and a vicious case of whiplash but it could have been so much worse. And the doctors had told her she only had to wear the surgical collar for a week.

A pretty nurse, pink-cheeked and sparkly-eyed, came hurrying up to them. 'Oh, you're just off? You've got another visitor!'

Grumpy Graham? Casey Kruger? More legal people? Turning stiffly to survey the double doors at the entrance to the ward, Cleo's heart did the rabbity, skippety thing it quite often did, nowadays, when she saw Johnny LaVenture.

'Why's she blushing?' Under his breath Ash murmured, 'Did he just give her one in the linen cupboard?'

He liked Johnny well enough as a person, but his effect on other women – OK, *on Fia* – was something Ash found hard to forgive.

'Hey.' Johnny smiled slightly when they reached him. 'So they're kicking you out.'

Nodding hurt. And, thanks to the high soft collar, probably gave her an unattractive double chin. Thinking that if Ash hadn't had a proprietary arm around her, Johnny might have greeted her with a kiss, Cleo said, 'I'm fine. Thanks for, you know, last night.'

'No problem. Glad I was able to help. He glanced at Ash. 'I can give her a lift home if you like. If you're busy . . . ?'

Yes please, yes please!

'It's OK, I came here to pick her up.' Ash's arm around her tightened. 'I'll take her back.'

Johnny nodded slowly. 'OK. I'll see you soon then. I'm heading up to London this evening, then back to Norfolk to organise Barbara's funeral.'

'Well, thanks again. For everything.' This time Cleo disentangled herself from Ash's grasp and leaned forward to plant a kiss on Johnny's cheek. Kissing was even more painful than nodding, but the smell of his aftershave and the warmth of his cheek made it worth it. Also, out of the corner of her eye she could see the envious expression on the face of the pretty nurse.

'You can thank me as well if you like,' said Ash on the way home.

'Thank you for what?'

'You wanted to go back with him, didn't you? And what would have been the point of that? You've got a thing for Johnny LaVenture. He might even have a bit of a thing for you, seeing as he hasn't had a chance yet to tick you off his To Do list.' Ash could be very blunt when he wanted. 'But let's face it, you're in no condition to do anything right now. Plus, you look dead rough. So leave him alone, that's all I'm saying. If you really want to make a fool of yourself, at least wait until you're better.'

As he drove through Winterbourne, Cleo pulled down the sun visor and studied her reflection in the tiny mirror. Hair a mess, cuts all over her face and a giant plastic-and-foam neck brace. Ash had a point.

Watching her, he added helpfully, 'You look as if you've been caught up in one of those vegetable-chopping machines.'

'Cheers.' You could always rely on your friends to give you a boost. To pay him back she said, 'How's it going with you and Fia?'

'I tell you what.' Ash kept his attention fixed on the road ahead. 'You don't ask me cruel questions. And I won't stop the car and make you walk.'

Fia couldn't believe she was having such a fantastic time. Who'd have thought a trip to the zoo could be so much fun? But it was, and it had all been her idea! When she'd invited Ash to come along with her, he'd looked stunned. But then he'd said yes and that had been the start of a truly brilliant day.

'Where next? Gorilla Island!' Taking his hand, she raced across the grass separating the lion enclosure from the monkey house. 'I want to see the baby gorillas . . .'

'No, no, penguins first.' Ash pulled her in another direction. 'They're being fed in ten minutes. Have you ever fed a penguin?'

'It's not allowed.' Fia had seen the signs. 'The keepers have to do it.'

'Ah, but I used to work here. Didn't you know that?' He shook his fair hair out of his eyes and gave her a wink. 'Which means we can.'

And unbelievably, they had. Taking off their shoes and socks, she and Ash had paddled barefoot in the shallows, feeding raw fish to the penguins and watching them swoop and dive through the water. The crowds of zoo-goers, watching enviously from behind the barriers, laughed and applauded Ash's comic antics as he interacted with the penguins. Finally she exclaimed, 'You're so different today! I love it when you're like this!'

And Ash replied, 'But I've always been like this. You've just never noticed before.' Then he reached for her hand and pulled her towards the ledge where the pebbles fell away and the deep water glittered in the sunlight. 'Come on, let's go for a swim!'

The crowd gasped as, together, they raised their arms and launched themselves like dolphins into the air. A split second before hitting the surface of the water, Fia woke up.

Wow, that had been bizarre. She gazed at the bedroom ceiling and wondered what had prompted it. She'd watched a wildlife documentary on TV last night, but that had been about meerkats. And she'd shopped at the supermarket yesterday but hadn't even visited the fresh fish counter . . .

Hang on, got it. Last night in the pub while she'd been bringing out food, Ash and Frank had been engaged in a passionate debate about the various merits of Wagon Wheels, Jaffa Cakes and, yes, P-p-p-penguins.

That was dreams for you. They were weird. God, though, this one had felt so real. And it wasn't fading away either, as dreams usually did. Every last detail was still vivid and intact.

Even thinking about Ash made her feel a bit funny. He'd been so brilliant in the dream, and there'd been this amazing connection between them, as if they'd been best friends for years. In fact, *more* than best friends . . .

Rolling over in bed, Fia turned off her alarm, switched on the radio and scrolled through the channels until she came to BWR. Did Ash's show start at seven?

'. . . on your marks then for the great Spacehoppathon. On the orange spacehopper we have Gay Pete and on the manly dark green spacehopper . . . *grrrr* . . . we have Big Bad Bruce in his motorbike boots. OK, twice round the studio, no pushing and shoving, three two one . . . go!'

Gosh, it felt strange to hear his voice again so soon after they'd been feeding penguins together. But Ash sounded just as jolly and relaxed on the radio as he had at the zoo. Anyway, time to get up. Hauling herself out of bed, Fia stumbled through to the bathroom and switched on the shower. At least this would be warmer than the icy blue waters of the penguin pool.

By seven thirty she was out of the shower and brushing her wet hair. On the radio Ash was consoling Gay Pete, who hadn't covered himself in glory during the race.

'Poor you, came last *and* broke the heel on your pink stiletto.'

'Bruce cheated! I would've won if he hadn't stabbed my space hopper with his penknife.'

'Oh now, come on, a bad hopper always blames his punctures. Just face up to it, Pete, you lost your race. Big Bad Bruce is the champion. And now I'm afraid you have to pay the price . . .'

By the time Fia had finished drying her hair, Rihanna was singing her latest single. When the music came to an end, Ash began chatting to Megan the traffic girl about the date she'd been out on last night with the drummer in a local band.

'It went fine. Really well.' Poor Megan, she was trying to be discreet; it couldn't be easy, being interrogated when her date could be listening in.

'I love it. This is so romantic,' Ash exclaimed gleefully. 'So who kissed who? OK, don't answer that, you kissed each other. How did the date come about, then? You can tell us that. How does a long-haired thrash-metal drummer with tattoos and multiple piercings go about romantically asking out a pretty little Doris Day type who loves puppies and hairbands and cupcakes with pink glittery icing?'

Fia pulled open her underwear drawer and selected her favourite peacock-blue bra and knicker set.

'Fine then.' Megan was laughing but her tone was defiant. 'If you must know, he didn't ask me out. I asked him.'

'*What?*' Ash affected shock. 'You mean he might not even *like* you?'

'Shush, I knew he liked me. I'd seen the way he looked at me. But I'd waited and waited and he *still* didn't say anything. In the end I knew I'd have to be the one to make the first move.'

'So why didn't he do it?'

'Because he was scared I'd turn him down.'

'Oh, right. You're telling me the long-haired tattooed thrash-metal drummer is shy.'

Megan sounded proud. 'He is. And you know what? I like that in a man. It's a very attractive quality. Not that you'd know anything about that.'

'Ha, now that's where you're wrong,' Ash countered. 'I have no confidence. Deep down, I'm very shy.'

Everyone in the studio was laughing now. Megan said, 'Yeah, yeah, you're about as shy as Russell Brand.'

'I can be shy. Sometimes.' He paused, and for a moment Fia almost believed him. Then he continued smoothly, 'So d'you fancy going out on a date with a real man now? What are you doing tomorrow night?'

They kept up the banter while Fia buttoned herself into her kitchen whites. Megan protested that her new drummer boyfriend probably wouldn't appreciate her going out with someone else and Ash told her she was a fool to throw away her big chance, that she didn't know what she was missing. Then female listeners started texting in, eagerly offering themselves as replacements and begging for a date with Ash.

'Right, all you girls out there have to calm down,' he ordered. 'There's only one of me to go around and, you know, I do still have my bad back. Oh God, and now we've had another text from

Keira Knightley. Keira, love, how many times do I have to say it? You're just not my type. Leave it now, give it a rest. Move on.'

Megan said, 'So who *do* you like?'

'Ah, a gentleman never tells. Plus, he definitely wouldn't be stupid enough to tell *you*. There might be someone capable of making my heart beat faster,' Ash's tone was playful, 'but that's my business, not yours.'

'Ooh!' Gay Pete chimed in. 'Is it me?'

Chapter 44

From the living-room sofa, Cleo listened to the sound of plates being taken out of kitchen cupboards and restacked in size order. Or according to colour and pattern. Being sorted in one way or another, anyway. With a lot of accompanying noise and clatter. Nor was it likely to stop in the foreseeable future.

Misery meant her sister didn't know what to do with her hands. In order to keep herself occupied, Abbie had embarked on a spring-clean the likes of which this cottage had never known.

Which was nice in one way, but also had its annoying side. Because if Cleo had been out at work, what could be lovelier than coming home at the end of the day to a sparkling, pristine, ultra-tidy house?

Except she wasn't out at work, was she? She was officially re-cuperating. And it was a lot less fun lying on the sofa when you had to listen to all the frenetic activity elsewhere in the house. As Abbie had previously been frustrated by Georgia's ironing in their living room, so she in turn was now frustrating Cleo, who had turned the volume up three times already and *still* couldn't hear the TV.

'Abbie? Abbie!'

'What?' Her sister appeared in the doorway. 'Do you want some scrambled eggs? Soup? Cup of tea?'

'No thanks. Why don't you come in here, just sit down and relax for a bit?' Cleo gave the sofa cushion an encouraging pat. 'Come on, it's *Masterchef*.'

Abbie shook her head. 'It's OK, I'm just scrubbing your cupboards. And then I'm going through all the food. There's a tin of treacle in there that's six years old!'

'I don't like treacle.'

'So why haven't you thrown it out?'

Because if you threw something out, sod's law dictated that you'd be desperately in need of it within the next fortnight. Cleo said, 'It might come in useful one day.'

'For throwing at someone, maybe, if you wanted to knock them out.'

Cleo hated to see her sister so unhappy. 'Look, why don't you let me have another talk with Tom? See if we can't get this sorted out?'

'I've tried. You've tried. It's no good.' Abbie shook her head. 'He hates me and he's not going to change his mind.'

In all honesty, this was true. Cleo's last attempt had been about as effective as a mouse stamping on an elephant's foot. Tom couldn't forgive Abbie for what she'd already admitted having done. The fact that she hadn't had actual sex with Des simply wasn't good enough.

Abbie turned and disappeared back into the kitchen. Within seconds the crash-bang-clatter of crockery resumed. In all likelihood it would still be going strong at midnight.

Picking up her mobile – her trusty, life-saving mobile – Cleo called a number. When it was answered, she whispered, '*Help*.'

★　★　★

By seven thirty, thanks to three glasses of wine, Cleo was feeling pleasantly fuzzy around the edges. A few people might still be giving her funny looks but she no longer minded. Here at the Hollybush she was among friends. And she knew she looked a fright, but that was car accidents for you; the healing phase, three days on from the crash, was in progress. She'd been lucky. The cuts and bruises on her face might be unsightly now, but at least they were only superficial. In another week they'd be gone.

If only she could say the same about her sister.

She heaved a sigh. 'What's going to happen? When's it going to end?'

Ash said, 'Are we talking about the world?'

Cleo gave him a prod. 'I'm talking about Abbie. My sitting tenant. Except she never does sit, she just keeps on cleaning. And having niggly little goes at me because I haven't polished the tops of the wardrobes or dusted the back of the TV in the last month.'

'When she's finished your place, send her round to do mine.'

'She can move in with you if you like.' Cleo sank her head back against her chair. 'Oh God, I'm horrible. She's my sister and I love her to bits, but I really don't want her living with me until I'm forty.'

'What makes you think she'd want to live with you?'

'Who wouldn't? I'm irresistible and gorgeous.' As she said it, her stomach rumbled.

Ash reached for a menu. 'And hungry?'

'Now you come to mention it,' said Cleo, 'that too.'

Fia put the finishing touches to Ash's hotpot and Cleo's chilli baked potato, ready to carry them out of the kitchen. Unbelievably, last night's dream was still vivid in her mind. Having felt compelled to listen to the rest of Ash's show this morning,

322

she now understood why it was so popular. In the studio he'd created a little world to which his listeners yearned to belong. Everyone joined in and the banter was a two-way process. Ash was razor-sharp, brilliantly funny and capable of going off on the most surreal of tangents when the mood took him. He was clearly adored by his many fans.

Yet when she'd taken their food order twenty minutes ago, he'd barely glanced at her. She still felt, in his presence, as if she'd inadvertently committed some hideous faux pas. Having intended to tell him about her dream, her nerve had failed her.

But this was ridiculous. Fia snipped flat-leaf parsley and sprinkled it over the hotpot. She loaded the plates on to a tray. If she'd done something to upset Ash, it was up to him to tell her what it was. He couldn't expect her to guess.

'There you go,' she said cheerfully as she put the plates down in front of them. 'One hotpot, one baked potato.'

Ash's jaw tightened. 'Thanks.'

'Yum!' Unwrapping her napkin, Cleo said, 'This is *just* what I need!'

OK, ignore the fact that Ash hadn't even bothered to look up. Fia said, 'I had the weirdest dream last night. And guess what? You were in it!'

'Me? Oh no, was I naked again?' Cleo pulled a face. 'I'm always dreaming that I'm out somewhere and I've forgotten to put any clothes on.'

'Not you. Ash.'

'You dreamed about Ash? Ha, was he naked?'

'No. We were at the zoo, feeding the penguins.'

'Oh now, that sounds *romantic*.'

When she'd mentioned his presence in her dream, Ash's shoulders had visibly stiffened. Now he shot Cleo a look of horror mingled with revulsion. Hurriedly Fia said, 'Oh God no, it wasn't romantic at all! That's the last thing it was. He was trying to make me dive into the freezing water with him . . . and there was this awful smell of raw fish and all these seals lolloping around . . . yeurgh, it was *gross*.'

'Sounds it.' Ash dug his fork through the layer of crispy potato slices on his hotpot; featuring in other people's dreams clearly wasn't something he enjoyed.

Embarrassed by the snub, Fia said, 'Yes, well, I didn't dream about you on purpose. If I had a choice I'd have preferred David Tennant.'

Ash looked as if he wished she'd leave them in peace. Evenly he said, 'Me too.'

'We'd all prefer David Tennant!' Cleo chipped in to cover the awkward silence.

See? She'd done it again. What *was* Ash's problem with her? It was on the tip of Fia's tongue to demand an answer, but the pub was busy and causing a scene would be awful. Instead she flushed and said evenly, 'Enjoy your meal,' before turning and heading back into the kitchen.

When she'd gone, Cleo said, 'You're such a div.'

'Shut up.'

'You went all weird again.'

'Look, I *know*, OK?'

'Why don't you just let me have a quiet word with—'

'Don't even think it. No way.' Vehemently Ash shook his head. 'If you do, you'll die a horrible death.'

'But—'

'You said her dream sounded romantic and she was appalled. I saw the look on her face. She couldn't have been more disgusted. Last week she saw me being massaged by Georgia and this week she dreamed about me swimming with a load of fat blubbery seals. So just leave it, OK?'

'OK. Could I just—?'

His voice rose. 'No no *no*.'

'Just—'

'Cleo, *NO*.'

'Just try a bit of your hotpot,' Cleo blurted out, 'to see what it's like.'

Ash sighed. 'Go on then. You're a nightmare.'

'Ooh, can I try some too?' Georgia had just come in. Bounding up to them, she snatched the fork from his hand and helped herself to a mouthful. 'Mmm, that's good. How are you, anyway?'

'Looking forward to the rest of my hotpot,' said Ash.

'How's your back?'

'Better.'

'See? That's all thanks to me! Didn't I tell you I was brilliant?' She waggled her hands at him. 'There's magic in these fingers. If you want me to give you another go with them, just say the word.'

Cleo looked hopefully at Tom, who had come in with Georgia. Maybe they could have a chat. In response he shook his head and said, 'I don't want to talk about Abbie. We've just come out for a quiet drink.'

'Not too quiet,' Georgia retorted. 'I'm not going to sit in a corner and be boring.'

Ash said, 'That would be too much to hope for.'

'You love me really.' Georgia's eyes danced. 'That was a wicked show you did this morning. I'm telling all my clients to listen to you.'

Cleo watched her with mixed feelings. Georgia was a sweet girl and great fun in lots of ways, but her arrival in their lives had caused all kinds of havoc. She still maintained she wasn't the one who had told Tom about Abbie's indiscretion with Des, but also insisted that he had deserved to learn the truth.

'Look, we'll leave you to eat your food. Join us afterwards if you fancy a game of doubles.' Indicating the pool table, Georgia said playfully, 'But only if you're brave enough to take us on.'

'Maybe later,' said Ash. 'If you promise not to cry like a baby when we whup your sorry ass.'

Georgia and Tom headed over to the pool table. Too busy watching them to pay attention to the food on her fork, Cleo dripped chilli down her front. 'Oh God, why does it always have to happen to me?'

Ash raised his eyebrows. 'And you were so flawless up until that moment.'

Cleo knew she wasn't looking great, what with the cuts all over her face, her super-attractive neck brace and her hair in need of a wash because Abbie's frenzy of cleaning had used up all the hot water in the tank. Oh well, never mind. As she rubbed at the stain on her top, she stuck her tongue out at Ash. 'Lucky I'm only here with you.'

Twenty minutes later the door swung open and Welsh Mac came in. Hoisting himself on to a stool at the bar, he said to Deborah, 'Pint of bitter, love. Johnny's back, just seen him. He's on his way over.'

Johnny was back? On his way over? Cleo sat up straight, simultaneously thrilled and mortified. This was something else that always seemed to happen to her.

Watching her with just a touch of *Schadenfreude*, Ash murmured, 'Bet you wish you'd bothered to wash your hair now.'

Some people just deserved to be kicked.

Under cover of the table, Cleo unzipped her handbag and furtively felt around to see if there was anything in there that might cover the marks on her face. Damn, no concealer, but she had a mini powder compact in there that would be better than nothing.

And yes, of course she wished she'd bothered to boil the kettle and shampoo her hair the hard way over the bathroom sink, but what would that have done to her neck?

'I'm just going to the loo for a second.'

'To try and tart yourself up?' Pretending to feel in his jacket pockets, Ash said innocently, 'Want to borrow my lipstick?'

'You're hilarious.'

'Damn, haven't got it with me. How about a brown paper bag to put over your head?'

Cleo aimed another kick at his legs beneath the table. 'How about I tell Fia you *luuurve* her, you want to *kiss* her, you want to *marry* her?'

Sorrowfully Ash shook his head. 'See, you had the chance to rush off and try to make yourself a bit less scary. But you didn't. And now it's too late, he's here.'

Chapter 45

Cleo swung round as the door opened. Oh well, it wasn't as if Johnny hadn't seen the cuts to her face before. Hastily she scrubbed with her serviette at the stain on her top. Then Johnny appeared and the sight of him prompted her strongest-yet adrenaline rush. Oh God, she'd really got it bad. He was wearing a white cotton shirt over a navy T-shirt and age-softened Levis. His dark hair was flopping over his forehead, his profile was chiselled and gorgeous, and he was laughing at a comment someone to the left of him had just made.

Then his previously obscured companion moved into view and the fizzing excitement deflated like a popped balloon. Not only was the girl tall, blonde and ridiculously attractive, but Cleo knew who she was. Thanks to the wonders of the internet, she knew far more than she wanted to know. Because this was Honor Donaldson, one of Australia's most famous exports. She was a plus-size supermodel, just short of six feet tall and not remotely plus-size in terms of the real world. But with her lusciously voluptuous size fourteen curves and flawless gilded skin, she had taken the modelling industry by storm. Then, when interviews followed and her vivacious character had become known, the rest of the world had fallen in love with her too.

One other small detail about her had come to Cleo's attention while she'd been – oh, the shame of it – Googling Johnny. This was that prior to his return to Channings Hill, for several months he and Honor had been a couple.

And now here she was, making Johnny laugh and holding his hand. Not to mention looking out-of-this-world stunning.

No, no, no, this isn't meant to happen.

Next to Cleo, Ash frowned and said, 'Isn't that thingy?'

'Yes.' If only she looked like a thingy.

'Oh my God!' Abandoning her game of pool, Georgia exclaimed, 'Are you Honor Donaldson? I love you!'

'Sweetie, thanks so much! And look at you, you're so gorgeous!' Honor, whose ability to charm was legendary, smiled at Georgia as if it was the nicest compliment she'd ever received. 'Hey, I like it here already! Johnny, you have to introduce me to *everyone*.' Even her voice was beautiful; she sounded like Nicole Kidman.

'Don't worry, I will. Just let me get some drinks in first.' For a brief moment Johnny's gaze met Cleo's and she saw him attempt to signal something . . . God knows what . . . with his eyes, before turning back to the bar.

'Wow,' murmured Ash.

Cleo realised that Fia was standing right beside her, a tray of dirty plates in her hands and a look of dismay on her face as she took in the sight of Johnny and Honor together. Evidently she wasn't the only one who'd just had her hopes dashed.

Under her breath Fia muttered, 'This is so unfair.'

Then Cleo saw the utter devastation in Ash's eyes, because more than anything he wanted Fia to feel that way about *him*. And it was clear that she never would. He was about as desirable, as far as she was concerned, as a mouldy old fridge.

Cleo zipped up her handbag, because a dab of powder was no longer worth even bothering with. It was a toss-up who she felt more sorry for, Ash or herself.

Within minutes, much like the dreaming-you-were-naked scenario where you prayed no one would notice, Johnny brought Honor Donaldson over to meet them. Up close she was even more golden, sheeny and jaw-droppingly beautiful. She was wearing a casual outfit of loose sand-coloured linen trousers, a paler sandy-gold top, cream waistcoat and espadrilles. Her hair was every shade of gold, her eyes chestnut brown.

'Oh my Lord, look at your face! And your neck! You poor *thing*.' Honor shook her head in sympathy. 'Are you the one who had the accident?'

What else could she say? Cleo nodded. 'That was me.'

'Johnny *told* me about it. Casey Kruger, right? I met him a couple of years back. Jeez, what an annoying little tit.'

Cleo's heart sank, because she'd wanted to dislike her. But how could you not love someone who said that? 'Well, yes.' It certainly summed Casey up.

'Anyway, great to meet you. It's so cool to finally be here, after hearing Johnny talk about this place for so long.' As she spoke, Honor leaned back against Johnny's chest, tilting her head affectionately towards his. 'And it's fantastic to be back with Johnny. I bet he's kept some of the girls around here on their toes, am I right?'

Cleo was numb. She said faintly, 'Oh, I'm sure he has.' Next to her, Ash was having trouble keeping his eyes off Honor's goddess-like cleavage. OK, now she definitely knew who she felt more sorry for. And it wasn't Ash.

In the harshly lit toilets, Cleo surveyed her reflection in the mirror. Flat chest, beige plastic neck brace, attractive chilli stain on T-shirt, face full of healing cuts. Nice. It was pointless but she took the mini powder compact out of her bag anyway and attempted to cover the unsightly marks.

If anything, that looked even worse, bumpy and seriously amateurish. Hopeless, hopeless. And what did it matter now, anyway?

Outside the toilets, she bumped into Johnny. *Of course.*

'I just wanted to say sorry.' He forced her to look at him. 'None of this was planned. Honor turned up out of the blue . . . but, you know, she's here now . . .'

Oh God, did this come under the category of Being Let Down Gently? Nausea crawled up Cleo's throat. It did, didn't it? His conscience had been pricking him, forcing him to acknowledge that up until recently he might have considered having a bit of a fling with her, but things were different now. His old girlfriend was back in his life and she just happened to be one of the most desired females in the world. So basically she, Cleo, had to understand that in comparison . . . well, sorry, there *was* no comparison. At all. End of.

Luckily these thoughts ricocheted through her mind in a nanosecond. Without missing a beat she was able to say breezily, 'Hey, no need to apologise. Honor's great, and she's so friendly. And it's about time you got yourself a nice girl and settled down. You're not so young as you used to be, after all!'

It actually sounded pretty convincing, even if she did say so herself.

'Thanks.' Johnny's gaze dropped to her front; was he looking at the mushroom sauce stain or at her sadly inferior breasts? 'Well, that's it, I just needed to explain.' Eager to change the subject he went on hurriedly, 'Anyway, how are you? How's the neck?'

Cleo's hand went up to the padded plastic contraption that was currently holding her head on her shoulders and forcing her to walk around looking as if she had a poker up her bottom. Cheerily she said, 'Not so bad.'

Unlike her heart.

'It could have been worse.' He looked as if he wanted to say more, but Cleo couldn't bear it. Her control was in danger of slipping and the only option was to head back to the bar before she said or did something she'd regret.

As the door swung shut behind them, she saw that Honor was busy getting a round in. Waving across, she called out, 'Cleo, there you are! Another white wine?'

'Um, no thanks.'

'Oh go on, we're all having a drink! Please let me get you one.'

OK, slightly surreal. Honor Donaldson, Australian supermodel, was begging to buy her a drink. Under other circumstances it would have been the highlight of her year.

But not when Honor had just triumphantly reclaimed the man she, Cleo, had been on the brink of plunging into a relationship with. No matter how unsuitable and doomed to disaster that relationship would undoubtedly have turned out to be. He had captured her heart, and maybe it wasn't completely shattered but it definitely now had a crack in it.

'I'd love to,' Cleo lied, 'but I'm shattered. I really need to get home.'

'She's a lightweight,' Ash explained to Honor. See? The presence of Fia rendered him practically mute but with Honor, whom he evidently didn't fancy, he was completely relaxed.

'And I'm taking strong painkillers that don't mix with alcohol.' Waving goodbye to everyone, Cleo said to Honor, 'Why don't you ask Ash to tell you what happened when he tried it?'

Outside the pub she stopped and gulped down lungfuls of cold air. At least she'd left with some shreds of dignity intact. Because a few more drinks and those shreds could so easily have deserted her.

And then where were you?

Rolling in the gutter with your knickers on show, like Auntie Jean.

It was eleven fifteen and Frank was kicking everyone out. Which was absolutely a good thing. Ash approved of this plan, particularly seeing as he had to be up at five to get to work. And he'd already had four . . . no, five . . . actually more like six or seven pints of lager tonight.

OK, maybe eight but definitely no more than that.

Eight pints. That meant a raging headache and having to take a taxi to the radio station tomorrow morning. Oh well, sometimes you just had to drink your own body weight in Kronenbourg and suffer the consequences.

And tonight this was what Ash had been compelled to do. Witnessing Fia's reaction to Honor Donaldson's arrival had hit him like a lorryload of bricks. Fia was besotted with Johnny. Fat ugly radio presenters didn't get a look in. If he'd ever seriously thought she might change her mind about him, he could give up now.

Anyway, sod it, there was always good old alcohol to soften the blow. And Fia wasn't the only fish in the sea, was she? Other girls found him attractive. Well, one in particular did.

'Ooh, I'm cold.' As they left the pub, Georgia pretended to shiver and snuggled up against him. 'Brrrrrr.'

Tom was beckoning her over. 'Georgia? Come on, let's get home.'

'It's OK, Dad. Ash is lending me a DVD so I'm just going back with him to pick it up.'

'But—'

'Dad, I'm fine! And I've got my key.' Georgia held it up to show him. 'I'll see you soon.'

Tom hesitated, clearly torn. Then he turned and strode off into the darkness.

Ash frowned. 'What DVD?'

'*Mamma Mia!*'

'What am I, some sort of girl? I don't have *Mamma Mia!*'

'No? Oh well, I'll borrow something else then. I'm not fussy.'

By the time they reached his house, Georgia had made her intentions crystal clear. She'd tried it on before, but each time Ash had fobbed her off. She wasn't his type, she was only eighteen, he didn't remotely fancy her, silly little reasons like that . . .

But that had been back when he'd still held out hope that Fia might come to her senses and give him a chance to persuade her he had his good points.

And this was now.

Chapter 46

Once inside the cottage, Georgia said brightly, 'Got anything to drink?'

'Um, there's a couple of beers in the fridge.' What the hell, one more wouldn't make any difference. Ash collapsed on to the sofa and said, 'Can you go and get them? And the DVDs are in that cupboard over there. Borrow anything you like.'

Moments later Georgia reappeared in the living room doorway, an opened bottle in each hand, silver-blond hair illuminated by the hall light behind her. 'I like you.' Pause. 'Does that mean I'm allowed to borrow you?'

Ash held her gaze. Normally at this point he'd make some flippant remark about her having to pay a fine if she didn't return him on time. But he wasn't in a flippant mood. Georgia was a wilful, entertaining eighteen-year-old who knew exactly what she wanted and went for it. She was pretty too; how many men would turn her down?

He didn't have to say a word. As if reading his mind, she crossed the room and put the bottles down out of the way. The next moment, like a small, turbo-powered heat-seeking missile, she was pinning him to the cushions with her arms planted either side of his shoulders, kissing him determinedly on the mouth.

Crikey, she meant business.

'I knew you'd change your mind in the end.' Pulling back for a moment, Georgia smiled at him.

The words reverberated in Ash's head. Ironically, they were what he'd envisaged saying to Fia when she eventually succumbed to his charms. But seeing as that wasn't going to happen, he wouldn't dwell on it now. Georgia had a lithe, dancer's body and how many men would turn her down? Reaching for her, he said, 'Do you always get what you want?'

Her eyes sparkled triumphantly. 'Oh yes.'

Except this time it turned out not to be true. He kissed her again, but in his mind's eye all he could see was Fia. Most men might not let that bother them, but Ash knew he wasn't like most men. Maybe it was old-fashioned in this day and age – OK, maybe it was downright laughable – but he never had been a fan of casual sex. If he slept with Georgia now, he would just be using her. And what effect would it have on their relationship after tonight?

'Look, I'm sorry.' Ash shook his head regretfully. 'I can't do this.'

She looked surprised. 'Why not?'

'It just doesn't feel right. We're *friends*.'

'But we could be more than friends!'

'No. It would be spoiled, trust me. It's not going to happen.' Gently he shifted her off his lap.

Georgia, her blond hair tousled, saw that he meant it. 'Well, *this* has never happened to me before.'

'It's not you. It's me,' said Ash.

'Well *duh*, I know that!'

336

'I mean, you're a beautiful girl. You haven't done anything wrong.'

'I know that too. Oh God,' Georgia blurted out, 'I like you so much! I really wanted us to do it!'

'Sorry. I don't know what else to say.'

She shook her head. 'I heard you on your show last week, going on about how you were shy. And I thought maybe that explained why you kept giving me the brush-off. So I decided the next opportunity that came up, I'd grab it.'

Ash smiled slightly at the unfortunate turn of phrase. She very nearly had.

'Well, that was the plan, anyway.' Rising to her feet, Georgia reached for her bag and slung it over her shoulder. 'Oh well, at least I gave it a try.'

Her tone was good-natured now. Ash stood up, relieved. 'You did. And you're a fantastic girl. Come on, I'll walk you home.'

'You don't have to. I can make my own way.'

'Hey, I know you can.' He put an arm around her shoulders and gave her an affectionate squeeze. 'But I'm a gentleman, so let me do it anyway. Please.'

Unable to sleep, Fia crept out of bed, padded down to the kitchen and made herself a cup of tea. Having carried it back upstairs, she pulled open the bedroom curtains and settled herself on to the cushioned window seat. It was the first place she'd ever lived that had a proper view, rather than just looking across to the other side of the street. From here, high up in the eaves of the pub, she was able to gaze out over the village green and the houses surrounding it. Then there were the hills, dotted with lights, rising up in the distance. It was a gorgeous sight.

But Fia was too unsettled to enjoy it. She was on edge for two reasons. Sipping her tea, she wondered what to do about the text she had received as she'd been getting ready for bed.

Hi, hope all's well. Molly and Rob send hugs. They miss you and would love to see you. Maybe this weekend? Love Will x

When she'd read the text, her eyes had filled with tears. Fond though she'd been of Rob and Molly, dear though they were to her, they hadn't been *hers*. Upon leaving Will, she had kind of assumed that she wouldn't see them again. But how unbearably sad must it be for children in that situation, the products of broken marriages, to be endlessly forced to adjust each time new partners appeared in their parents' lives?

Fia rubbed her face. She *had* missed Rob and Molly. But the prospect of seeing Will again was less enticing.

So that was one thing occupying her mind. Then there was Johnny and Honor Donaldson. Their arrival in the pub this evening – Honor's arrival back in Johnny's life – had knocked her for six. Her hopes and fantasies had been dashed, because who could begin to compete with someone like that? Talk about a reality check.

She took a sip of tea. It had been weird in the pub tonight. And what had been going on between Ash and Georgia, for heaven's sake? Ash had been knocking back drinks like nobody's business and Georgia had been even more openly adoring than usual. It was an odd situation, without a doubt. And they'd left the pub together, although nothing would have happened, surely. Of course it wouldn't; Tom had been there with them. Oh God, so much to think about, no wonder she couldn't sleep . . .

Across the green, a front door opened and golden light spilled out. Pressing her forehead against the cool glass, Fia peered through the window as two instantly recognisable figures emerged from

Ash's cottage. Ash and Georgia made their way down the front path and headed off along the lane. Their heads were bent together, they were talking intently, Georgia's arm was around Ash's waist and his was wrapped around her shoulders. At one point they stopped and Ash planted a tender kiss on her forehead. Fia jerked back from the window, feeling as if she'd been punched in the stomach. She had no idea why the sight of them should make her feel like that, but the jolt was undeniably there.

She watched, condensation from her hot breath forming on the glass, as the two of them made their way towards Georgia's house. They looked like a couple, which was something she hadn't expected to happen. And they'd just spent time together in Ash's cottage . . .

When they moved out of view, Fia stayed where she was. Her tea grew tepid as she went over the various events in her mind. A fox slunk across the road and disappeared into a garden. An owl hooted in the distance and the more accustomed her eyes grew to the darkness, the more stars Fia was able to see glittering in the velvety dark sky. Eventually Ash reappeared, strolling along with his hands in his pockets. Illuminated by the orange glow of the street light, he paused then turned and for a moment seemed to be gazing directly at Fia. She shrank back, heart thudding, but of course he wasn't looking at her, he'd either heard the fox sloping through the undergrowth or was simply looking at the pub.

Then he headed on up the lane to his cottage, unlocked the front door and disappeared inside.

Sliding off the window seat, Fia closed the curtains and climbed back into bed. After the amount of lager he'd sunk tonight, Ash was going to have his work cut out putting together a good show in the morning.

★ ★ ★

'Is it weird to be asking you this?' When she'd finished running through the whole Will's children scenario, Fia looked at Cleo. 'I want to see Rob and Molly again, but I can't bear the thought of spending time with them *and* Will. And wouldn't they find that confusing? I'd hate them to think we might be getting back together.'

Cleo nodded. 'So why don't you tell him that? Say you'd like to take the kids out on your own.'

'I know. And I *could* do that. But the thing is, it's months since I last saw them. And I've never actually done anything with them on my own. Every time they came over, Will was always there. He's their dad. I'd love to see them, but I don't know if it'd feel a bit funny.' Fia pulled a face. 'And I'm not really sure what I'd do with them either. There's the cinema, but then we'd just be sitting in the dark watching a film. And they're sick to death of the zoo . . .'

Eek, the zoo . . .

Cleo was looking at her curiously. 'Are you blushing?'

Good grief, the mere thought of the zoo was enough to set her off; that penguin dream was destined to haunt her for life. Fia vigorously flapped the collar of her shirt. 'I'm just panicking, wondering what to do.'

Cleo thought for a moment. 'OK, how about Sunday afternoon?'

Fia nodded; having already asked Frank for time off, this she could do. If she prepared and cooked the lunches beforehand, he'd agreed to take care of the rest. 'I can be free from one o'clock onwards.'

'Right.' Pressing a button on her phone, Cleo said, 'Hi, Shelley, what's Saskia up to on Sunday? Nothing? Ask her if she'd like to come out with her lovely Auntie Cleo. Great, I'll see her at one o'clock. Bye!'

She hung up and nodded triumphantly at Fia. 'There, all sorted, we'll go together. You, me and the kids. It's Treasure Hunt day — they'll love it.'

'God, thanks.' Fia was touched. 'That's really nice of you.'

'I know!' Cleo beamed, delighted with herself. 'Well, I haven't seen Sass for a while, so we're due a day out. And I'm signed off work until next week, what with being so scary to look at.'

'You aren't.' Which was nearly true; the unsightly marks on Cleo's face were lessening day by day. 'Anyway, a treasure hunt sounds perfect. Where's it held?'

'Marcombe Arboretum.'

Fia clapped a hand over her mouth. 'The Father Christmas place?'

'I know, but that's where they have them.' Breaking into a grin, Cleo said, 'I'd call it kind of apt.'

Chapter 47

As she made her way along the lane, Abbie felt her palms grow damp. How ridiculous, it was her own house, she was entitled to take whatever she wanted from it and there were things she genuinely needed. But she'd waited until she knew the place was empty. Tom would be at work and she'd seen Georgia driving off in her van twenty minutes ago.

Right, nearly there now. She had to pick up her sewing box and kitchen scales – because Cleo didn't own any – plus a couple of Pyrex dishes. Also, she was going to take the table lamp with the ostrich-feather trimmed shade because it belonged to her and she loved it.

No cars on the driveway, good. It seemed wrong, somehow, that from the outside the house could look so exactly the same, while her own world had changed so completely. Bracing herself, Abbie fitted her key in the lock and opened the front door. She bet it would be messier on the inside; Tom had never been that hot on tidying up. And there would be bags of clothes waiting to be ironed by Georgia, ironed clothes hanging from the picture rails, abandoned coffee cups everywhere—

'*Oh my God.*' Having pushed open the living room door, her

knees almost buckled beneath her. Not expecting to see anyone on the sofa was bad enough. Seeing *who* was lying on the sofa knocked the air from her lungs harder than any cricket bat.

'Bloody hell, look at you! Hello!' Unfolding her crossed legs and pulling the iPod headphones out of her ears, Patty Summers put down the copy of *Heat* she'd been reading. 'Long time no see!'

The loud buzzing of white noise rang in Abbie's ears. She stared at Patty, tanned and blonde and wearing a white satin dressing gown. Her *own* white satin dressing gown. Finally she managed to stammer, 'Wh-what are you doing here?'

'Oh gosh, long story!' Shaking her head, Patty said, 'Basically, it's all over between me and Ted. Did Georgia tell you about Ted? Well, he turned out to be a dud. All that golf with his mates . . . it did my head in. So we ended up having a bit of a barney about it and he kicked me out. Men are such dicks, aren't they? I thought I'd come back to the UK and see how my beautiful daughter's getting on with her daddy! She'd told me about you moving out, so I knew there'd be room if I wanted to stay for a bit. So there you go, that's it, really. Here I am!'

Silence. Abbie stared at Patty on the sofa. Finally she said, 'That's my dressing gown.'

'I know, Georgia told me to wear it because I don't have one. Look, it's way too big for me!'

Was she for real? 'That's because it's mine.'

'What are you saying? That you want it back?' Patty's blond eyebrows rose. 'Do you want me to take it off now?'

Was she even wearing anything under it? Probably not. Abbie's skin prickled with anger.

Reading her expression, Patty said, 'Oh, I get it, you're still mad at me over the baby thing. Shouldn't you be over that by now?'

The buzzing was louder. 'Why would I be?'

'Because it happened nearly twenty years ago.'

'You stole my baby.' As she said it, tears sprang into Abbie's eyes.

'I didn't. She was *my* baby. I kept her because I loved her.'

'I wanted her so much.'

'And now you've got her! She turned up and moved in with you, and you moved out! Look, I'm sorry if I mucked up your plans back then, but you can't blame me for the mess you've made of the rest of your life.' Patty's eyes glittered as she stated her point. 'I've heard all about what you got up to with your boss, so don't make out you're Miss Innocent.'

Abbie concentrated on her breathing. Patty Summers was now living in *her* house with *her* husband and *her* daughter. She was even wearing *her* best satin dressing gown. Grief, raw and painful, surged up inside her chest; how long would it be before Patty was sharing Tom's bed, or had that happened already? Oh God, don't think about it, *don't think about it*.

'Anyway, what are you doing here? Come to sort out the kitchen? Because let me tell you,' Patty said blithely, 'it could do with a clean-up.'

But not badly enough, evidently, to persuade her to get up off the sofa and do it herself.

'I've come to collect some things.' Crossing the room to unplug the feather-trimmed lamp, Abbie discovered that one of the intricate pottery branches of the lampstand had been snapped off and the shade had a rip in it.

'I noticed that,' said Patty. 'It was Georgia, she knocked it off the table.'

Abbie put her favourite lamp back down. So much for treasured possessions.

Ten minutes later she'd gathered together the other items she'd come for.

'I'll tell Tom you dropped by,' said Patty.

'Fine.'

'They make a good team, don't they? Tom and Georgia.'

'Oh yes.' Abbie just wanted to be gone.

'I'm so pleased for her that she found him. And he says she's changed his life.' Pausing, Patty pointed to the key visible through the cotton of Abbie's shirt pocket. 'Do you still need that key? Because Tom doesn't have a spare and I could really do with one.'

The bloody cheek of the woman. Then again, refusing would seem childish. And after today, why would she want to come back again anyway? Abbie took the front door key out of her pocket and placed it – *click* – on the glass-topped table.

Patty said, 'Thanks!'

Baby. Husband. House. Dressing gown. Key. Might she be interested in a heart, freshly torn out of a broken rival's chest so she could trample on it?

With a lump the size of an egg in her throat, Abbie said, 'Don't mention it.'

It was going to be a good day, but just at the moment it wasn't being *that* good. It had come as a guilty relief to be escaping from Abbie at home; Cleo's spirits had risen as she'd made her way over to the Hollybush on Sunday lunchtime. Her face had pretty much healed up, it was her first time out without her neck brace and she was actually looking normal again. Furthermore, the sun was out and the temperature had rocketed into the seventies, which made everyone feel better. Well, apart from Abbie, who was currently scrubbing the utility room, occupying herself by getting it up to operating-theatre levels of cleanliness.

345

So Cleo's high hopes were currently taking a bit of a tumble, because while Honor Donaldson was undoubtedly cheerful, chatty company and a genuinely nice person, having to listen to her chattering on about just how ecstatically happy she and Johnny were together wasn't exactly top of Cleo's want-to-hear list.

'I mean, it was all my fault in the first place. When I look back now, I can't believe I was so stupid. But that's what we're like, isn't it? Stuff happens and we get carried away. This other guy came into my life and I was just, like, wow, this is *amazing*, because I had all his attention and he was so full-on. And he was a movie producer, which helped. He knew everyone, all the A-listers. That makes me a horrible person, right? I'm not proud of myself, but at the time I really thought I was in love with him. So I left Johnny, just like that. Broke his heart. And he was *devastated*.' Honor shook her head sorrowfully at the memory. 'I felt bad about it, of course I did, but I was so wrapped up in this fantastic new relation-ship I told myself I was doing the right thing.'

She stopped, waiting for the reaction. Forced to oblige, Cleo said, 'But you weren't?'

'Of course I wasn't! The guy was a complete nightmare, super-possessive, paranoid, the works. I realised I'd made the biggest mistake of my life. I mean, he bought me stuff, diamond bracelets, a Maybach, a Picasso . . . but he wasn't making me happy. And all the parties we went to? They were pretty dull. So I was really missing Johnny by then, but I told myself I shouldn't contact him. I'd made him so unhappy, he deserved the chance to rebuild his life. Then I bumped into his New York agent at a gallery opening and he told me about Johnny's aunt. Well, that was it.' Honor pressed her clenched fist to her chest and said, 'I couldn't help myself, I knew I had to call him. Oh God, and then the moment I heard his voice again, I knew what I had to do. He was all on his own in Norfolk and I just couldn't bear it. I packed my bags, went straight to the airport and caught the first flight to London. Do you know how I knew I really loved him?'

'Um . . . no.'

'They didn't have any seats left in first class *or* in business.' Honor said proudly, 'So I flew economy.'

Cleo shook her head. The unimaginable horror.

'But it was worth it. I caught a cab to Norfolk and turned up at Johnny's hotel. Then I got the manager to call him down to reception . . . oh wow, it was like something out of a movie.' Her eyes shining, Honor said, 'All these people were watching as Johnny came down the stairs. I just held out my arms and said, "Oh baby, I love you so much! I'm here for you now." And the tourists were all going "Aaaahhh," and it was the most amazing romantic moment . . . oh jeez, look at me, I'm welling up just thinking about it!'

She was, too. In the prettiest way imaginable. Even the whites of her eyes stayed Persil-white. Cleo watched as, half laughing and half sobbing, Honor wiped away a Swarovski crystal tear. 'If I tried something like that, it'd all go pear-shaped. I'd turn up and the guy'd say, "Sorry, love, bit late, I've met someone else now."'

Honor said confidently, 'Oh, I knew that hadn't happened.'

'Did you?' Cleo felt sick. 'How?'

'I Googled him. Typed in his name plus new girlfriend.' Honor shrugged as if it were obvious. 'Not a bean.'

'What if he was seeing someone secretly?' God, was she some kind of masochist?

'It's OK, I did double-check.' Smiling, Honor said, 'I asked him myself. There hasn't been anyone else. And now we're back together there isn't going to be, I can promise you that!'

So, officially a masochist.

Rescue arrived minutes later in the form of Johnny himself, come to take Honor away. They were driving back to Norfolk ahead of tomorrow's funeral. Sliding gracefully off her bar stool, Honor planted a lingering kiss on his mouth. 'We've just been talking about you.'

Cleo's own mouth was dry; how did it feel to be kissed by Johnny? She'd never find out now. And look at the two of them together; they made such a perfect couple. Honor was stunning in an amethyst wrap-around dress and silver jewellery. Johnny was wearing a pale grey shirt and black trousers. They were visiting Aunt Clarice in the nursing home and making the final arrangements for the service. For a second he met Cleo's gaze and her heart turned over.

'You're on the mend. Looking better. How's the neck?'

'Good, thanks.' She nodded to prove it, as through the window a turquoise Fiat whizzed into the car park. Shelley and Saskia had arrived.

'Great. Well, we need to get off.' He jangled his keys at Honor.

'Hope the funeral's OK tomorrow.' Was that a ridiculous thing to say? But what else was there?

'Thanks. Bye.' Johnny's hand rested in the small of Honor's back as he ushered her out. *She remembered what that felt like . . .*

'See you when we get back, guys!' Honor waved over her shoulder.

Fia, finished in the kitchen, said resignedly, 'She's so nice, isn't she? I suppose he was always going to end up with someone like that.'

'I suppose so,' murmured Cleo.

Johnny and Honor left, and Saskia and Shelley came in. Glad of the distraction, she held out her arms.

'Mum said you had an accident and I mustn't say if you look funny.' Saskia gave Cleo a hug. 'But you don't look too bad.'

'I was much worse last week,' Cleo promised.

Saskia's face fell. 'Oh. I wish I'd seen you then. Was there all loads of blood?'

'Oh yes. Bucket-loads.'

'I love blood! I fell off a climbing frame once and all blood came out of my nose!' Shaking her head like an old pro, Saskia said, 'The doctor at the hospital said I was *very* brave.'

Cleo nodded solemnly. 'We remember that.' Behind Saskia, Shelley was rolling her eyes; Saskia might think she'd been brave but in reality she'd screamed the place down. 'Anyway, this is my friend Fia and she's coming along on the Treasure Hunt too.' OK, slightly weird to be describing Fia as a friend, but what else could she say? *And here's Fia, whose marriage I broke up when I had an affair with her husband?*

Shelley left. Minutes later, Will drove into the car park with Rob and Molly. Fia went outside to greet the children she hadn't seen for five months and they seemed touchingly delighted to see her.

Then it was Cleo's turn to take Saskia out to meet them.

Chapter 48

Will looked Cleo up and down and said evenly, 'Hello.'

'Hi.' It was always nice to see someone completely crumble after your relationship with them had broken up. Sadly this hadn't happened with Will. He was looking trim and fit in a pink polo shirt and pressed chinos, with a shorter-than-usual haircut. He was wearing plenty of Armani aftershave, highly polished loafers and a new expensive watch. The good thing, though, was that the sight of him was having absolutely no effect on her. Not a twinge, not a flicker, not so much as an iota of attraction or regret.

Wouldn't it be great if she could feel the same way about Johnny? If only there was an Off switch you could just press.

'So this is where you're living now.' Will turned back to Fia.

'And working.' She indicated the pub behind them. 'I love it.'

He smirked a bit. 'Mum said she bumped into you the other week. You were with some fat drunk guy. So that's who you're seeing now, is it?'

Fia said pleasantly, 'I'm not seeing anyone. Right then, shall we go?' She reached for Molly's hand. 'We'll be back by six.'

'Fine. I'll be here to pick them up.'

'We're going on a treasure hunt,' Saskia informed Molly like a kindly teacher. 'We have to find caterpillars and leaves and things.'

Molly, who was five, gazed wide-eyed up at six-year-old Saskia. 'Do we have to eat them?'

'No, they're made out of paper and they have clues written on them.'

'I can't read.'

'Don't worry.' Saskia, in her element, said happily, 'I'll help you.'

Ash, playing pool with Welsh Mac, watched Will Newman order half a pint of lager shandy at the bar, then take a seat at a corner table. He never had liked Will when Cleo had been seeing him. He'd liked him even less when he'd found out how he'd treated Fia. What a tosser. Anyway, none of that mattered now. They didn't have to be polite and speak to each other. In a few minutes Will would finish his drink and leave. And he wouldn't have to be jealous of the man who had married Fia and treated her with so little love and respect that—

'*Yesss!*' cried Welsh Mac as Ash potted the white. 'Four away, that makes it my game. You owe me a fiver.'

They set up the table for the next match. Blaming Will entirely for his lapse in concentration, Ash now disliked him even more.

Halfway through the second game, Georgia's mother walked into the pub. Not that Ash had seen her before, but everyone in Channings Hill knew she was staying here in the village and, frankly, she wouldn't have needed to wear a name badge. Apart from the fact that her eyes were brown instead of bright blue, she was eerily similar to Georgia. Tall and slender, she was wearing a cream lace strappy top and the kind of short, pale-green skirt that most forty-year-olds couldn't have got away with. Many heads turned to look at her, Will Newman's included.

Within five minutes Ash had witnessed a masterclass in how to chat up a complete stranger. It was a revelation, like watching a neatly choreographed dance. While Georgia's mother bought herself a gin and tonic and glanced artlessly around the pub, Will drained his drink and moved over to stand next to her at the bar. Looks and polite-on-the-surface smiles were exchanged. Followed by rather more meaningful smiles. Then Georgia's mother — Patty Summers, that was her name — rested a finger lightly on Will's right forearm and admired his wristwatch. In response to this, he leaned in and murmured something that made her throw back her head and laugh. Then she swung round on her stool so her bare knees were almost but not quite brushing against his super-ironed trousers. Will had her undivided attention and he was loving it. You could feel the testosterone in the air, experience the frisson, practically breathe in the seductive charm.

'Watch and learn, lad,' said Welsh Mac, pausing to chalk his cue.

Well, quite. Except this was a skill he'd never be able to pick up. Because Patty and Will were physically attracted to each other and for that to happen you had to *be* physically attractive in the first place. Observing the goings-on over at the bar, Ash noted the similarities to a wildlife documentary about animal mating habits. There was preening, there was significant eye contact, there was touching and animated interaction, Will was smiling flirtatiously and Patty was wriggling out of her clothes . . .

OK, not really, but give her another ten minutes and she might. And if she did, it was fairly obvious that Will Newman wouldn't object.

It had been a fun afternoon. The treasure hunt had been a huge success, the children had got along well together, the sun had blazed down all afternoon and people had finally stopped gazing at Cleo in horror as if she were the Elephant Man. Who could ask for more?

'And Will's here waiting for us.' Cleo pointed to the car as they pulled into the pub car park.

Except there was no sign of him. The car was empty, the Hollybush was closed for the afternoon and the pub garden was deserted.

'He must have gone for a walk. I'll call him.' Fia took out her phone, dialled and hung up. 'Switched off.' Drily she murmured, 'Just like old times.'

'I'm thirsty.' Saskia, from the back seat, said, 'Can I have a drink?'

'I need a wee,' Molly announced.

Rob said, 'I'm hungry. Are there any biscuits?'

'OK, no problem, let's go to mine.' Cleo swung the car back out on to the road. 'Where on earth could Will have got to?'

Having heard them pull up outside the cottages, Ash emerged to greet them. 'Good time?'

'Great,' said Cleo. 'You haven't seen Will, have you?'

Ash waited until she'd let the children out of the car and into the house. Without meeting Fia's eye, he said in a low voice, 'He left the pub with Georgia's mother.'

Cleo frowned. 'Why? He doesn't even know her.'

'I think he probably does now,' said Ash.

'But his car's still here, so where could they have gone?'

Ash shrugged. 'Tom and Georgia went off to a motocross thing in Devon this morning.'

Oh, for heaven's sake. In disbelief, Cleo whipped out her phone and dialled the number of Abbie's old home. It rang and rang. 'No answer.'

Abbie, bringing the children outside with drinks and biscuits, said, 'What's going on?'

Cleo brought her up to date. 'But where else can they be? And you gave her your key, so we can't even get into the house.'

Abbie gave her a look. 'I'm not completely stupid. That was the front door key. I've still got the one for the back.'

Will had said he'd be here to pick up the children at six. It was now six thirty. Not that they seemed bothered; Saskia, who adored Ash, was demonstrating his ability to race around the garden with her hanging from one arm and balancing on one of his feet. Molly and Rob, charging after them, were bellowing, 'My turn, me next, I want to do it too!'

Cleo came to a decision. Leaving the kids with Fia and Ash, she and Abbie headed over to the house. When they got there, Abbie peered through the living-room window. 'No sign of anyone.'

Cleo rang the doorbell and waited. Nothing. Then she stepped back, gazed up at the house and glimpsed furtive movement at the bedroom window. 'There's someone up there.'

Abbie hissed indignantly, 'That's *our* bedroom.'

'Might be burglars,' Cleo tut-tutted. 'We'd better check.'

They slipped along the path that led around to the back of the house. Abbie unlocked the kitchen door and Cleo followed her in. There was a mountain of washing-up in the sink, the work-tops hadn't been wiped down and the thin, sharp smell of alcohol hung in the air. Childhood memories came flooding back. It was like being ten years old again, coming home from school and wondering if you were going to find Auntie Jean passed out on your sofa.

Upstairs, Abbie opened the bedroom door and a great wave of gin fumes whooshed out. Together they surveyed the scene. Patty Summers was passed out on the bed, sprawled naked on her front and snoring gently. An empty gin bottle lay on the floor. Snow

354

Patrol were blaring from the CD player and the carpet was littered with popcorn and discarded items of clothing.

Cleo nudged the black Armani boxer shorts on the floor and flipped them over with her foot. Of course, Armani. Will had always liked to match his aftershave to his underpants.

Abbie said, 'Where's he gone?'

It didn't take a genius to work it out, since he was unlikely to have hidden himself in one of the bedside drawers. Cleo, who had always had a soft spot for theatrical farce, went over to the wardrobe and pulled it open with a flourish.

'OK, OK.' Naked, covering himself with cupped hands and looking defensive, Will shook his head. 'I fell asleep, all right? Just let me get dressed and I'll be along to collect the kids.'

'Not if you've been drinking, you won't.'

'I haven't. Just a couple at lunchtime.' He nodded over at the bed. 'She did enough drinking for the both of us.'

The corners of her mouth twitched. 'Why were you hiding in the wardrobe?'

'I heard the door open downstairs. Didn't know it was you, did I? Could have been some bloke of hers.'

Cleo said brightly, 'But at least you've had fun. That's the import-ant thing.'

Will shot her a filthy look. 'How did you get in here anyway?'

'Oh, didn't you know? Remember my sister?' Cleo indicated Abbie. 'Well, this is her house. And guess what? That's her bed.'

'Oh God.' Will went pale. 'Look, I didn't know that.' He shook his head. 'I only met this one at lunchtime. She's completely mental.'

'Hey, watch what you're saying.' Having rolled over and opened her eyes, Patty smiled blearily at them and waggled her fingers in greeting. 'What's going on? I didn't know we had an audience.'

She was about to have even more of one. From downstairs came the sound of a key being fitted into the front door, followed by the door opening and being slammed shut.

'For God's sake,' groaned Will, still shielding himself with his hands. Turning to Cleo he pleaded, 'Any chance of a bit of privacy so I can get dressed?'

'Don't worry, it's nothing I haven't seen before.' Cleo beamed and kept her foot firmly on the Armani boxers. Wiggling her little finger she added cheerfully, 'And I've told my sister all about it.'

'Mum?' The next thing they heard was Georgia's footsteps on the stairs.

Blinking and hauling herself into a semi-sitting position, Patty pushed swathes of blond hair out of her mascara-smudged eyes and called out over the music, 'Hi, baby, come on up, we're in here.'

Cleo bent down, gathered together the boxers and chinos, and threw them at Will. She followed Abbie out of the bedroom and closed the door behind her just as Georgia reached the landing.

'What's going on?' Sunburned from her day out at the motocross, Georgia regarded them both warily. 'What are you doing here? Is she drunk?'

Abbie nodded. 'Yes, but she's OK. Don't go in there, sweetheart.'

'Oh please, this is my mother we're talking about. Do you think I haven't seen it all before?'

'I know, but there's someone else in there with her.'

'What a surprise.' Georgia's tone was detached but the irony was mixed with shame.

The bedroom door was wrenched open and Will, having dressed at the speed of light, rushed out past them.

'Bit young for you, Mum, isn't he?' Georgia stood in the doorway and gazed at her barely decent mother on the bed.

Patty drawled, 'Oh, don't *start*.'

Exhaling, Georgia glanced at Abbie. 'Sorry.'

'Oh, sweetheart, it's not—'

'Let me deal with her now.' Georgia's body language was stiff, her manner brusque. 'I'm used to it. Could you just go?'

Downstairs they passed Tom on their way out. He deliberately didn't look at them.

'Patty's in your bed.' Unable to help herself, Abbie said, 'Does that mean you've been sleeping with her too?'

Tom's jaw was rigid. 'No, I haven't slept with anyone else. *Unlike you.*'

'Come on.' Since it wasn't the moment for yet another show-down, Cleo ushered her sister through the front door. 'Let's leave them to it. We need to get back.'

Fia was watching Molly and Rob cavort with Ash and Saskia around the garden. Ash, yelling out instructions, had them tackling an impromptu assault course. They let out screams of delight as he helped them run along low walls, roll across the grass between the fence and the apple tree, wriggle under the wooden seat and over the row of flower pots.

'My turn, my turn!' screamed Molly, grabbing hold of Ash's hands almost before he'd had a chance to let go of Rob.

Fia couldn't help smiling; Ash had such an easy way with them. Who knew he'd be so brilliant with children?

Then her attention was diverted by the sight of Will heading towards them, striding along, with Cleo and Abbie following twenty yards behind him. Will was looking distinctly pissed off.

'They found you, then.' Fia wondered if, deep down, Cleo wished she and Will were still together.

'Looks like it, doesn't it?' He raised an arm to attract Rob and Molly's attention. 'Come on, you two. Time to go.'

'Daddy, you're *late*.' Rob was proud of his just-learned ability to tell the time.

'Can we stay longer?' Molly begged. '*Please?* We're doing a salsa course!'

'No, we need to get back.' Eyeing Ash with suspicion, Will said to Fia, 'Is this the fat bloke my mother saw you with?'

He really was despicable. And to think she'd actually married him. Fia said, 'Yes, we had a great night out.'

Five minutes later, once she'd hugged and kissed the children goodbye, Will walked Molly and Rob back across the village green to the pub car park.

Ash watched them go. 'If he hadn't had those kids with him, I'd have broken his nose.'

Cleo said, 'I'd have cheered you on.'

Having spent the day snapping away with her digital camera, Fia said, 'I'd have taken photos and put them up on the internet.'

Only Abbie's mind was elsewhere. No longer thinking of Will, she said distractedly, 'Poor Georgia.'

Chapter 49

By Tuesday night the weekend's fabulous weather was a dim and distant memory. Peering out of the bedroom window, Abbie shivered at the sight of the rain hammering down and the branches of the trees behind the house being battered and swept sideways by the howling gale. Poor Cleo, on her first day back at work, was having to drive a car full of executives up to Gatwick.

Guilt kicked in then, because at least she was warm and dry and comfortable, and shouldn't that be enough to make her happy? But it wasn't. Unrelenting misery was now an inescapable part of her life and she knew she was no fun to live with. How Cleo was managing to put up with her, she had no idea. It was time to sort herself out and start thinking about the future. She couldn't impose indefinitely. She also needed to get another job.

Abbie headed downstairs in her dressing gown. She would make herself a cup of tea, curl up on the sofa and find something easy to watch on TV.

The doorbell rang halfway through *Britain's Got Talent*. A manic magician had just – apparently – sliced off his arm with a circular saw. The audience let out a collective gasp of horror as blood fountained out and spurted across the stage. Abbie gasped too when she opened the front door and saw Des Kilgour standing wet and windswept on her doorstep.

'Abbie? Can I come in?'

She hesitated. 'Why?'

'I need to talk to you.'

'Des, I don't think so.' God, had he come here to tell her he still loved her? Her pulse quickened with anxiety. 'Really, there's nothing to say.'

'Look, this isn't like last time. It's nothing to do with that.' He paused, clearly embarrassed. 'It's about . . . something I've found out.'

Abbie wavered. Des was a good-hearted soul; it wasn't as if she was afraid of him.

'Please,' he said again.

She took off the chain and opened the door properly. 'OK.'

Rain dripped from Des's Barbour and formed puddles on the parquet floor. Sitting back down on the sofa and wrapping her dressing gown tightly around herself, Abbie said, 'What's this about, then?'

Des stayed standing in front of the fireplace, his hands thrust deep into his pockets. 'You know you thought it was Georgia who told Tom about us?'

Us. She wished he wouldn't use that word. 'It had to be Georgia. No one else knew anything.'

'It wasn't her.' He shook his head, causing Abbie to feel sick.

'So what are you telling me? It was you?'

'God no!' Stricken, Des said, 'Of course it wasn't me!'

'Who, then? Who wrote that letter and stuck it on Tom's windscreen?'

'Glynis.'

'*What?* Glynis from the shop?' This made no sense. How could Glynis have found out? It wasn't physically possible.

'She wasn't snooping. She just . . . heard us.'

Abbie still couldn't believe it. 'And she actually told you this?'

'Huw did,' said Des. 'She only told him last night. He came to see me this evening, thought I should know.'

'I don't see how it happened.'

'It was my fault.' He shifted awkwardly from foot to foot. 'Glynis was working in the shop when the phone rang. She picked it up and heard our voices. I know, I know how it happened,' Des hurried on. 'I worked it out. Before you came into my office that morning, I'd been trying to contact Huw at home. Then when you turned up and we were talking I must have accidentally knocked my phone . . .' He demonstrated, patting the shirt pocket where his mobile was invariably kept. '. . . and hit redial. Glynis answered the phone and heard us. I suppose it sounded as if we were having a full-on affair. And she's pretty straight, you know. It shocked her. She didn't want to be seen to be the one spreading gossip, but she thought Tom deserved to know what was going on behind his back.'

'Oh God.' Abbie rubbed her face as the information sank in. It made sense.

'Sorry. But I had to tell you.' Des raked his fingers through his reddish fair hair. 'Huw feels bad about it too.'

'Right. Well, thanks. At least now we know.'

As she showed him out, Des said, 'Everyone misses you at work, you know. Not just me. If you wanted to, we'd have you back tomorrow.'

'Thanks, but it'd be too difficult. I couldn't.' Abbie knew that Tom wasn't going to take her back, but the superstitious part of her wouldn't let her even consider returning to Kilgour's in case he found out just as he might be on the verge of changing his mind.

* * *

The trees creaked and swayed and leaves swirled up like ghosts as the storm raged around her. Everyone else was inside tonight. Abbie's umbrella had been blown inside out; giving up on it, she let the rain hit her in the face. Within minutes she'd reached her old home. It was eleven o'clock but there were still plenty of lights on. And it didn't matter how horrendous the weather was, she wasn't going inside.

Not that she was likely to be invited.

Abbie braced herself. She didn't even know yet if Georgia was there. She could be out. And Georgia was the only person she wanted to speak to.

Adrenaline pounded through her veins. Oh well, only one way to find out.

But it was Georgia who answered the door and was visibly shocked to see her. 'Oh. Dad's not here.'

Good. 'That's OK, it's you I wanted to see.' Abbie noted the bandage on Georgia's right hand.

Opening the door wider, Georgia stepped aside and said, 'You'd better come in.'

'No, um, I'd rather not . . .' As she spoke, a blast of wind hit Abbie from behind, almost knocking her off her feet.

Georgia read her mind. 'It's all right, Mum's not here either. I'm on my own.'

Relieved, Abbie said, 'OK then.'

The living room was festooned with more clothes than ever. Georgia winced with pain as she picked up the steaming iron.

Right, let's get this done before Tom and Patty come back. Abbie plunged straight in. 'Look, I've come to apologise. I accused you of telling Tom about . . . you know. And you told me you hadn't, but I didn't believe you. Well, now I know it wasn't you. I was wrong and I'm so, so sorry.'

362

Georgia stopped ironing. She carefully upended the iron on its rest and said, 'So who was it, then?'

Abbie explained who had composed the anonymous letter and how it had come to be written. 'I think Glynis's conscience was pricking her, because she knew I thought it was you.' She shook her head and clutched at her battered umbrella. 'Anyway, that's how it happened. And I'm sorry.'

'Thanks. But you should have believed me.' Georgia looked relieved and sad at the same time. 'I'm a very honest person.'

'I know. And there's nothing worse than being accused of something you didn't do. That's why I had to come over and tell you, because I felt so terrible . . .' Abbie's voice trailed off as Georgia bent her head and a tear plopped on to the ironing board. First one, then – *plop* – another. 'Oh please, don't cry. You didn't do anything wrong!'

'That's not quite true though, is it?' Raising her chin, Georgia said unsteadily, 'I've messed up everything. I should never have come here. No wonder you hate me, look what's happened since I turned up. I've ruined your life.'

Oh God. Abbie was horrified. 'You haven't . . . you didn't . . .'

'I have.' Georgia's mouth wobbled with the effort of not bursting into tears. 'I'm not stupid, I know what it's been like for you. I've wrecked everything and I'm s-sorry . . . if I hadn't come along, you and Tom would still be t-together.'

Unable to bear it a moment longer, Abbie rushed over. Georgia let out a howl of misery and crumpled into her arms.

'Oh sweetheart, don't cry, ssshhh.' A lump sprang into Abbie's throat as she folded her into a hug.

'*Ow* . . .' Flinching, Georgia pulled her bandaged hand free.

'I'm sorry, I'm sorry.' Attempting to let her go, Abbie discovered she couldn't; Georgia was clinging to her like a baby koala.

'And you mustn't blame yourself. I'm the one who messed up. It's not your fault . . . oh God, now you've set me off . . . listen to me, you haven't done *anything* wrong.' Her own tears were now falling into the hair of the daughter she'd never had. She stroked Georgia's silky head and patted her like a baby. 'Don't cry. Goodness, what do we look like? If your mum comes in now, what's she going to say?'

'She won't be coming in. She's in Portugal.'

'What?'

Georgia sniffed and rubbed her wet face. 'She's my mum and I love her, but she's a nightmare to live with. I told her she had to go.'

'She's gone back to Portugal? But I thought her boyfriend kicked her out of the house.'

'Ted did. He was the last one. She's back with Christian now, the one before Ted.'

Abbie took this in. 'And where's your dad?'

'He's got a job on in Bournemouth so he's staying down there for a couple of days. It's just me here tonight.'

'And your hand? What happened to that?'

'Burned it with the iron.'

'Let me see.'

Georgia reluctantly peeled off the bandage.

'*Ouch.*' Abbie winced at the sight of the livid, triangular burn on her palm.

'I know. I sent the iron flying and tried to catch it.' Georgia said wryly, 'That's how smart I am.'

'How can you even *hold* an iron now?' It had to be agonisingly painful.

Georgia indicated the bags of clothes. 'That's how. It all has to be done and I can't let people down. I took Sunday off to go out with Dad, so yesterday I was ironing for eighteen hours straight. And I still haven't caught up.'

She was pale, in pain, emotionally wrung out and physically exhausted. Abbie said, 'Oh sweetheart, just look at you,' and took off her coat.

'It's OK, you don't have to help me.' Georgia's eyes filled with fresh tears as she watched Abbie roll up her sleeves.

'I know I don't. But I want to.' Abbie smiled at the girl she would have been unbelievably proud to call her daughter. 'And I'll keep going for as long as it takes. If you want to do something useful you could put the kettle on. I'd love a cup of tea.'

Chapter 50

'Hi, can you pop over? I've got something for you to say thanks for the other night.'

'Oh sweetheart, you didn't need to do that.' Abbie melted at the sound of Georgia's voice; it was so lovely to hear her sounding cheerful again. 'You don't have to buy me presents.'

'Ha, bit late now, it's here. I'd bring it over in the van,' said Georgia, 'but it's too heavy for me to lift on my own.'

Was it a bay tree in a pot, a garden table, a gigantic vase, a life-size pottery crocodile? With Georgia, who knew? As Abbie reached the house and raised her hand to ring the bell, the front door was pulled open and Georgia threw her arms around her.

'Hello, I've got to go! Your present's in the living room . . . hope you like it!'

And she was gone. The van sped off down the lane and Abbie's knees turned to spaghetti. Because her present was no longer in the living room. It had moved into the hallway.

'I've been given a big talking-to by my daughter,' said Tom. 'And she's explained some things I should have been adult enough to work out for myself.'

Abbie's heart was in her mouth. Tom's voice wasn't completely steady. Instead of his dusty work clothes he was wearing clean jeans and the blue and green striped shirt she had bought him for Christmas. She could tell by the set of his shoulders that he wasn't comfortable; talking about his feelings had never come naturally to him. Aloud she said faintly, 'What kind of things?'

'Oh, I don't know . . .' Tom licked his lips and gazed up at the ceiling. 'Things like I've missed you so much and I love you and the last couple of weeks have been the most miserable of my life . . .' Now that he'd started, the words came tumbling out. 'And I can either carry on being proud and miserable or I can get over what happened and put it behind me and tell you I don't want to live without you. Because that other stuff doesn't matter, it was a mistake and I just want us to be like we were before.' He shook his head. 'I overreacted. I said I couldn't forgive you, but that was just cutting my nose off to spite my face. And I've been thinking and *thinking* about it ever since. I knew I had to sort things out, but it took Georgia to bring me to my senses and realise that I need to do it now. It was just my stupid pride stopping me.' This time Tom's voice cracked with emotion. 'I was an idiot and I'm sorry, and I might have left it too late because you could be loving every minute of your new single life. But I love you so much, I really do. And if you do want to come back, you'd make me the happiest man in the world.'

Abbie managed a wobbly smile. This was why she'd spent her entire adult life loving him. Tom was honest, principled, loyal and strong. He might find it hard to express his feelings but that only made it all the more special when he did. Her throat tightening, she said, 'Are you sure?'

'I'm sure.' He nodded, keeping his gaze fixed on her. 'And you'd make Georgia pretty happy too.'

Was this really happening? She threw herself into his arms and this time Tom was the one whose eyes were damp with tears. Tom, who never ever cried.

'I'm sorry too. I wish it hadn't happened but it did. I was out of my mind with misery and I made a hideous mistake. But I didn't have sex with Des Kilgour, I swear I didn't—'

'Sshh. It's OK, I believe you. I just want you back.'

Dizzy with joy, Abbie kissed him. 'I've missed you so much. I want to come back more than anything.'

He squeezed her, overcome with emotion. 'Good. And there are going to be some changes around here.'

Was he laying down the law? Were there going to be *rules*? Taken aback, Abbie said, 'Like what?'

Tom took a half-step back and drew her into the living-room doorway. 'Take a look. Notice anything different?'

What was different? And then she saw. *Oh, good grief!* There were no clothes hung up, no crammed-full bags, no ironing board set up in front of the TV. The room was back to its pristine, uncluttered, pre-Georgia state. It looked so *empty* . . .

Abbie's heart thudded with fear. Her initial instinct was horror. Oh no, this was the very last thing she wanted. 'Is Georgia leaving? Is she moving out?'

Tom looked carefully at her. 'Would it help if she did?'

'No! I don't want her to go!'

He relaxed, broke into a smile. 'That's OK then. She's not going anywhere.'

Abbie gestured around the room. 'So where's . . . everything?'

'You know Georgia, she doesn't hang about. One of her clients runs an ad agency in Cheltenham. He offered her a job as his receptionist. She's taken on Ethel and Myrtle Mason to do the ironing at their house from now on. She'll take care of the pick-ups and deliveries before and after work. So that's it, all sorted. We've got our house back.'

'I've got my husband back.' Abbie stroked his dear oh-so-familiar face.

'And I've got my beautiful wife back.' Kissing her, then kissing her again, Tom said, 'Now that's what I call a result.'

An hour later, Abbie's phone went. Smiling when she saw who was calling, she answered and said, 'Hi.'

'I've waited and waited, and now I can't wait a single second more. *Well?*' demanded Georgia.

Patience had never been one of her strong points.

Abbie said, 'What time are you coming home and what would you like for dinner?'

'Yay! Is everything really OK now?'

'It's more than OK. Thanks to you. How about roast chicken?'

'Yes please! With loads of roast potatoes. And can you do the stuffing separately? Because—'

'It's OK, I know.' Abbie realised that what she was feeling was unconditional love. Her happiness knew no bounds. Squeezing Tom's hand, she said into the phone, 'Because stuffing's always better when it's crunchy.'

It was like turning up at Cabot Circus for a major shopping splurge, only to discover that all the shops were shut. Fia, having switched on the radio expecting to hear Ash, couldn't believe it when she found herself listening to the voice of a complete stranger.

Had somebody moved the dial to another station without telling her? No, it was still on BWR. For heaven's sake, who was this man burbling on about supermarket queues? He wasn't even funny! What was he doing on Ash's show? How dare he!

Was it weird to be this indignant and put out? Oh well, too

bad. Fia carried on listening until the usurper said chummily, 'And for those just joining us, a big hello from me, Max Margason, filling in for Ash this morning. Poor old Ash, he's only gone and lost his voice! Has he tried looking under the sofa cushions, that's what I want to know, ha ha ha! When I lose my car keys that's usually where they've ended up!'

God, he was so *annoying*. But at least now she knew what had happened to Ash. Laryngitis, hardly ideal for a radio presenter. Poor thing, hopefully he wasn't feeling too rotten. Maybe she'd call round after lunch and see if there was anything he needed.

'Unless he's pulling a sickie,' Max burbled on. 'Eh, Megan? That could be it, couldn't it? Maybe he had a damn good night, met a pretty young thing and . . . well, wa-heyyyy, just didn't feel like getting out of bed this morning, ha ha ha!'

How dare he say that? What an idiot, what an annoying, unfunny *prat*. Fia had never wanted to slap someone so badly in her life.

Emerging from the kitchen at lunchtime, Fia was startled to see Ash sitting up at the bar. So he wasn't ill after all. Did that mean he'd lied to his bosses at the radio station? *Had* he pulled a sickie because he'd had a riotous night last night?

More to the point, who had he spent it with?

'Hi.' She felt . . . not jealous exactly. Just kind of really needing to know.

Ash looked up and waggled his fingers by way of greeting. His fair hair was tousled and still damp from the shower. He was wearing a blue and white striped cotton shirt over a white T-shirt and faded jeans. Beckoning her over, he scribbled something on a fluorescent pink Post-It pad:

Laryngitis. Hi!

Oh, the relief. Fia knew she was beaming like an idiot but she couldn't help herself. She was glad he hadn't got lucky last night, glad he hadn't been lying.

'I know. I heard the other guy on the radio this morning.'

Ash raised an eyebrow and wrote: He's a dickhead.

'You can say that again.'

He tore off the Post-It and wrote on the next sheet: He's a dickhead.

Fia laughed. 'I thought you'd be at home in bed. How are you feeling?'

Ash scrawled: Fine! It's just my voice that's gone. Saw Dr and he said rest it completely.

'Poor you.'

Ash wasn't looking at her. Instead he concentrated on writing the next message: When did you start listening to my show???

The fact that his eyes were fixed on the Post-It pad meant she didn't have to blush. 'Oh, a while back. I like it. I can listen to classical music during the rest of the day. You and Megan make me laugh.'

As he scribbled the next words, she noticed that Ash's neck was reddening. Maybe he was running a temperature and didn't realise it. Fia watched him write: Excellent! But I'm funnier than Megan.

'That goes without saying.'

Smiling slightly, Ash scrawled: That's why I didn't say it.

'Are you hungry? Does it hurt to eat?'

He nodded then shook his head.

'So you'd like . . . ?' Fia indicated the blackboard with today's offerings chalked up.

Ash made horns of his index fingers.

'Chicken.'

He gave her a look.

'Sorry. Beef. OK, salad or curry?'

Ash fanned his mouth vigorously.

She smiled as his phone started to ring. 'Coming right up. Want me to answer that for you?'

He glanced at caller ID, shook his head and scribbled: Only my agent.

Ten minutes later, returning with the curry, she found Ash gazing into space and looking preoccupied.

'Everything OK?'

He paused, then grimly passed his mobile over to her, indicating that she should listen to the message.

Never mind preoccupied, he was in a state of shock. Had someone died? Had he been sacked? Fia put down the plate of beef Madras and took the phone.

'Ash? Listen, kid, we've had an approach from KCL. I've just taken a call from the big boss – he's a major fan of yours. He wants you to fly over there, meet the team, see what you make of the place.' Ash's agent had a gravelly, intense, agenty type of voice, the kind that was skilled in the art of building up his clients. His words sent an icy tremor down Fia's spine. 'But they really want you, so it's pretty much a done deal. And they're talking big bucks. So how about that then? Bit of a result, eh? Told you it was worth a shot. Call me back, kid. See ya!'

Fia switched the phone off and swallowed hard. 'Wow. That sounds . . . fantastic. Where's KCL?'

She peered at the pad as he wrote: Sydney.

'Australia?' Idiotic question. And she already knew how many enthusiastic Australian fans he had; they were endlessly emailing the show. Ash called them his Possum Posse.

He nodded.

God, Australia. The other side of the world. Stunned, she said, 'I didn't know you were thinking of moving abroad.'

He shrugged helplessly.

'Well, good for you. Sydney. Wow.' OK, this was getting stupid, she had to stop saying wow. Fia dredged up a smile. 'Bondi Beach. Barbeques. Beer . . . all that *sun* . . .' Oh God, listen to her, and now she was practically pushing him on to the plane.

Deborah joined them. 'Fia, table three are ready to order. D'you want me to do it?'

Did she? Fia couldn't even tell. All she knew was that she was seized with a strange panicky fear teetering on the edge of tearfulness.

OK, get a grip. She shook her head at Deborah. 'No . . . no, it's fine, I'll take care of them now.'

Probably just as well, before she made a massive fool of herself in the middle of the pub without even quite understanding why.

Chapter 51

Sometimes dreams trick you into believing they're real. And then there are other times when, completely out of the blue, life suddenly becomes so surreal that you wonder if perhaps you're dreaming after all.

Cleo stared at Fia, who had come hurtling across the green to see her. It was nine o'clock in the morning, bright and sunny, and she'd been washing the red Bentley prior to picking up a married couple later who were celebrating their ruby wedding anniversary. She switched off the power hose.

'Sorry, say that again?'

'I don't want Ash to move to Australia. I don't want him to go.' Out of breath and with an air of desperation about her, Fia blurted out, 'The thing is, I really like him but he's always been really weird with me . . . I didn't know what I'd done wrong but he obviously couldn't stand me, then something changed and he seemed different and then *I* started to feel differently, but it's all so weird and confusing, and now there's this Australia thing happening and I'm just so *scared* . . .'

Blimey. Cleo was stunned; she'd never seen Fia in a state like this. 'So what do you want me to do?'

'Oh God.' Fia raked her fingers through her hair. 'I suppose I'm asking if he's said anything to you.'

'About Australia?'

'About me! I'm asking if he's said he really doesn't like me.' She paused, shaking her head. 'Or if you think, deep down, maybe he likes me a little bit . . . you know, just enough to give me something to work with.'

Cleo surveyed her seriously, taking in the ruffled blond hair, the absence of make-up, the air of agitation. 'It's neither of those.'

'Oh. Oh.'

'He doesn't dislike you.'

'Oh?' Hope flared in Fia's eyes.

'He doesn't like you a little bit.'

'Oh.' Fia's shoulders slumped. 'Right.'

'He likes you a lot.'

Confusion reigned. 'What?'

Honestly, how could some people be so blind? Cleo said, 'I thought you knew! It was so obvious, I thought you'd figured it out and were just being polite and pretending you hadn't noticed.'

Fia did a double-take. 'He ignored me! He hardly ever *spoke*. Most of the time he wouldn't even look at me!'

'Hello?' Cleo gave her a *duh* look. 'That's kind of what shy people do.'

'*Shy?*' Fia clapped a hand over her mouth in disbelief. 'He said he was shy once, on the radio. I thought it was a joke.'

'Uh-uh.' Cleo broke into a grin and shook her head. 'Ash has had a massive crush on you from day one. I did offer to tell you but he threatened to chop me into small pieces. And to be honest, I never thought for one minute you'd go for him. The only person you were interested in was Johnny.'

'Maybe I was, at first. But some things are never going to

375

happen, are they?' Fia shrugged, casually eradicating that idea. 'Anyway, forget about that. Let's talk about Ash. What am I going to *do*?'

Cleo wished she could fall in love with someone else and dismiss Johnny from her life as easily as Fia. Sadly he appeared to be stuck in her brain for good. But never mind that now; if there was anyone with a more disastrous love life than hers, it was Ash. This was stunning news for him.

'Easy. Just tell him.'

'Oh God, my *heart*. I don't know if I can.' Fia was trembling and clutching her chest at the mere thought of it. 'He hasn't been over to the pub for the last two days. And I'm working tonight . . . look, could you tell him?'

'What, my mate really fancies you? Bit teenagey, isn't it?' Cleo pulled a face. 'It'd be a lot better coming from you.'

Visibly losing her nerve, Fia hesitated and fiddled with her watch strap. 'The thing is, I don't think I can. Well, perhaps I'll leave it for a bit. Maybe until the weekend . . .'

Honestly, how could people *do* that? Never one of life's procrastinators – at least where good news was concerned – Cleo exclaimed, 'This is something *nice*! We're not talking about filling in a tax return here. You want to tell him straight away!'

'I know, but this is all a bit sudden.' Fia was hyperventilating and edging backwards. 'I kind of need to think about how to say it.'

Right, enough faffing about. A kick up the backside was definitely called for. Thinking on her feet, Cleo said, 'Except you can't afford to hang about, can you? Because it'll be too late by then. You have to do it now!'

Fia's eyes widened. 'Why?'

'Because he's jacking in his job, didn't you know?' Cleo shook her head and crossed her fingers behind her back. 'He told me yesterday, said there was nothing to keep him here so he may as well go to Australia. And did he tell you about his boss?'

'No, what about him?'

'They can't stand each other! And Ash is going to resign live on air this morning . . . God only knows what he's going to say.'

'He's doing it *today*?' Fia's throat went blotchy with shock.

'At the end of the show. He told me he had some stuff he wanted to get off his chest about the way the place was run. I said it would stir up all kinds of trouble but Ash doesn't care, because he's off anyway.' Cleo ran out of breath. God, though, she was brilliant.

Fia checked her watch. 'It's ten past nine. Oh no, you have to stop him!'

'*You* have to stop him,' said Cleo.

'How can I do that?'

'Phone him. Now.'

'Oh God, no, I couldn't. On the phone?' Vehemently Fia shook her head. 'No way.'

Cleo put down the power hose and gave her a measured look. Then she eased her mobile out of her jeans pocket. Finally she said in a firm but kind voice, 'If you don't want to lose him, you really don't have any choice.'

Panicking and caving in, Fia whispered fearfully, 'OK then.'

Hee!

Inside the cottage, Cleo made her sit on the sofa. She pressed out the number of the radio station and asked to speak to Megan. The call was transferred in a matter of moments.

'Megan? Hi, it's Cleo Quinn. Now listen, have you ever wanted to be a fairy godmother?'

Megan, Ash's traffic and weather girl and all-round sidekick, was always up for some fun. 'Hi, Cleo! You mean with a wand and a tiara? Always!'

'Well, listen, don't let Ash know who's calling, but I've got a friend here who has something very important she'd like to say to him. And let me tell you, it'll be good.'

'Yeah?' Megan was immediately interested. 'Ooh, give me a clue!'

'I can't, it's better if it's a surprise, but you'll love it, I promise. So, can you put her on after the next record?'

Fia let out a squeak of alarm. 'I'm not saying it on the radio! Can't I just talk to him off-air?'

'No, because the hands-free thingy's broken on my phone so I wouldn't be able to hear what's going on at the other end. This way,' Cleo explained cheerfully, 'I can!'

'Is that her in the background?' Megan said, 'What's her name?'

'Oh God,' wailed Fia, 'don't tell her my name.'

'It's Fia.'

'Oh no, I can't do this! It's no good, I feel sick, I just *can't*.'

'Oh, *Fia*.' Megan sounded even more intrigued. 'The one who does the food in the pub? Ash is always talking about her.'

'That's because he's secretly in luuuuurve with her.' Beaming across at Fia, Cleo said, 'But nobody else knows it yet.'

'Hallelujah, I am loving the sound of this.' Megan, who spent her life being mercilessly teased by Ash, let out a whoop of delight. 'This is going to make up for the time he told everyone I was born with a willy. Let's do it, baby. Put her on!'

Fia's palms were slick with perspiration. Gripped with terror, she almost dropped the phone when Cleo passed it across. How was this happening to her?

'Listen,' said Cleo encouragingly, 'it's got to be easier than doing it face to face.'

But Fia could barely hear what Cleo was telling her, because Megan was saying in her other ear, 'Fia? Hi there, I've heard so much about you! OK, I'm going to bring you in at the end of this track that's playing now. You just say what you have to say to Ash, but do keep it clean, OK? And don't try to listen to yourself on the radio there, because we operate with a two-second delay and you'd get in a muddle.'

Fia croaked, 'Right.' How much more of a muddle could she get into than the one she was already in? She appeared to be having an out-of-body experience. Glancing across at Cleo, who was busy fiddling with the tuner on her old transistor, she shook her head and said, 'You can't have it on in here. And I can't do it with you listening. Take it into the kitchen.' She couldn't cope with Cleo watching while she possibly turned herself into an international laughing stock.

Then the track that had been playing on the radio came to an end and in her ear Fia heard Megan announcing, 'That was Leona Lewis with her new single, and now we have a mystery caller on the line for our Ash. And I want all of you out there to pay attention to this, because I have it on good authority that it's going to be worth listening to.'

Chapter 52

'What's this?' protested Ash. 'Some kind of set-up? It had better not be that barking psychotherapist again, calling from Arizona to tell me—'

'It's not the psychotherapist,' Megan interrupted. 'It's actually a lady by the name of Fia, who I believe you already know. Hello, Fia! Ooh, and can I just tell everyone that Ash has just gone a very fetching shade of pink!'

'Hi. It's me.' Fia discovered that her mouth was managing to produce the words despite the fact that her brain felt as if it had just been whizzed up in a blender.

'Fia?' Ash sounded stunned.

OK. Fia closed her eyes; she had to do this, she just had to. Don't think about who else might be listening. This was just the two of them now. She cleared her throat and said, 'The thing is . . . someone's just told me that, um, you might quite, um, like me. And I wondered if it was true. Because if it is, I just want you to know that I feel the same way about you, and the reason I'm telling you this now is in case it might make you change your mind about Australia.'

'Australia . . .' Ash repeated the word as if in a trance.

She couldn't give up now. She'd started, so she'd finish. 'So basically, I don't want you to go.'

Ash said dazedly, 'Why not?'

Fia unstuck her tongue from the roof of her mouth. 'Because I'd miss you. I can't believe I'm saying this on the radio. And if you're taking up the job in Sydney because it's what you want more than anything in the world, that's fine. Just forget any of this happened. But if it makes any difference at all, I need you to know that if you *did* decide to stay here . . . well, I'd be glad about that, because I really really like you. A lot.'

'This *liking* thing,' said Ash. 'Excuse me for asking, but can I just double-check that this isn't liking in a platonic, just-good-friends kind of way?'

Fia took a deep breath. 'No, definitely not platonic.'

Oh heavens, she'd actually said it now.

Ash cleared his throat and said huskily, 'Fia? Is this true?'

As if she'd be doing this if it wasn't. 'Yes, it's true.'

'God, I can't believe it.'

A laugh bubbled up without any warning at all. 'Neither can I!'

'This is . . . amazing.'

'I know. Do you really like me?'

'Yes. Oh yes. You have no idea.'

'Are you going to Australia?'

'No no no. I called them days ago and told them I wasn't taking the job.'

Jolted, Fia wailed, '*Days ago?* But I thought you were handing in your notice today . . . I mean, er . . .'

The kitchen door swung open, bursting the bubble and bringing her crashing back to reality. Cleo poked her head round and said gaily, 'Whoops, sorry, I made that bit up!'

What? 'Why?'

'Duh. Otherwise you wouldn't have done this!'

On the other end of the line, Fia realised, Megan and assorted other people in the studio were now whistling and cheering. Megan was saying gleefully, 'Oh my word, you should see how many texts and emails we've got coming in – this console's lit up like the Starship *Enterprise*!'

'Look, I've just got to finish the show,' said Ash, 'then I'm coming home. I can be there in an hour. Where will you be?'

Oh God, she was so happy. What a morning, and it wasn't over yet. Unable to wipe the ridiculous smile off her face, Fia said joyfully, 'I'll be right here, waiting for you.'

In Channings Hill, Abbie and Georgia listened to the rest of the show in silence, then Abbie switched off the radio. 'Oh sweetie, are you upset? I know how much you liked him.'

Georgia dabbed a finger across her plate, carefully collecting up crumbs and wondering how she felt. So that was it, Fia from the pub was in love with Ash. And Ash, it turned out, had been secretly in love with her for months. And now they were a couple, so besotted with each other that you could almost *feel* it over the airwaves.

Whereas Ash might have been her type but, for whatever reason, she hadn't been his.

Anyone would be disappointed, wouldn't they? But the thing was, it wasn't her fault. The reason he hadn't wanted to sleep with her wasn't because she was unattractive and a complete turn-off, but simply because she hadn't been Fia Newman.

Which was actually quite a comforting thing to know.

'I liked him. But it's no big deal.' Georgia shrugged and shook back her hair. 'Ash had his chance and he blew it.'

Abbie gave her shoulder an affectionate squeeze on her way to the sink. 'Don't let it get you down. You're a gorgeous girl and you'll find someone else. It's his loss.'

Georgia smiled and relaxed. So far this year she'd acquired a new home, a new family and two new jobs, which was probably enough for anyone to be going along with for now. Aloud she said happily, 'Yeah.'

When Ash arrived home fifty minutes later, Fia was waiting for him outside his cottage. His heart began to thud at the sight of her, in her grey top and skirt, her gold-brown hair lifting in the morning breeze.

Somewhat less romantically, Cleo was there too, looking incredibly pleased with herself. They weren't going to hear the end of this for some time; she was a nightmare when she knew she'd done something right.

Ash climbed out of the car, pointed to her open front door and said, 'Off you go.'

'Spoilsport.' Triumphantly Cleo said, 'This is all thanks to me, you know.'

'All the same. Bye.'

Amazingly, she disappeared inside her cottage. He turned his attention back to Fia. Her amber eyes were glowing. His voice cracking with emotion, Ash said, 'You're beautiful.'

Fia visibly relaxed. She broke into a huge, uncontrollable smile. Without even hesitating, she moved towards him and kissed him on the mouth. Oh God, this was fantastic . . . her lips were warm and soft . . . she was pressing her body against his . . . Like magic, he discovered that all the excruciating shyness had melted away. It was no longer there, paralysing his mind and rendering him practically unable to think, let alone speak. Still holding her, Ash broke away and said, 'Not that I'm complaining, but what brought this on?'

'You didn't come to the pub,' said Fia. 'It's been three days since you got that message from your agent. Last night I couldn't sleep for thinking about you. Then I came over here this morning to see Cleo and she said you were off to Australia.'

'Oh.' How had he guessed that Cleo was behind it?

'And she told me all about you resigning live on air at the end of today's show, telling your boss what you really thought of him.' Fia shook her head. 'So I realised I had to stop you before you did that. Except what I didn't know was that she'd made the whole story up.'

Ash stroked her face. Her skin was like silk. 'You're amazing.'

Fia wrapped her arms tightly around him. 'And as it seems to have worked, I suppose I can't be too cross with her. Tell me why you decided against Australia.'

He regarded her with amusement. 'OK, can you seriously picture me on Bondi Beach? A million fit tanned bodies and one beached whale?'

'Stop it. You're not fat. OK,' Fia amended, 'you're a *bit* fat. But I like it. You're *you*.' She ran her hand down his front. 'And you're definitely not a whale.'

'I'll never have a six-pack,' said Ash.

'My husband had one of those. Six-packs are nothing to write home about. They're not even comfortable, just rock-hard and bumpy.'

Ash smiled. 'That's it then, I definitely don't want one now.'

Then he took her by the hand and led her up the path and into his house. The real reason he hadn't seriously considered taking the job in Sydney was because Fia was here. But he'd tell her that later.

Right now they had more important things to do.

Chapter 53

'Hi, it's me.' The moment she heard his voice on the other end of the line, Cleo's stomach did its habitual swoop-and-dive. 'Look, I have a big favour to ask you.'

Cleo hesitated; did she even want to do Johnny any more favours? Since returning from Norfolk last week following the funeral, he and Honor had been seen coming and going. In yesterday's *Daily Mail* there had been a photo of them arriving at a high-profile fashion event in Knightsbridge. Honor had looked stunning in a scarlet taffeta mermaid-style dress that showed off her signature curves. Johnny had been wearing a designer suit. Honor was quoted as saying, 'Sacrifice? What sacrifice? Love's all that matters and I've never been happier in my life!'

Which was how Cleo, upon reading the accompanying piece, had learned that Honor Donaldson had turned down a multimillion-dollar deal to front a major cosmetics campaign because it would have meant working in Venezuela and being apart from Johnny for three months. Explaining her decision, Honor had said, 'It was pressure of work that broke us up last time. We're not going to let that happen again. Being together is more important than any amount of money in the bank.'

Which was undoubtedly true, but didn't make it any easier to read. There was something about other people's happiness – well, Johnny and Honor's happiness – that was hard to bear. Anyway, back to the present. Cleo braced herself. 'What kind of favour?'

Unless . . . wouldn't it be great if he was calling to say that it was all over between him and Honor and could she possibly come over and give them a hand packing up her stuff?

God, that would be fantastic.

Johnny said, 'Are you doing anything this evening?'

Hmm, one of *those* questions, the kind where you had to commit yourself before discovering what you were letting yourself in for. Well, she wasn't going to fall for *that* old trick.

Cleo said cautiously, 'What's the favour?'

'The thing is, we've got Clarice here at the house. She's come to stay for a few days. Now mentally she's fine, but physically she's pretty frail and I don't want to leave her on her own. But we've been invited to a gallery opening tonight and they're raising money for charity . . . I promised to help out and I don't want to let them down.'

That was it, then. Basically, she would be Cinderella left at home while he and Honor swanned off to the prince's ball.

'So you're wanting me to babysit.'

'Just for a few hours. We'd be home by midnight. But only if you want to. If you're busy, that's fine,' said Johnny. 'I'll ask someone else.'

Cleo hesitated; the way her brain was programmed meant she found it hard to refuse anyone requesting a favour. It was one of those genetic things; you could either do it without a qualm or you couldn't.

Plus, it wasn't as if she had anything else planned for this evening. Slapping on a face pack and eating her way through a giant bag of Kettle chips probably didn't count.

'OK, I'll do it. What time do you want me?'

For a moment there was no reply and she wondered if her phone had gone dead. Then Johnny said, 'You will? That's great, you're a star. Eight o'clock all right with you?'

He'd come to her rescue when she'd crashed into a ditch. Of course she had to help him in return. And anyway, it might turn out to be fun. Forcing herself to sound cheerful, Cleo said, 'No problem. Eight's fine.'

'Oh hooray, you're here, come on in, thanks so much for doing this!' Honor greeted her warmly at the door and ushered her through to the living room. 'Come and meet Clarice. Poor old darling, she's a bit crotchety but we've only got her for a few days. Here we are, then!' She pushed open the door and raised her voice. 'Aunt Clarice, this is Cleo, she's going to be keeping you company this evening, isn't that nice?'

'How would I know if it's nice? She might be the most boring creature on the planet.'

Okaaaaaay.

'Well, she isn't,' said Honor. 'She's lovely, so there.'

'And I'm crotchety.' Johnny's aged aunt eyed her over the top of her reading glasses. 'Mainly because you keep calling me a poor old darling and acting as if I'm stone deaf.'

'Hey, how's it going? Thanks for doing this.' Johnny hurried into the room, pulling on his jacket. He nodded at Cleo, then at his aunt. 'You'll be fine with Cleo. There's whisky in the cupboard and food in the fridge. Just help yourselves to anything you want. We won't be late home.'

'Baby, can you do this for me?' Honor approached Johnny, holding out a narrow gold chain. Sweeping up her hair and turning her flawless back to him, she waited while he fastened it around her neck.

'There, done.' He stepped back.

'And that's us all ready to go!' Flashing them the kind of smile that made Cleo feel about as alluring as a squashed frog, Honor waggled her French-manicured fingers and said, 'See you later! Have fun!'

They let themselves out of the house and Clarice echoed drily, 'Have fun. If only I'd remembered to bring my time machine with me.'

She was in her late seventies, as thin as a whippet and with practically translucent skin. Her hair was grey and fastened back in a ballerina's bun. She was wearing a plain white shirt, pale green wool skirt and darker green cardigan. No make-up. Miss-nothing grey eyes. Impressive diamond studs in her ears and a hefty steel watch on her left wrist.

Cleo sat down opposite her. 'I'm so sorry about your sister.'

'Thank you. Yes.' Clarice nodded briefly and closed the book on her lap. She removed her rimless reading glasses and said, 'First Lawrence, then Barbara. Only one of us left now.'

'Are you down here for long?'

'Just a few days. Then it's back to the nursing home.'

'What's that like?'

'Full of old people. Who keep *dying*. Oh, it's a laugh a minute. The conversation just sparkles.' Clarice heaved a sigh.

'If you don't like it,' said Cleo, 'why are you there?'

'Oh, God knows. It was Barbara's idea, when the house got too much for us. And she seemed to like it. She was happy there.' Clarice paused. 'I wouldn't call it my idea of heaven.'

'So couldn't you leave?'

'What, run away and join the circus?' With a brief smile, Clarice said, 'Unfortunately I'm a decrepit old bat, just in case you hadn't noticed. I have heart problems, joint problems, eye problems, you name it. Oh yes, it's a bundle of laughs being old and in possession of a body that's falling to bits.' She dismissed the topic with a shrug. 'Anyway, enough about me and my disintegrating bones. Why don't we talk about something more interesting? Johnny tells me you're a chauffeuse . . .'

The next couple of hours passed effortlessly. Contrary to expectations, Cleo really enjoyed herself. Clarice might be a decrepit old bat, but she was hugely entertaining, as sharp and scurrilous as Paul O'Grady and with a wicked sense of humour to boot. Having slightly dreaded the prospect of having to spend an entire evening keeping her company, she was now glad she'd come over. Clarice asked plenty of questions and provided acerbic comments. She also spoke about her family and told brilliant tales of Johnny's childhood.

'He came to stay with me once when he was . . . ooh, six or seven. I was driving us along when all of a sudden a mouse ran across my foot. Damn near crashed the car! And Johnny said, "Oh no, I forgot I had Harry in my pocket. Poor Harry, if we'd had an accident he could have been *killed*."'

Hopeless case that she was, just the mention of Johnny was enough to cause a flutter of excitement in her chest. Quelling it, Cleo said, 'That almost happened to me once. I had a client in the back of the car and we were heading along the M5 when he said, "Now don't panic, Miss Quinn, but I have to warn you that my snake is heading for your gearstick."'

'Ha!' Clarice almost spilled her tumbler of whisky and water. 'I once had a work colleague like that.'

'Except this was a real snake.' Shuddering at the memory, Cleo said, 'And I was doing eighty in the outside lane.'

Clarice took a sip of her drink and surveyed her through narrowed eyes. 'Quinn . . . Quinn . . . that's interesting. Are you just a few months younger than Johnny?'

Cleo nodded. 'Yes.'

'Hmm. Birthday at the end of August?'

OK, slightly spooky. Was she Derek Acorah in her spare time?

'Um, that's right,' said Cleo. 'August the twenty-fifth. How do you know that?'

Clarice looked pleased with herself. 'We've met before, dear.'

'Well, I was at Lawrence's funeral. I saw you there, and in the Hollybush afterwards, but we didn't get a chance to talk . . .'

'No, not then. Many years before that.' Clarice watched her with amusement. 'It's all right, I'm being unfair. You won't remember. In fact, it happened before you were born.'

Cleo hesitated; now they were wandering into the realms of the downright bizarre. Warily she said, 'I don't understand.'

'I was down here visiting Lawrence and his family. It was the middle of August and there was a summer fair being held out on the village green. It was a sunny day,' Clarice remembered. 'Very hot. I was holding Johnny in my arms and he kept trying to pull his little sun hat off.'

The image of Johnny in a cotton sun hat was one to treasure. Cleo said, 'Go on.'

'I was with Johnny's mother when we were approached by a man. His wife was pregnant and in something of a state, because she was almost at full term but her baby had stopped kicking. In fact they were both beside themselves, worried sick, but because it was a Sunday there was no doctor's surgery open. And they were terrified that something had happened to the baby. So I offered to examine his wife.'

Cleo made the connection at last. 'Because you were a doctor.'

'I was a consultant obstetrician,' Clarice crisply corrected her. 'And the couple's name was Quinn. We went back to their cottage on the other side of the green and I examined your mother, whose name I *do* remember, because that was the name of my secretary at the time. And I was able to assure Belinda that you were still alive in there. In fact I woke you up and you started kicking like a donkey. Your parents were so relieved. You were a very much longed-for baby, you know. So there you go.' Pleased with herself, Clarice said, 'And a week or so later, Lawrence called to let me know that Belinda Quinn had given birth to a healthy baby girl. So you and I may not have exchanged too much in the way of conversation, but I gave you a jolly good prod and a poke, and you kicked me in return, which seems only— Good Lord!' She stopped abruptly. 'My dear girl, are you *crying*?'

Embarrassed, Cleo shook her head. 'No, not really . . .' Using the backs of her fingers she wiped her wet cheeks. 'OK, maybe a bit . . .'

'Well, it's been a while since I retired but they look like tears to me. I'm sorry, my dear, did I say something wrong? I didn't mean to upset you.'

'It's all right, I'm fine.' This time Cleo managed to smile. 'Sorry about that. My mum died when I was eleven, so it's just nice to hear you talking about her.'

'She was a nice lady. Very grateful. I was happy to help. Now, could you be an angel and fetch some cheese and biscuits from the kitchen? Then we'll have a chat about you. Oh, and here . . .' Diamonds flashed on Clarice's arthritic fingers as she held out her empty tumbler. 'Pour me another whisky, dear, if you would.'

Johnny and Honor arrived back just before midnight.

'We're home!' sang Honor, and Cleo's heart sank, because she said it as if she meant it. Ravenswood was her home now, and she and Johnny were a proper couple. A stunning, golden couple with everything going for them.

Johnny surveyed them from the doorway. 'Everything OK?'

'Perfect. We've had a wonderful evening.' Patting Cleo's hand, Clarice said, 'Couldn't have asked for a nicer babysitter.'

He smiled briefly. 'Good.'

'How about you two?'

'Great.' Johnny shrugged. 'The evening was a success. The art was . . . interesting.'

'It was modern,' Honor cut in. 'Basically, it looked like it had been done by a bunch of drunken monkeys. Paint spattered everywhere. But we raised a ton of money, so that's the main thing. Right, I'm off to bed. Night, everyone! See you, Clarice!' She blew kisses and retired upstairs.

Clarice said drily, 'See you.'

Chapter 54

Clarice isn't happy in that nursing home. She was only putting
up with it to keep her sister company. And now she doesn't have
to stay there any more.'

Johnny had offered to walk her home and Cleo had taken him
up on it. This was something he needed to hear and she suspected
that for all her straight talking, Clarice wouldn't dream of telling
him herself.

He nodded thoughtfully. 'I did wonder.'

'She calls it God's waiting room. She hates it.'

'That bad?'

'Yes.' She was firm.

Johnny shoved his hands into his jacket pockets as they made
their way across the wet grass. 'Well then, we need to get something else organised.'

'Can I say something?'

In the darkness she detected a glimmer of a smile. 'Can I stop
you?'

*Only with a kiss. But that's not going to happen, so don't even think
about it.*

Aloud she said, 'Your aunt is brilliant. I really like her.'

'So do I.'

'But when she told me about how much she hated the nursing home, I said hadn't she thought about moving to this part of the country? And she said she couldn't do that because then you'd feel obliged to visit her all the time. She doesn't want to be a nuisance and put you under pressure.'

Johnny stopped walking. 'She's my only living relative. Why would she think I'd feel pressurised?'

'Because she says you have your own life to live and you don't need some ancient relative taking up your time. Which is why I'm telling you now.' Cleo looked at him. 'Even though she made me promise I wouldn't. But I do happen to know a good nursing home in Bristol. One of my regular customers lives there and she loves it.'

'And when I'm at home she could come and stay here . . . it'd be easy if she was that close.' Johnny said, 'Whereabouts is this nursing home? What's it called? God, she spent forty years terrifying the life out of young doctors. She's such a professional battleaxe I can't believe Clarice didn't want to ask me herself.'

'She's considerate. She doesn't want to be a burden.' Brimming with fresh emotion, Cleo said, 'Look, if you ever needed a hand with her, I'd be more than happy to help out.' Oh God, did that make her sound like a creep, desperate for contact with him no matter how tenuous it might be?

They'd reached the cottage. Johnny lightly touched her on the arm and the unexpected contact made her shiver with suppressed longing.

He looked down at her and said, 'What is it?'

Cleo shook her head helplessly; it wasn't as if she could blurt out how she felt about him and how utterly bereft Honor's re-appearance in his life had made her feel.

'Nothing. I'm OK, just . . . you know, tired . . .'

Johnny's dark eyes glittered. 'I meant what's the name of the nursing home?'

'Oh God, sorry . . .' Just as well it was dark; she squeezed her eyes tight shut and felt her cheeks heat up. 'It's Neild House in Clifton, up on the Downs.'

'I'll have a look at the website when I get home.' He paused. 'Thanks for tonight. I owe you one.'

Owed her one what? A favour? A moment of rampant passion? For a long moment they looked at each other and Cleo wondered if he was thinking what she was thinking. What would happen if she were to grab him now, just go for it and, God, *launch* herself at him? And was she imagining it or did he—

'Yee-ha!' The whoop came out of the darkness, closely followed by the sound of running footsteps and panting and muffled laughter. Together they turned and saw Ash racing across the grass towards them with his striped shirt untucked and Fia in his arms giggling and shrieking to be put down. On their way back from the pub, it wasn't hard to guess why they were in such a hurry to get home. Watching them, Cleo was glad they were so ecstatically happy, but Ash's timing definitely left something to be desired.

Then again, maybe it was just as well.

'Evening!' Grinning broadly at the sight of them, Ash lowered Fia to the ground but kept his arm around her; practically inseparable for the past few days, it was as if they couldn't bear to let each other go.

'Evening.' Johnny nodded, smiled briefly and said, 'Right, I'd better get back then.' He looked at Cleo, his expression unreadable. 'Thanks again.'

She dragged her gaze away from his mouth and heard herself

say as chirpily as a Girl Guide, 'No problem, I really enjoyed it. Goodnight!'

Ash gave Fia's waist a squeeze and murmured, 'It isn't over yet.'

Smiling, Fia whispered back, 'But the next bit's going to be even better.'

God, newly-in-love people. They could really make you sick.

From her darkened bedroom window Cleo watched as Johnny made his way back across the green to Ravenswood. And to Honor Donaldson, curvy and irresistible and more than likely currently lying naked in his huge king-sized bed.

Not that she'd ever seen it, but she'd bet any money it was king-sized.

From next door came whoops and squeals of helpless laughter. Cleo rubbed her hands over her face and turned away from the window. It wasn't much fun feeling unwanted, unloved and like a gooseberry in your own house.

The last eight days had been a whirlwind of work. The upside to this, Cleo had discovered, was that it kept your mind occupied and stopped you daydreaming hopelessly about your last unsatisfactory encounter with Johnny LaVenture before he and Honor had disappeared from the village. Well, it almost stopped you daydreaming about him. The downside was that she was exhausted, and today had been another long day. A long, looooonnnngggg day. Nor, sadly, was it over yet. When she called Grumpy Graham and tried to wriggle out of the third booking, he informed her in no uncertain terms that she was out of luck.

'But I did the Heathrow run this morning.' She wondered if he had a heart at all. 'And I've done the wedding anniversary thing in Devon. Couldn't someone else do this one?'

'Bloody hell, no, they flaming well can't.' Graham heaved a sigh of annoyance. 'I've already told you, everyone else is *busy*.'

Cleo flexed her spine; she was shattered and seizing up. 'What about Shelley?'

'Taking that kid of hers to the dentist.'

For crying out loud, did Shelley really have to? Saskia was only six. Wasn't the whole point of baby teeth that they were all just going to fall out anyway?

OK, she probably shouldn't use that as an argument. With resignation Cleo gave up and ended the call. Despite starting work at eight o'clock this morning and having driven over four hundred miles *so far*, it looked as if she had a couple more hours to go yet. And another hundred miles at least, in order to collect someone called Lady Rosemary from her home outside Stratford-upon-Avon and take her to her daughter's home in Shepton Mallet.

Because some people simply didn't *do* trains, dahling.

Cleo could guess what Lady Rosemary would be like. Loud for a start, with an offhand, peremptory manner. She would complain about bumps in the road, be wearing too much make-up and nostril-shrivelling perfume, and she would exhale with irritation every time they were forced to stop at a zebra crossing, because how *dare* people in crimplene skirts and ghastly tracksuits want to cross the road . . .

Oh well, no point dwelling on it. Cleo gave herself a mental shake; she was tired, her back was aching and her life was shit. But hey, the job was booked and she had to do it. Served her right for being indispensable.

An hour later she was almost there. Compton Court was in the depths of the Warwickshire countryside, and it was proving to be extremely well hidden. The battery on the satnav had died and she was due to pick up Lady Rosemary at eight o'clock. Finally arriving at a junction, Cleo saw that the rustic wooden road sign had had its arms wrenched off – evidently what passed for teenage entertainment in these parts. Pulling in to one side of the narrow lane, she reached across to retrieve her map from the glove compartment. Maps didn't have annoying robotic voices, they didn't run out of battery and stop functioning, they were reliable and trustworthy and they—

Oh *fuck*.

And they were held together with a spiral of wire that had sharp ends capable of snagging a hole in your tights just when you *really* didn't need it to happen.

Fuck and bugger, a hole *and* a ladder now, on the one day she didn't have an emergency pair stashed in her bag. If this wasn't a shining example of how completely crappy her life was at the moment, she didn't know what was.

Two miles down the road, possible salvation presented itself in the form of a tiny petrol station of the post-war kind. Two old-fashioned pumps stood on a minuscule forecourt amid piles of used tyres and several dusty, rusty cars. But by some miracle it appeared to be open. A fat man in dusty overalls was tinkering with the engine of an old van. Cleo jumped out of the car and said, 'Hi, I'm looking for Compton Court.'

He straightened up and wiped sausagey fingers on a cloth. 'Lady Rosemary's place? Straight along this road, take the second right, then half a mile along and you'll see the entrance on your left.'

'Thanks. Um, is your shop open?'

The man nodded and said, 'Feel free.'

Calling it a shop was possibly overstating the case. The tiny room was part of the garage and the air tasted of dust and oil. There were crisps on sale, cartons of UHT milk, bottles of limeade and crates of fresh-from-the-garden vegetables. In addition, on a series of shelves, were piled assorted motoring magazines, petrol cans, bottles of engine oil, stretchy steering wheel covers and a box of wheel nuts.

And then, the second miracle, Cleo spotted a selection of rain hats, plastic macs and packets of tights.

This was the good news. The bad news was that the tights were all forty denier, extra large and American Tan in colour. The worst kind you could imagine.

Cleo turned to the man who had followed her into the shop. 'Um, do you have any other tights?'

'No, sorry.'

'Oh. It's just that I've got a hole in mine. And these are a bit grannyish.'

He lit a cigarette. 'They're my wife's tights.'

Eek.

'Oh. Sorry.'

'She died last year.' He breathed out a lungful of smoke. 'So I thought I might as well sell them.'

Oh, good grief. At least they were still in their packets; his wife hadn't actually worn them. 'I'm sorry. I'll have this pair.' Cleo hurriedly paid for them; bare legs would look so much better, but her uniform demanded that she wear tights and Lady Rosemary would be bound to complain if she didn't.

A mile down the road she pulled into a gateway and changed into the Nora Batty tights. They were the colour of really strong tea and absolutely huge, wrinkling around her legs like a snake halfway through shedding its skin. Oh well, never mind.

Cleo followed the garage owner's instructions and finally reached the entrance to Compton Court. The sun had just set, a misty dusk was falling and the driveway leading up to the house was lined with chestnut trees.

Very nice too. It was like one of those houses you saw featured in the pages of *Country Life* when you were sitting in the dentist waiting room. Quite Jane Austen-esque, in fact. Cleo's mood began to improve as she reached the top of the driveway. You could imagine the lady of the house holding a Regency ball here, greeting her guests on the steps and graciously—

'Oh hi, you the driver?' The front door had swung open to reveal a teenage girl with multiple facial piercings, fluorescent pink eyeshadow and leopard-print jeans. Clutching her mobile phone to one ear and gesturing with her free hand, she said, 'They're round the back, just follow the path down past the rose garden and go through the arch in the yew hedge . . . yah, I know, I *told* Zan she was a slapper but he didn't believe me!'

Probably not Lady Rosemary. Engrossed once more in her phone conversation, the girl wandered back into the house and kicked the door shut with her bare foot. The good news was that she hadn't even noticed Cleo's legs.

The tights were loose around the waist too. She was forced to hold them up as she made her way through the misty gloom. Her shoes crunched on the gravel and the smell of freshly mown grass hung in the air. Rooks were cawing in the trees, disturbed by the drone of a single-engined plane as it crossed overhead, leaving a silvery vapour trail in the darkening sky. At ground level, a thickening low mist floated like white ectoplasm above the lawns. As Cleo passed the carefully tended rose garden, she began to hear voices in the distance. Ahead of her stood the yew hedge, twelve feet tall and with an eight-foot arch carved into it. Something was happening beyond the arch; as she moved towards it, the voices grew louder and she glimpsed flashes of colour and movement through the gap.

Some kind of garden party, by the look of things. Although the timing was bizarre, what with it getting darker by the minute. Cleo bent and attempted to smooth out the accordion pleats in her tights then grabbed the waistband and yanked them up Benny Hill style as high as they'd go.

Then it all began to make sense. As she reached the archway a switch was flicked, the area beyond it was suddenly flooded with light and the assembled audience burst into applause.

Behind them, Cleo's heart did a dolphin leap of disbelief. A surge of adrenaline shot through her body and her skin prickled with recognition, because there in the centre of the clearing, illuminated by the expertly angled uplighters, stood a family of deer. The proud stag, antlers stretched out like wings, directly faced them. To his right stood the graceful female, her neck bent as she grazed. And between them, playful and inquisitive, was their fawn.

Not a real family of deer, but constructed from stainless steel and larger than life-size. The stag was over twelve feet high. Bathed in silvery-white light and surrounded by trees, the effect was ethereal and other-worldly. And the woman leading the applause was now drawing their creator forward.

Chapter 55

Johnny was smiling, wearing a dark blue shirt and jeans, looking modest and unbelievably gorgeous. Cleo couldn't help herself; just seeing him unexpectedly like this was enough to set off a whole cascade of emotions. Ravenswood had been standing empty for the past week. No one had known where he was.

'Thanks so much to Johnny for making my dream come true. He's absolutely exceeded my expectations, I couldn't be happier with my beautiful sculptures and I know I'm going to love them until the day I die!' The woman — could this be Lady Rosemary? — was in her early fifties, plump and smiley in a padded gilet and threadbare corduroy trousers. So much for preconceptions. She hugged Johnny before announcing, 'Well, it's getting a bit chilly so shall we all head back inside? Ooh, hello!' Spotting Cleo hovering at the back of the crowd by the giant yew hedge, she added, 'We have a new arrival. Have you come to whisk my favourite artist away?'

As they passed her on their way back up to the house, Cleo felt herself being scrutinised by the assembled guests. Were they laughing at her Nora Batty corrugated tights? When it was just the three of them left, the woman clasped Cleo's hand in both of hers and said warmly, 'I've heard all about you, my dear. I'm Rose, by the way.'

What was going on? Cleo said, 'Hello, I'm Cleo. Um . . . am I driving you to Shepton Mallet?'

'No, dear, you're taking Johnny home. Now, I'll just go and start pouring drinks for my thirsty friends. And you're both more than welcome to join us if you'd like to.' Beaming at Johnny over her shoulder as she disappeared through the archway, Rose said cheerfully, 'Pretty girl. Gorgeous freckles. Funny tights!'

And then it was just the two of them left in the clearing, with the surrounding trees and the family of silver deer artfully spotlit, dusk falling around them and the grass wreathed in white mist.

Cleo met Johnny's gaze for the first time. Something was definitely going on and nobody was explaining it to her. It was like one of those dreams where you find yourself on stage but nobody's told you the name of the play you're meant to be appearing in.

OK, first things first. Her mouth dry, she said, 'What happened to Shepton Mallet?'

Johnny took a deep breath. 'Sorry, that was down to Rose.' He sounded less sure of himself than usual, which was weird for a start.

'Why has she heard all about me?'

'I've been working here for the last eight days. We got talking.' He paused. 'I had to talk to someone or I'd have gone mad. And getting you here like this was all her idea. If you'd known you were coming over to see me, it wouldn't have been a surprise.' Drily Johnny added, 'Surprises are very much Rose's thing.'

Cleo's heart had never beaten so fast. To give herself time to think, she said, 'How's Clarice?'

'Very well. She's going to be moving into Neild House next month.'

'That's . . . great.'

'I know.'

She braced herself. 'And how's things with Honor?'

'Honor's fine. She's very well too.' Another pause. 'We're not together any more. I finished with Honor last week.'

Oh good grief, was he serious? Unable to contain herself, Cleo blurted out, 'You did? Why? Why would you *do* that?'

He held up his hand to stop her. 'OK, let me explain something. When I was living in the States, Honor and I were seeing each other and things weren't really working out. The relationship had pretty much run its course, but Honor panicked when I tried to end it. Then she met this other guy and told me our relationship was over. That way, she wasn't the one being dumped. Which was absolutely fine by me. I was relieved. But then last month that all went pear-shaped when she realised what a prat he was. And that was when she called me, while I was in Norfolk and Barbara was about to die. The next thing I knew, she'd jumped on the next plane. And she'd turned down this multi-million-dollar deal to be with me, so what could I say? Tell her thanks but no thanks?' He shook his head. 'I couldn't do that to her. She's a sweet girl with a good heart. So I felt I had to go along with it, give it another try.'

'Until a week ago.' Cleo's teeth were chattering. 'What happened?'

'You really want to know?' He gazed steadily at her. 'OK, I'll say it. You happened.'

'What?'

'Remember when I asked you to come over to the house and keep Clarice company for the evening?'

'Yes.' *Oh God, what was she supposed to do with all this adrenaline?*

'You said you'd do it. Then you said, what time do you want

404

me?' Johnny waited, then dipped his head. 'And I wanted to say, *All the time.*'

Silence. In the distance an owl screeched. Cleo shivered; was this really happening? It *felt* as if it was happening, but how could she be absolutely sure?

'And that was the moment I knew what I had to do,' said Johnny. 'Even if I end up looking like a complete idiot. Because maybe you don't feel the same way about me, but ever since I came back to Channings Hill, I haven't been able to stop thinking about you.'

Could he hear how fast her heart was beating? It was like a kangaroo trying to batter its way out of her chest. Risking a brief smile, Cleo said, 'Thinking what about me?'

'Only good things. I'm serious now. Since the day of Dad's funeral, you've been . . . in here.' He tapped the side of his head.

Oh God, how brilliant. 'Why me, though? Why me and not Honor?'

'OK, off the top of my head.' Johnny counted off on his fingers. 'If you broke one of your nails, would you call up your manicurist and tell her to get on a plane and come and sort it out?'

'I might,' said Cleo.

'If I frowned and my forehead moved, would you go on and on and on at me, telling me I really should get myself Botoxed?'

'It's a possibility.'

'If I told you I was making arrangements for my aunt to move down to a nursing home in Bristol, would you say, "Ah Jeez, does she have to? That means she'll keep wanting to come and stay!"'

He'd captured Honor's accent to perfection. Shocked but at the same time delighted, Cleo said, 'God, did she really say that?'

Johnny shrugged. 'It's not why I finished with her. I did that because she wasn't you. OK, shall I make a confession now?'

'Yes please.'

'You're funny and stroppy and you have no idea how gorgeous you are.' He paused. 'You're the reason I came back to live in Channings Hill.'

She blinked. 'I don't believe you.'

'It's true. Would you like another confession?'

'Definitely,' said Cleo.

'This is a shameful one.'

'My favourite kind.'

'When I bet you couldn't last six months without a boyfriend, it was because I didn't want you getting involved with anyone else.'

Cleo's stomach squirmed with joy. 'Remind me again how much money was involved? I can't wait to win this bet.'

'I haven't finished yet with the confessions.'

'Sorry. Carry on.'

'All these months I've wanted to kiss you.' Johnny shook his head. 'So badly. God, all this time and I haven't even *kissed* you . . .'

Cleo swallowed. 'You're making me nervous now.'

'Why?'

'Because what if I'm rubbish at it? I might kiss like a washing machine.'

Johnny said, 'Has it occurred to you that I might be nervous too?'

She shook her head. 'Now you're the one talking rubbish. You're never nervous.'

'I never have been before.' He moved closer. 'But I am now. Apart from anything else, I've told you how I feel about you and you haven't said anything back. You could be about to tell me to take a running jump.'

Cleo gazed up at him. He sounded as if he meant it, but this was the most confident man she'd ever encountered in her life. Without warning she reached out and pressed the flat of her hand against the warm triangle of chest exposed by his open-necked shirt . . .

Thudthudthudthudthudthud . . .

Johnny exhaled, mortified. 'Oh God, could you *hear* my heart beating?'

How funny that in all these years it had never once occurred to her that men might worry about this too. A smile spread across Cleo's face as she reached for his hand and placed it at the base of her own throat.

Dahdahdahdahdahdah . . .

Johnny felt it, then visibly relaxed. 'Nearly as fast as mine.'

Did he kiss her or did she kiss him? Cleo had no idea how it happened; all she knew was that they met in the middle, their mouths touching and magically appearing to already know each other. Johnny wrapped his arms around her, she ran her fingers through his hair and it felt so perfect she never wanted it to end.

Which, for quite a long time, it didn't. Until finally they had to come up for air.

Johnny was smiling and stroking her face. 'Not a bit like a washing machine.'

'Nor you.'

He touched the freckle below her right eye. 'Final confession?'

'Go ahead.' How were her legs still managing to hold her up?

'I love you. I really do. And I feel like such a novice, because I've never felt this way about anyone else before.'

I love you. There it was. The last time someone had said those words to her, it had been Will, in the pub that day when she'd told him she wanted nothing more to do with him. Her very first *I love you*, and it had been horrible, so completely wrong.

But this time it felt wonderful. Johnny was saying it and it felt blissfully, perfectly *right*. Cleo swallowed; she wasn't at all sure her legs *were* still holding her up. If he hadn't been holding her, she'd be in a heap on the grass. Faintly she said, 'This had better not be a joke . . .'

'Oh God, don't even think that! I've felt guilty about that for *years . . .*'

'Guilty about what?'

'That stupid bet. The night of the school disco.' Johnny shook his head, mortified. 'I've wanted to apologise for that so many times, but I just didn't have the nerve. Then I thought – hoped – that maybe you'd forgotten all about it, so what would be the point of bringing it up again? But you hadn't forgotten about it, had you? I'm so sorry.'

He truly meant it. Magically, the burden of embarrassment rose up and floated away. Cleo said happily, 'I've forgotten about it now. Anyway, carry on with what you were saying.'

'OK, maybe this is jumping the gun,' Johnny went on, 'but all these years, you're the one I've been waiting for. Because I know I could spend the rest of my life with you. I *want* to spend the rest of my life with you . . .' Another kiss, then he said in a voice that wasn't completely steady, 'Will you give me a chance to prove it?'

Cleo said, 'Don't make promises you might not be able to keep. Let's just take it one day at a time, shall we?'

'Fine, but I know how I feel, and I know this is a promise I can keep. I'm not going to change my mind about you.' The look in his eyes told her how much he meant it. 'You're everything I've ever wanted.'

Cleo felt her heart expand with joy. Until he'd said them, she hadn't dared to admit even to herself that hearing those words from Johnny LaVenture was all she'd ever wanted too. If it had happened years ago, it would never have worked. But now . . . now it was right, it was *perfect*. She tilted her head. *Hang on . . .*

'What's that noise?'

Johnny straightened up and listened. It was only faint but there was some kind of whooping.

'Oh, don't worry about that.' Having turned to look behind him, he said with amusement, 'It's just Rose, celebrating because she's been proved right.'

Earlier, Cleo had briefly wondered why anyone would commission a truly spectacular sculpture and situate it in a wooded clearing, obscured from general view by a twelve-foot-high yew hedge.

Now she discovered that, like Stonehenge, the sculpture had been carefully positioned so that from the glass orangery at the side of the house you had a perfect view of it through the archway cut in the hedge.

It was also apparent that, along with the family of steel deer behind them, she and Johnny were illuminated in the glow of the silvery spotlights.

And Rose wasn't the only one waving and cheering. All her guests were gathered at the full-length windows; they were quite the centre of attention.

'We'll have to stay for a quick drink,' said Johnny. 'Let her have her moment of glory.'

'This is going to be so embarrassing,' said Cleo.

'It won't, it'll be fine, I promise. Hey, where are you going? Jesus, are you taking all your clothes off?' Alarmed, Johnny said, 'Hey, I don't want to wait either but we can't do anything here, not with everyone watching.'

Behind the hedge, just about hidden from view of the orangery, Cleo did what she had to do and said, 'Don't panic, I'm not getting naked. Just taking these God-awful tights off. Here, hide them in your pocket.'

Johnny held them up and fondly contemplated them, wrinkled and ugly and the colour of builder's tea. 'Fine, but we're never going to throw these away. They'll be a memento of an unforgettable day.' Sliding his arm around Cleo's waist as they made their way beneath the yew arch, he murmured, 'You can wear them under your wedding dress when we get married.'

Did he think she was completely stupid? 'I've got a better idea,' said Cleo. 'Why don't you?'